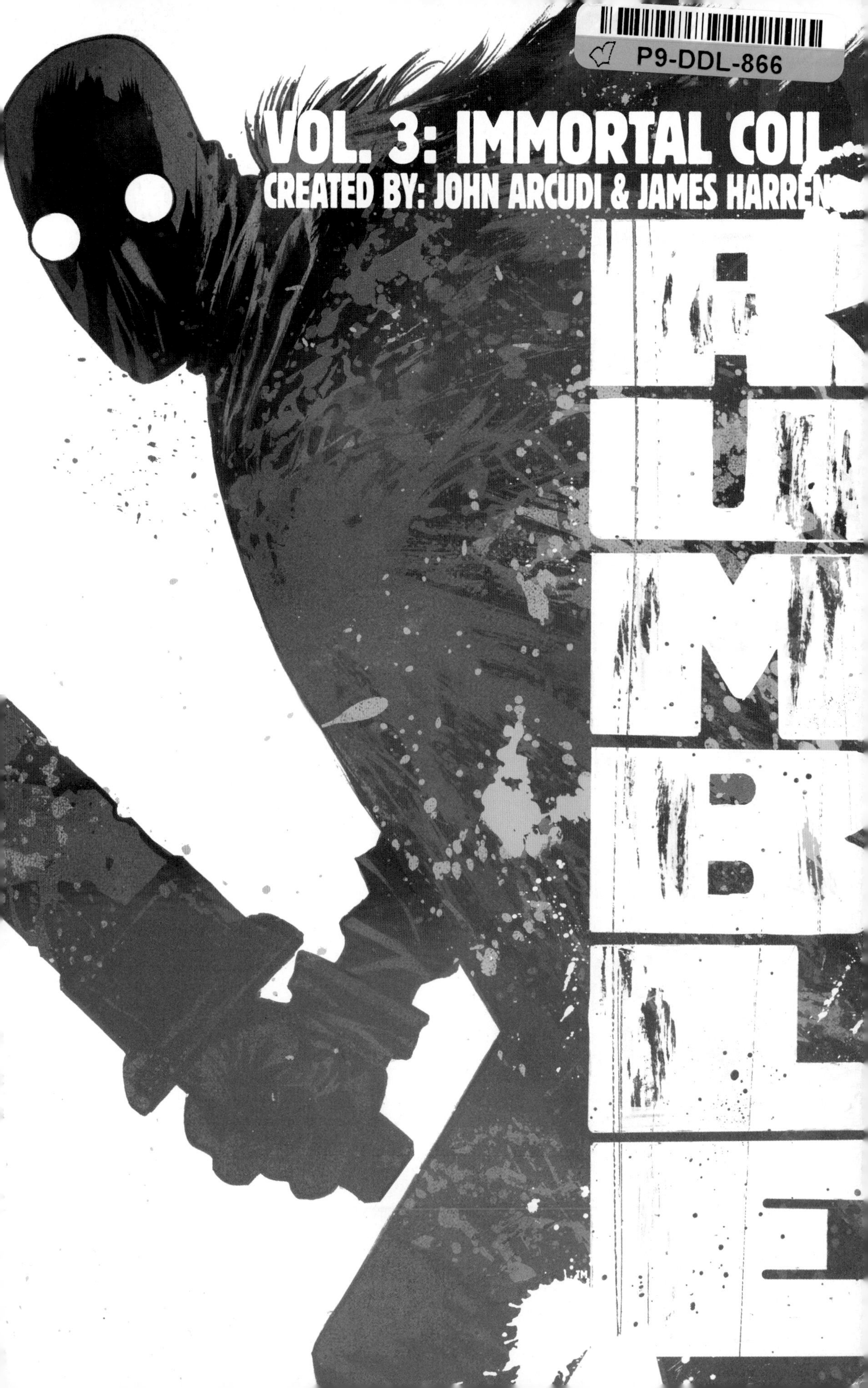
VOL. 3: IMMORTAL COIL
CREATED BY: JOHN ARCUDI & JAMES HARREN
RUMBLE™

JOHN ARCUDI
JAMES HARREN
Co-creators

DAVE STEWART
Color Art

JOE SABINO
Letters

VINCENT KUKUA
Book Design

FOR IMAGE COMICS, INC:

ROBERT KIRKMAN - Chief Operating Officer
ERIK LARSEN - Chief Financial Officer
TODD MCFARLANE - President
MARC SILVESTRI - Chief Executive Officer
JIM VALENTINO - Vice-President

ERIC STEPHENSON - Publisher
COREY MURPHY - Director of Sales
JEFF BOISON - Director of Publishing Planning & Book Trade Sales
JEREMY SULLIVAN - Director of Digital Sales
KAT SALAZAR - Director of PR & Marketing
BRANWYN BIGGLESTONE - Controller
DREW GILL - Art Director
JONATHAN CHAN - Production Manager
MEREDITH WALLACE - Print Manager
BRIAH SKELLY - Publicist
SASHA HEAD - Sales & Marketing Production Designer
RANDY OKAMURA - Digital Marketing Designer
DAVID BROTHERS - Branding Manager
OLIVIA NGAI - Content Manager
ADDISON DUKE - Production Artist
TRICIA RAMOS - Production Artist
VINCENT KUKUA - Production Artist
JEFF STANG - Direct Market Sales Representative
EMILIO BAUTISTA - Digital Sales Associate
LEANNA CAUNTER - Accounting Assistant
CHLOE RAMOS-PETERSON - Library Market Sales Representative

IMAGECOMICS.COM

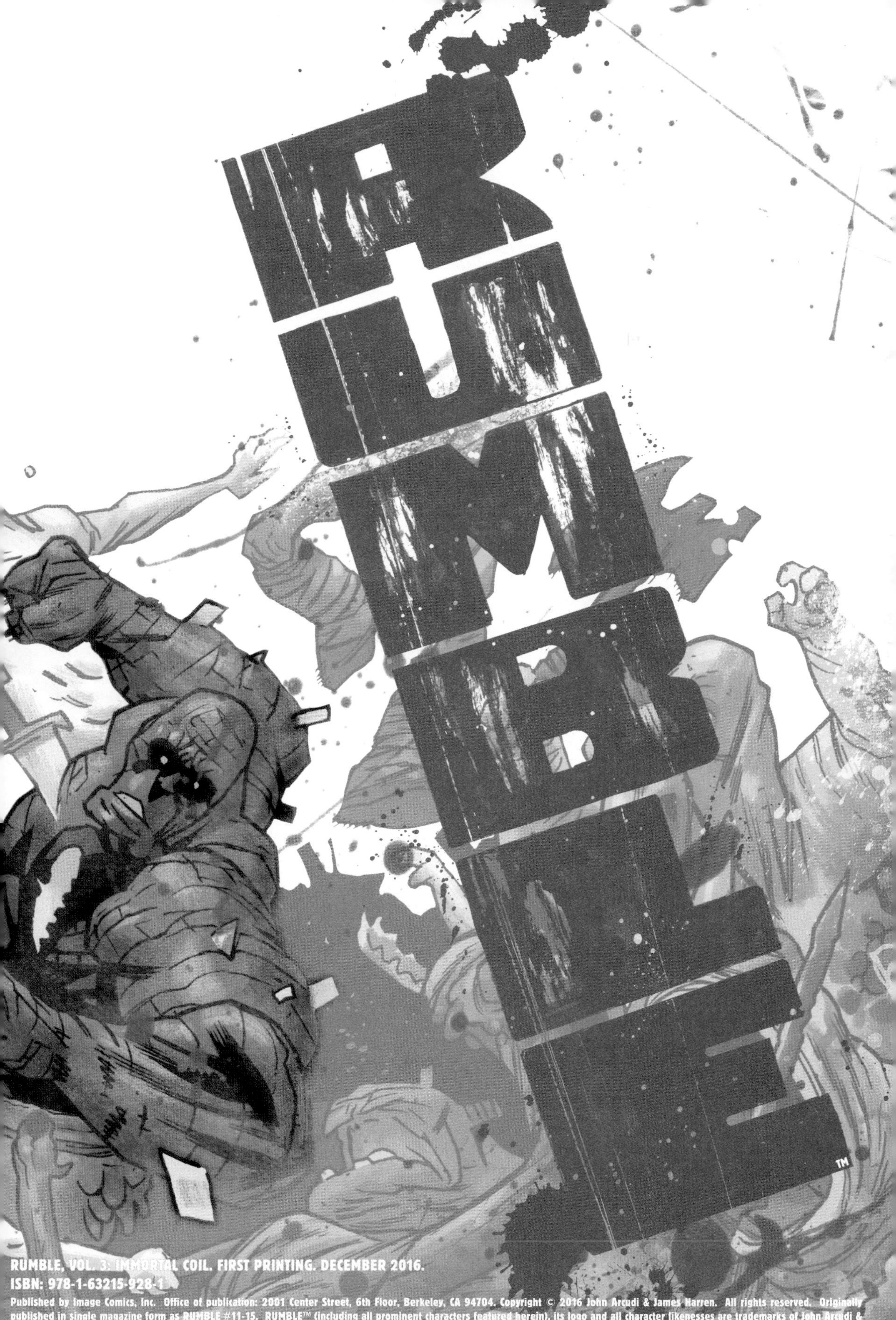
RUMBLE™

RUMBLE, VOL. 3: IMMORTAL COIL. FIRST PRINTING. DECEMBER 2016.
ISBN: 978-1-63215-928-1
Published by Image Comics, Inc. Office of publication: 2001 Center Street, 6th Floor, Berkeley, CA 94704. PRINTED IN THE U.S.A. For information regarding the CPSIA on this printed material call: 203-595-3636 and provide reference: RICH–716158.

For international rights inquiries, contact: foreignlicensing@imagecomics.com

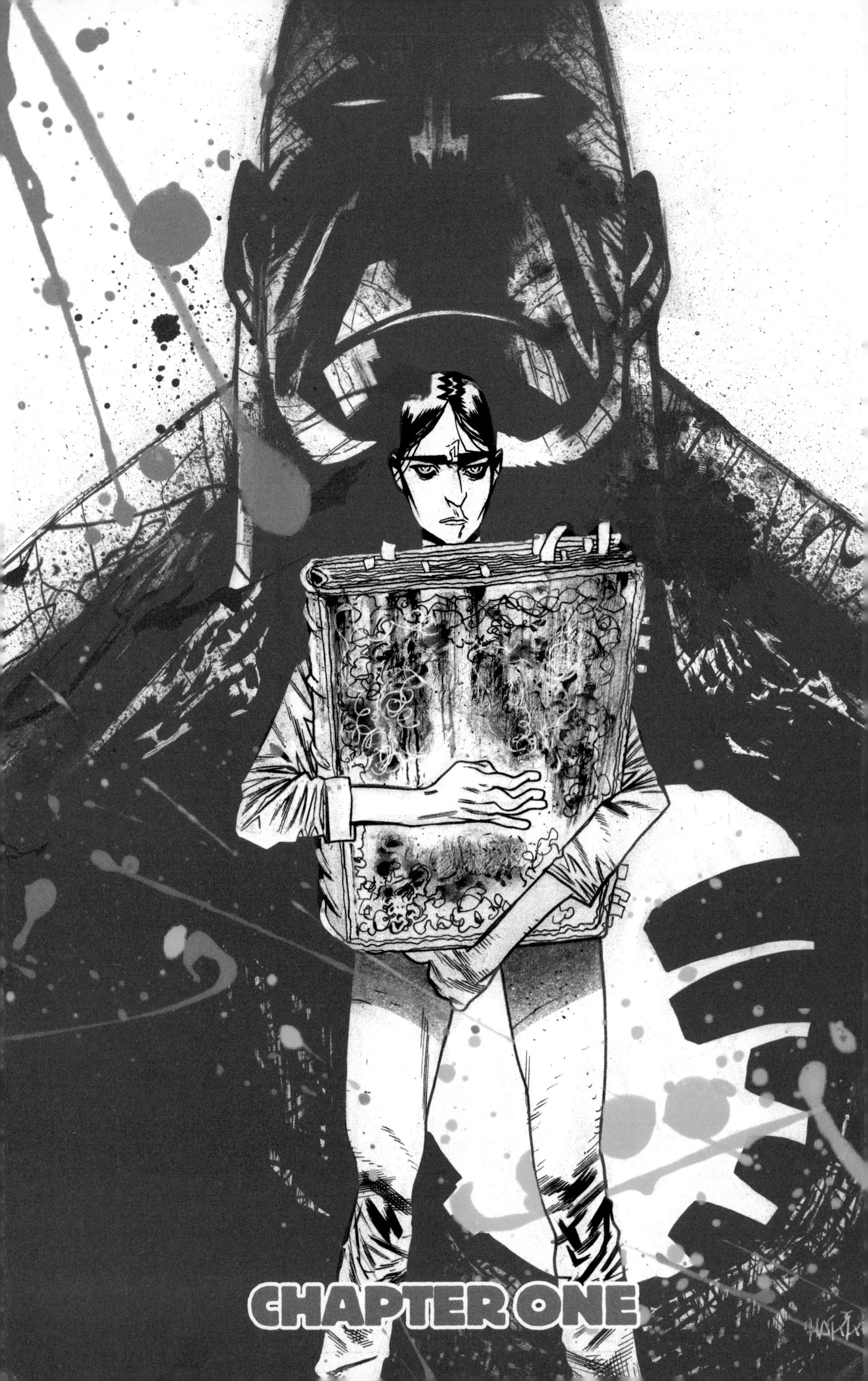

CHAPTER ONE

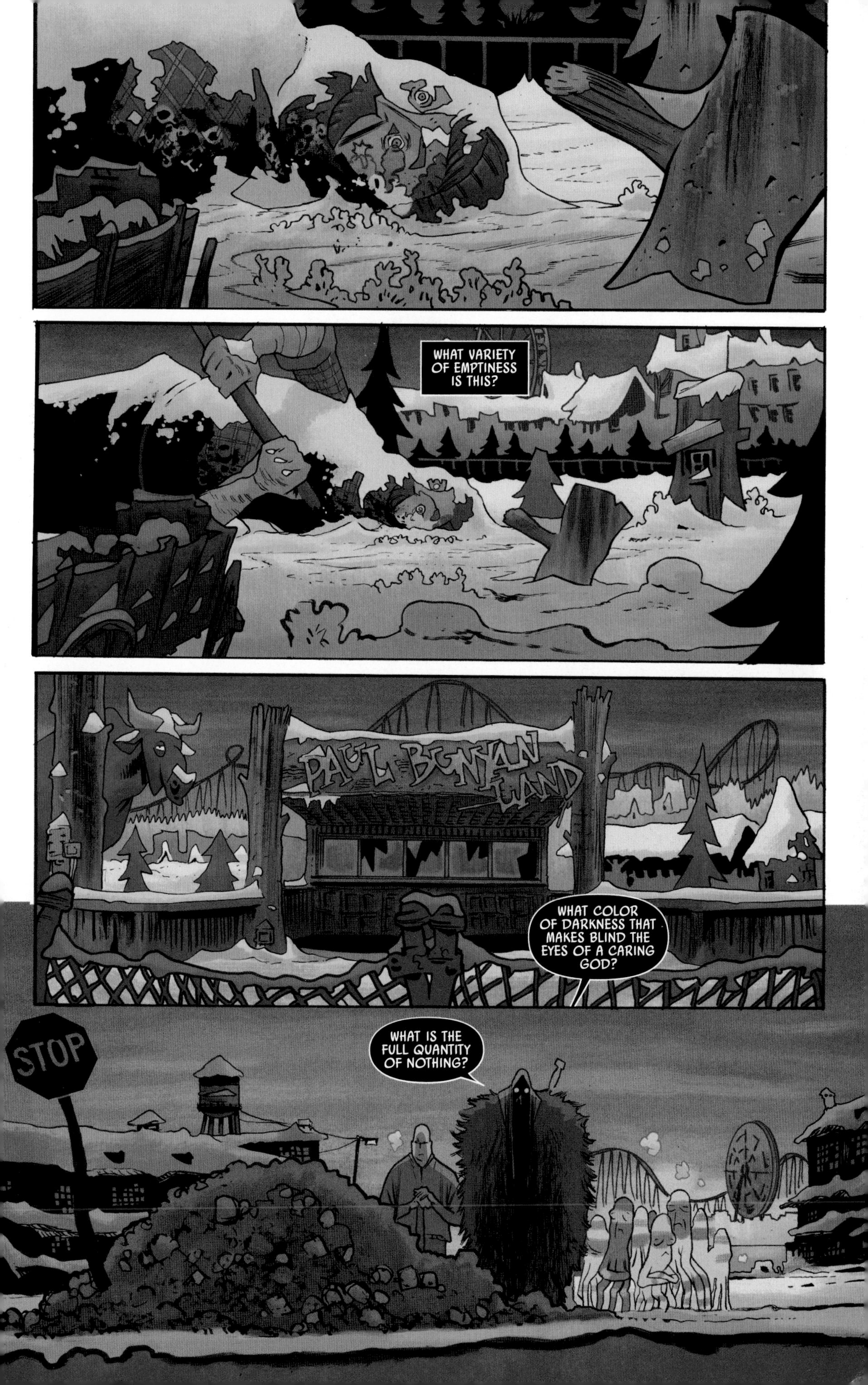
WHAT VARIETY OF EMPTINESS IS THIS?
PAUL BUNYAN LAND
WHAT COLOR OF DARKNESS THAT MAKES BLIND THE EYES OF A CARING GOD?
STOP
WHAT IS THE FULL QUANTITY OF NOTHING?

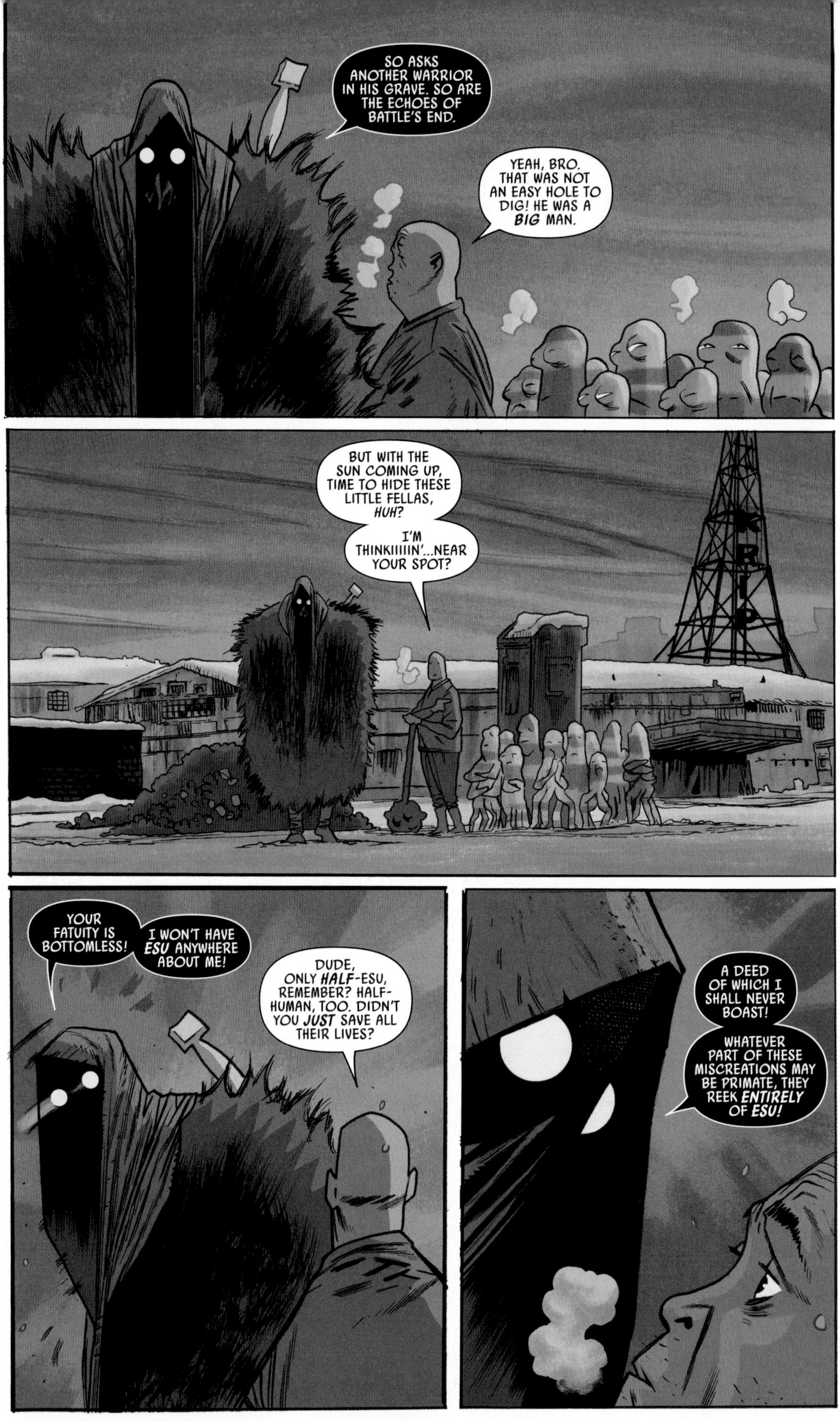
SO ASKS ANOTHER WARRIOR IN HIS GRAVE. SO ARE THE ECHOES OF BATTLE'S END.
YEAH, BRO. THAT WAS NOT AN EASY HOLE TO DIG! HE WAS A BIG MAN.
BUT WITH THE SUN COMING UP, TIME TO HIDE THESE LITTLE FELLAS, HUH?
I'M THINKIIIIIN'...NEAR YOUR SPOT?
YOUR FATUITY IS BOTTOMLESS!
I WON'T HAVE ESU ANYWHERE ABOUT ME!
DUDE, ONLY HALF-ESU, REMEMBER? HALF-HUMAN, TOO. DIDN'T YOU JUST SAVE ALL THEIR LIVES?
A DEED OF WHICH I SHALL NEVER BOAST!
WHATEVER PART OF THESE MISCREATIONS MAY BE PRIMATE, THEY REEK ENTIRELY OF ESU!

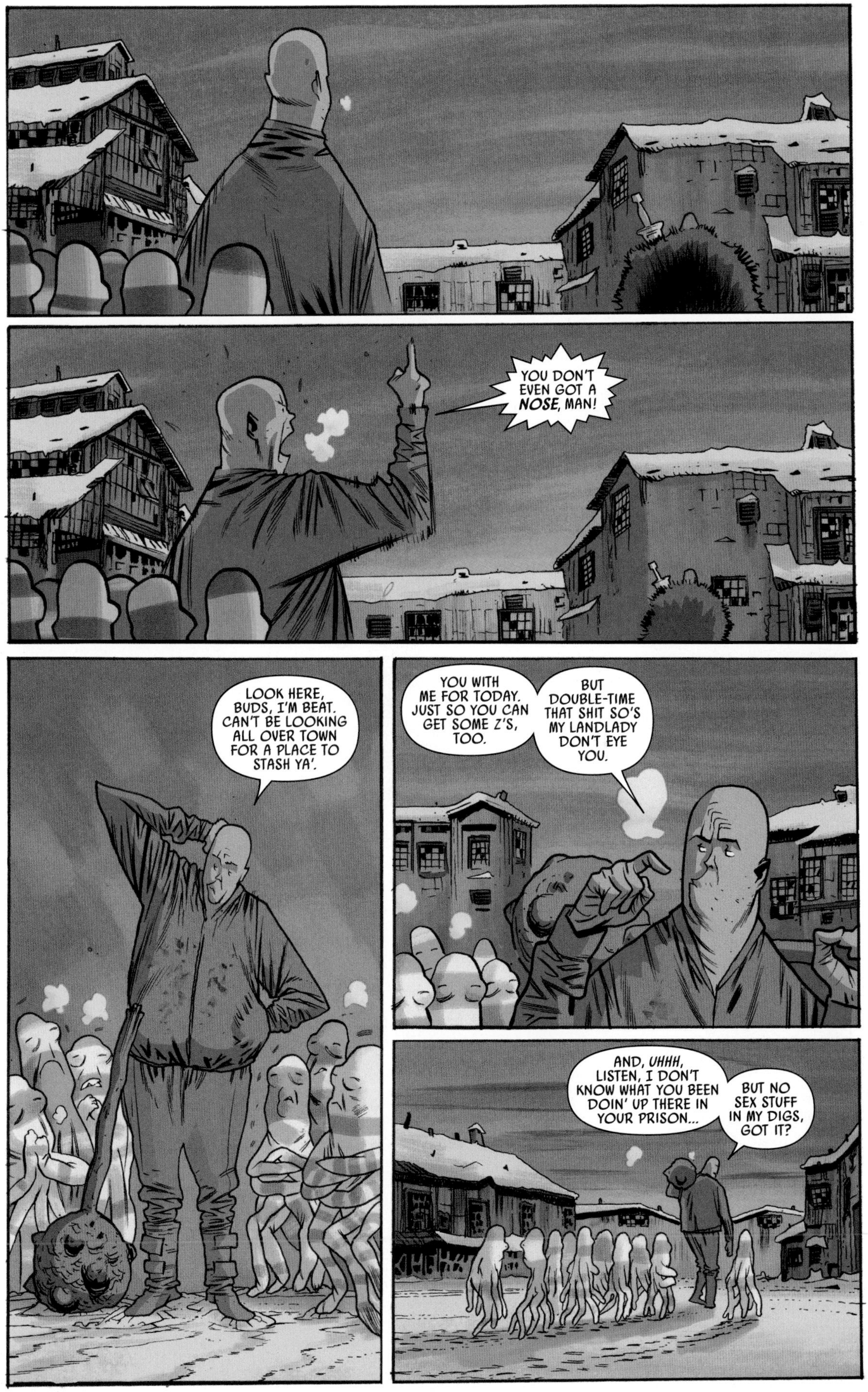
YOU DON'T EVEN GOT A NOSE, MAN!
LOOK HERE, BUDS, I'M BEAT. CAN'T BE LOOKING ALL OVER TOWN FOR A PLACE TO STASH YA'.
YOU WITH ME FOR TODAY. JUST SO YOU CAN GET SOME Z'S, TOO.
BUT DOUBLE-TIME THAT SHIT SO'S MY LANDLADY DON'T EYE YOU.
AND, UHHH, LISTEN, I DON'T KNOW WHAT YOU BEEN DOIN' UP THERE IN YOUR PRISON...
BUT NO SEX STUFF IN MY DIGS, GOT IT?

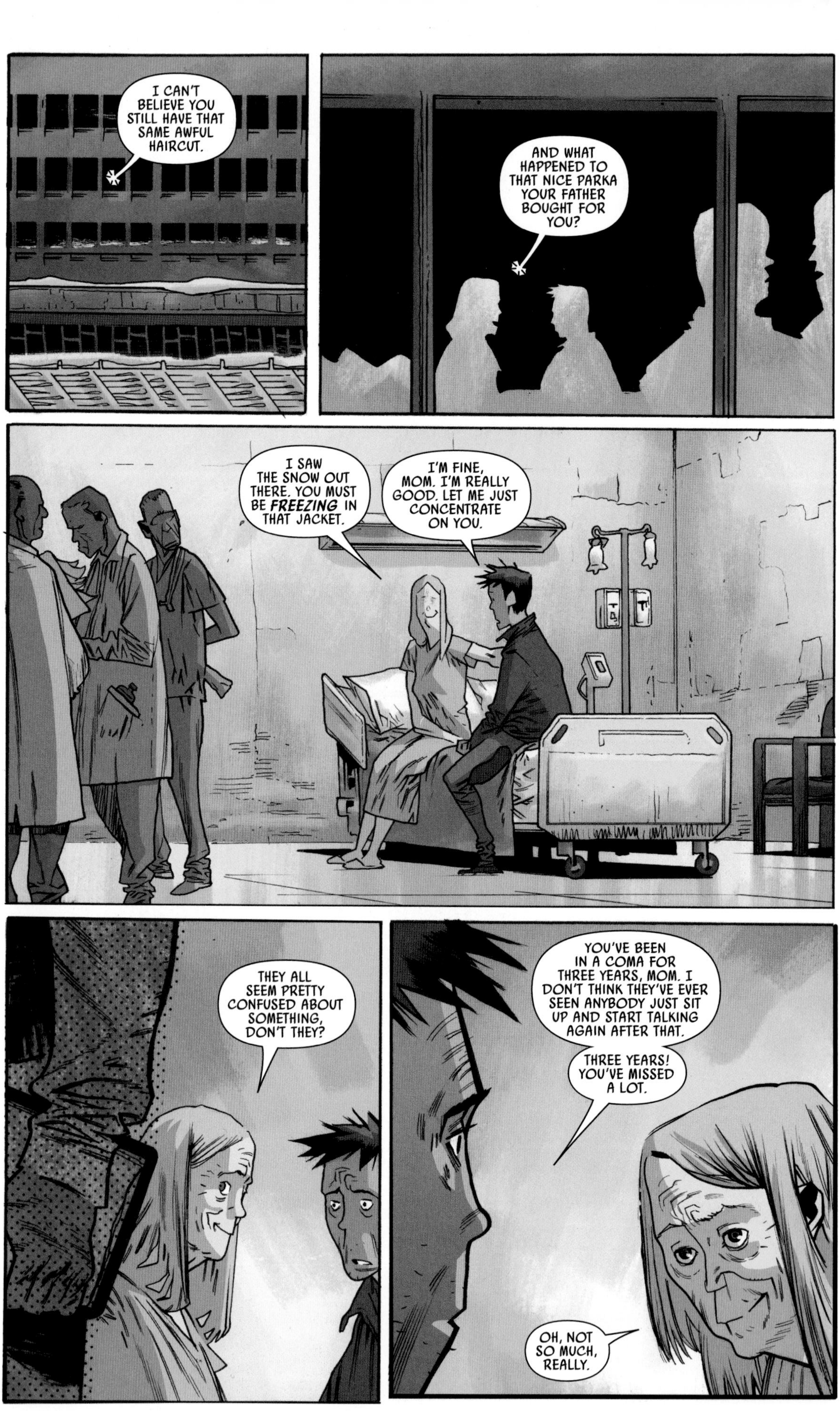
I CAN'T BELIEVE YOU STILL HAVE THAT SAME AWFUL HAIRCUT.
AND WHAT HAPPENED TO THAT NICE PARKA YOUR FATHER BOUGHT FOR YOU?
I SAW THE SNOW OUT THERE. YOU MUST BE *FREEZING* IN THAT JACKET.
I'M FINE, MOM. I'M REALLY GOOD. LET ME JUST CONCENTRATE ON YOU.
THEY ALL SEEM PRETTY CONFUSED ABOUT SOMETHING, DON'T THEY?
YOU'VE BEEN IN A COMA FOR THREE YEARS, MOM. I DON'T THINK THEY'VE EVER SEEN ANYBODY JUST SIT UP AND START TALKING AGAIN AFTER THAT.
THREE YEARS! YOU'VE MISSED A LOT.
OH, NOT SO MUCH, REALLY.

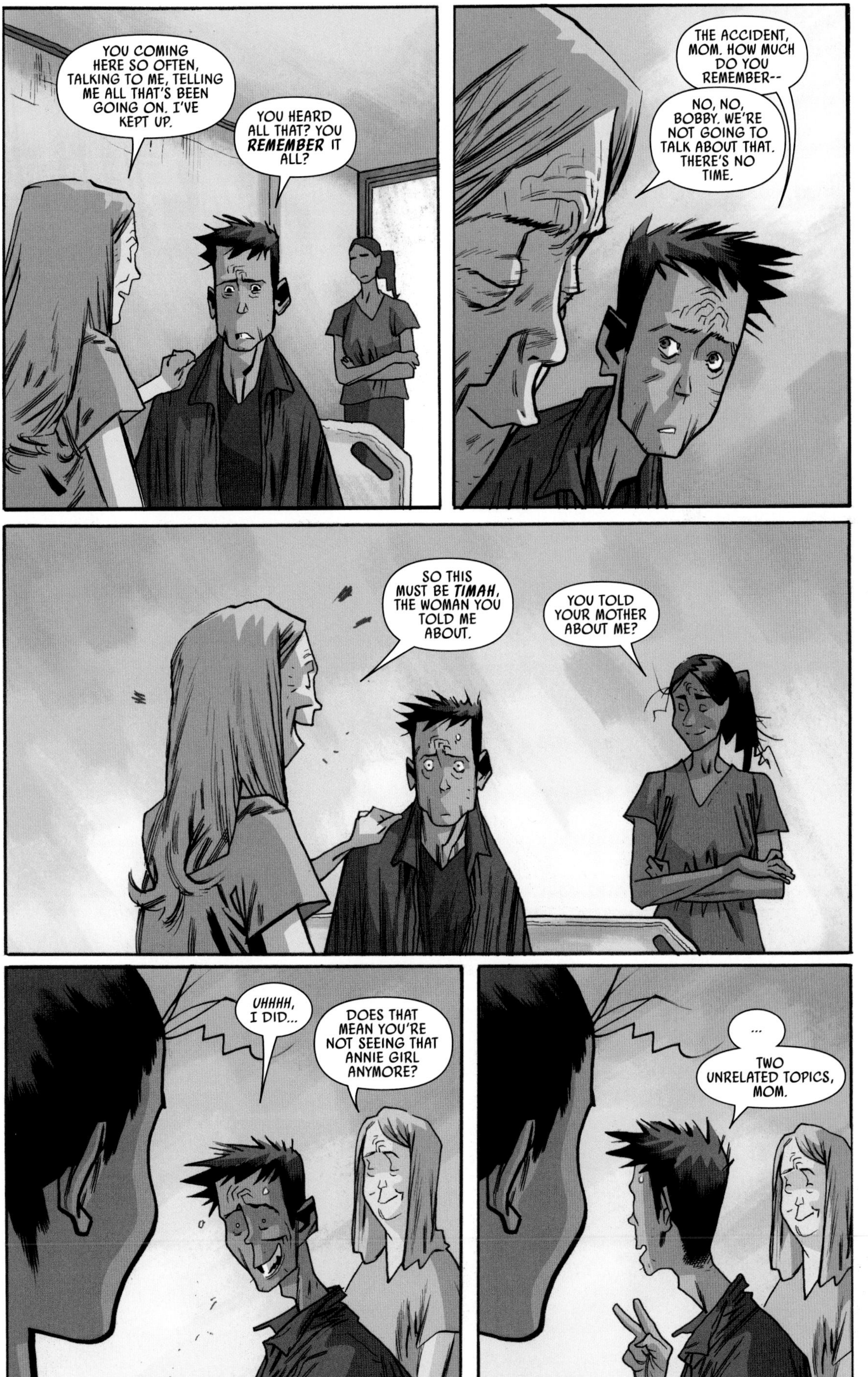
YOU COMING HERE SO OFTEN, TALKING TO ME, TELLING ME ALL THAT'S BEEN GOING ON. I'VE KEPT UP.
YOU HEARD ALL THAT? YOU *REMEMBER* IT ALL?
THE ACCIDENT, MOM. HOW MUCH DO YOU REMEMBER--
NO, NO, BOBBY. WE'RE NOT GOING TO TALK ABOUT THAT. THERE'S NO TIME.
SO THIS MUST BE *TIMAH*, THE WOMAN YOU TOLD ME ABOUT.
YOU TOLD YOUR MOTHER ABOUT ME?
UHHHH, I DID...
DOES THAT MEAN YOU'RE NOT SEEING THAT ANNIE GIRL ANYMORE?
...
TWO UNRELATED TOPICS, MOM.

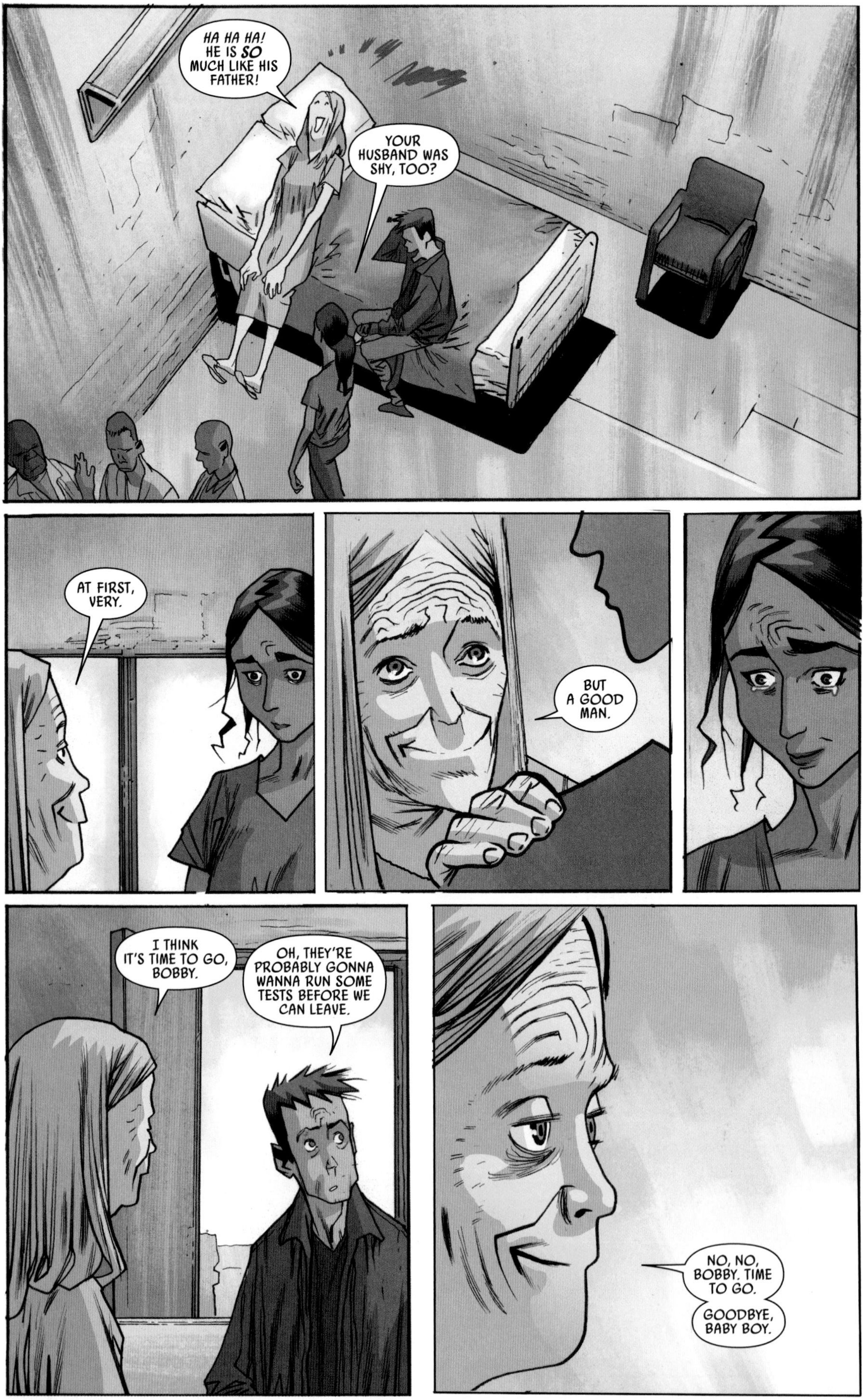

HA HA HA! HE IS SO MUCH LIKE HIS FATHER!
YOUR HUSBAND WAS SHY, TOO?
AT FIRST, VERY.
BUT A GOOD MAN.
I THINK IT'S TIME TO GO, BOBBY.
OH, THEY'RE PROBABLY GONNA WANNA RUN SOME TESTS BEFORE WE CAN LEAVE.
NO, NO, BOBBY. TIME TO GO.
GOODBYE, BABY BOY.

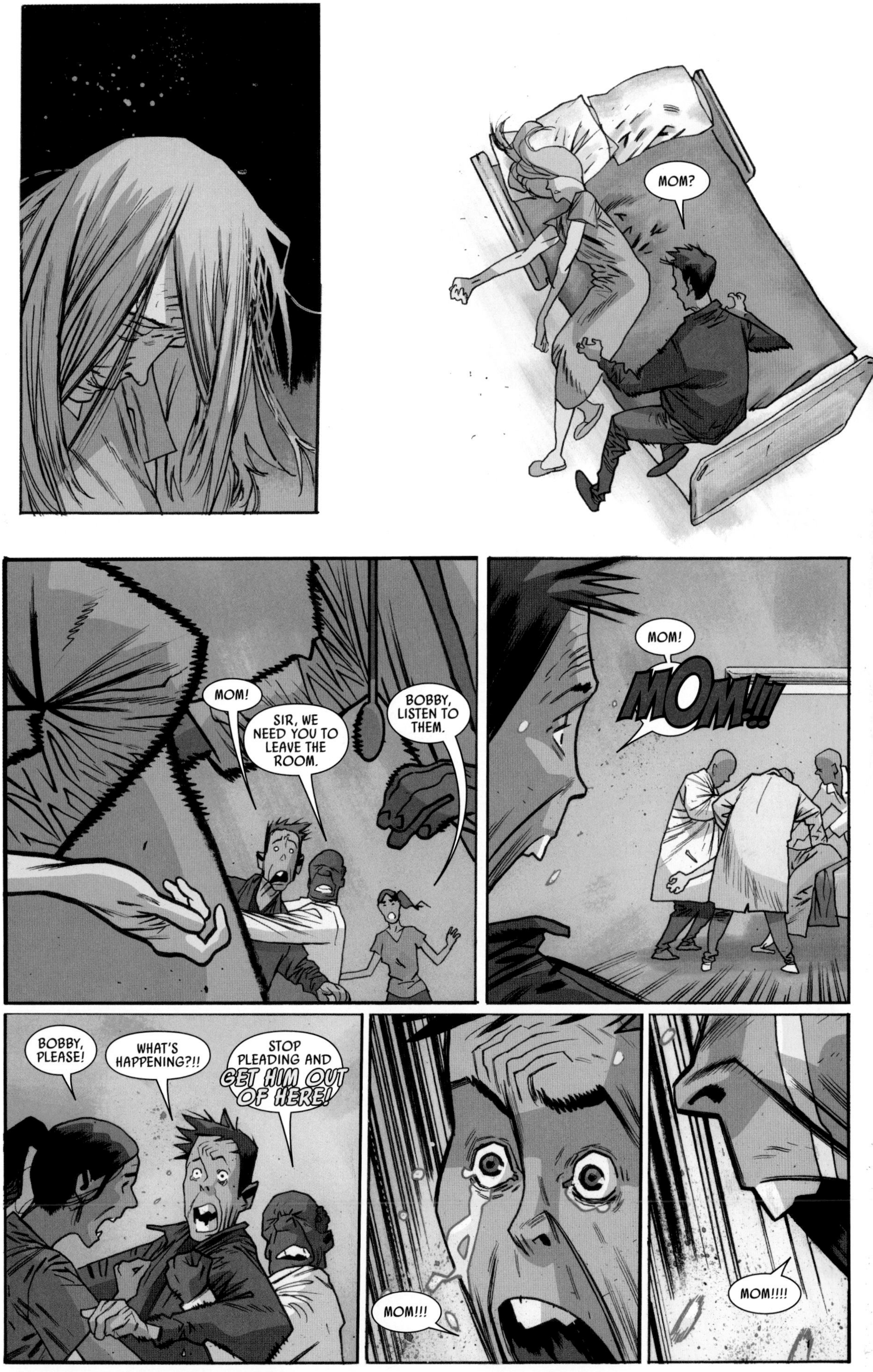
MOM?
MOM!
SIR, WE NEED YOU TO LEAVE THE ROOM.
BOBBY, LISTEN TO THEM.
MOM!
MOM!!!
BOBBY, PLEASE!
WHAT'S HAPPENING?!!
STOP PLEADING AND GET HIM OUT OF HERE!
MOM!!!
MOM!!!!

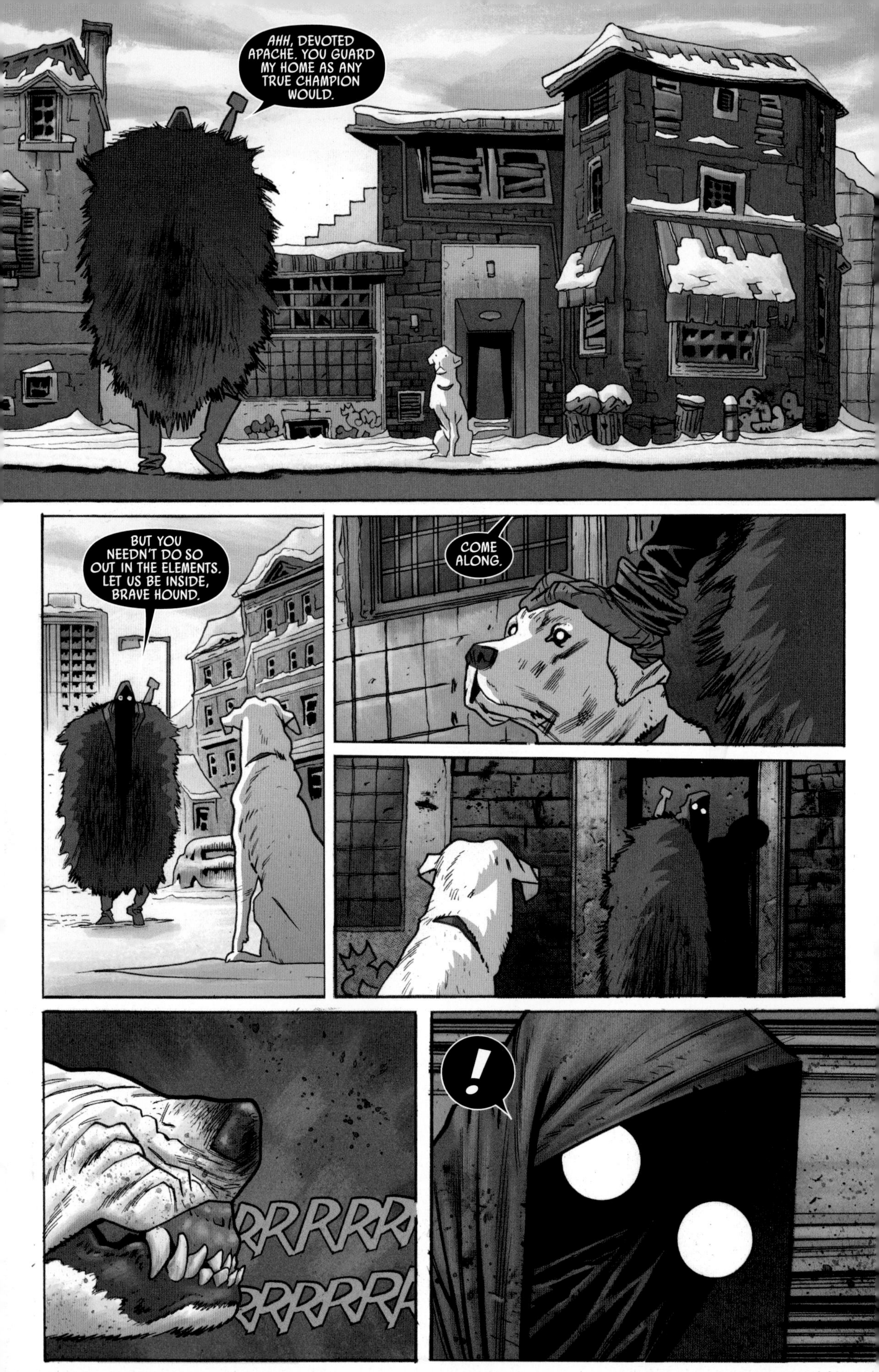
AHH, DEVOTED APACHE. YOU GUARD MY HOME AS ANY TRUE CHAMPION WOULD.
BUT YOU NEEDN'T DO SO OUT IN THE ELEMENTS. LET US BE INSIDE, BRAVE HOUND.
COME ALONG.
RRRRRR
RRRRRR
!

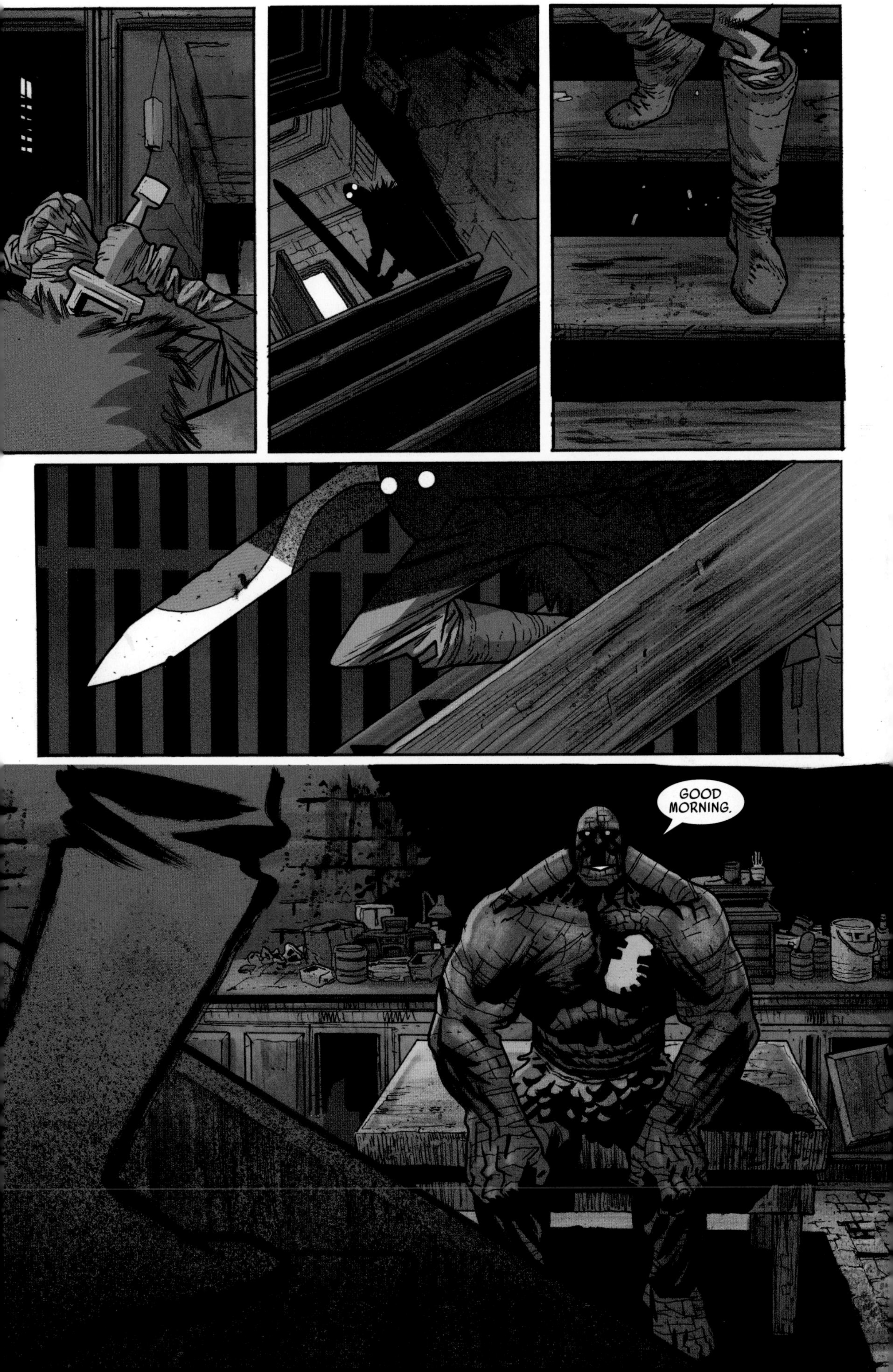
GOOD MORNING.

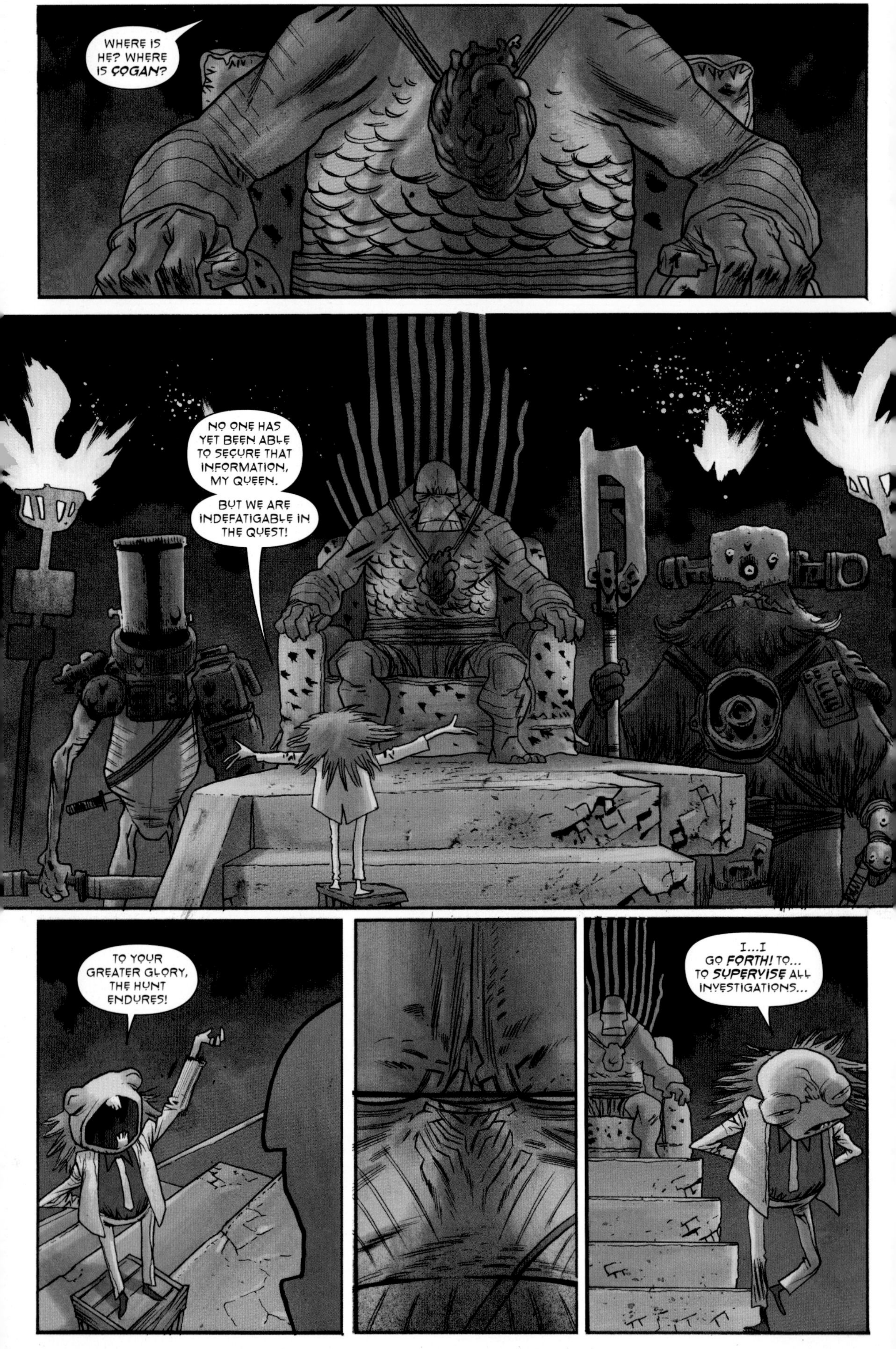
WHERE IS HE? WHERE IS COGAN?
NO ONE HAS YET BEEN ABLE TO SECURE THAT INFORMATION, MY QUEEN.
BUT WE ARE INDEFATIGABLE IN THE QUEST!
TO YOUR GREATER GLORY, THE HUNT ENDURES!
I...I GO FORTH! TO... TO SUPERVISE ALL INVESTIGATIONS...

SNIFF

SNIFF

WHIMPER

WHIIIINE

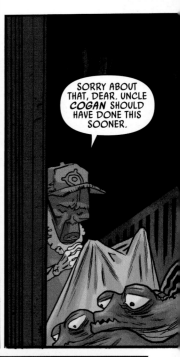

SORRY ABOUT THAT, DEAR. UNCLE *COGAN* SHOULD HAVE DONE THIS SOONER.

NOT MUCH BETTER, IS IT? BUT LISTEN: THIS IS JUST--IT'S *TEMPORARY*, UNDERSTAND? I MEAN, YOU REMEMBER WHAT ASURA SAID TO YOU, DON'T YOU?

"*DADDY'S GONNA BE BACK REALLY SOON*," HE SAID, SO YOU *HAVE* TO EAT. NEED TO GROW THOSE HEADS BACK FOR WHEN HE COMES HOME.

PLEASE, COME ALONG, *LERNA!* HAVE SOMETHING TO EAT AND THEN WE'LL...I DON'T KNOW, WE'LL...WE'LL PLAY BALL?

"*BALL*"? THAT'S THE MAGIC WORD? OKAY, WELL, EAT UP.

ASURA, YOU ARE GOING TO ANSWER FOR THIS!

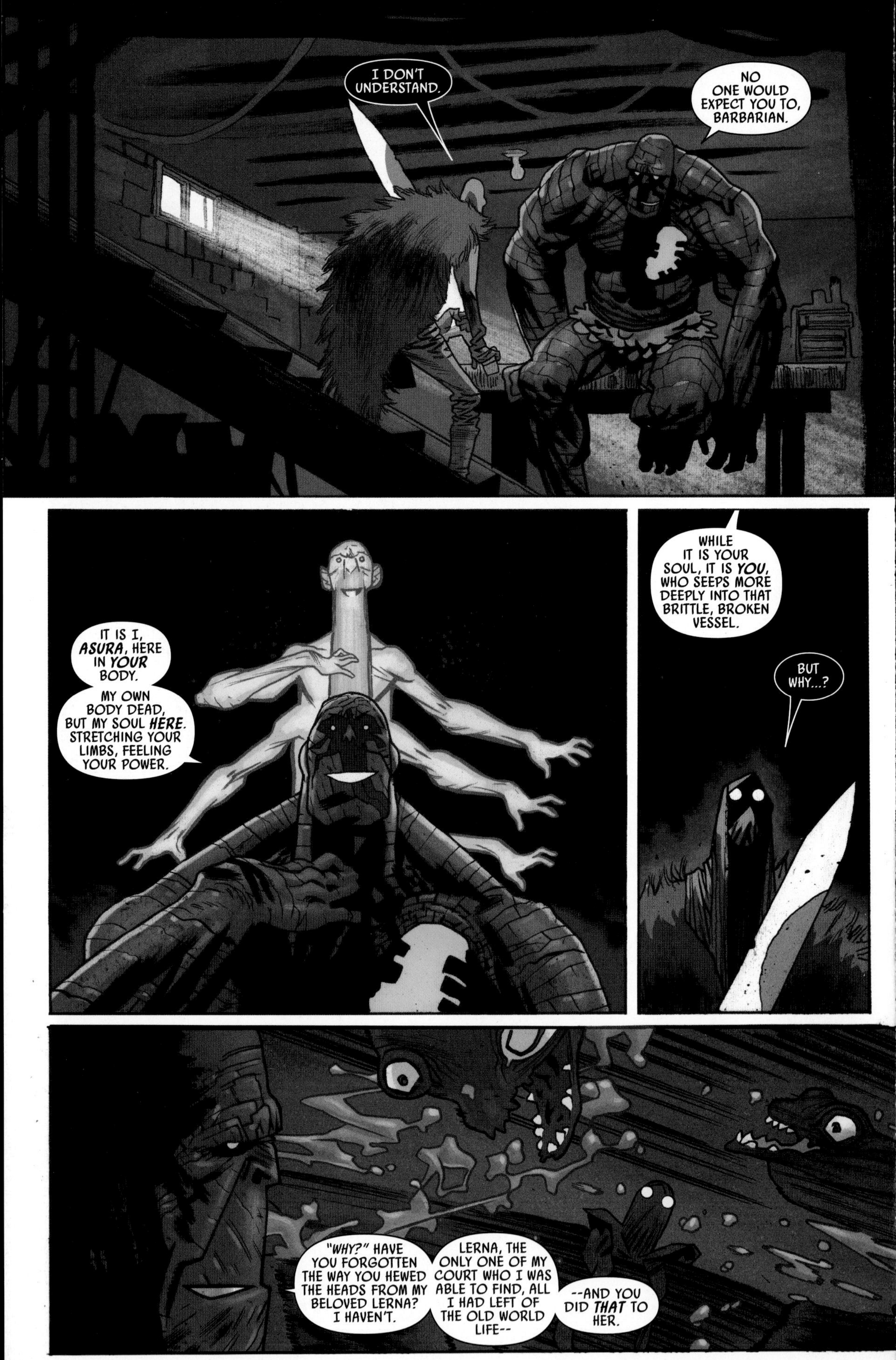
I DON'T UNDERSTAND.
NO ONE WOULD EXPECT YOU TO, BARBARIAN.
IT IS I, ASURA, HERE IN YOUR BODY.
MY OWN BODY DEAD, BUT MY SOUL HERE. STRETCHING YOUR LIMBS, FEELING YOUR POWER.
WHILE IT IS YOUR SOUL, IT IS YOU, WHO SEEPS MORE DEEPLY INTO THAT BRITTLE, BROKEN VESSEL.
BUT WHY...?
"WHY?" HAVE YOU FORGOTTEN THE WAY YOU HEWED THE HEADS FROM MY BELOVED LERNA? I HAVEN'T.
LERNA, THE ONLY ONE OF MY COURT WHO I WAS ABLE TO FIND, ALL I HAD LEFT OF THE OLD WORLD LIFE--
--AND YOU DID THAT TO HER.

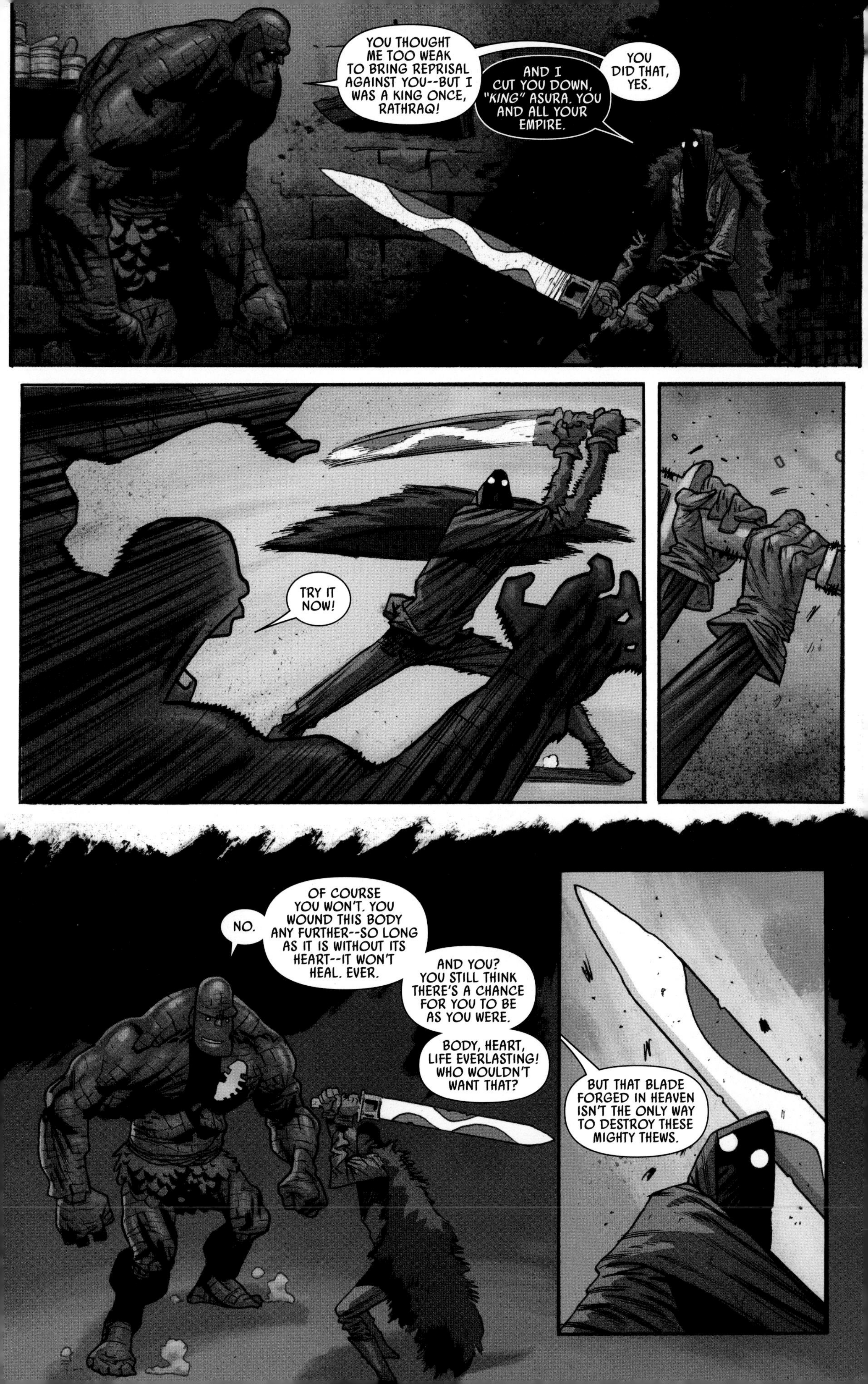
YOU THOUGHT ME TOO WEAK TO BRING REPRISAL AGAINST YOU--BUT I WAS A KING ONCE, RATHRAQ!
AND I CUT YOU DOWN, "KING" ASURA. YOU AND ALL YOUR EMPIRE.
YOU DID THAT, YES.
TRY IT NOW!
NO.
OF COURSE YOU WON'T. YOU WOUND THIS BODY ANY FURTHER--SO LONG AS IT IS WITHOUT ITS HEART--IT WON'T HEAL. EVER.
AND YOU? YOU STILL THINK THERE'S A CHANCE FOR YOU TO BE AS YOU WERE.
BODY, HEART, LIFE EVERLASTING! WHO WOULDN'T WANT THAT?
BUT THAT BLADE FORGED IN HEAVEN ISN'T THE ONLY WAY TO DESTROY THESE MIGHTY THEWS.

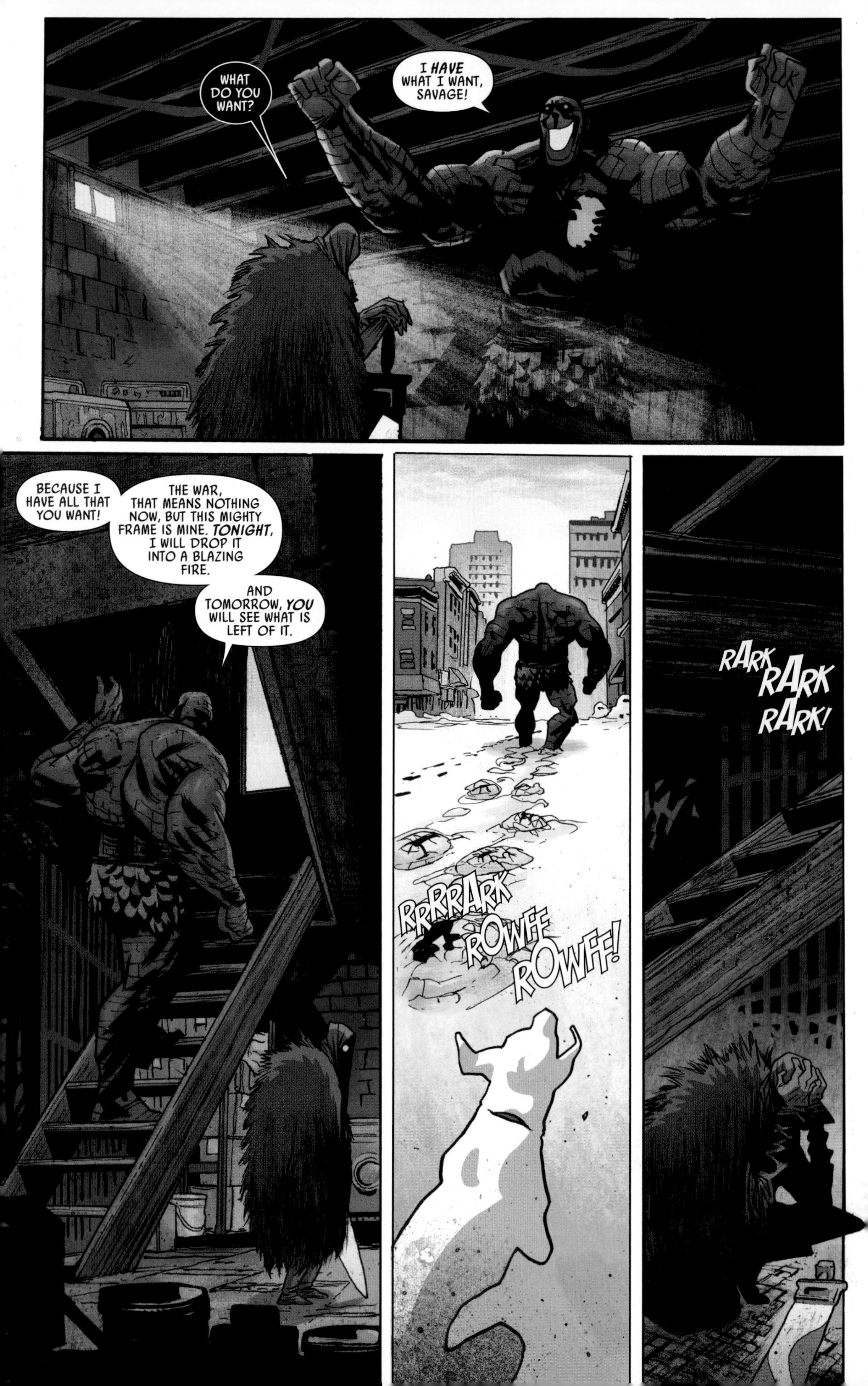
WHAT DO YOU WANT?
I HAVE WHAT I WANT, SAVAGE!
BECAUSE I HAVE ALL THAT YOU WANT!
THE WAR, THAT MEANS NOTHING NOW, BUT THIS MIGHTY FRAME IS MINE. TONIGHT, I WILL DROP IT INTO A BLAZING FIRE.
AND TOMORROW, YOU WILL SEE WHAT IS LEFT OF IT.
RRRRARK ROWFF ROWFF!
RARK RARK RARK!

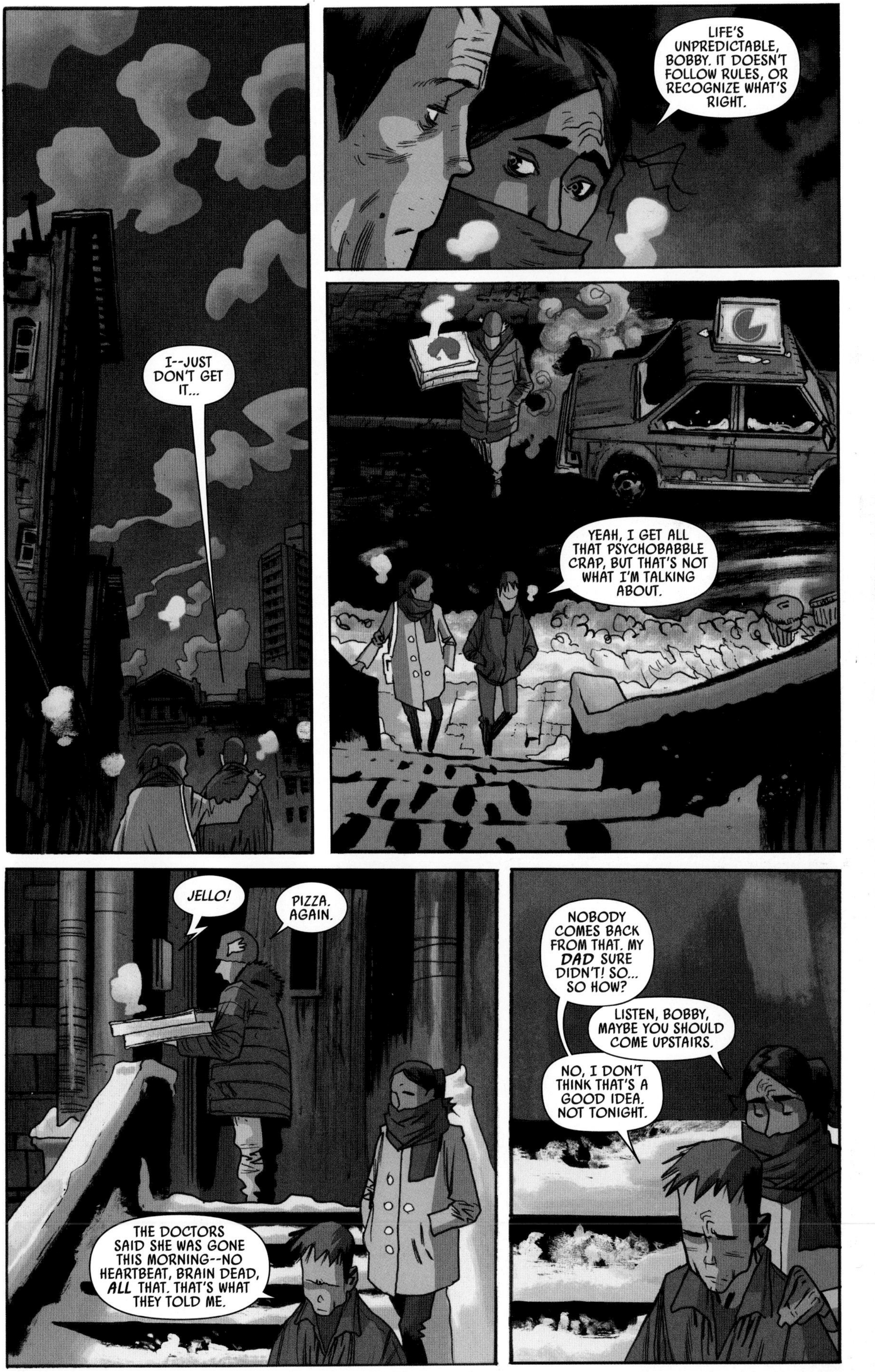
I--JUST DON'T GET IT...
LIFE'S UNPREDICTABLE, BOBBY. IT DOESN'T FOLLOW RULES, OR RECOGNIZE WHAT'S RIGHT.
YEAH, I GET ALL THAT PSYCHOBABBLE CRAP, BUT THAT'S NOT WHAT I'M TALKING ABOUT.
JELLO!
PIZZA. AGAIN.
THE DOCTORS SAID SHE WAS GONE THIS MORNING--NO HEARTBEAT, BRAIN DEAD, ALL THAT. THAT'S WHAT THEY TOLD ME.
NOBODY COMES BACK FROM THAT. MY DAD SURE DIDN'T! SO... SO HOW?
LISTEN, BOBBY, MAYBE YOU SHOULD COME UPSTAIRS.
NO, I DON'T THINK THAT'S A GOOD IDEA. NOT TONIGHT.

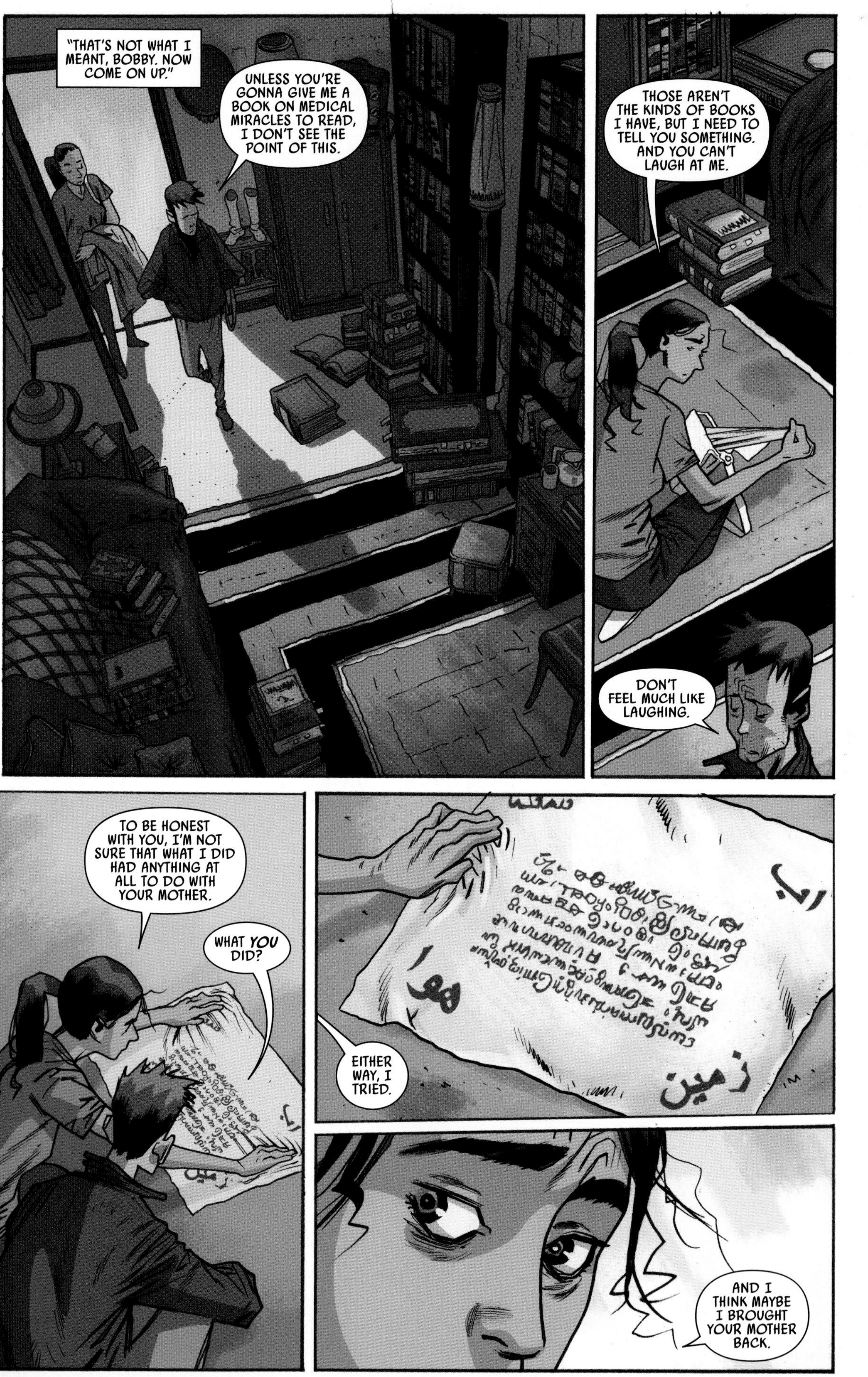
"THAT'S NOT WHAT I MEANT, BOBBY. NOW COME ON UP."
UNLESS YOU'RE GONNA GIVE ME A BOOK ON MEDICAL MIRACLES TO READ, I DON'T SEE THE POINT OF THIS.
THOSE AREN'T THE KINDS OF BOOKS I HAVE, BUT I NEED TO TELL YOU SOMETHING. AND YOU CAN'T LAUGH AT ME.
DON'T FEEL MUCH LIKE LAUGHING.
TO BE HONEST WITH YOU, I'M NOT SURE THAT WHAT I DID HAD ANYTHING AT ALL TO DO WITH YOUR MOTHER.
WHAT *YOU* DID?
EITHER WAY, I TRIED.
AND I THINK MAYBE I BROUGHT YOUR MOTHER BACK.

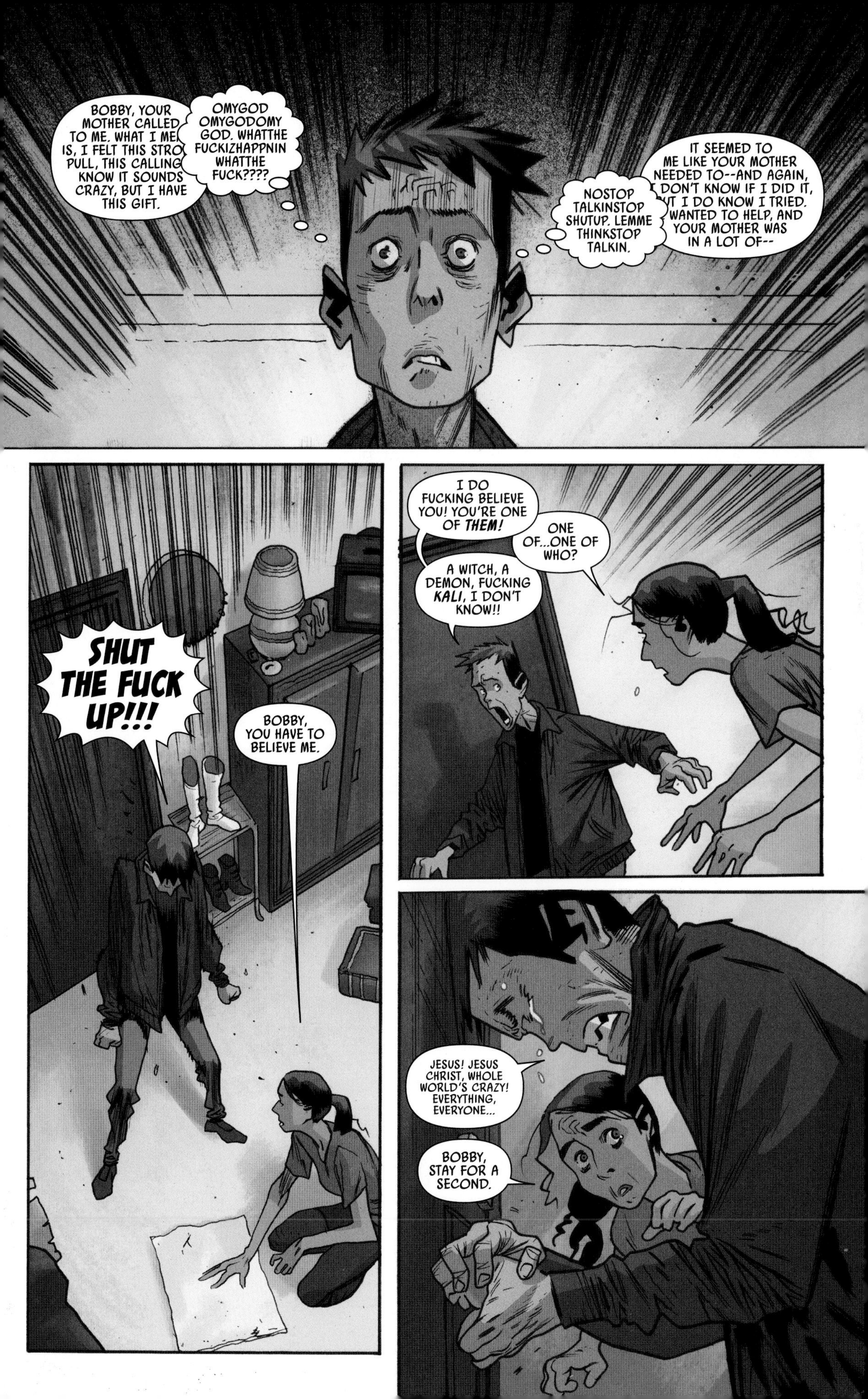
BOBBY, YOUR MOTHER CALLED TO ME. WHAT I ME IS, I FELT THIS STRO PULL, THIS CALLING KNOW IT SOUNDS CRAZY, BUT I HAVE THIS GIFT.
OMYGOD OMYGODOMY GOD. WHATTHE FUCKIZHAPPNIN WHATTHE FUCK????
IT SEEMED TO ME LIKE YOUR MOTHER NEEDED TO--AND AGAIN, I DON'T KNOW IF I DID IT, UT I DO KNOW I TRIED. WANTED TO HELP, AND YOUR MOTHER WAS IN A LOT OF--
NOSTOP TALKINSTOP SHUTUP. LEMME THINKSTOP TALKIN.
SHUT THE FUCK UP!!!
BOBBY, YOU HAVE TO BELIEVE ME.
I DO FUCKING BELIEVE YOU! YOU'RE ONE OF THEM!
ONE OF...ONE OF WHO?
A WITCH, A DEMON, FUCKING KALI, I DON'T KNOW!!
JESUS! JESUS CHRIST, WHOLE WORLD'S CRAZY! EVERYTHING, EVERYONE...
BOBBY, STAY FOR A SECOND.

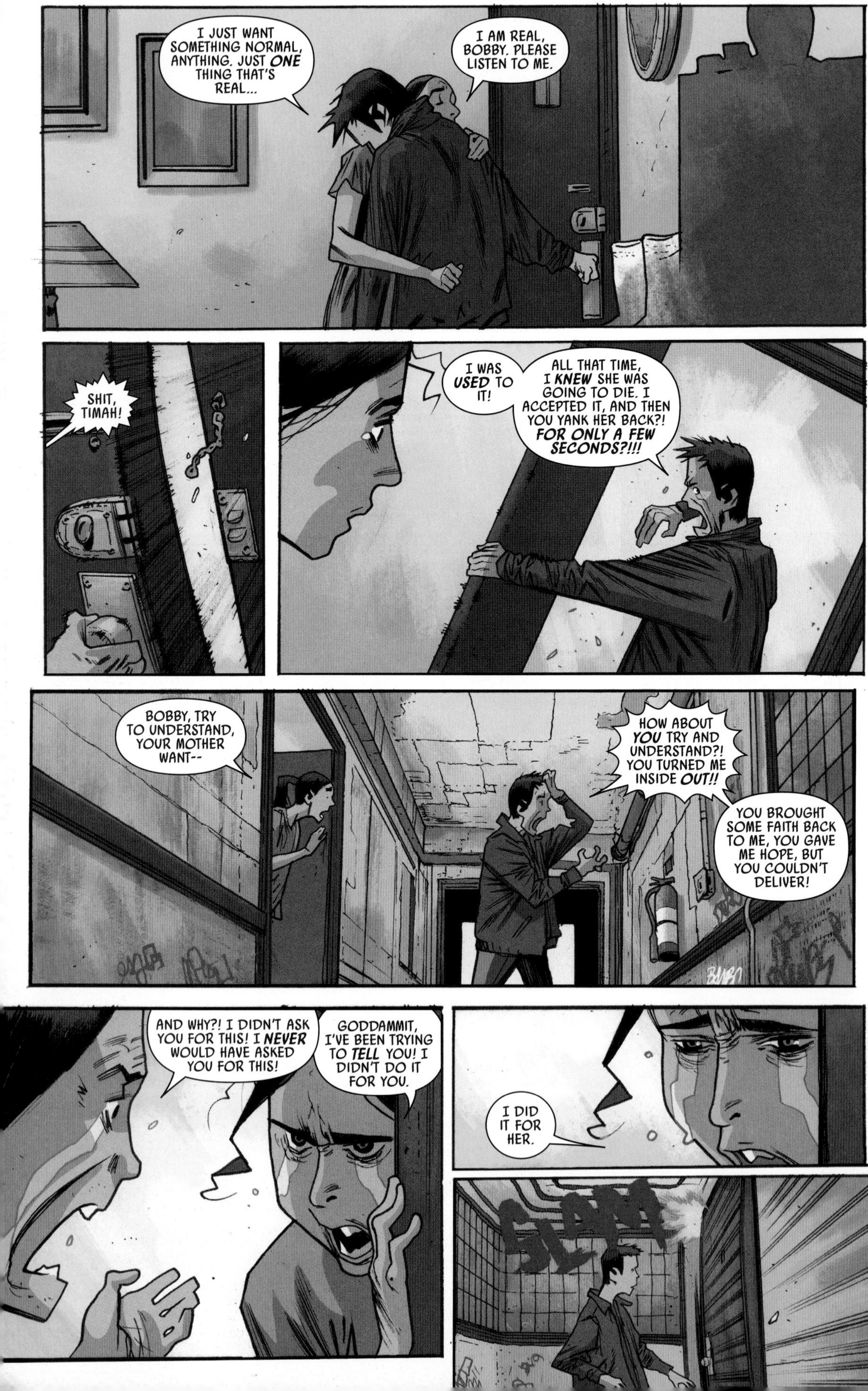
I JUST WANT SOMETHING NORMAL, ANYTHING. JUST ONE THING THAT'S REAL...
I AM REAL, BOBBY. PLEASE LISTEN TO ME.
SHIT, TIMAH!
I WAS USED TO IT!
ALL THAT TIME, I KNEW SHE WAS GOING TO DIE. I ACCEPTED IT, AND THEN YOU YANK HER BACK?! FOR ONLY A FEW SECONDS?!!!
BOBBY, TRY TO UNDERSTAND, YOUR MOTHER WANT--
HOW ABOUT YOU TRY AND UNDERSTAND?! YOU TURNED ME INSIDE OUT!!
YOU BROUGHT SOME FAITH BACK TO ME, YOU GAVE ME HOPE, BUT YOU COULDN'T DELIVER!
AND WHY?! I DIDN'T ASK YOU FOR THIS! I NEVER WOULD HAVE ASKED YOU FOR THIS!
GODDAMMIT, I'VE BEEN TRYING TO TELL YOU! I DIDN'T DO IT FOR YOU.
I DID IT FOR HER.
SLAM

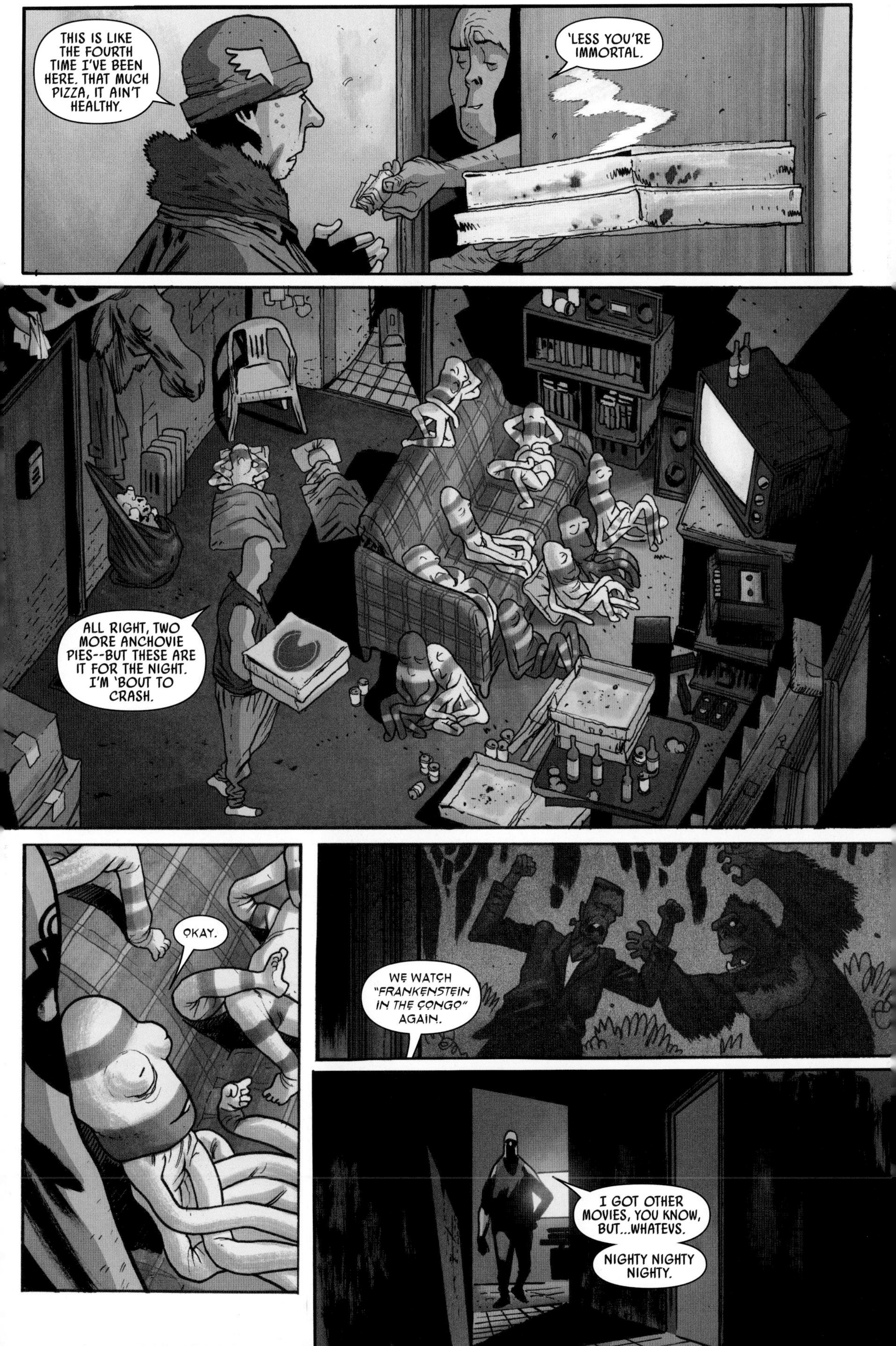
THIS IS LIKE THE FOURTH TIME I'VE BEEN HERE. THAT MUCH PIZZA, IT AIN'T HEALTHY.
'LESS YOU'RE IMMORTAL.
ALL RIGHT, TWO MORE ANCHOVIE PIES--BUT THESE ARE IT FOR THE NIGHT. I'M 'BOUT TO CRASH.
OKAY.
WE WATCH "FRANKENSTEIN IN THE CONGO" AGAIN.
I GOT OTHER MOVIES, YOU KNOW, BUT...WHATEVS.
NIGHTY NIGHTY NIGHTY.

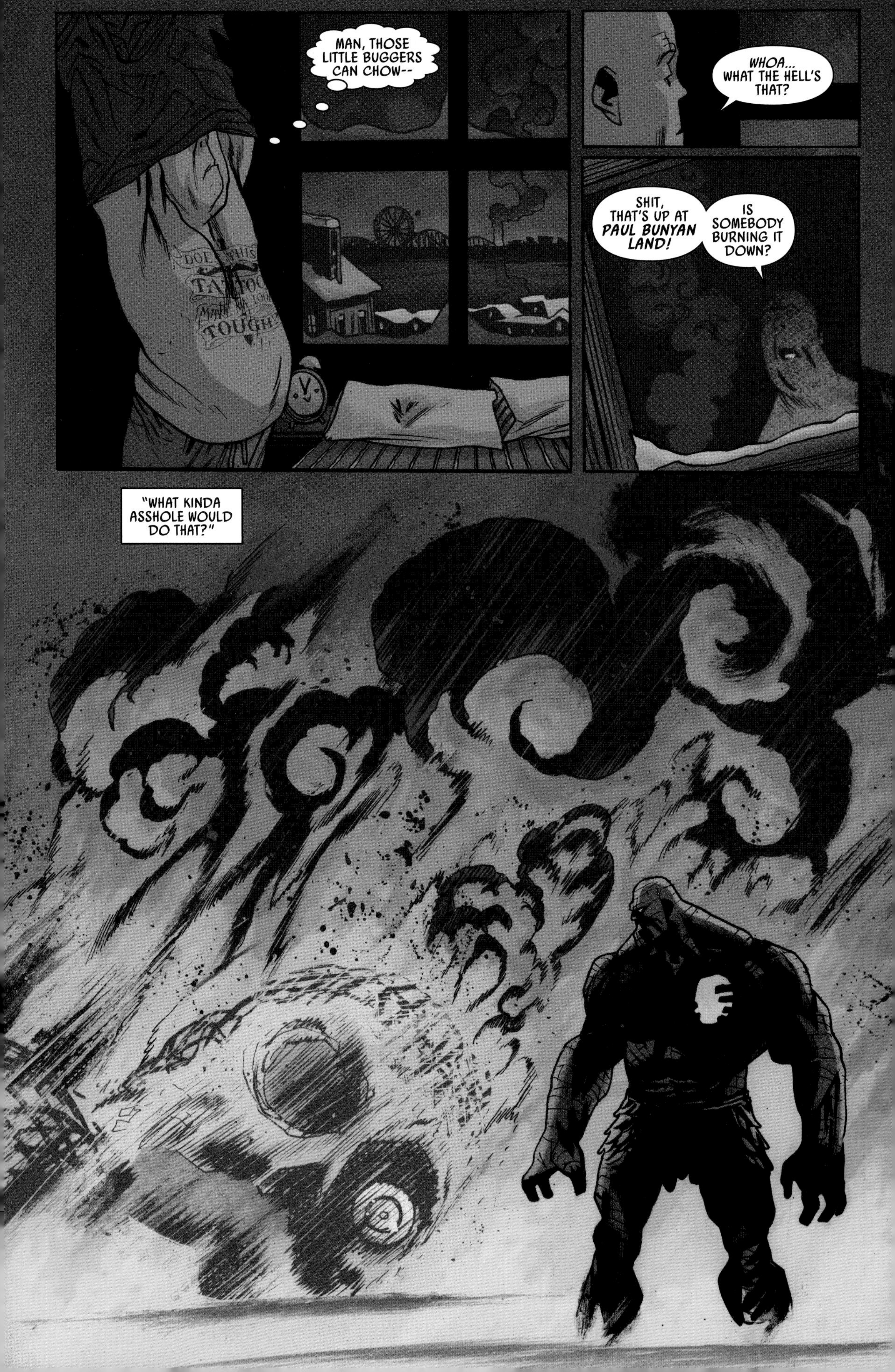
MAN, THOSE LITTLE BUGGERS CAN CHOW--
WHOA... WHAT THE HELL'S THAT?
SHIT, THAT'S UP AT *PAUL BUNYAN LAND!*
IS SOMEBODY BURNING IT DOWN?
"WHAT KINDA ASSHOLE WOULD DO THAT?"

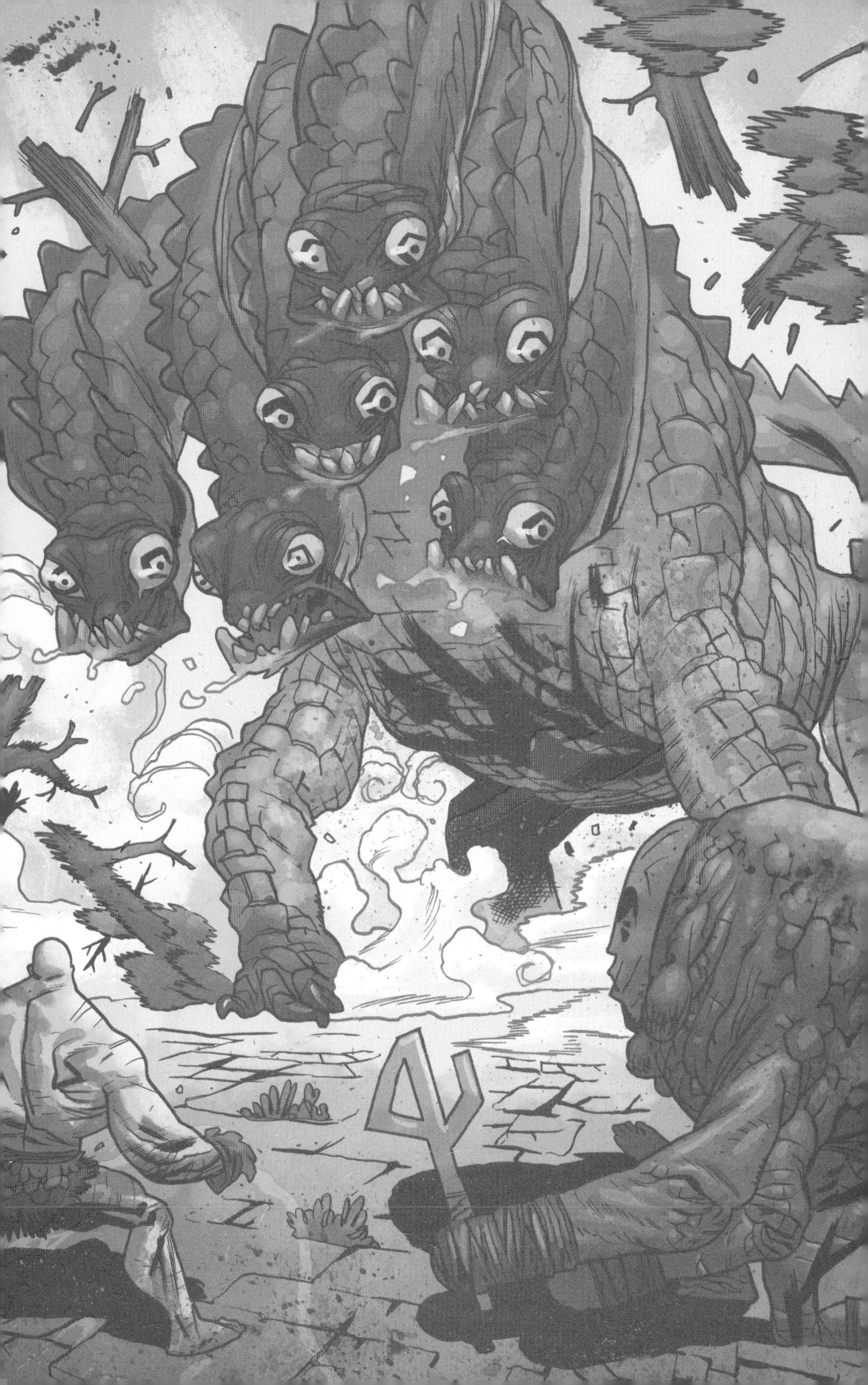

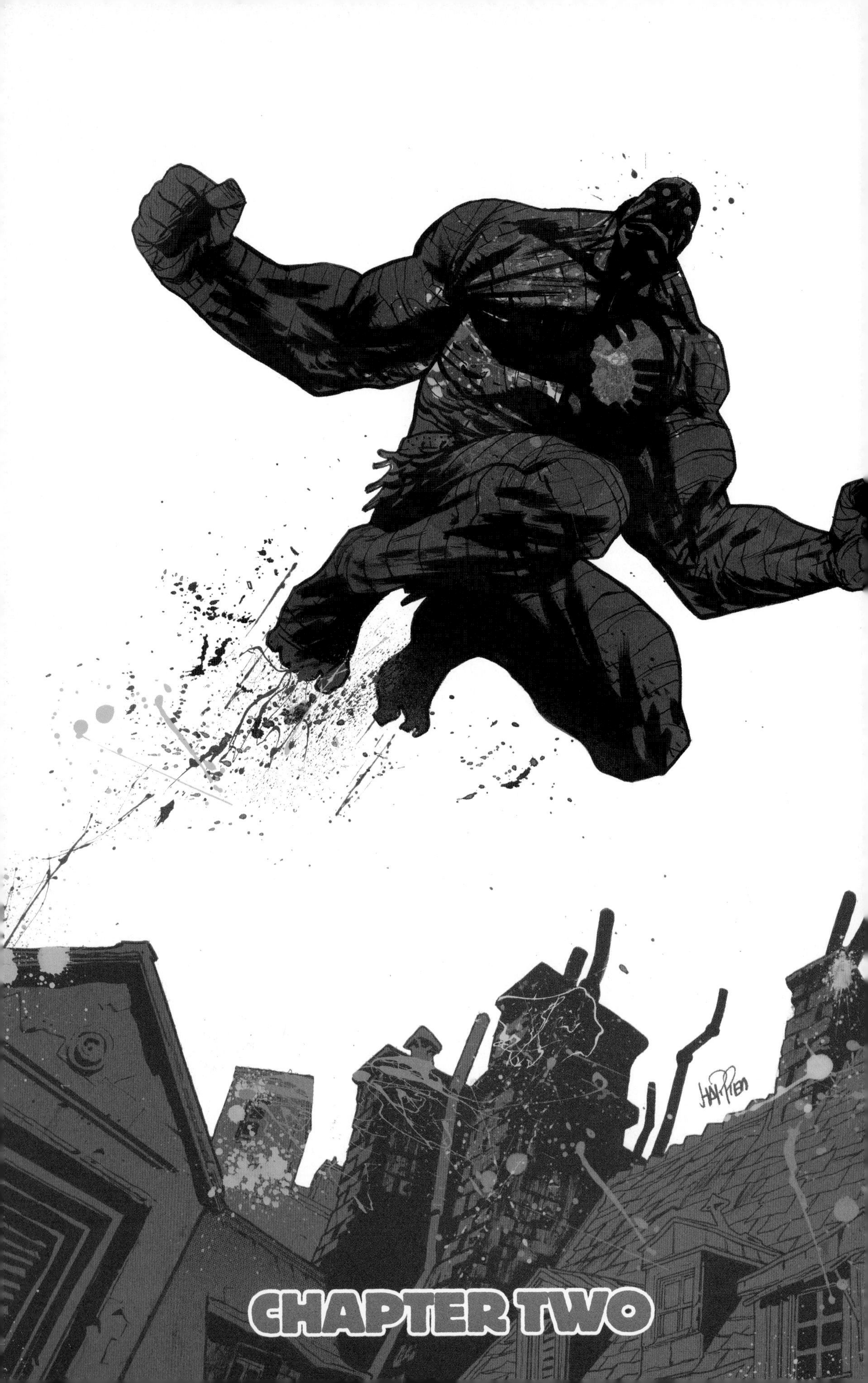

CHAPTER TWO

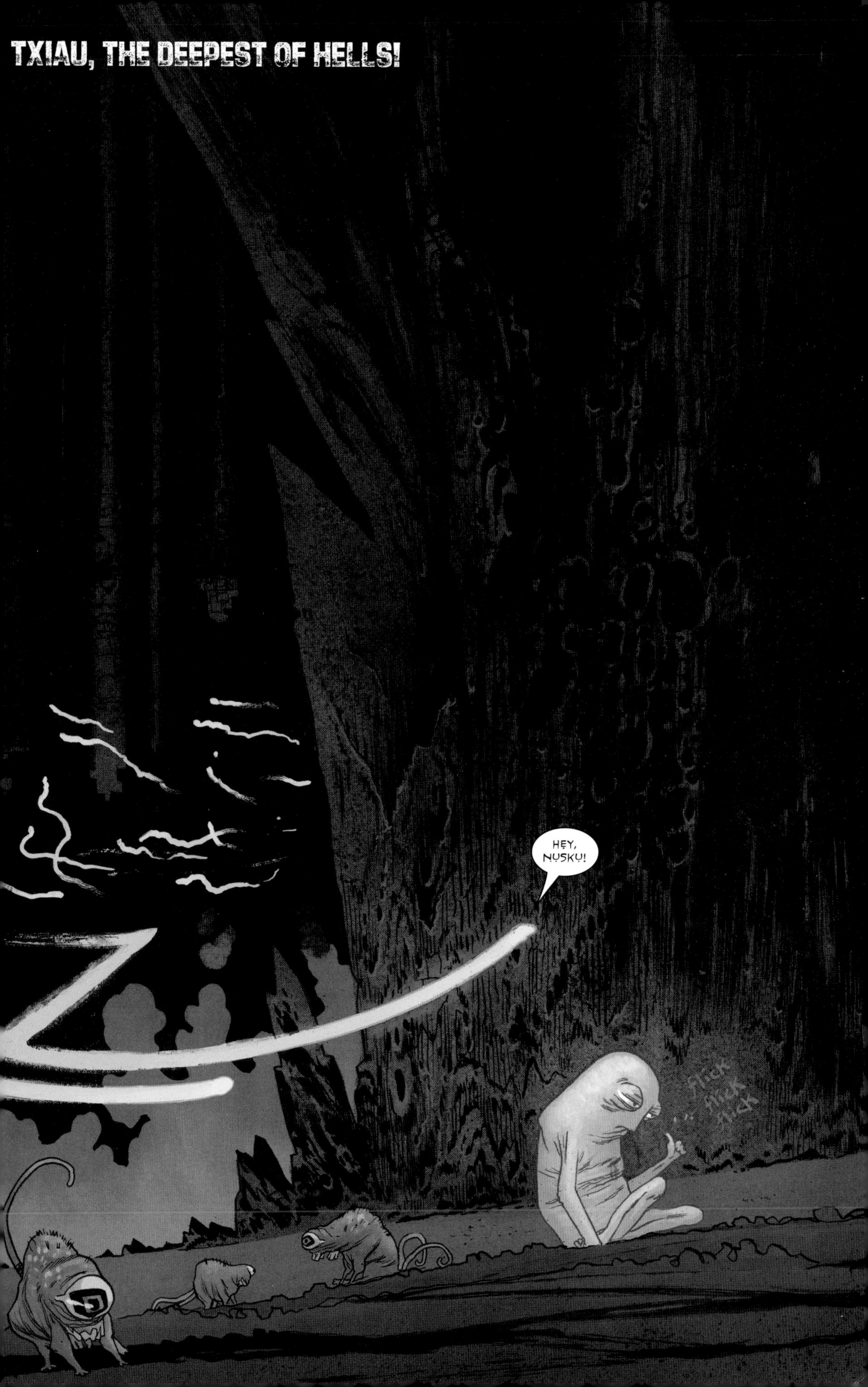
TXIAU, THE DEEPEST OF HELLS!
HEY, NUSKU!
flick flick flick

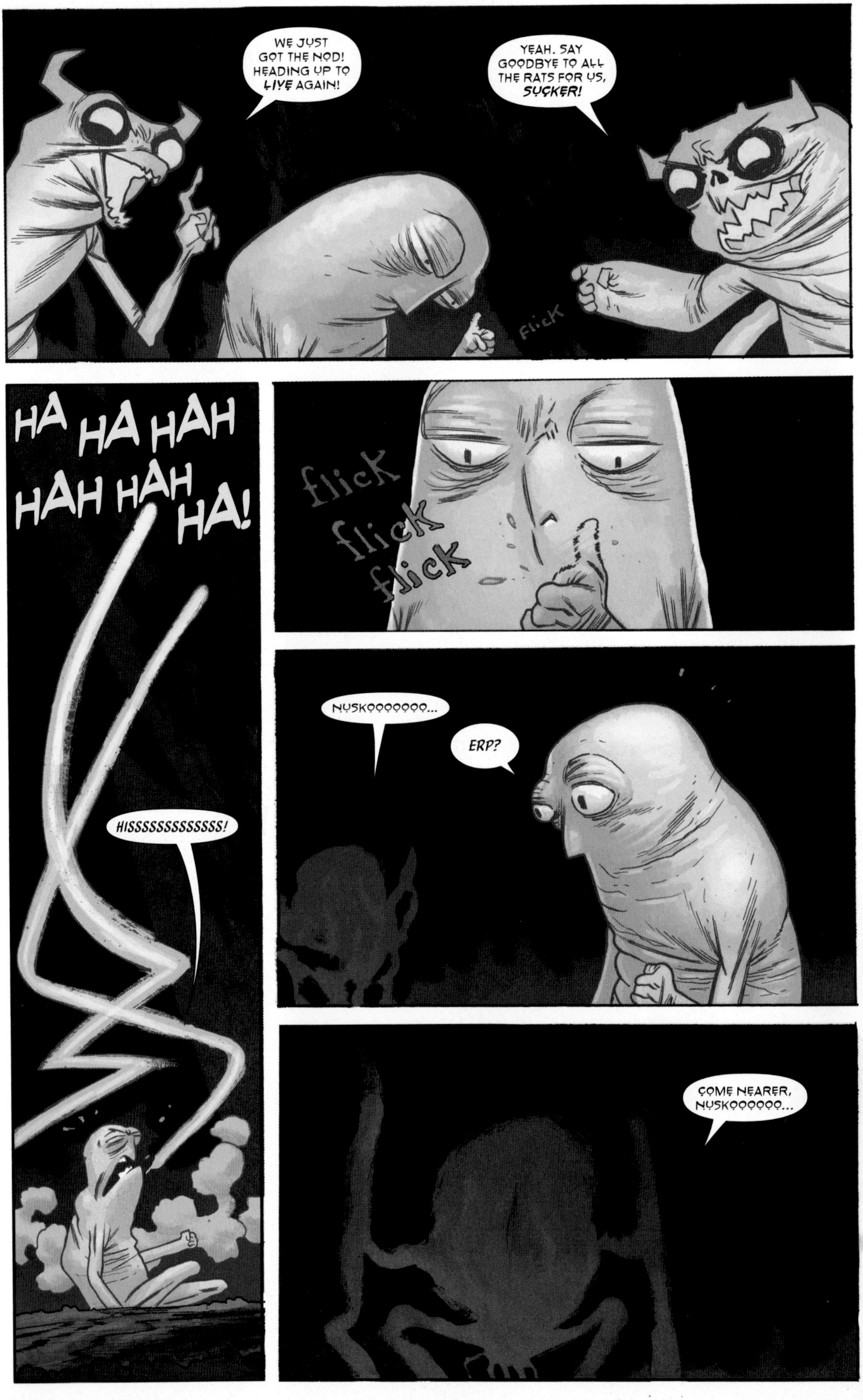
WE JUST GOT THE NOD! HEADING UP TO LIVE AGAIN!
YEAH. SAY GOODBYE TO ALL THE RATS FOR US, SUCKER!
FLICK
HA HA HAH HAH HAH HA!
HISSSSSSSSSSSSS!
flick flick flick
NUSKOOOOOOO...
ERP?
COME NEARER, NUSKOOOOOO...

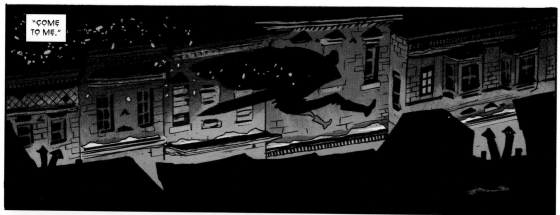

"COME TO ME."

ZZZZZZZZ

WHURZA...?

TO ARMS, DEL! MY BODY HAS BEEN STOLEN!

WHACHOO TALKIN' BOUT? STANDIN' RIGHT FRONTA ME...

MY *IMMORTAL* BODY! AN ENEMY'S SOUL HAS POSSESSED IT!

HE WILL DESTROY IT-- BURN IT--FOR REVENGE! I SEE THE FIRE ACROSS THE RIVER, WHERE THE GOD STATUES HAVE FALLEN!

MAN, YOU *ALWAYS* GOT SHIT GOIN' ON, DON'T YOU?

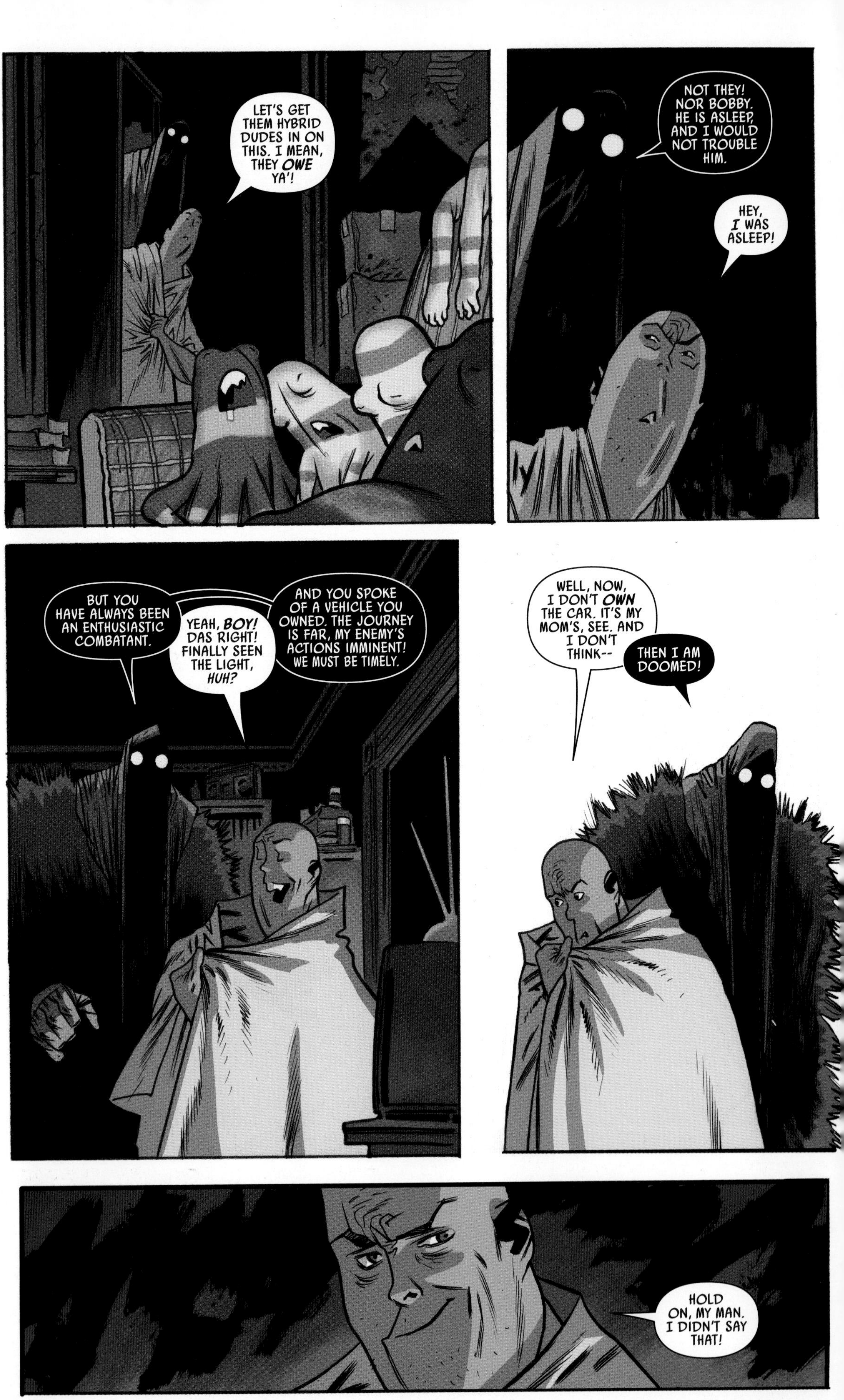
LET'S GET THEM HYBRID DUDES IN ON THIS. I MEAN, THEY OWE YA'!
NOT THEY! NOR BOBBY. HE IS ASLEEP, AND I WOULD NOT TROUBLE HIM.
HEY, I WAS ASLEEP!
BUT YOU HAVE ALWAYS BEEN AN ENTHUSIASTIC COMBATANT.
AND YOU SPOKE OF A VEHICLE YOU OWNED. THE JOURNEY IS FAR, MY ENEMY'S ACTIONS IMMINENT! WE MUST BE TIMELY.
YEAH, BOY! DAS RIGHT! FINALLY SEEN THE LIGHT, HUH?
WELL, NOW, I DON'T OWN THE CAR. IT'S MY MOM'S, SEE. AND I DON'T THINK--
THEN I AM DOOMED!
HOLD ON, MY MAN. I DIDN'T SAY THAT!

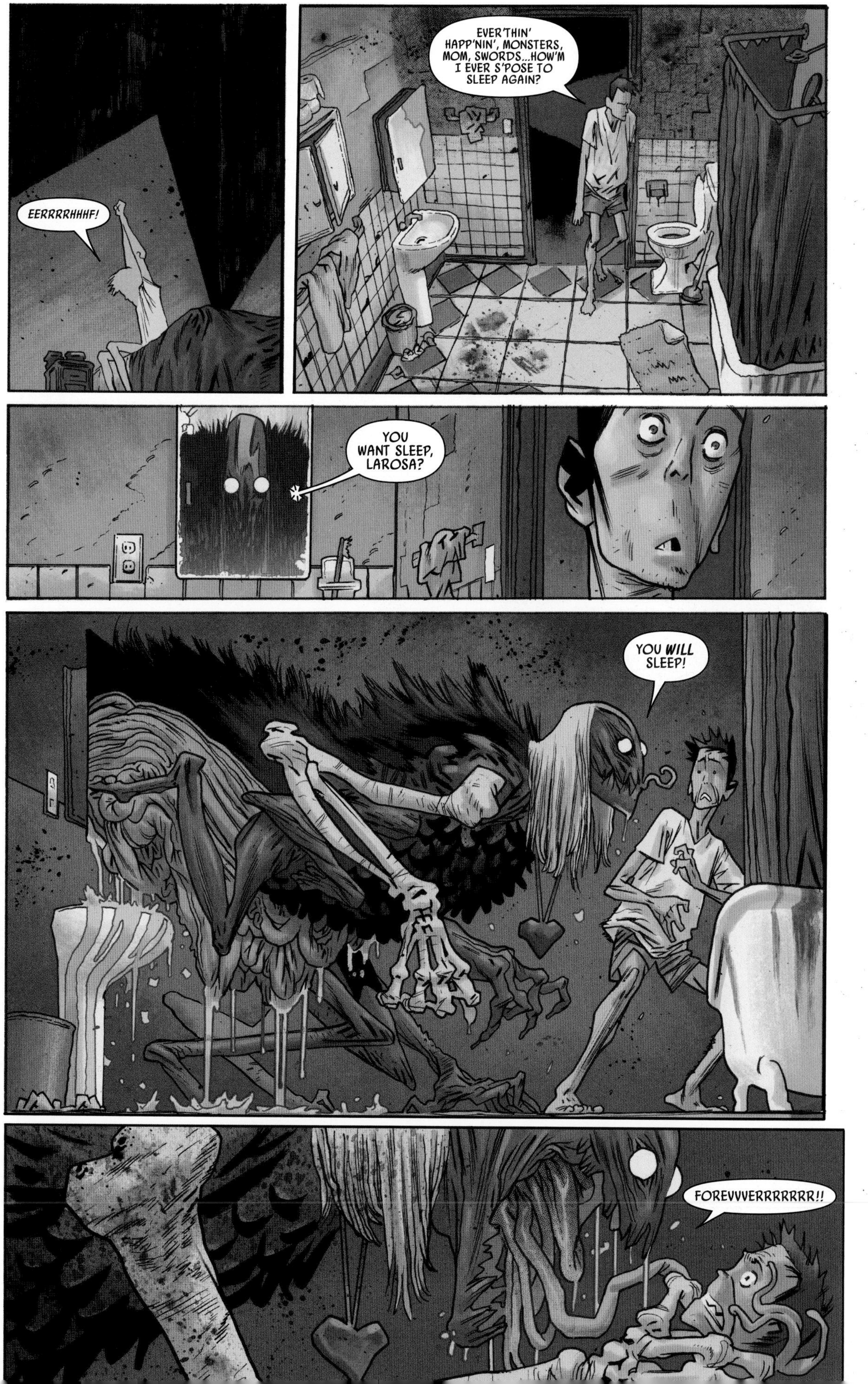
EERRRRHHHF!
EVER'THIN' HAPP'NIN', MONSTERS, MOM, SWORDS...HOW'M I EVER S'POSE TO SLEEP AGAIN?
YOU WANT SLEEP, LAROSA?
YOU WILL SLEEP!
FOREVVVERRRRRRR!!

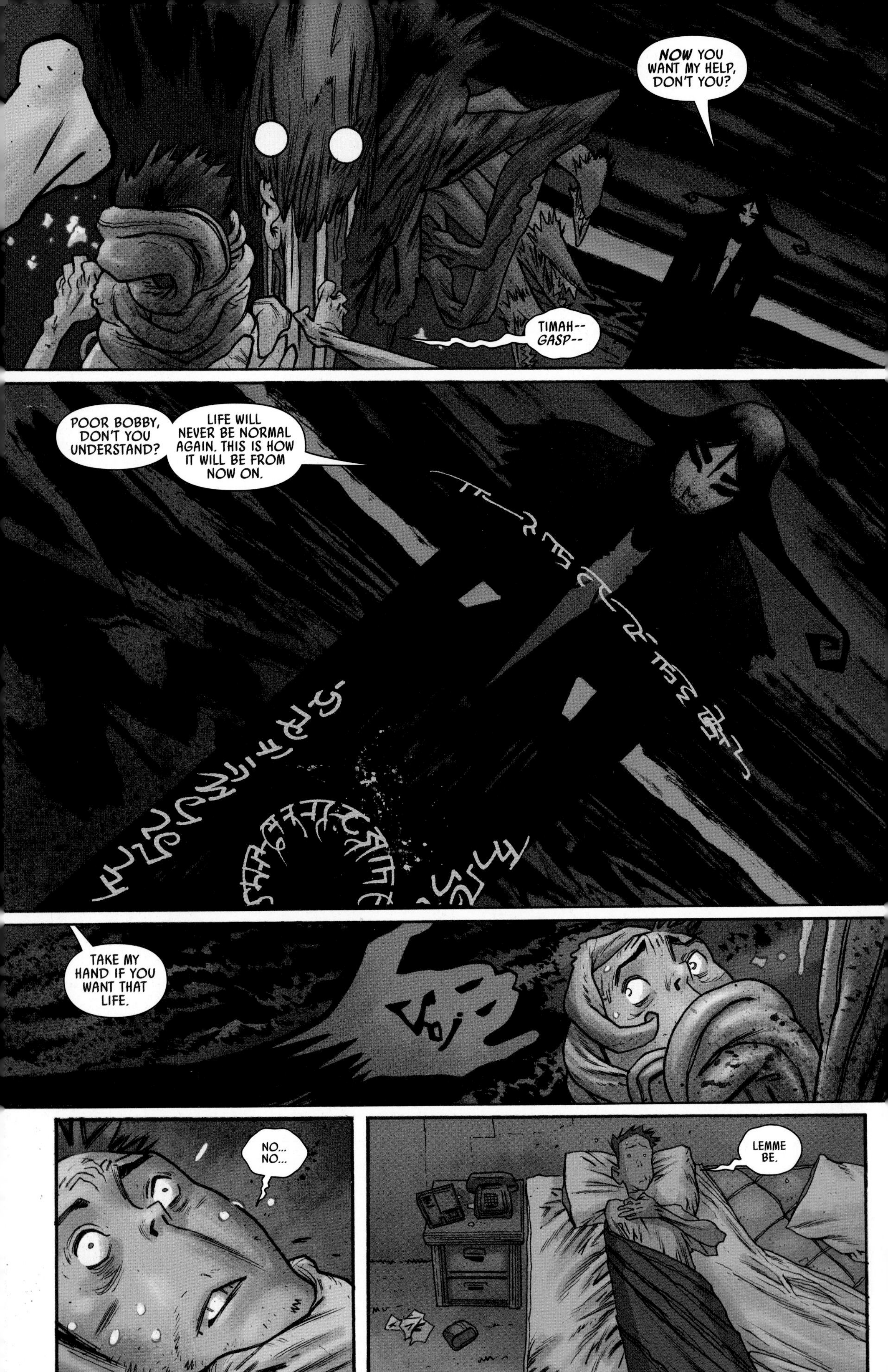
NOW YOU WANT MY HELP, DON'T YOU?
TIMAH-- GASP--
POOR BOBBY, DON'T YOU UNDERSTAND?
LIFE WILL NEVER BE NORMAL AGAIN. THIS IS HOW IT WILL BE FROM NOW ON.
TAKE MY HAND IF YOU WANT THAT LIFE.
NO... NO...
LEMME BE.

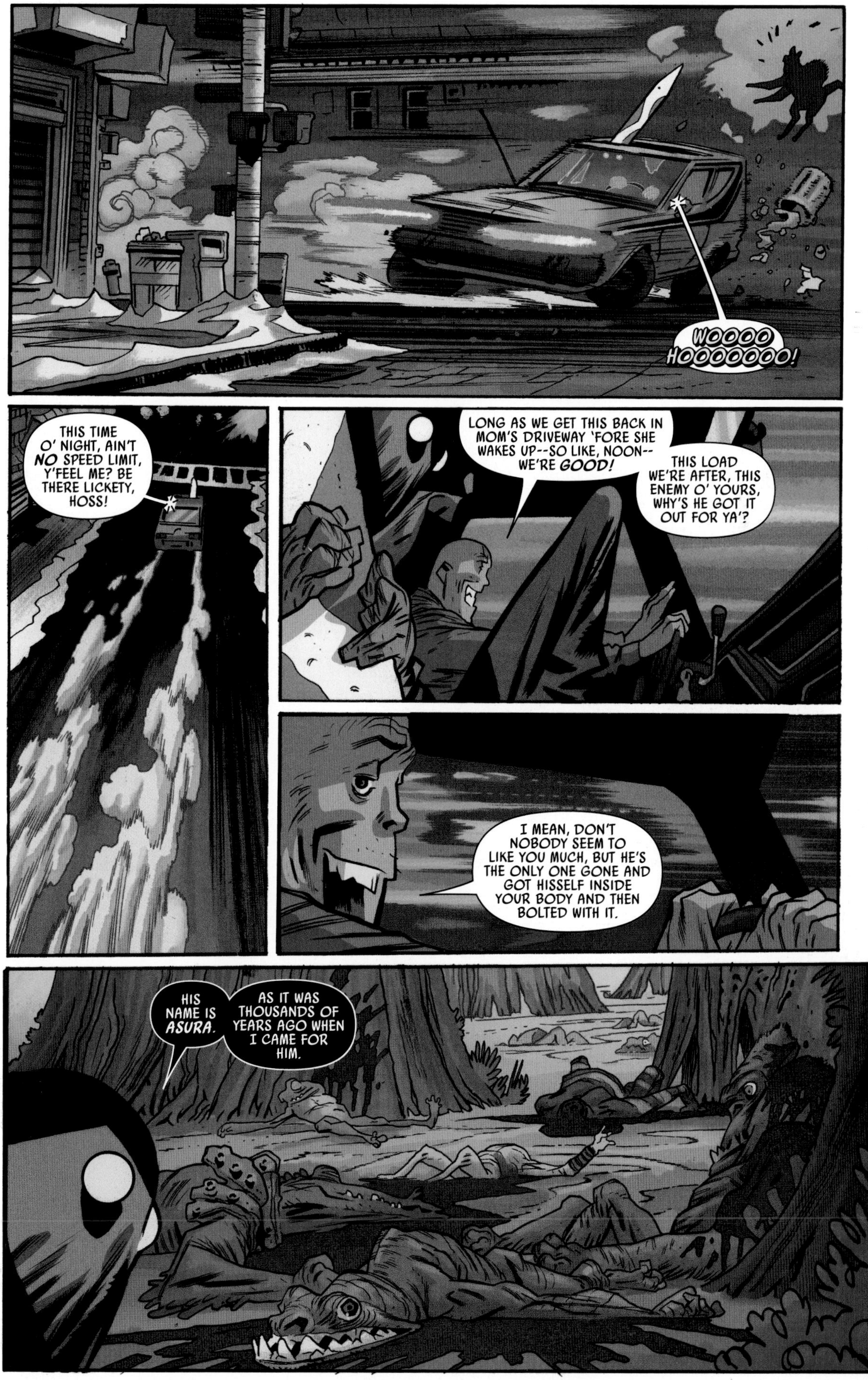
WOOOO HOOOOOOOO!
THIS TIME O' NIGHT, AIN'T **NO** SPEED LIMIT, Y'FEEL ME? BE THERE LICKETY, HOSS!
LONG AS WE GET THIS BACK IN MOM'S DRIVEWAY 'FORE SHE WAKES UP--SO LIKE, NOON--WE'RE **GOOD!**
THIS LOAD WE'RE AFTER, THIS ENEMY O' YOURS, WHY'S HE GOT IT OUT FOR YA'?
I MEAN, DON'T NOBODY SEEM TO LIKE YOU MUCH, BUT HE'S THE ONLY ONE GONE AND GOT HISSELF INSIDE YOUR BODY AND THEN BOLTED WITH IT.
HIS NAME IS *ASURA*.
AS IT WAS THOUSANDS OF YEARS AGO WHEN I CAME FOR HIM.

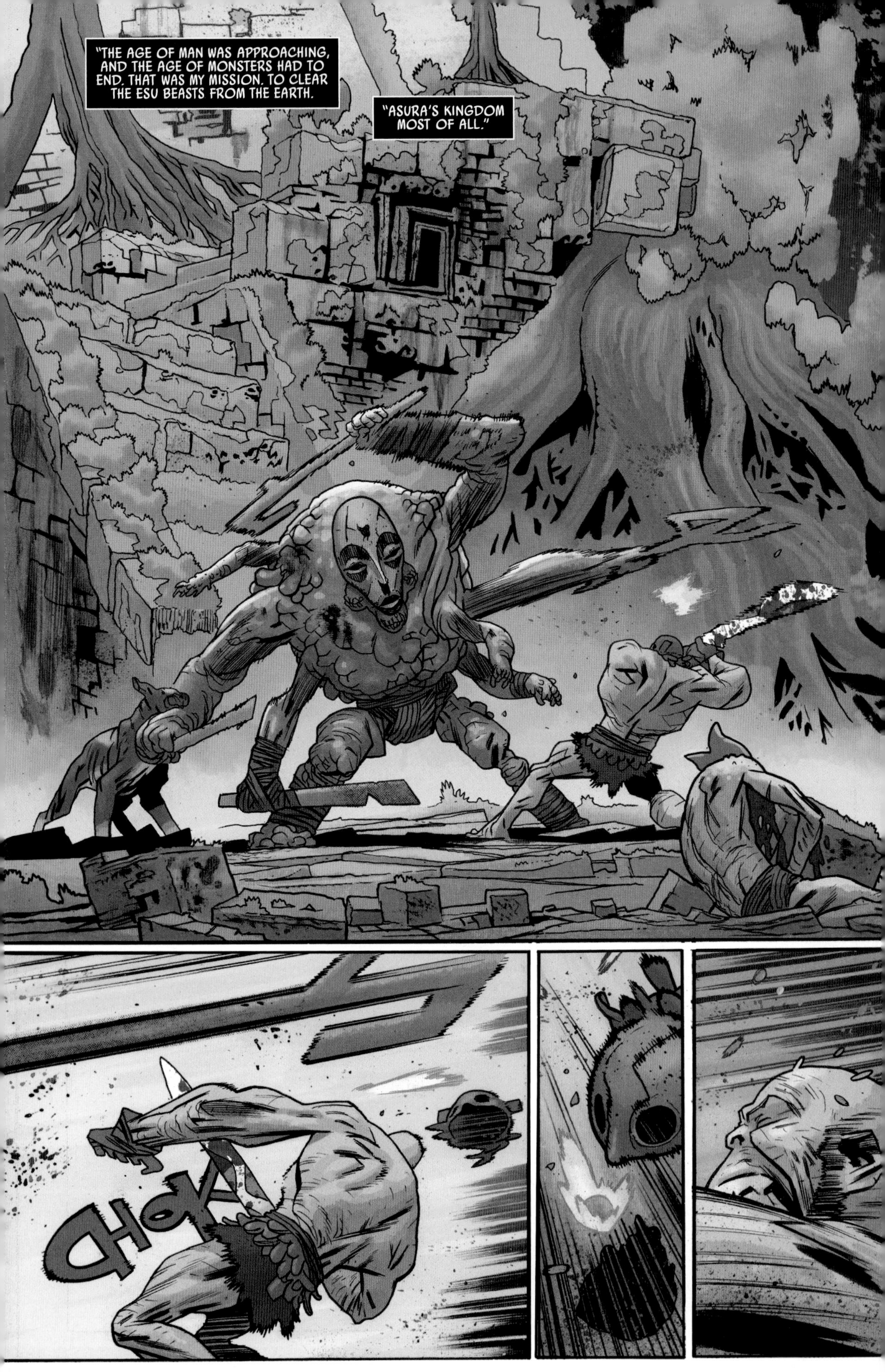
"THE AGE OF MAN WAS APPROACHING, AND THE AGE OF MONSTERS HAD TO END. THAT WAS MY MISSION. TO CLEAR THE ESU BEASTS FROM THE EARTH.
"ASURA'S KINGDOM MOST OF ALL."
CHOK

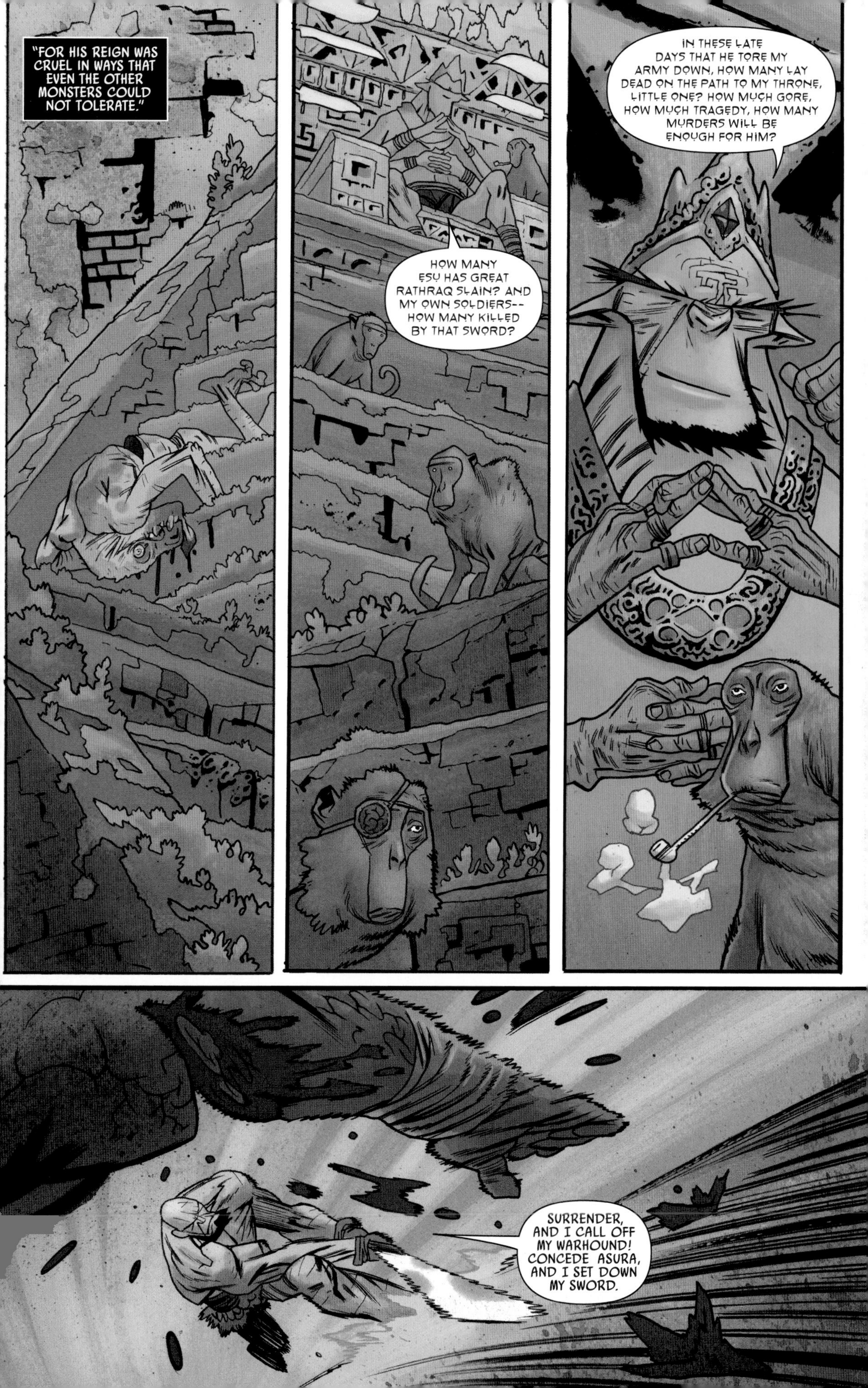
"FOR HIS REIGN WAS CRUEL IN WAYS THAT EVEN THE OTHER MONSTERS COULD NOT TOLERATE."
HOW MANY ESU HAS GREAT RATHRAQ SLAIN? AND MY OWN SOLDIERS-- HOW MANY KILLED BY THAT SWORD?
IN THESE LATE DAYS THAT HE TORE MY ARMY DOWN, HOW MANY LAY DEAD ON THE PATH TO MY THRONE, LITTLE ONE? HOW MUCH GORE, HOW MUCH TRAGEDY, HOW MANY MURDERS WILL BE ENOUGH FOR HIM?
SURRENDER, AND I CALL OFF MY WARHOUND! CONCEDE ASURA, AND I SET DOWN MY SWORD.

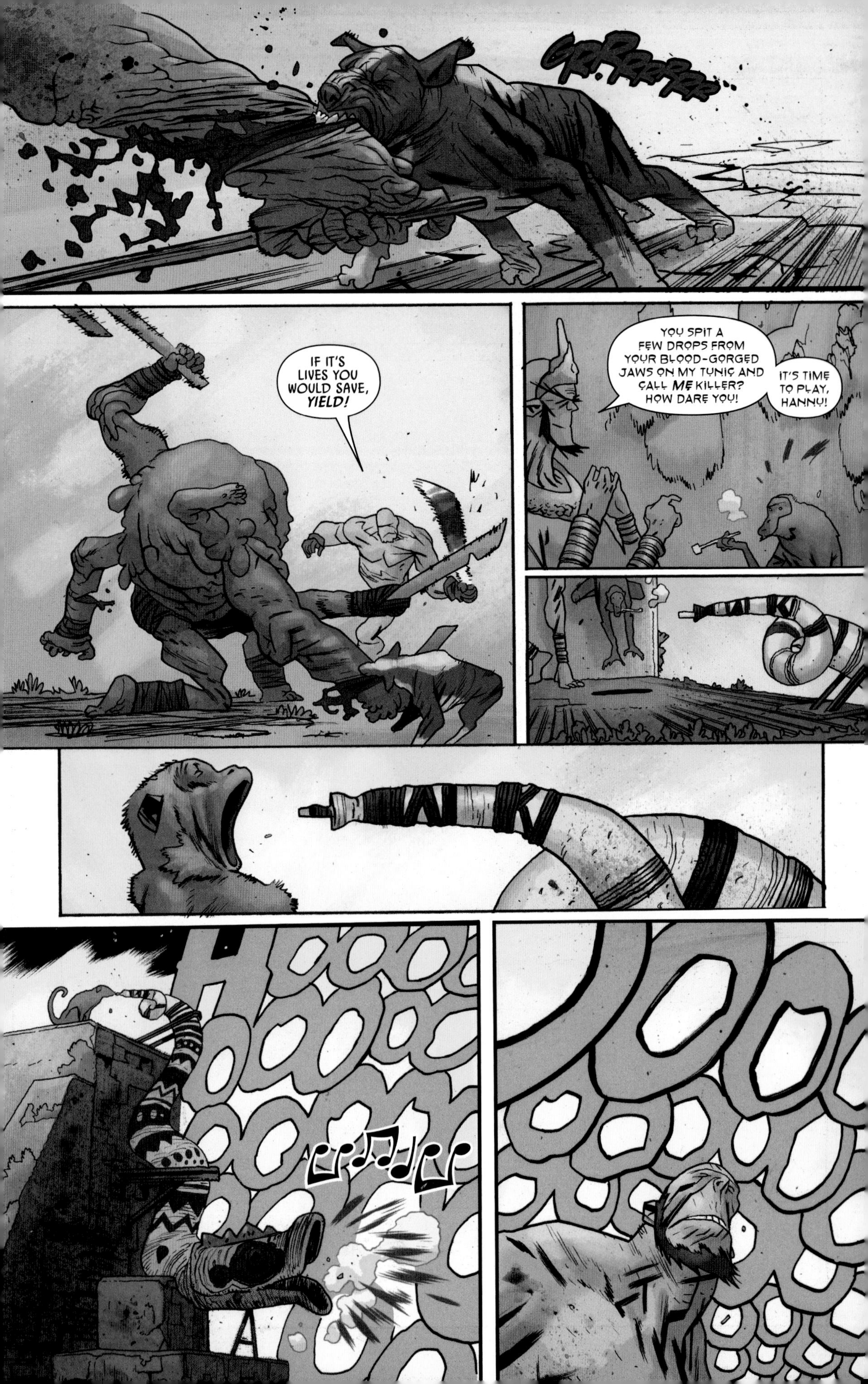
GRRRRRRR
IF IT'S LIVES YOU WOULD SAVE, *YIELD!*
YOU SPIT A FEW DROPS FROM YOUR BLOOD-GORGED JAWS ON MY TUNIC AND CALL *ME* KILLER? HOW DARE YOU!
IT'S TIME TO PLAY, HANNU!

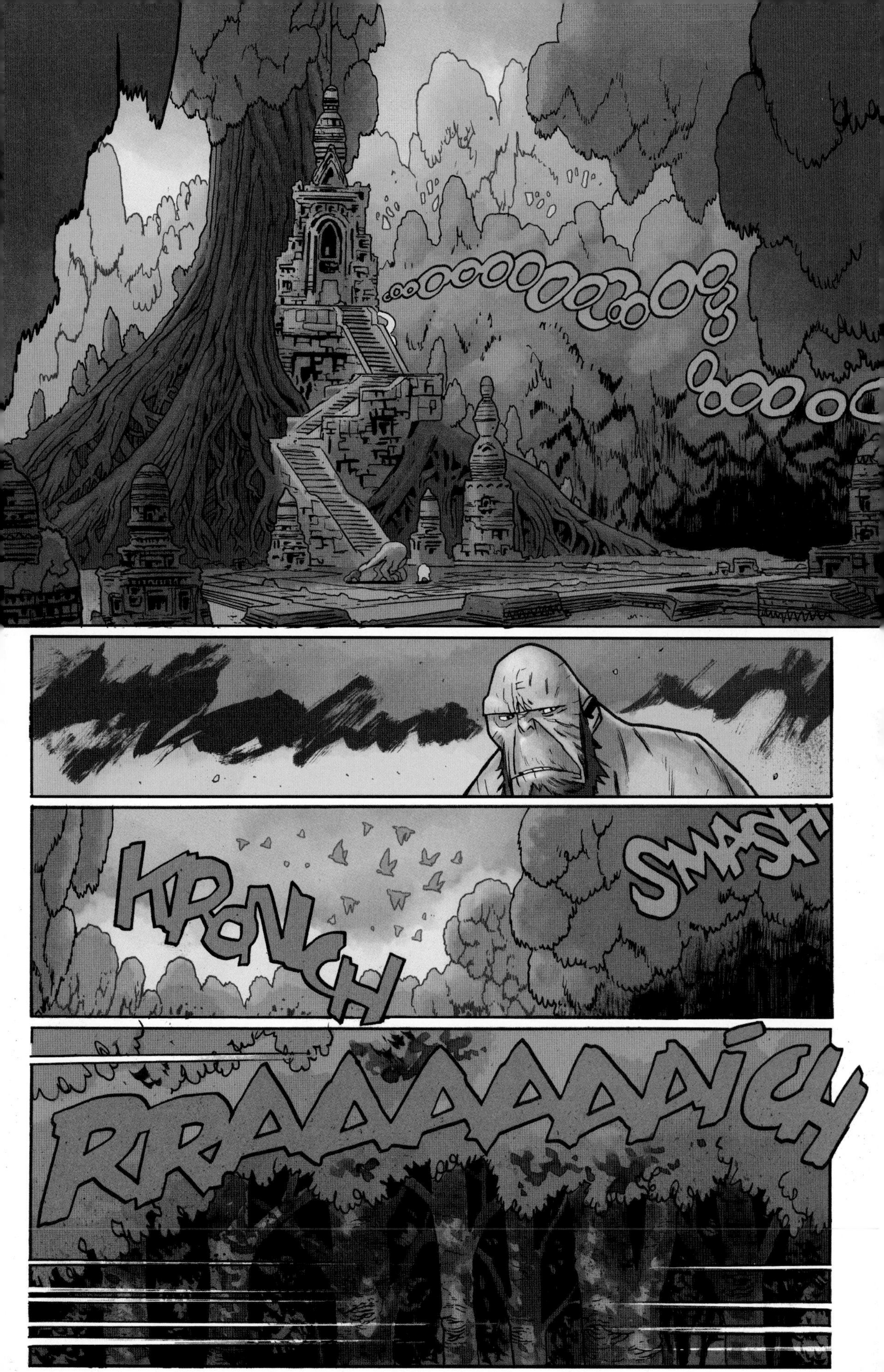
KRONCH
SMASH
RRAAAAAAAICH

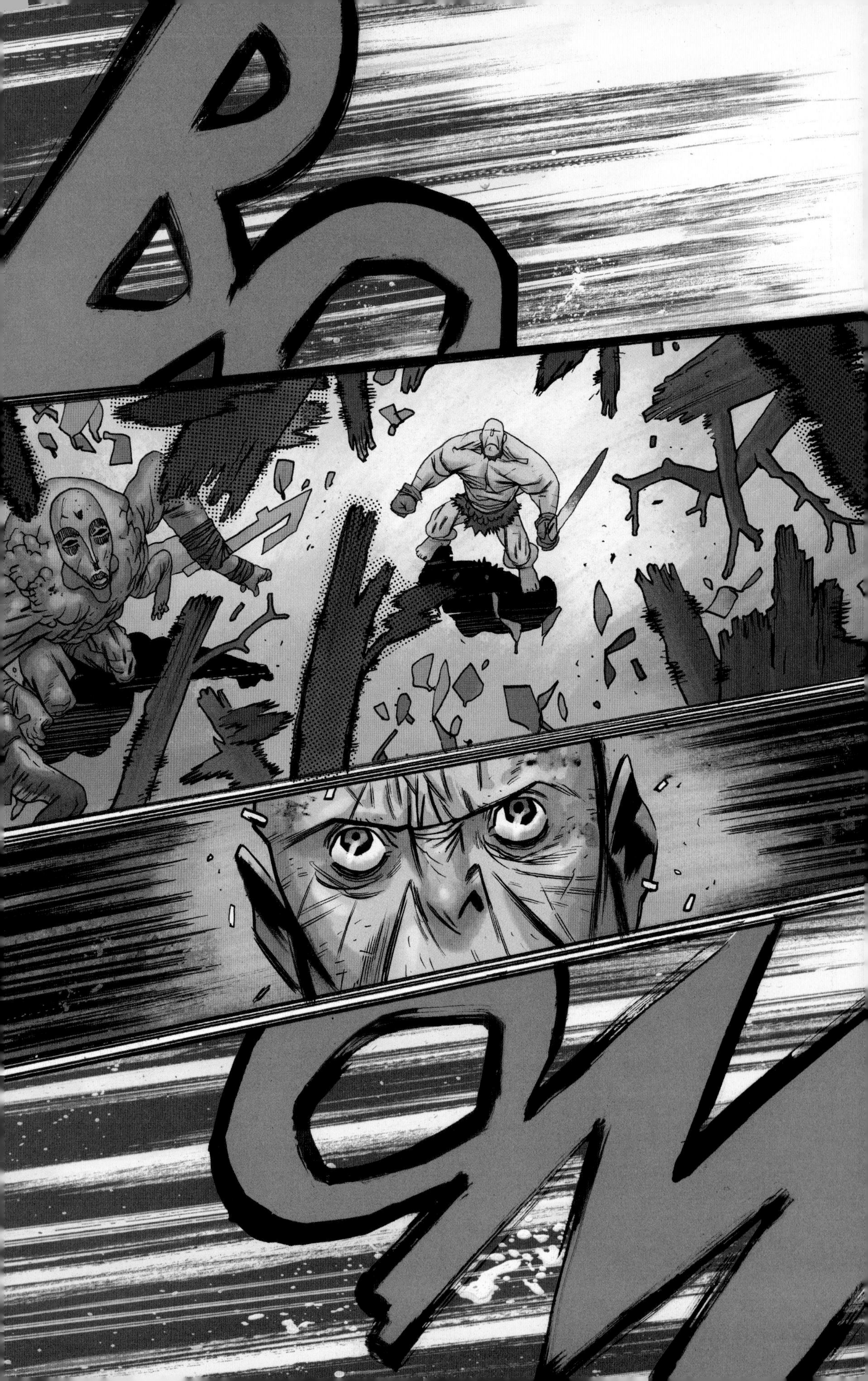

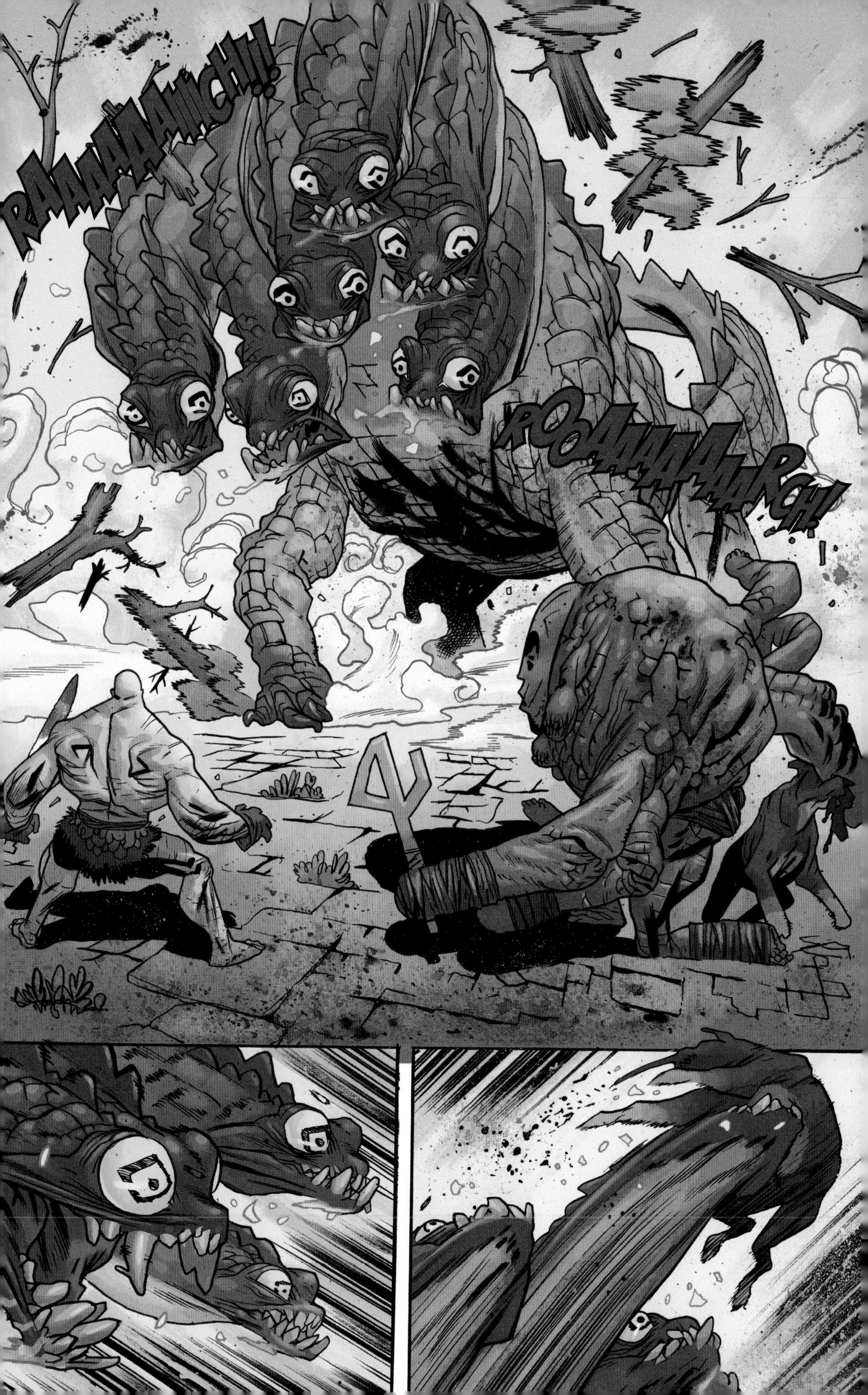
RAAAAAAWCH!!!
ROOAAAAAARCH!

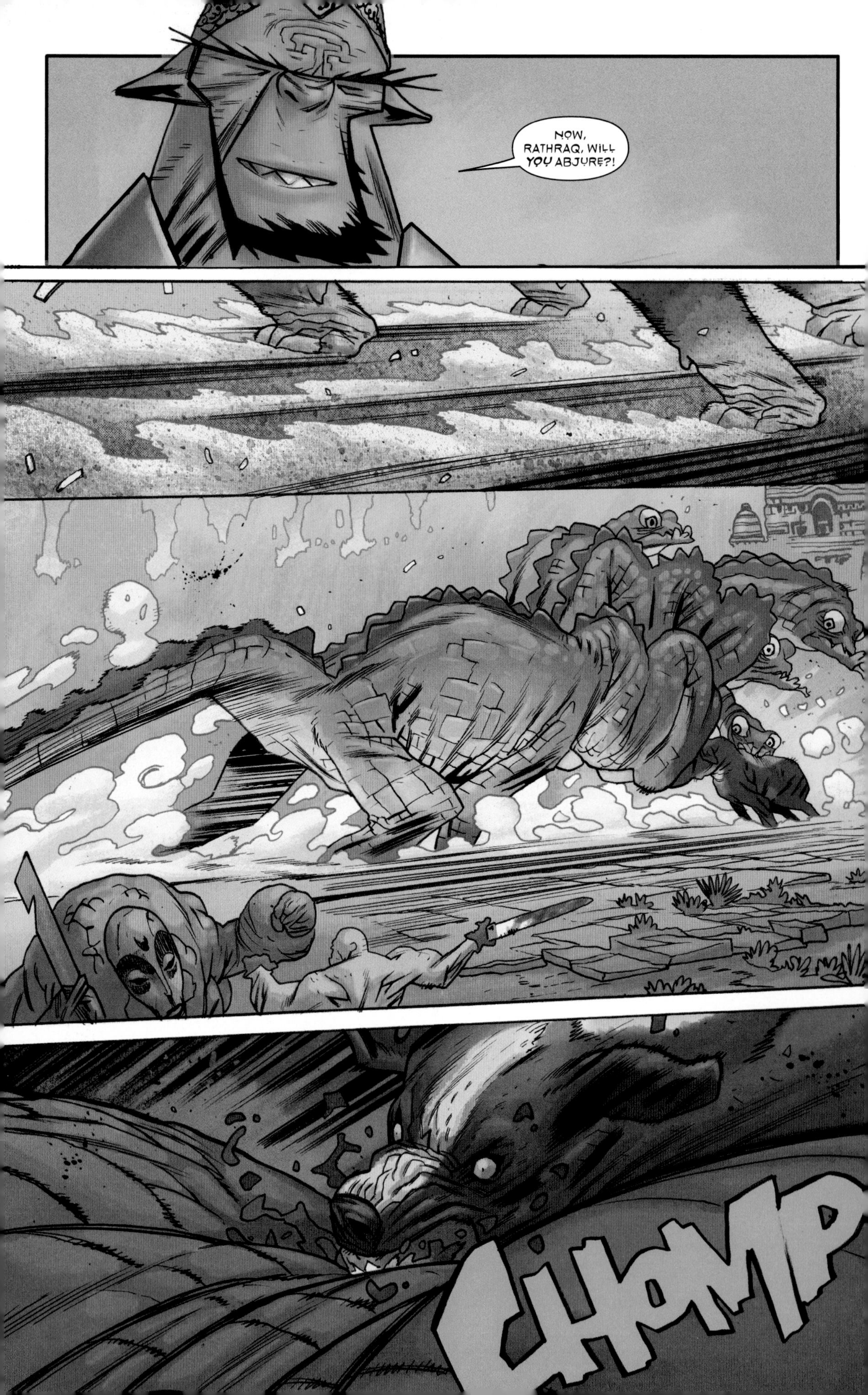
NOW, RATHRAQ, WILL YOU ABJURE?!
CHOMP

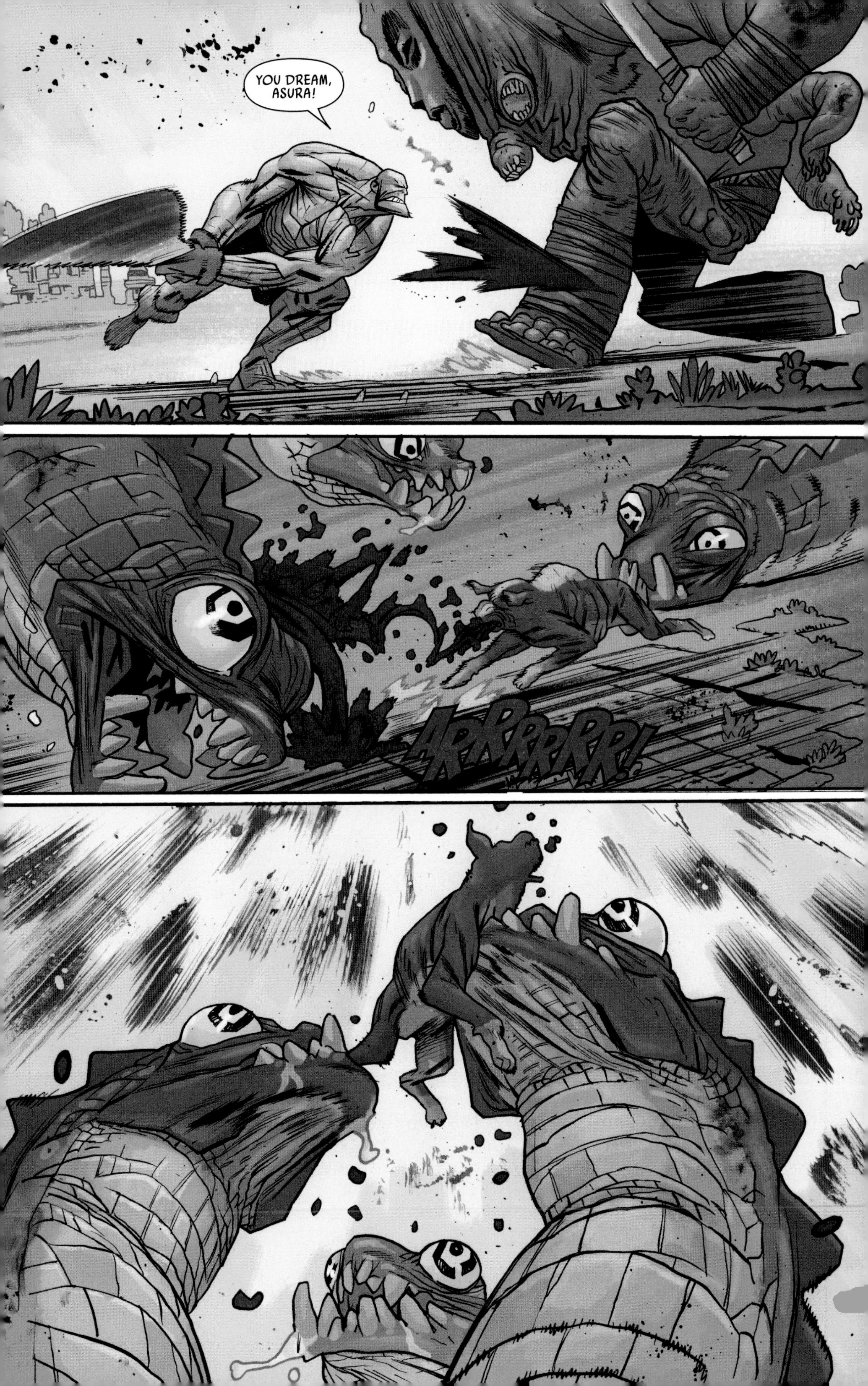
YOU DREAM, ASURA!
ARRRRRRR!

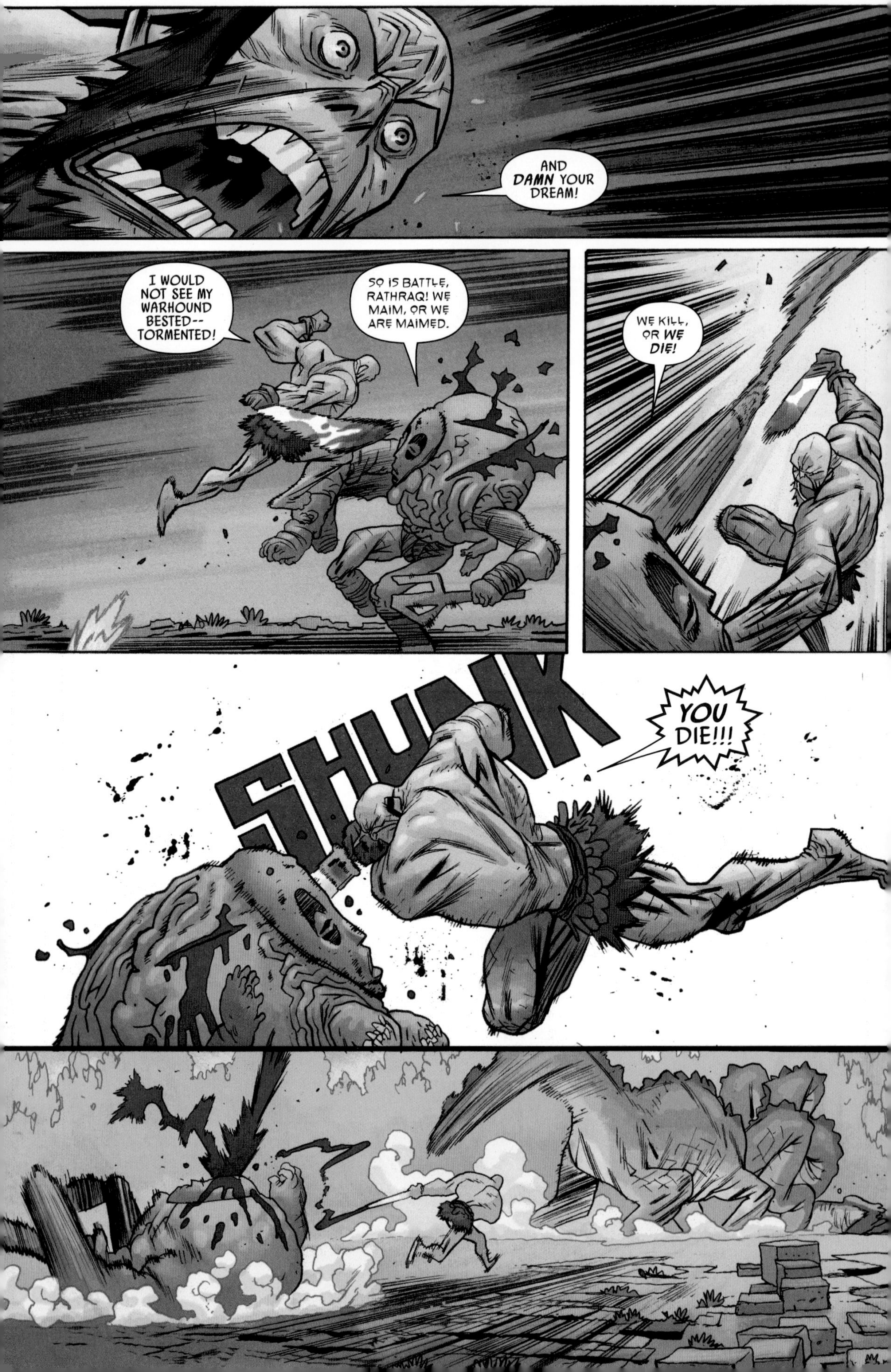
AND DAMN YOUR DREAM!
I WOULD NOT SEE MY WARHOUND BESTED-- TORMENTED!
SO IS BATTLE, RATHRAQ! WE MAIM, OR WE ARE MAIMED.
WE KILL, OR WE DIE!
SHUNK
YOU DIE!!!

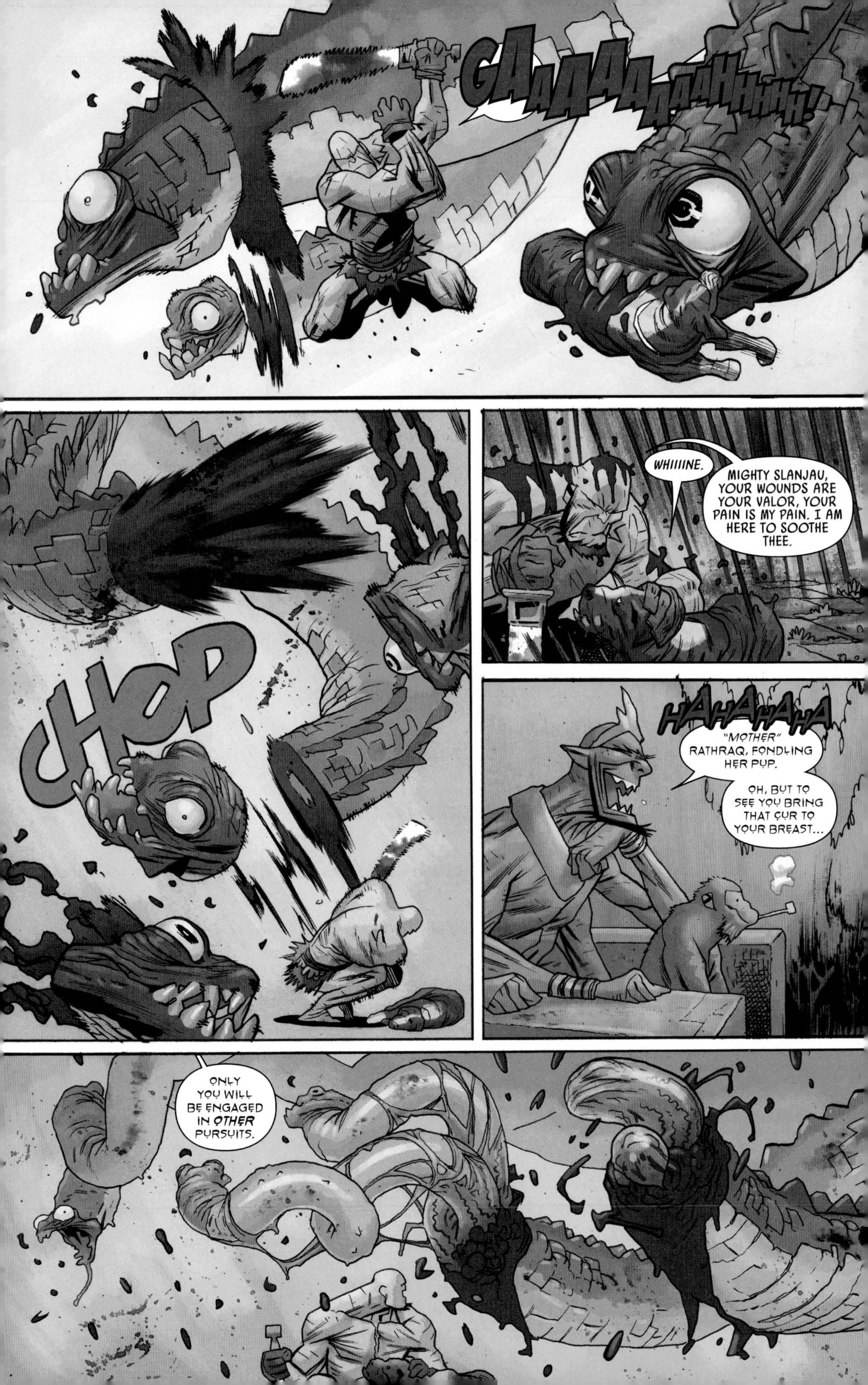
GAAAAAAAAHHHHH!
CHOP
WHIIIINE.
MIGHTY SLANJAU, YOUR WOUNDS ARE YOUR VALOR, YOUR PAIN IS MY PAIN. I AM HERE TO SOOTHE THEE.
HAHAHAHA
"MOTHER" RATHRAQ, FONDLING HER PUP.
OH, BUT TO SEE YOU BRING THAT CUR TO YOUR BREAST...
ONLY YOU WILL BE ENGAGED IN OTHER PURSUITS.

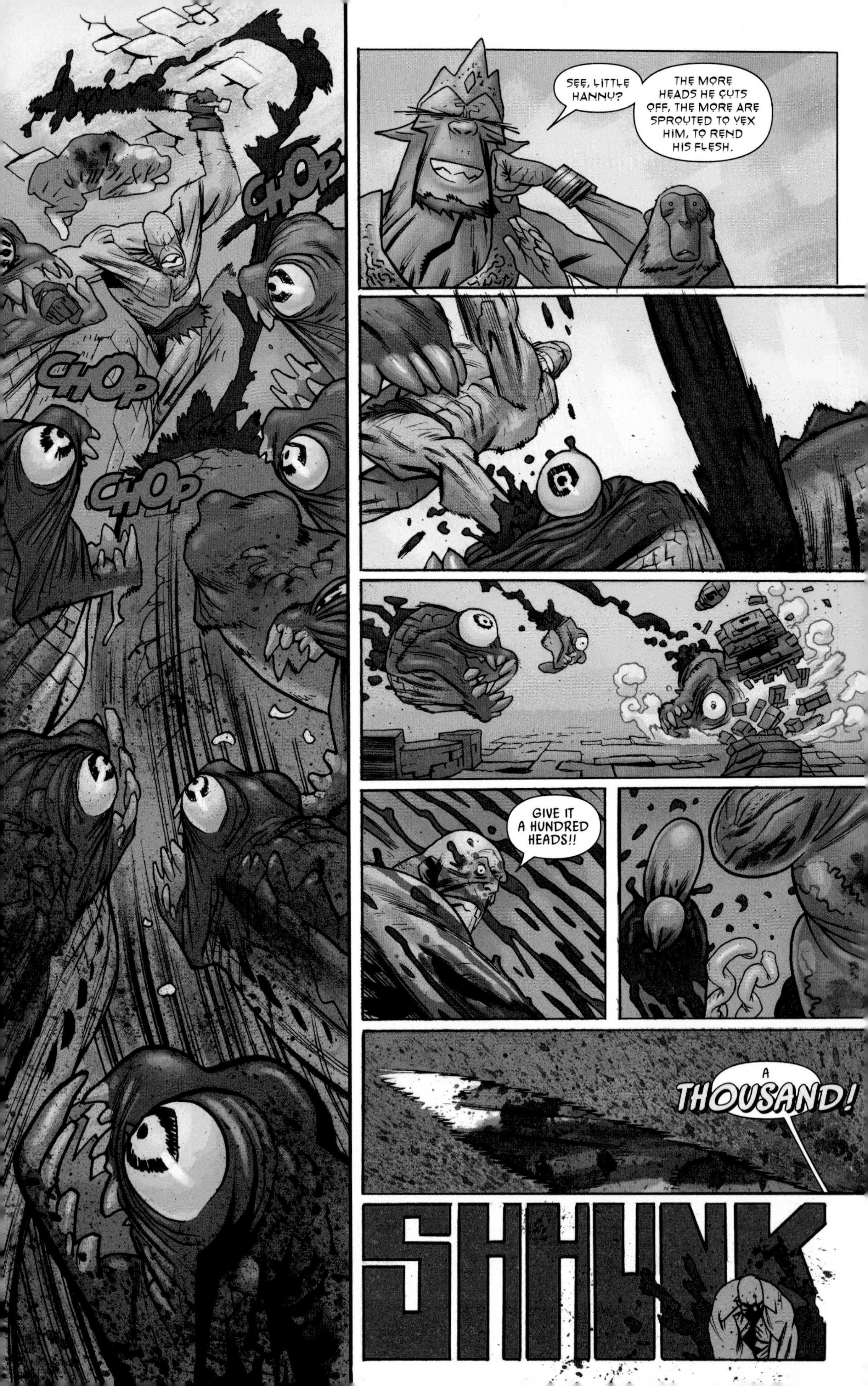
CHOP
CHOP
CHOP
SEE, LITTLE HANNU?
THE MORE HEADS HE CUTS OFF, THE MORE ARE SPROUTED TO VEX HIM, TO REND HIS FLESH.
GIVE IT A HUNDRED HEADS!!
A THOUSAND!
SHHUNK

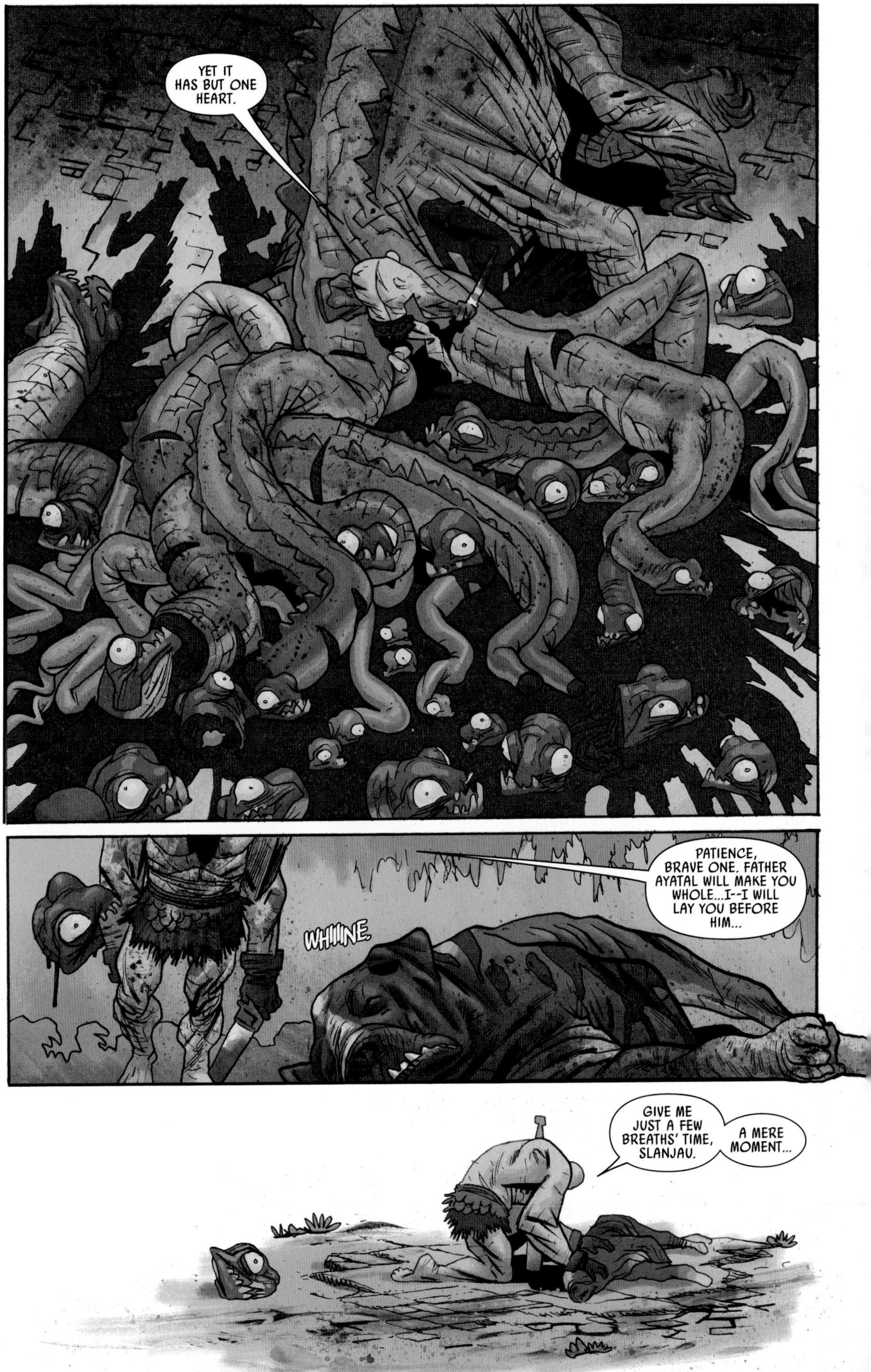
YET IT HAS BUT ONE HEART.
PATIENCE, BRAVE ONE. FATHER AYATAL WILL MAKE YOU WHOLE...I--I WILL LAY YOU BEFORE HIM...
WHIIINE
GIVE ME JUST A FEW BREATHS' TIME, SLANJAU.
A MERE MOMENT...

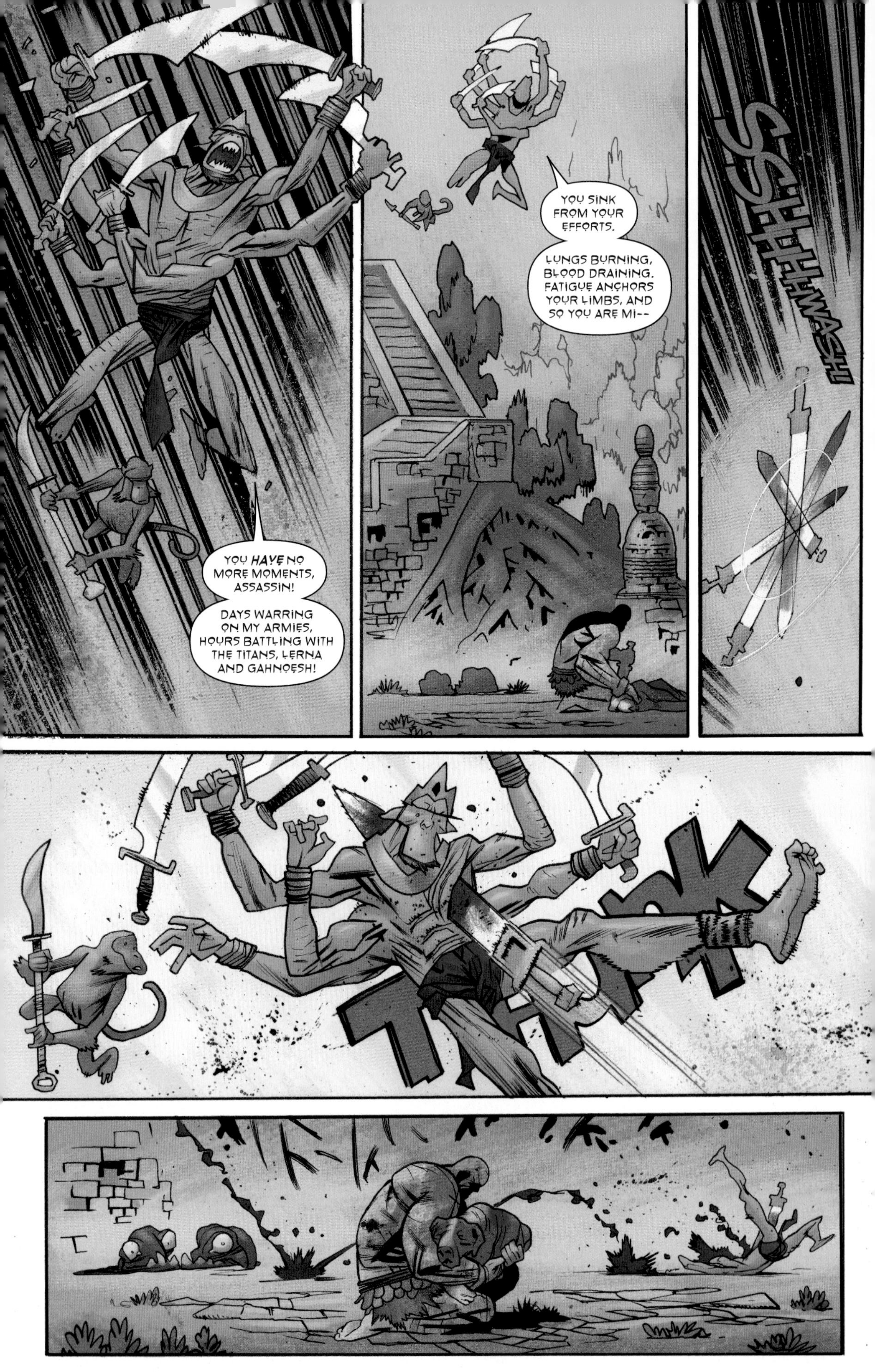
YOU HAVE NO MORE MOMENTS, ASSASSIN!
DAYS WARRING ON MY ARMIES, HOURS BATTLING WITH THE TITANS, LERNA AND GAHNOESH!
YOU SINK FROM YOUR EFFORTS.
LUNGS BURNING, BLOOD DRAINING. FATIGUE ANCHORS YOUR LIMBS, AND SO YOU ARE MI--
SSHHHWASH!

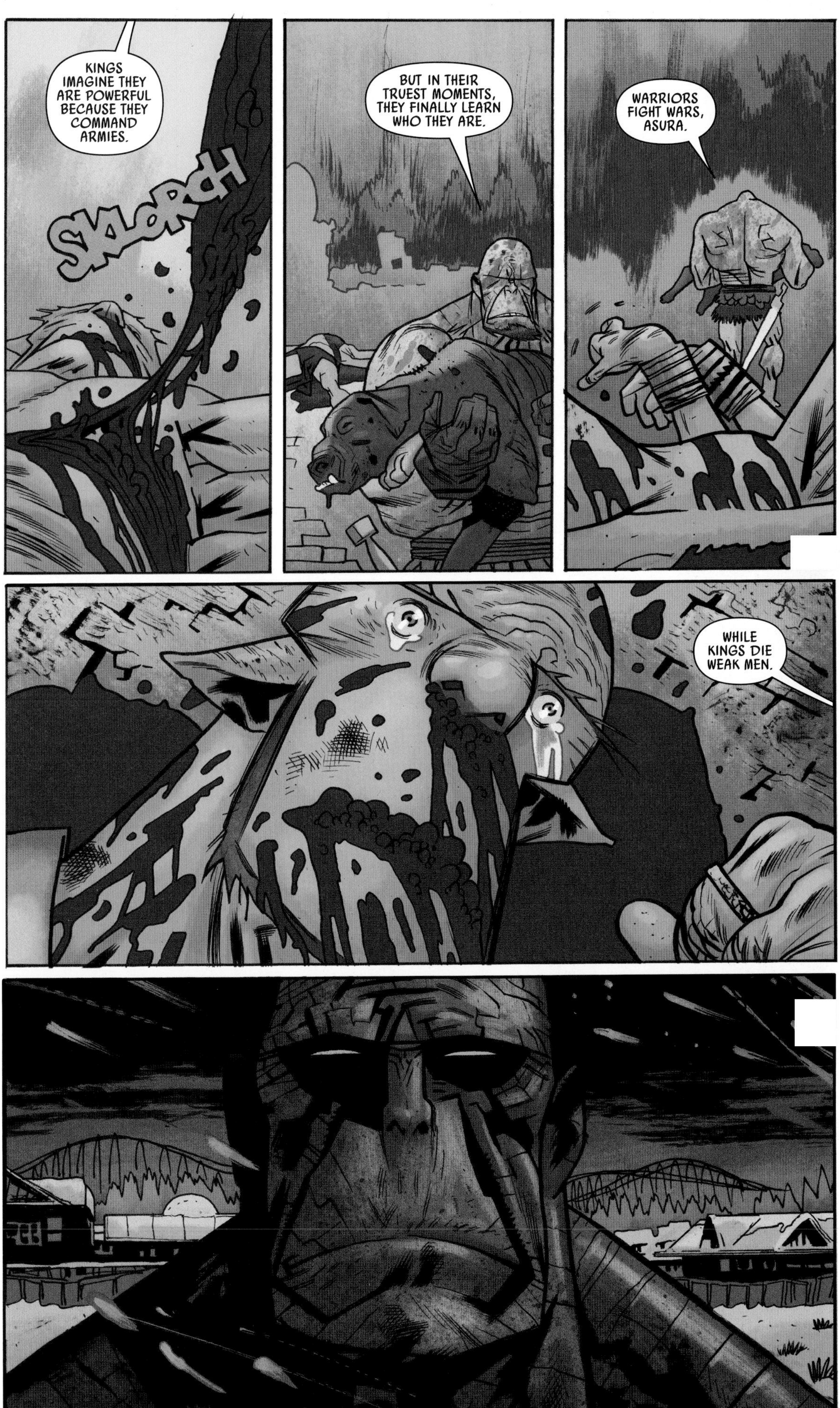
KINGS IMAGINE THEY ARE POWERFUL BECAUSE THEY COMMAND ARMIES.
SKLORCH
BUT IN THEIR TRUEST MOMENTS, THEY FINALLY LEARN WHO THEY ARE.
WARRIORS FIGHT WARS, ASURA.
WHILE KINGS DIE WEAK MEN.

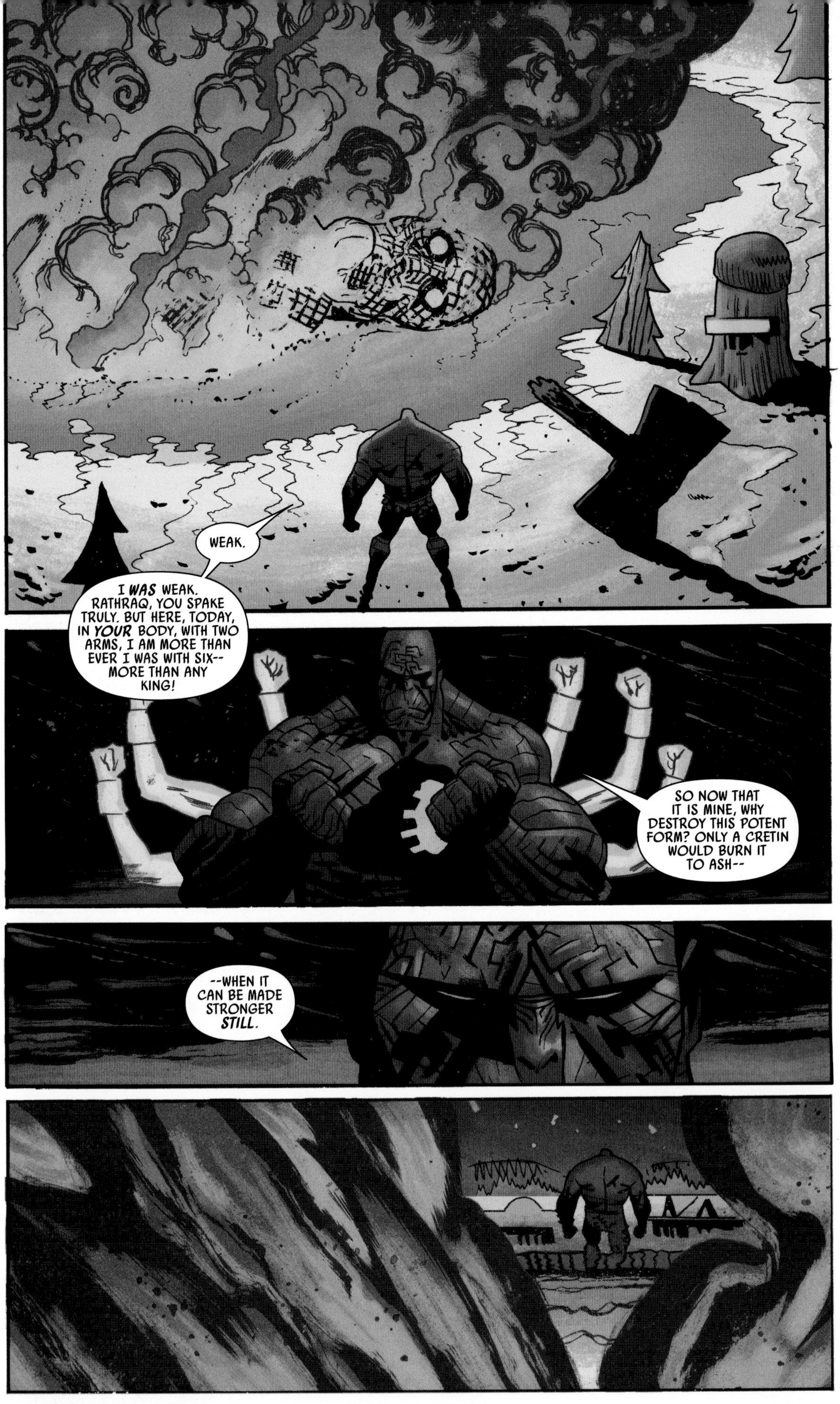
WEAK.
I WAS WEAK. RATHRAQ, YOU SPAKE TRULY. BUT HERE, TODAY, IN YOUR BODY, WITH TWO ARMS, I AM MORE THAN EVER I WAS WITH SIX--MORE THAN ANY KING!
SO NOW THAT IT IS MINE, WHY DESTROY THIS POTENT FORM? ONLY A CRETIN WOULD BURN IT TO ASH--
--WHEN IT CAN BE MADE STRONGER STILL.

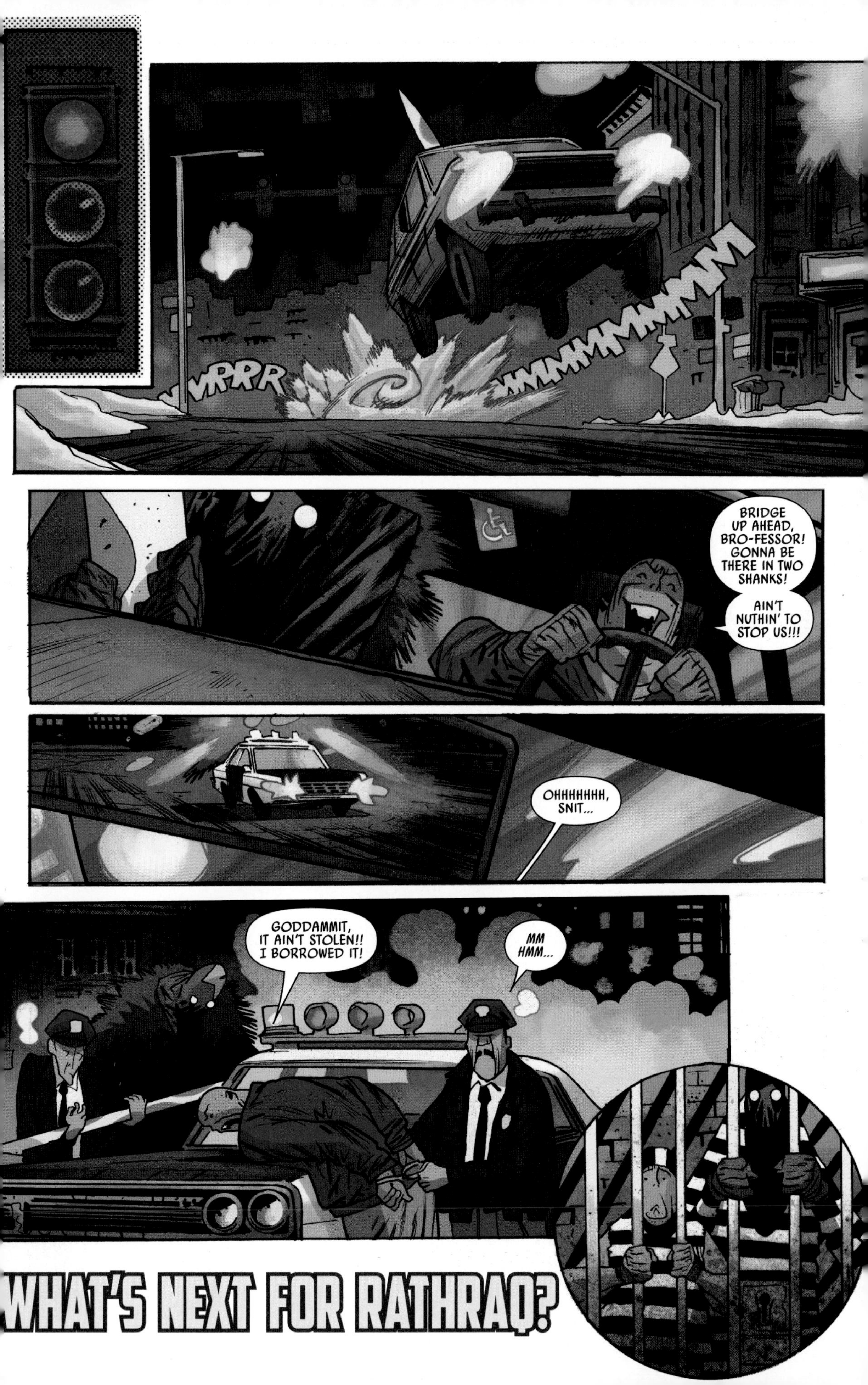
VRRRR
MMMMMMMMMM
BRIDGE UP AHEAD, BRO-FESSOR! GONNA BE THERE IN TWO SHANKS!
AIN'T NUTHIN' TO STOP US!!!
OHHHHHHH, SNIT...
GODDAMMIT, IT AIN'T STOLEN!! I BORROWED IT!
MM HMM...
WHAT'S NEXT FOR RATHRAQ?

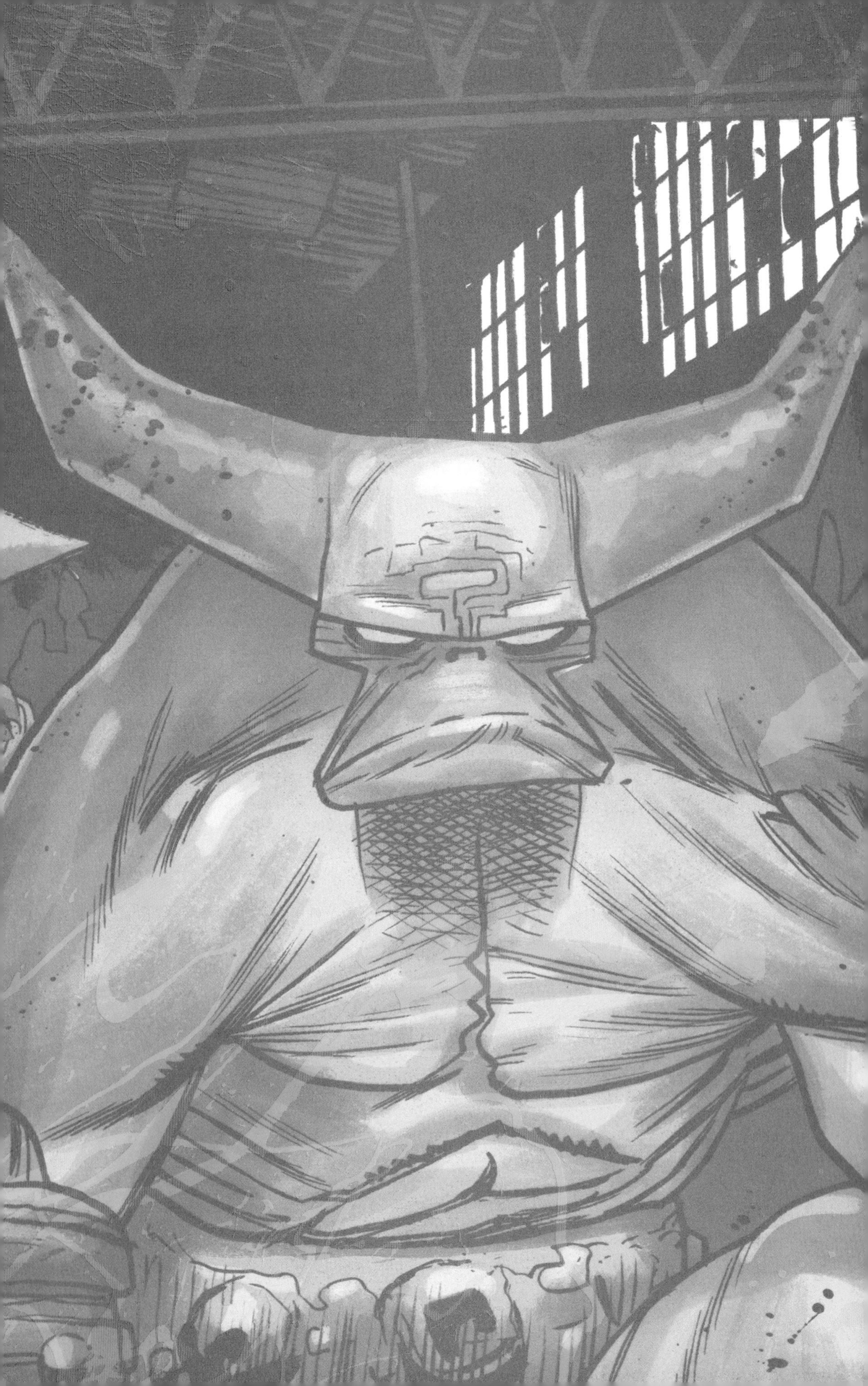

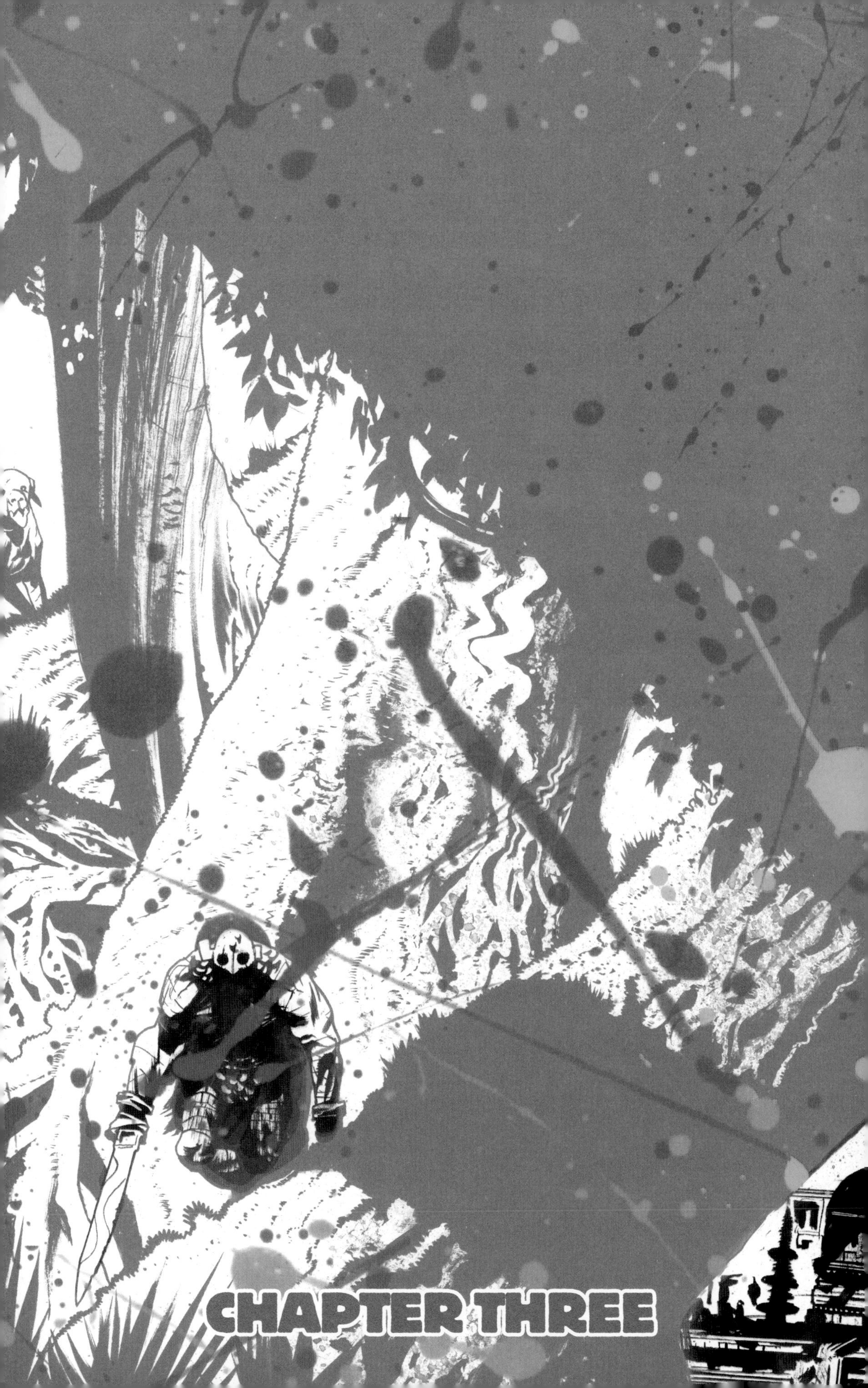
CHAPTER THREE

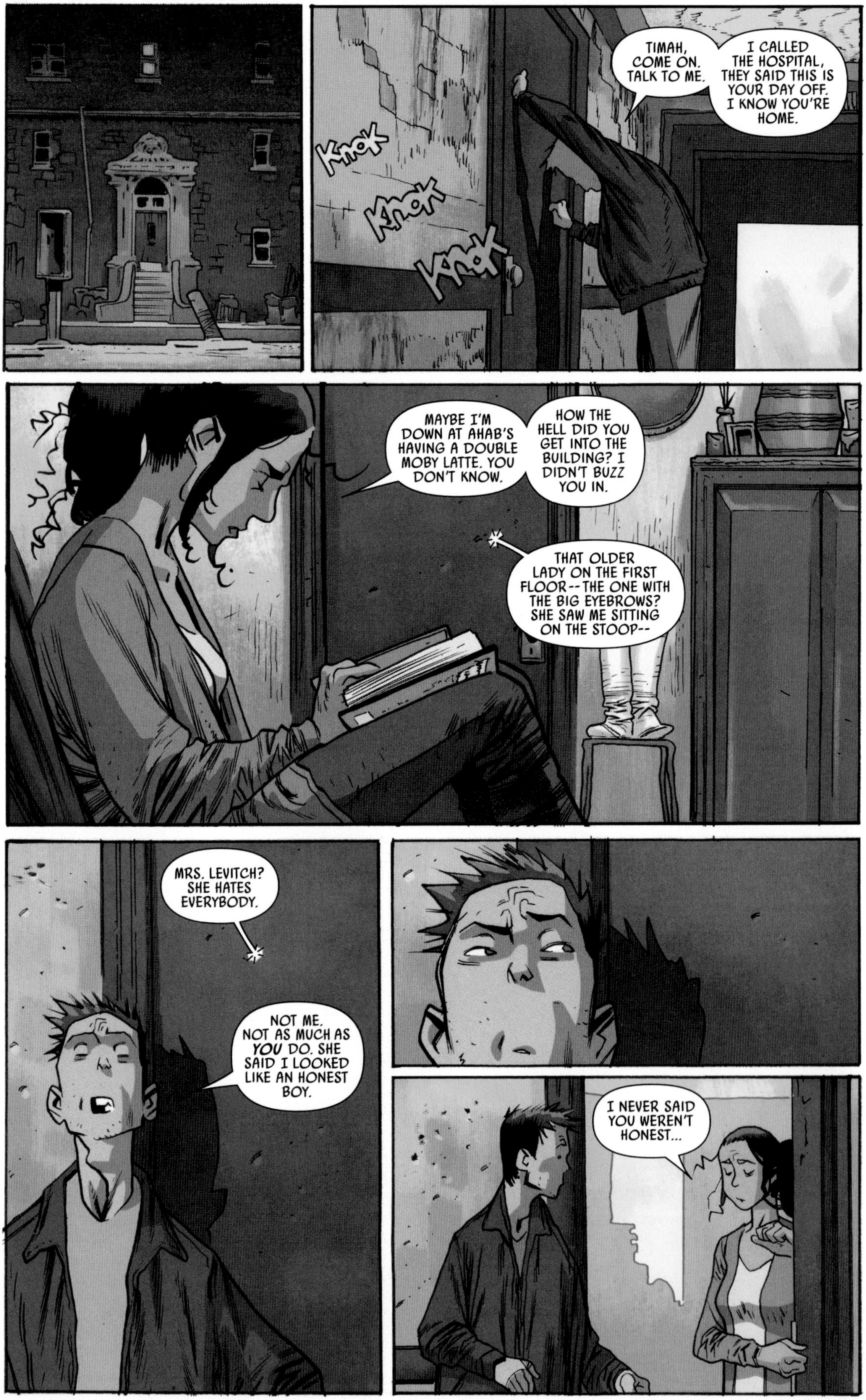
KNOK
KNOK
KNOK
TIMAH, COME ON. TALK TO ME.
I CALLED THE HOSPITAL, THEY SAID THIS IS YOUR DAY OFF. I KNOW YOU'RE HOME.
MAYBE I'M DOWN AT AHAB'S HAVING A DOUBLE MOBY LATTE. YOU DON'T KNOW.
HOW THE HELL DID YOU GET INTO THE BUILDING? I DIDN'T BUZZ YOU IN.
THAT OLDER LADY ON THE FIRST FLOOR--THE ONE WITH THE BIG EYEBROWS? SHE SAW ME SITTING ON THE STOOP--
MRS. LEVITCH? SHE HATES EVERYBODY.
NOT ME. NOT AS MUCH AS *YOU* DO. SHE SAID I LOOKED LIKE AN HONEST BOY.
I NEVER SAID YOU WEREN'T HONEST...

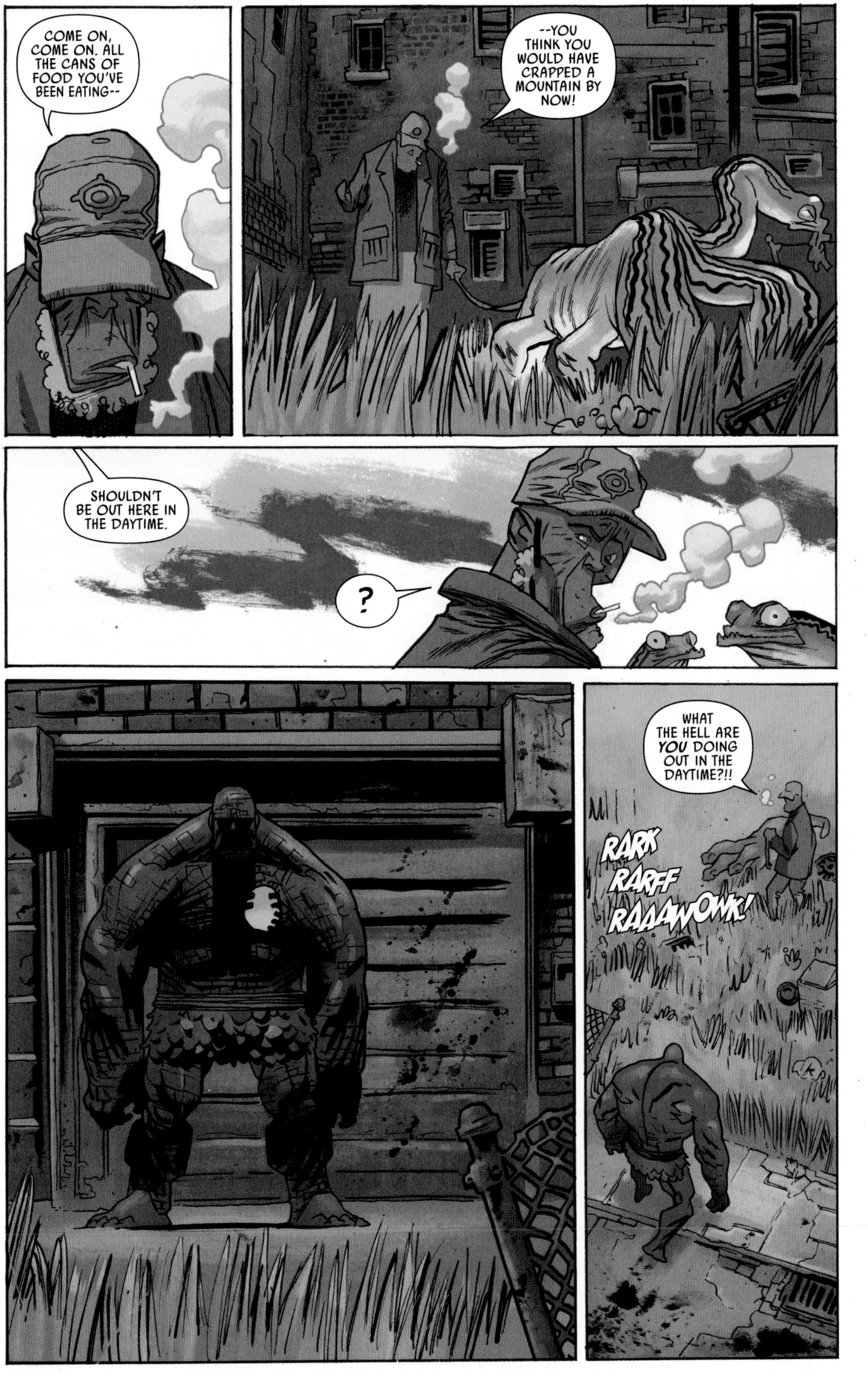
COME ON, COME ON. ALL THE CANS OF FOOD YOU'VE BEEN EATING--
--YOU THINK YOU WOULD HAVE CRAPPED A MOUNTAIN BY NOW!
SHOULDN'T BE OUT HERE IN THE DAYTIME.
?
WHAT THE HELL ARE YOU DOING OUT IN THE DAYTIME?!!
RARK
RARFF
RAAAWOWK!

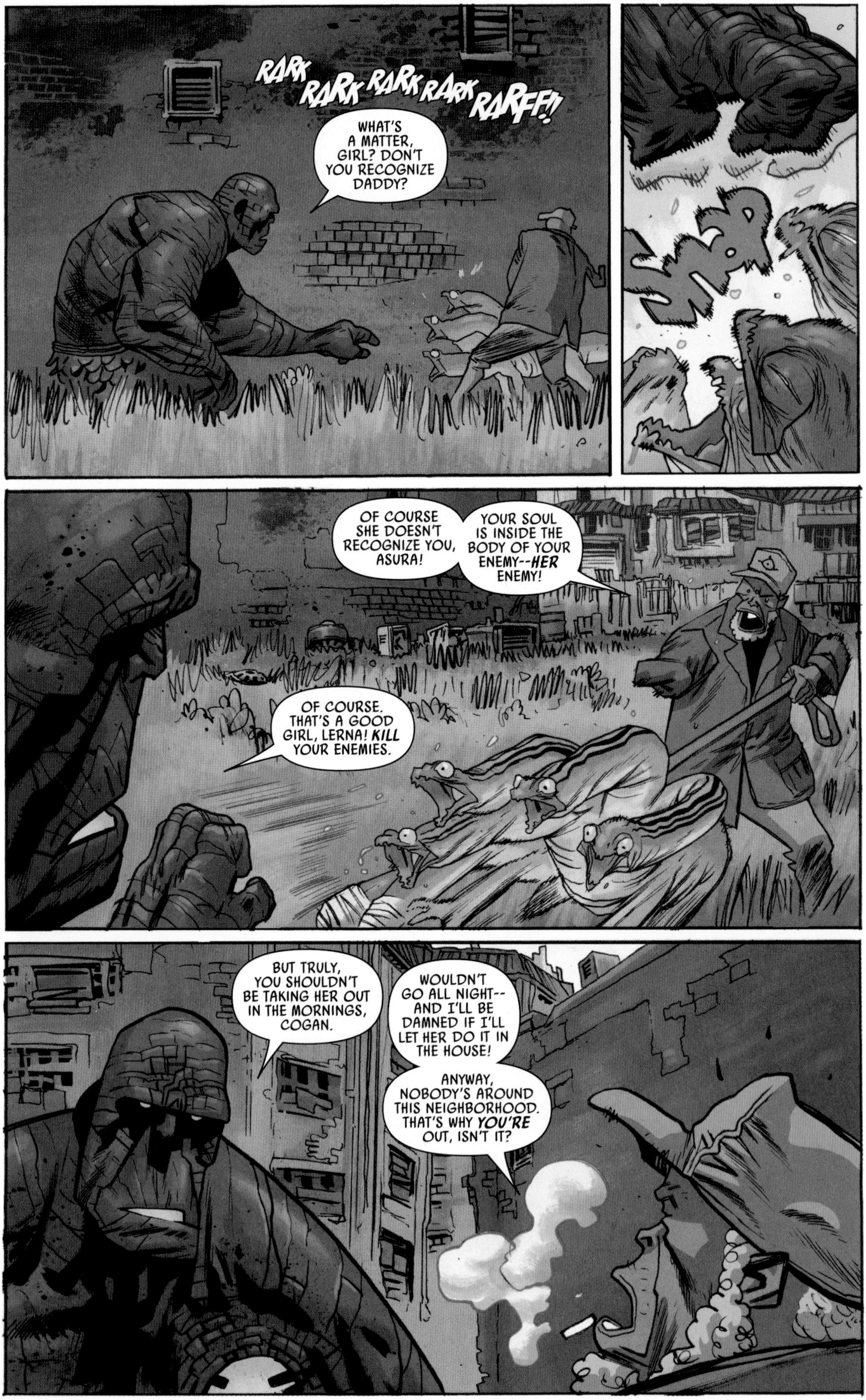
RARK RARK RARK RARK RARFF!!
WHAT'S A MATTER, GIRL? DON'T YOU RECOGNIZE DADDY?
WHAP
OF COURSE SHE DOESN'T RECOGNIZE YOU, ASURA!
YOUR SOUL IS INSIDE THE BODY OF YOUR ENEMY--HER ENEMY!
OF COURSE. THAT'S A GOOD GIRL, LERNA! KILL YOUR ENEMIES.
BUT TRULY, YOU SHOULDN'T BE TAKING HER OUT IN THE MORNINGS, COGAN.
WOULDN'T GO ALL NIGHT-- AND I'LL BE DAMNED IF I'LL LET HER DO IT IN THE HOUSE!
ANYWAY, NOBODY'S AROUND THIS NEIGHBORHOOD. THAT'S WHY YOU'RE OUT, ISN'T IT?

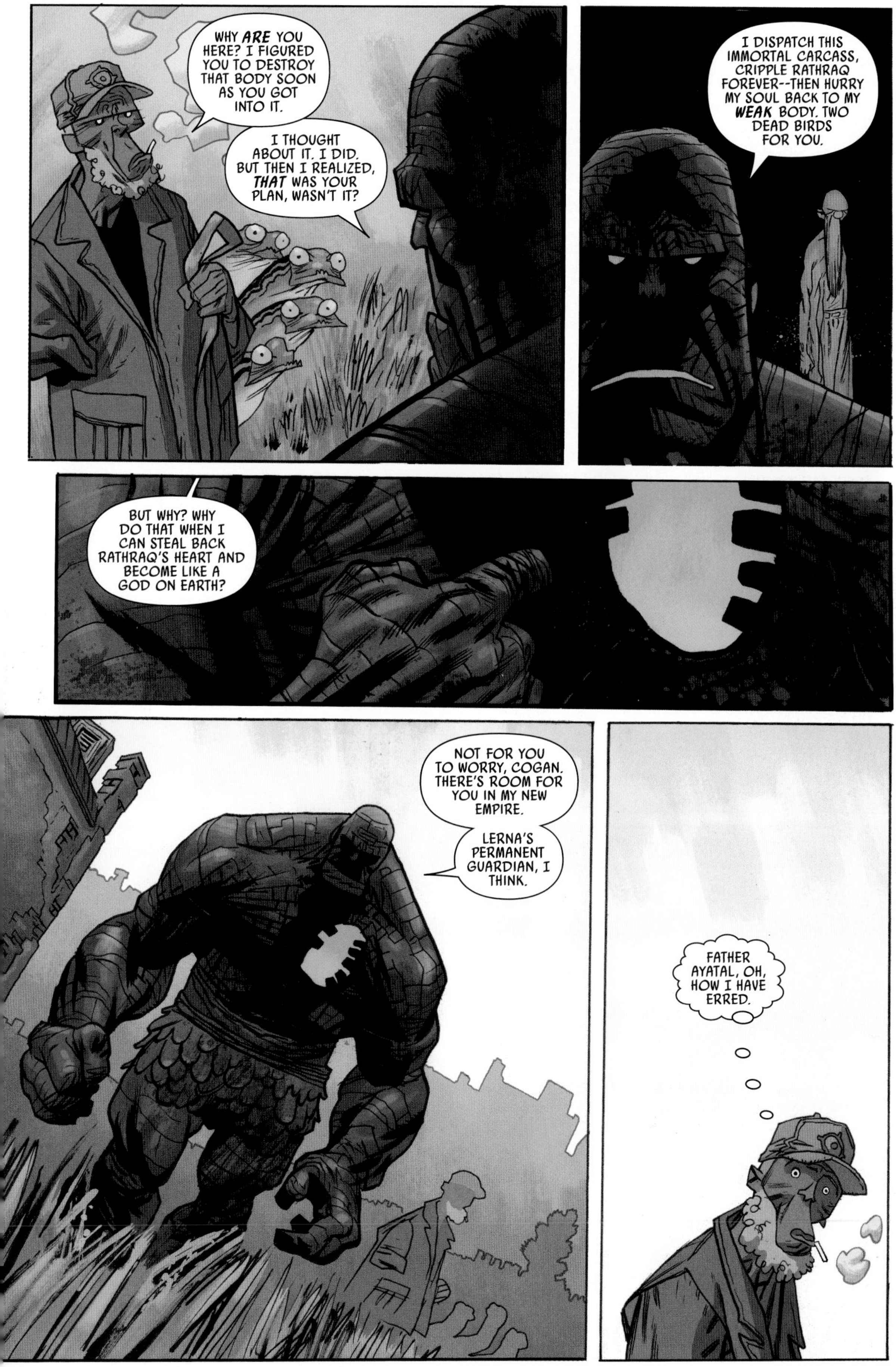
WHY ARE YOU HERE? I FIGURED YOU TO DESTROY THAT BODY SOON AS YOU GOT INTO IT.
I THOUGHT ABOUT IT. I DID. BUT THEN I REALIZED, THAT WAS YOUR PLAN, WASN'T IT?
I DISPATCH THIS IMMORTAL CARCASS, CRIPPLE RATHRAQ FOREVER--THEN HURRY MY SOUL BACK TO MY WEAK BODY. TWO DEAD BIRDS FOR YOU.
BUT WHY? WHY DO THAT WHEN I CAN STEAL BACK RATHRAQ'S HEART AND BECOME LIKE A GOD ON EARTH?
NOT FOR YOU TO WORRY, COGAN. THERE'S ROOM FOR YOU IN MY NEW EMPIRE.
LERNA'S PERMANENT GUARDIAN, I THINK.
FATHER AYATAL, OH, HOW I HAVE ERRED.

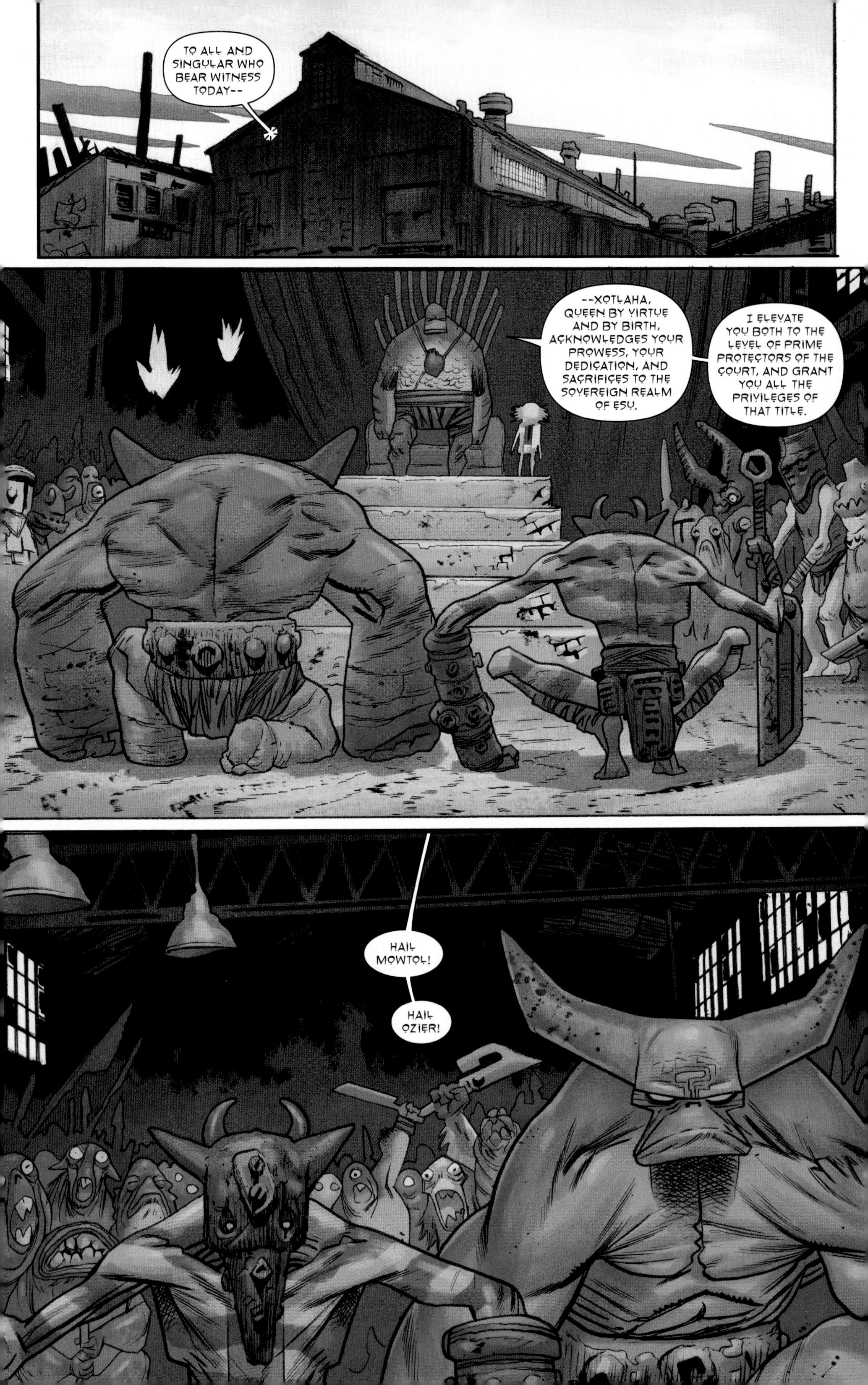
TO ALL AND SINGULAR WHO BEAR WITNESS TODAY--
--XOTLAHA, QUEEN BY VIRTUE AND BY BIRTH, ACKNOWLEDGES YOUR PROWESS, YOUR DEDICATION, AND SACRIFICES TO THE SOVEREIGN REALM OF ESU.
I ELEVATE YOU BOTH TO THE LEVEL OF PRIME PROTECTORS OF THE COURT, AND GRANT YOU ALL THE PRIVILEGES OF THAT TITLE.
HAIL MOWTOL!
HAIL OZIER!

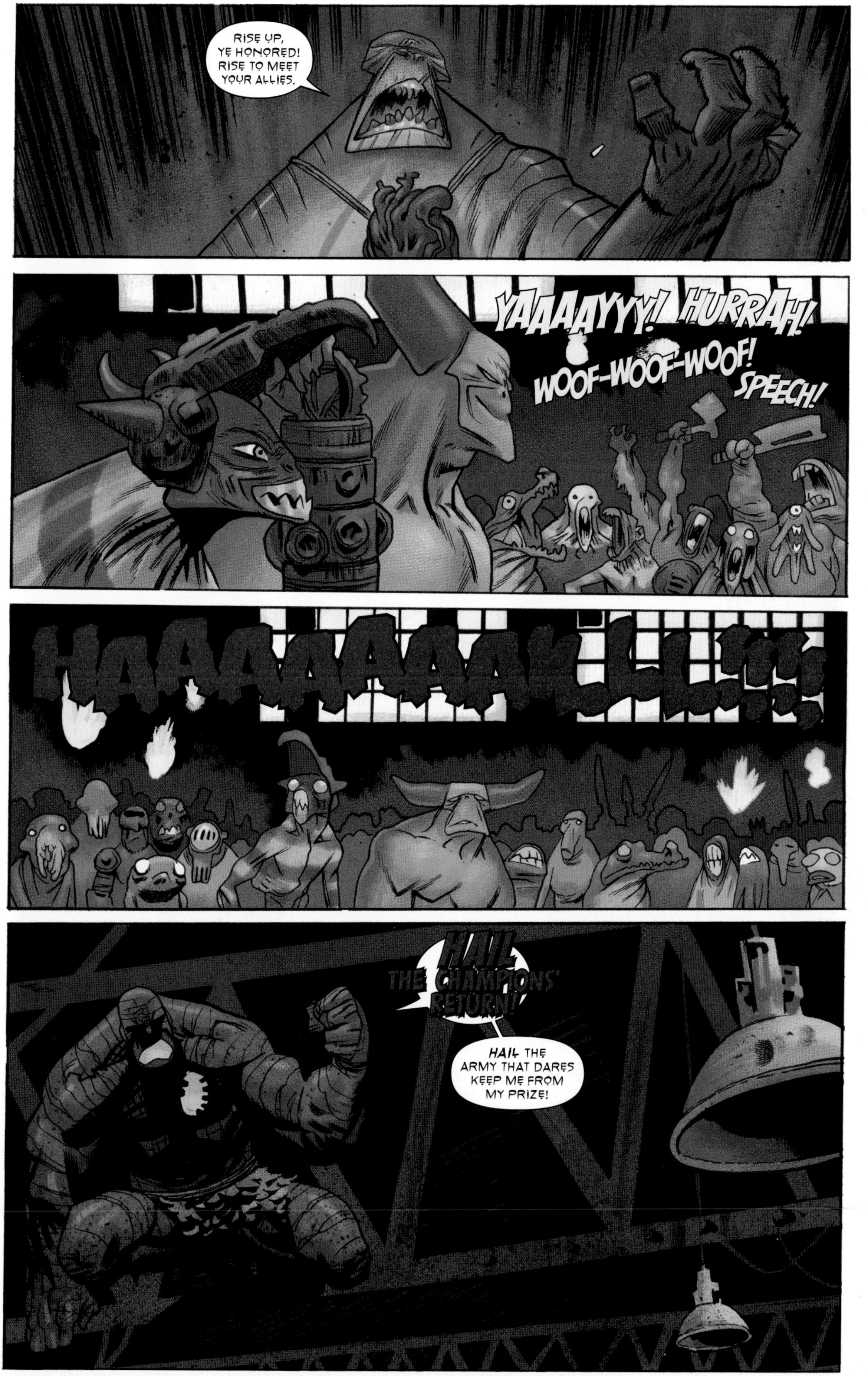
RISE UP, YE HONORED! RISE TO MEET YOUR ALLIES.
YAAAAYYY! HURRAH!
WOOF-WOOF-WOOF!
SPEECH!
HAAAAAAALLL!!!
HAIL THE CHAMPIONS' RETURN!
HAIL THE ARMY THAT DARES KEEP ME FROM MY PRIZE!

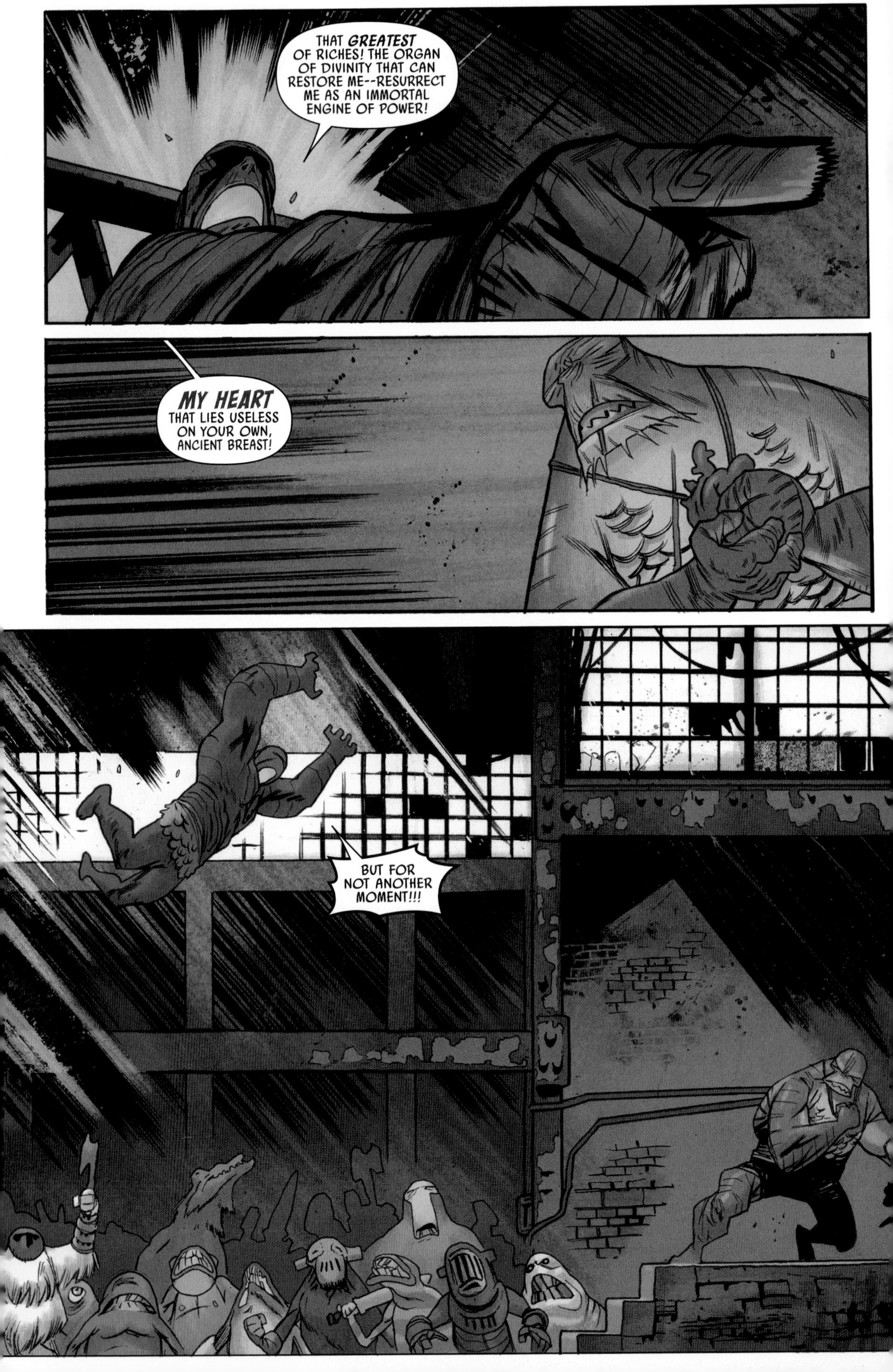
THAT GREATEST OF RICHES! THE ORGAN OF DIVINITY THAT CAN RESTORE ME--RESURRECT ME AS AN IMMORTAL ENGINE OF POWER!
MY HEART THAT LIES USELESS ON YOUR OWN, ANCIENT BREAST!
BUT FOR NOT ANOTHER MOMENT!!!

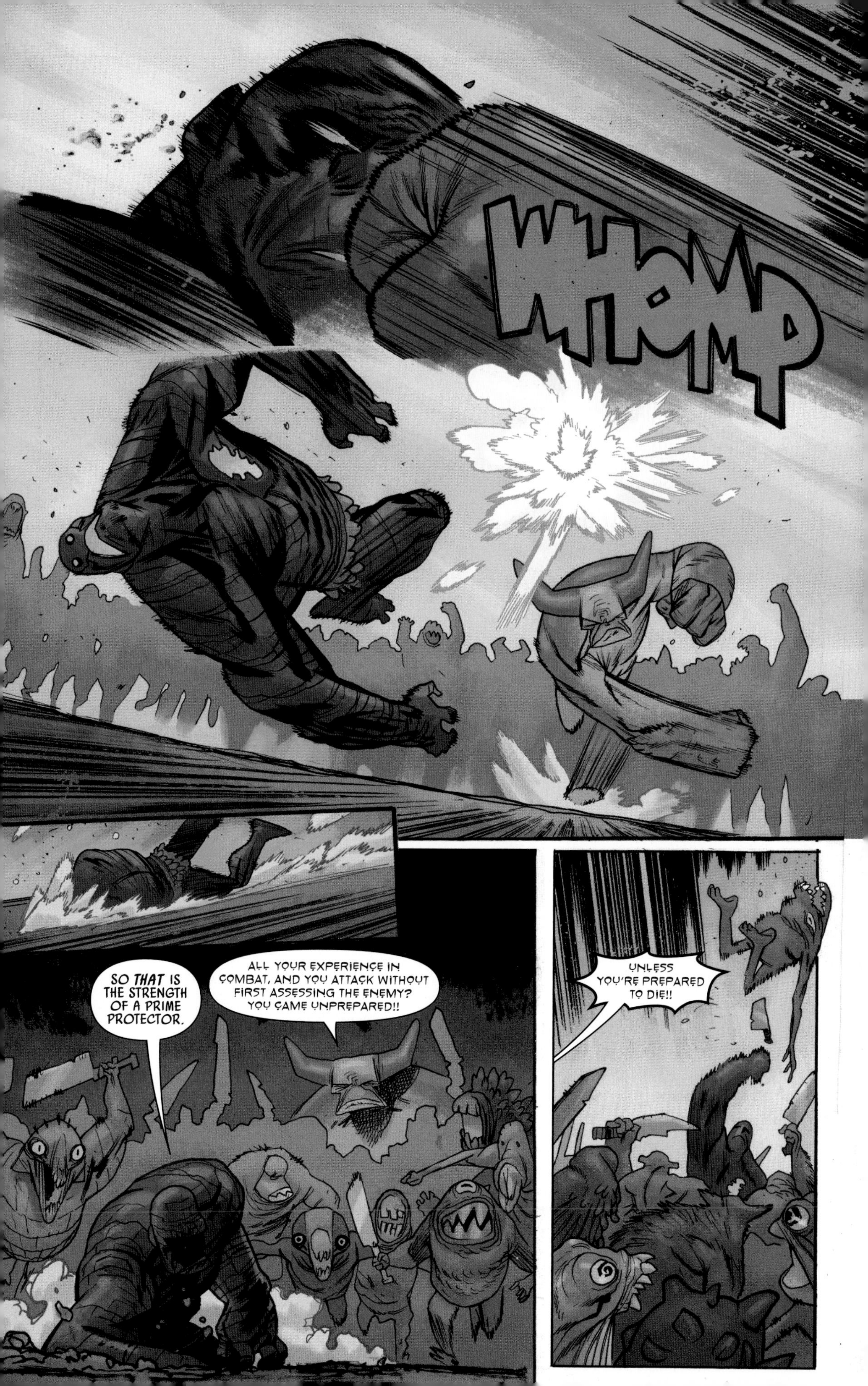
WHOMP
SO THAT IS THE STRENGTH OF A PRIME PROTECTOR.
ALL YOUR EXPERIENCE IN COMBAT, AND YOU ATTACK WITHOUT FIRST ASSESSING THE ENEMY? YOU CAME UNPREPARED!!
UNLESS YOU'RE PREPARED TO DIE!!

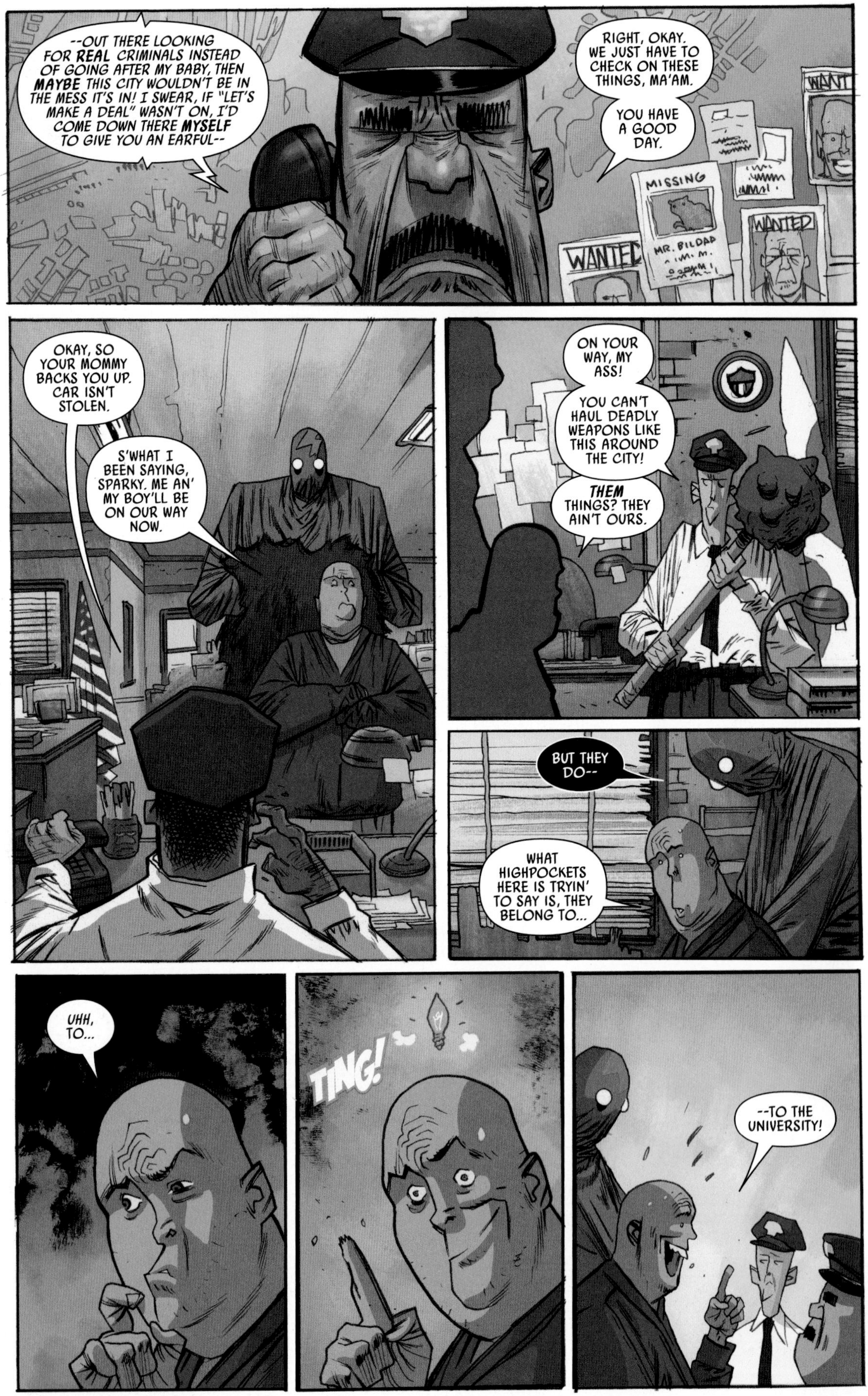
--OUT THERE LOOKING FOR REAL CRIMINALS INSTEAD OF GOING AFTER MY BABY, THEN MAYBE THIS CITY WOULDN'T BE IN THE MESS IT'S IN! I SWEAR, IF "LET'S MAKE A DEAL" WASN'T ON, I'D COME DOWN THERE MYSELF TO GIVE YOU AN EARFUL--
RIGHT, OKAY. WE JUST HAVE TO CHECK ON THESE THINGS, MA'AM.
YOU HAVE A GOOD DAY.
MISSING
MR. BILDAD
WANTED
WANTED
OKAY, SO YOUR MOMMY BACKS YOU UP. CAR ISN'T STOLEN.
S'WHAT I BEEN SAYING, SPARKY. ME AN' MY BOY'LL BE ON OUR WAY NOW.
ON YOUR WAY, MY ASS!
YOU CAN'T HAUL DEADLY WEAPONS LIKE THIS AROUND THE CITY!
THEM THINGS? THEY AIN'T OURS.
BUT THEY DO--
WHAT HIGHPOCKETS HERE IS TRYIN' TO SAY IS, THEY BELONG TO...
UHH, TO...
TING!
--TO THE UNIVERSITY!

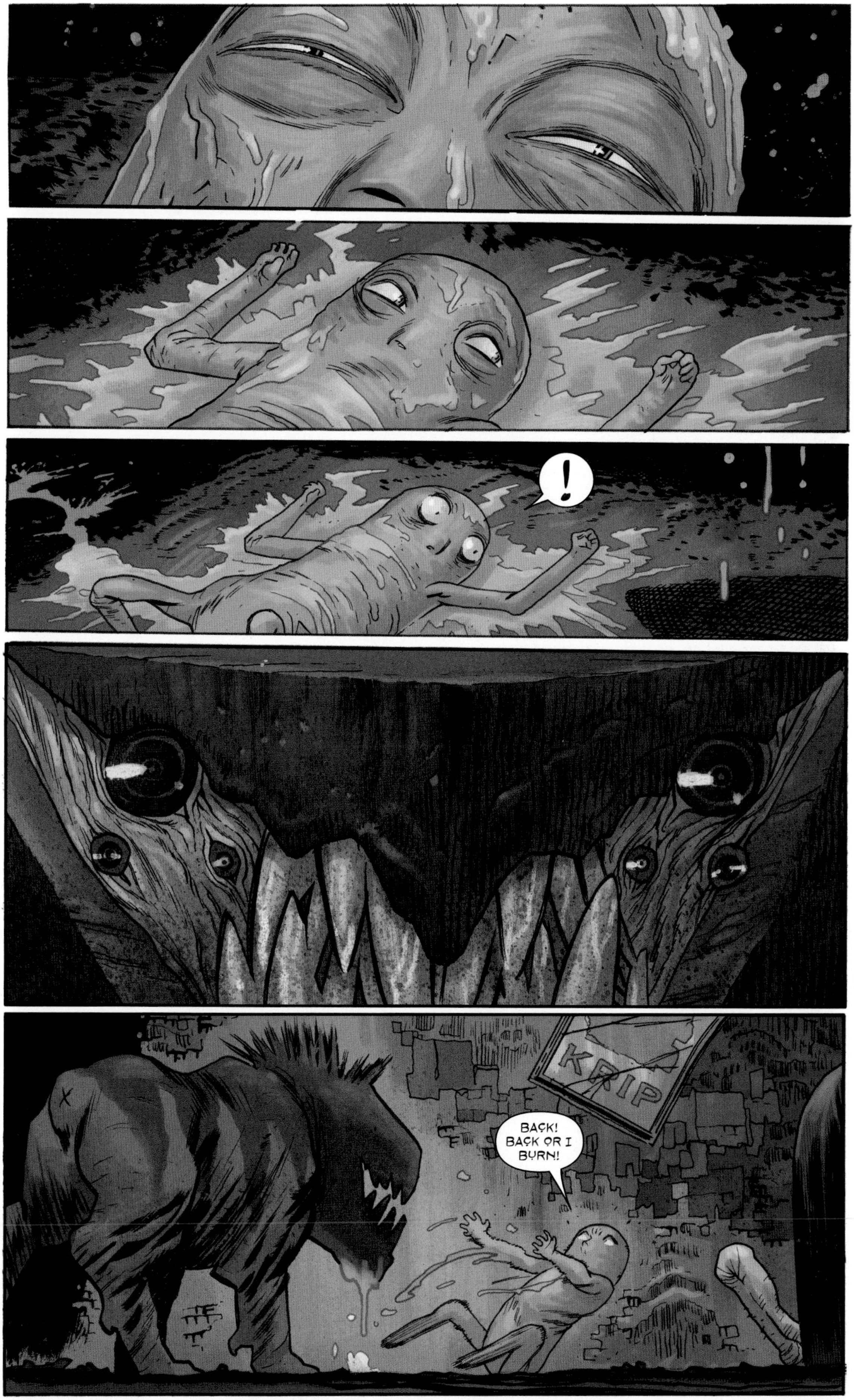
!
BACK! BACK OR I BURN!
KRIP

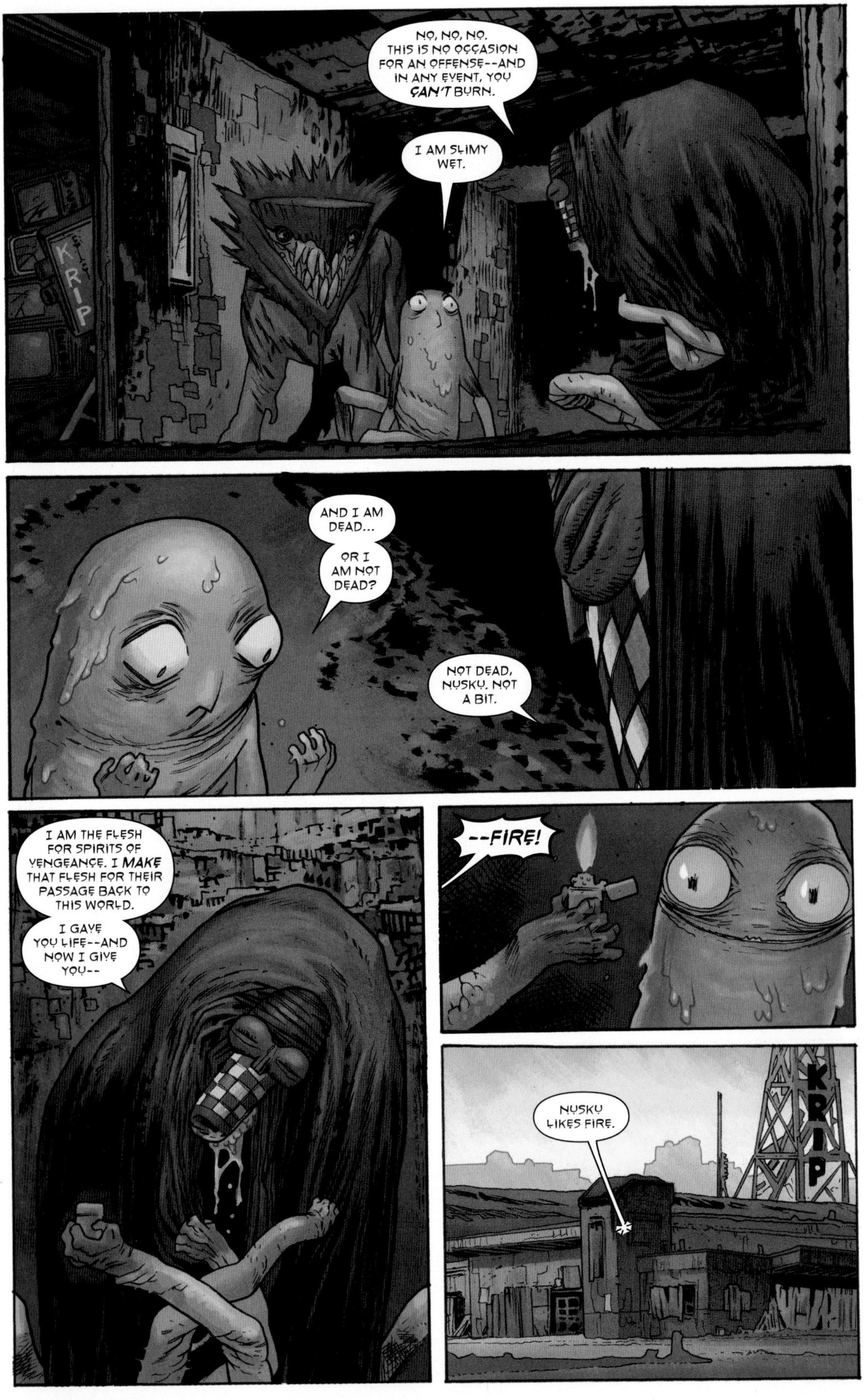
KRIP
NO, NO, NO. THIS IS NO OCCASION FOR AN OFFENSE--AND IN ANY EVENT, YOU CAN'T BURN.
I AM SLIMY WET.
AND I AM DEAD...
OR I AM NOT DEAD?
NOT DEAD, NUSKU. NOT A BIT.
I AM THE FLESH FOR SPIRITS OF VENGEANCE. I MAKE THAT FLESH FOR THEIR PASSAGE BACK TO THIS WORLD.
I GAVE YOU LIFE--AND NOW I GIVE YOU--
--FIRE!
NUSKU LIKES FIRE.
KRIP

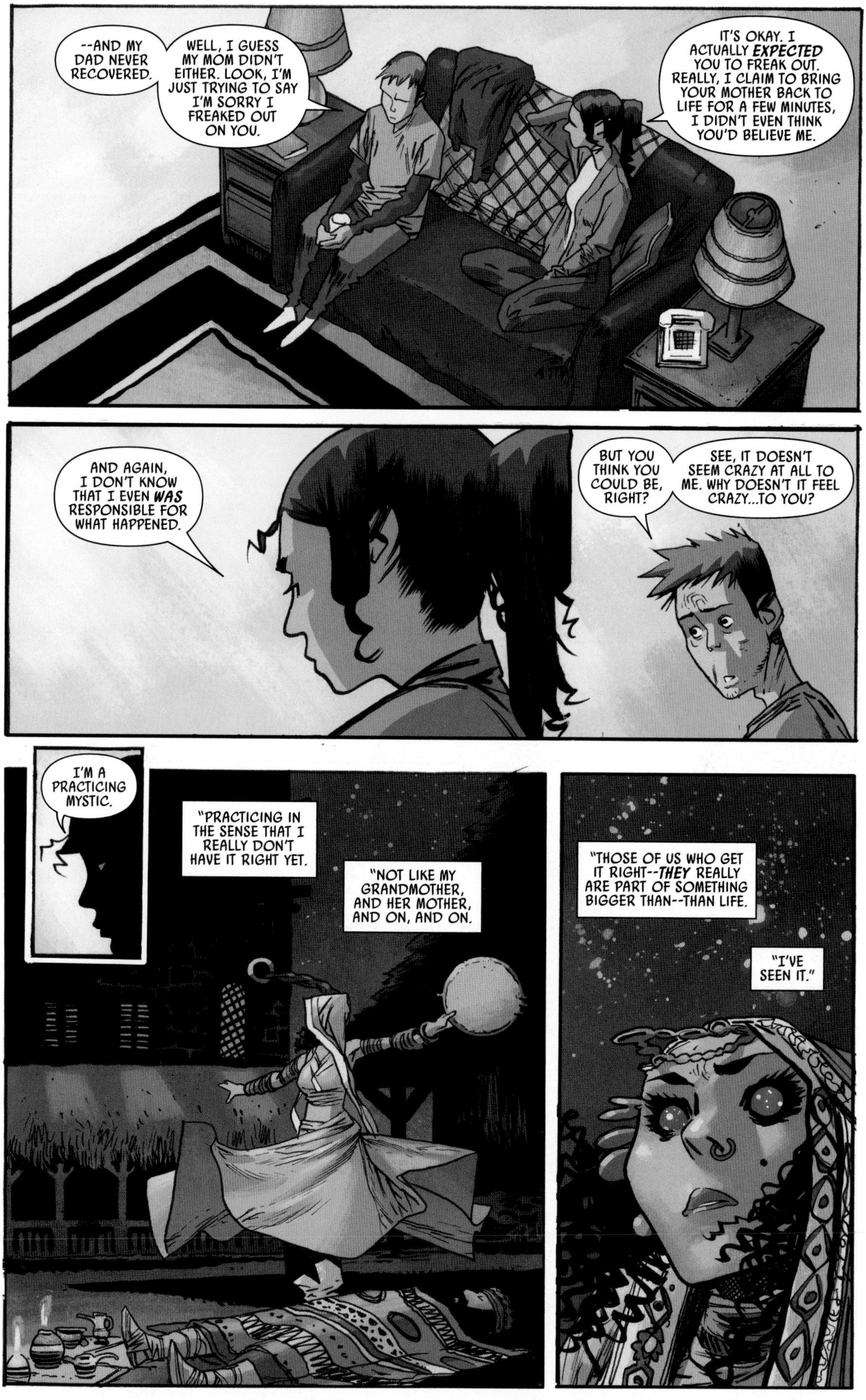
--AND MY DAD NEVER RECOVERED.
WELL, I GUESS MY MOM DIDN'T EITHER. LOOK, I'M JUST TRYING TO SAY I'M SORRY I FREAKED OUT ON YOU.
IT'S OKAY. I ACTUALLY EXPECTED YOU TO FREAK OUT. REALLY, I CLAIM TO BRING YOUR MOTHER BACK TO LIFE FOR A FEW MINUTES, I DIDN'T EVEN THINK YOU'D BELIEVE ME.
AND AGAIN, I DON'T KNOW THAT I EVEN WAS RESPONSIBLE FOR WHAT HAPPENED.
BUT YOU THINK YOU COULD BE, RIGHT?
SEE, IT DOESN'T SEEM CRAZY AT ALL TO ME. WHY DOESN'T IT FEEL CRAZY...TO YOU?
I'M A PRACTICING MYSTIC.
"PRACTICING IN THE SENSE THAT I REALLY DON'T HAVE IT RIGHT YET.
"NOT LIKE MY GRANDMOTHER, AND HER MOTHER, AND ON, AND ON.
"THOSE OF US WHO GET IT RIGHT--THEY REALLY ARE PART OF SOMETHING BIGGER THAN--THAN LIFE.
"I'VE SEEN IT."

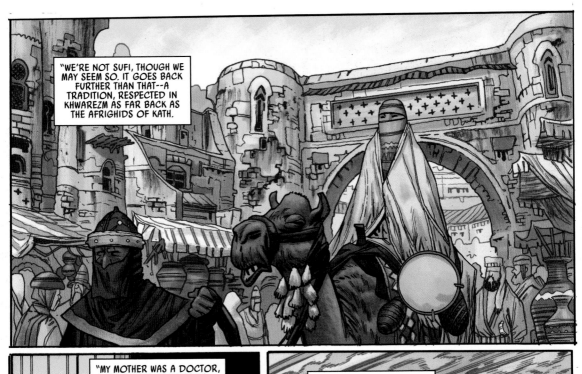

"WE'RE NOT SUFI, THOUGH WE MAY SEEM SO. IT GOES BACK FURTHER THAN THAT--A TRADITION, RESPECTED IN KHWAREZM AS FAR BACK AS THE AFRIGHIDS OF KATH.

"MY MOTHER WAS A DOCTOR, AND THAT'S MEANINGFUL. HELPING SICK PEOPLE, IT'S ESSENTIAL--BUT GRANDMA TAUGHT ME IT DIDN'T END THERE.

"SHE TREATED THOSE THAT MEDICINE COULDN'T HELP. PEOPLE WHO WERE *SPIRITUALLY* SICK.

"ONLY THE *OTHERWORLD*, THE SPIRITS, COULD HELP THEM--AND ONLY GRANDMA COULD REACH THE SPIRITS.

"WHEN SHE DIED, AND I SAW THE HUGE CROWDS AT HER FUNERAL, I FELT THIS GREAT ABSENCE-- THIS VOID IN THEIR WORLD--

"I THOUGHT, MAYBE I COULD HELP."

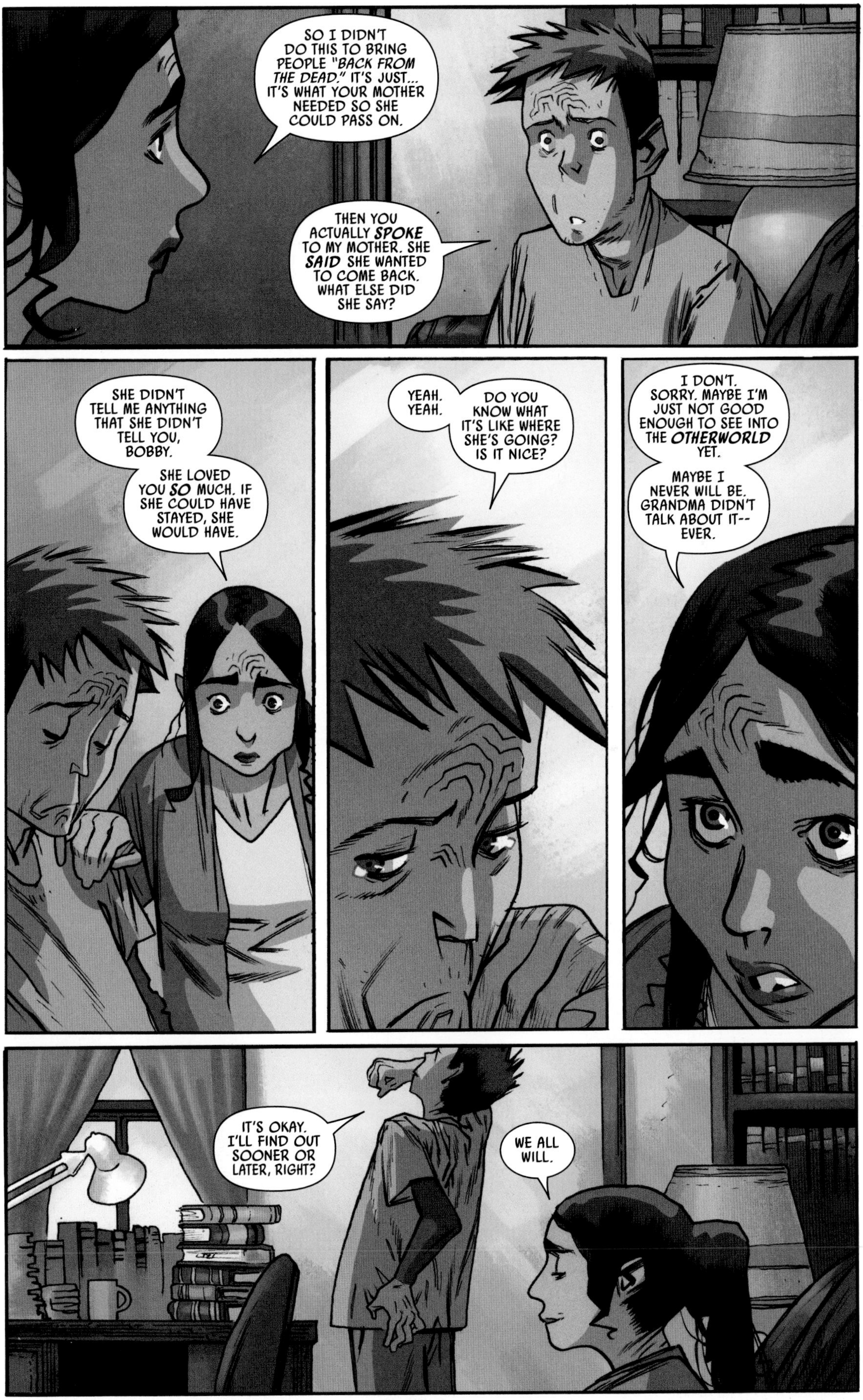
SO I DIDN'T DO THIS TO BRING PEOPLE "BACK FROM THE DEAD." IT'S JUST... IT'S WHAT YOUR MOTHER NEEDED SO SHE COULD PASS ON.
THEN YOU ACTUALLY SPOKE TO MY MOTHER. SHE SAID SHE WANTED TO COME BACK. WHAT ELSE DID SHE SAY?
SHE DIDN'T TELL ME ANYTHING THAT SHE DIDN'T TELL YOU, BOBBY.
SHE LOVED YOU SO MUCH. IF SHE COULD HAVE STAYED, SHE WOULD HAVE.
YEAH. YEAH.
DO YOU KNOW WHAT IT'S LIKE WHERE SHE'S GOING? IS IT NICE?
I DON'T. SORRY. MAYBE I'M JUST NOT GOOD ENOUGH TO SEE INTO THE OTHERWORLD YET.
MAYBE I NEVER WILL BE. GRANDMA DIDN'T TALK ABOUT IT-- EVER.
IT'S OKAY. I'LL FIND OUT SOONER OR LATER, RIGHT?
WE ALL WILL.

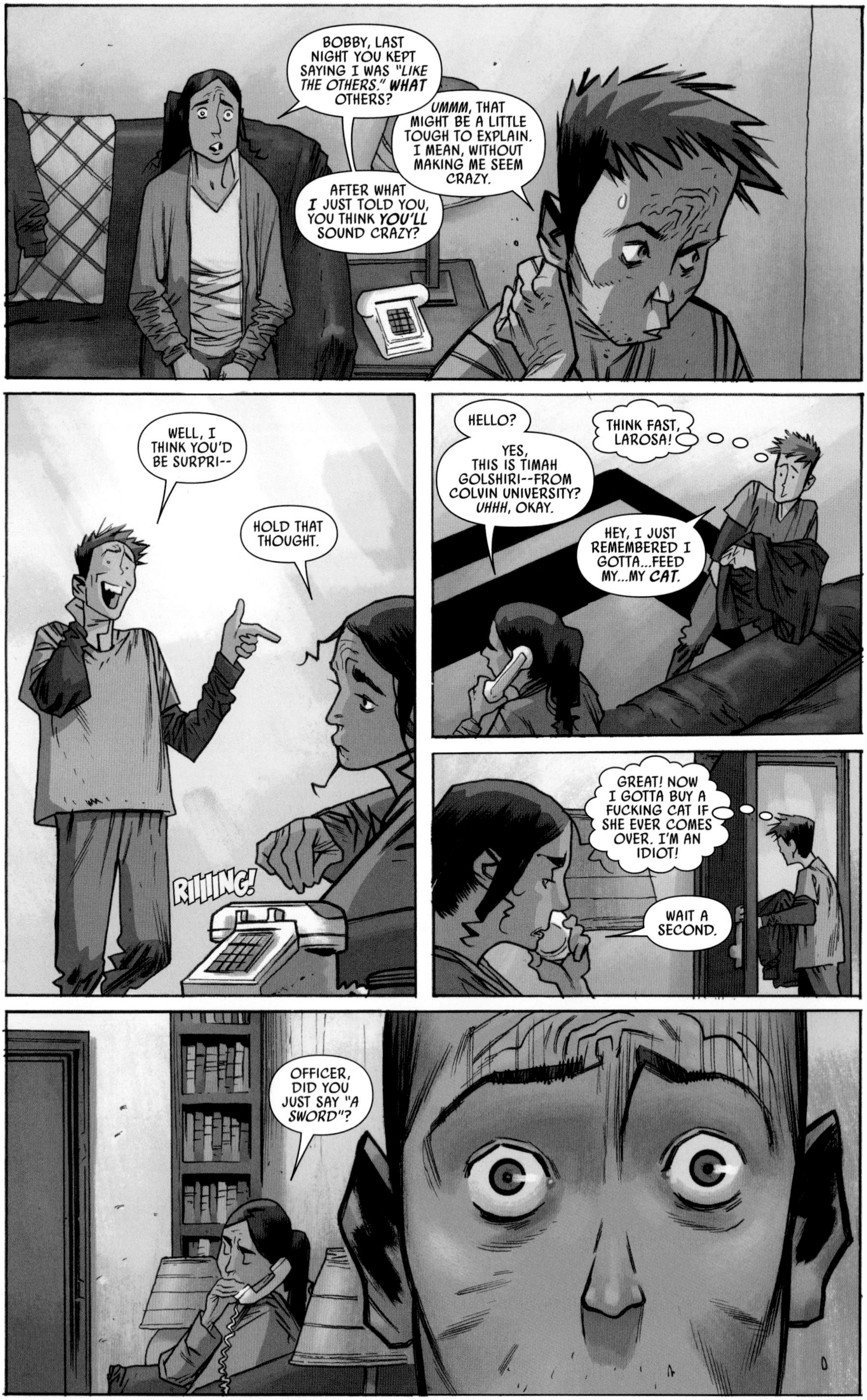
BOBBY, LAST NIGHT YOU KEPT SAYING I WAS "LIKE THE OTHERS." WHAT OTHERS?
UMMM, THAT MIGHT BE A LITTLE TOUGH TO EXPLAIN. I MEAN, WITHOUT MAKING ME SEEM CRAZY.
AFTER WHAT I JUST TOLD YOU, YOU THINK YOU'LL SOUND CRAZY?
WELL, I THINK YOU'D BE SURPRI--
HOLD THAT THOUGHT.
RIIIING!
HELLO?
YES, THIS IS TIMAH GOLSHIRI--FROM COLVIN UNIVERSITY? UHHH, OKAY.
THINK FAST, LAROSA!
HEY, I JUST REMEMBERED I GOTTA...FEED MY...MY CAT.
GREAT! NOW I GOTTA BUY A FUCKING CAT IF SHE EVER COMES OVER. I'M AN IDIOT!
WAIT A SECOND.
OFFICER, DID YOU JUST SAY "A SWORD"?

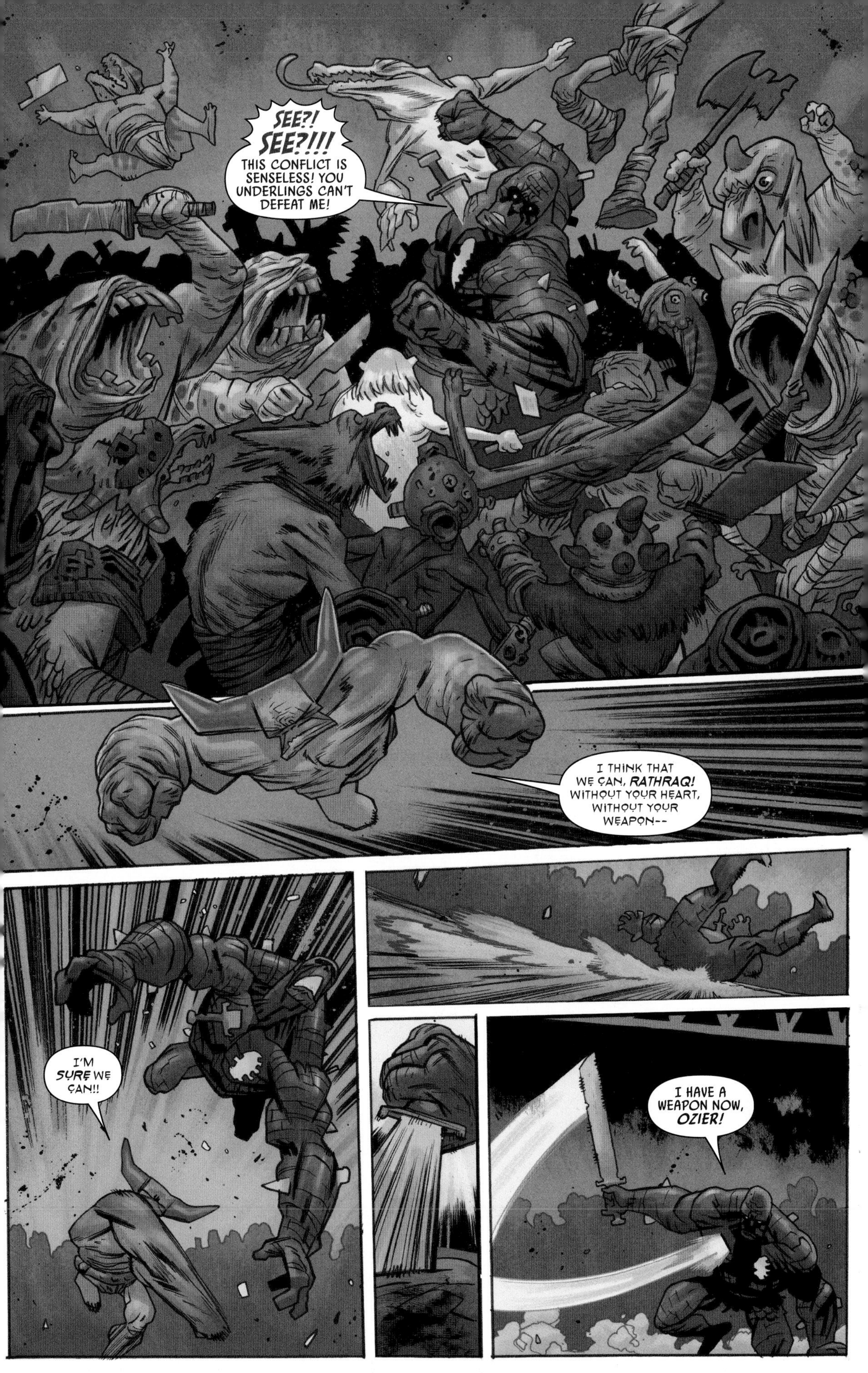
SEE?! SEE?!!! THIS CONFLICT IS SENSELESS! YOU UNDERLINGS CAN'T DEFEAT ME!
I THINK THAT WE CAN, RATHRAQ! WITHOUT YOUR HEART, WITHOUT YOUR WEAPON--
I'M SURE WE CAN!!
I HAVE A WEAPON NOW, OZIER!

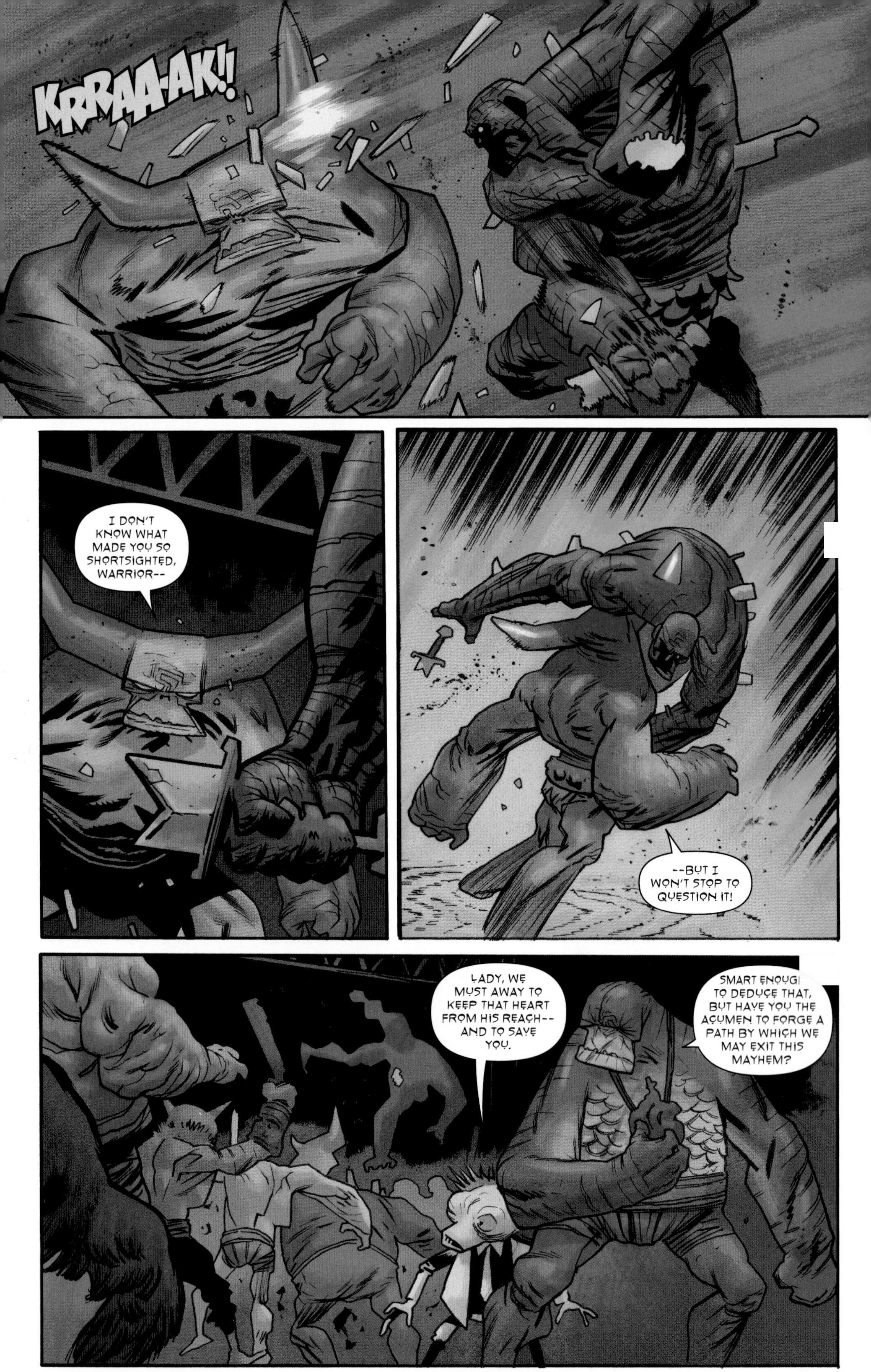
KRRAA-AK!!
I DON'T KNOW WHAT MADE YOU SO SHORTSIGHTED, WARRIOR--
--BUT I WON'T STOP TO QUESTION IT!
LADY, WE MUST AWAY TO KEEP THAT HEART FROM HIS REACH--AND TO SAVE YOU.
SMART ENOUGH TO DEDUCE THAT, BUT HAVE YOU THE ACUMEN TO FORGE A PATH BY WHICH WE MAY EXIT THIS MAYHEM?

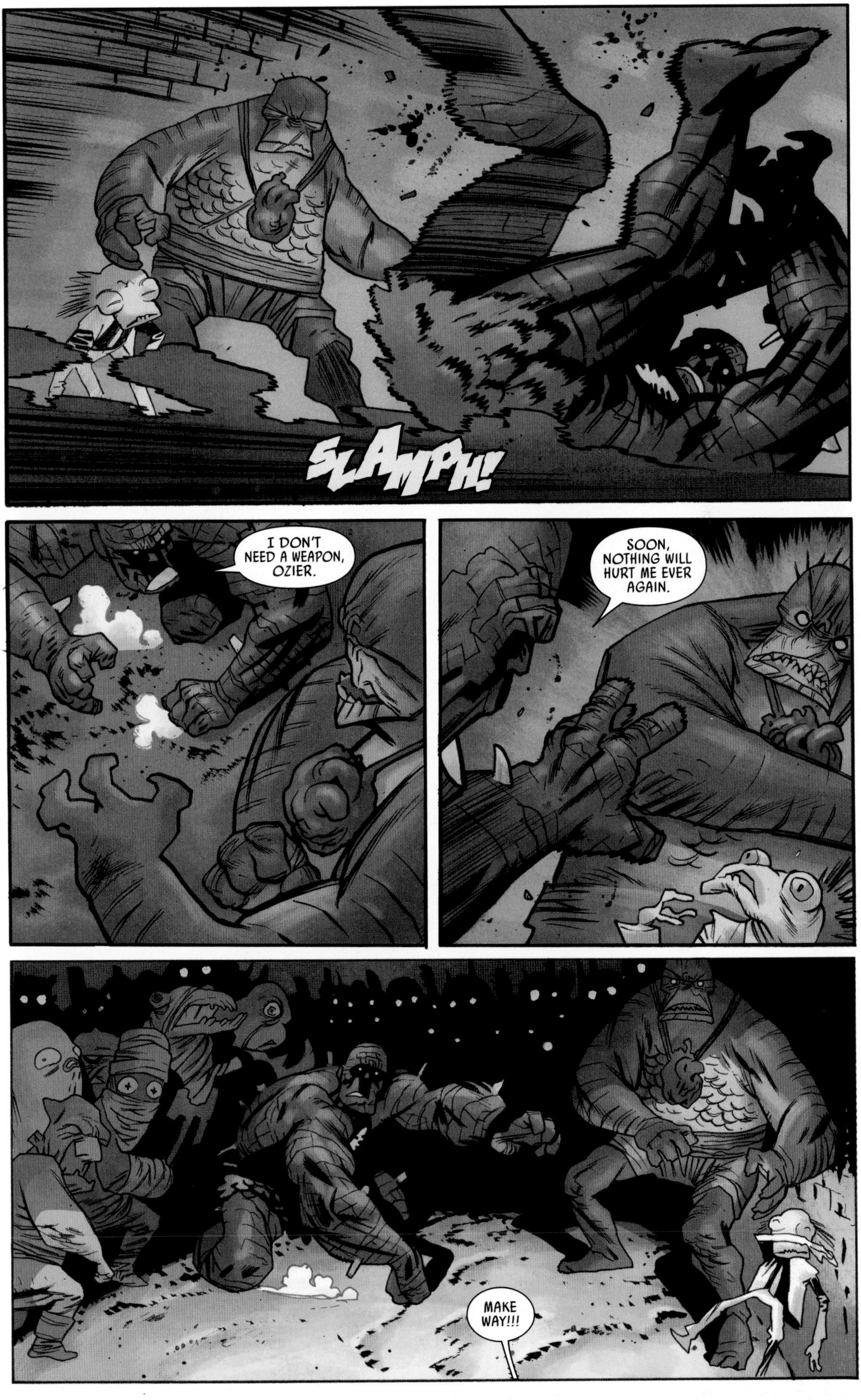
SLAMPH!
I DON'T NEED A WEAPON, OZIER.
SOON, NOTHING WILL HURT ME EVER AGAIN.
MAKE WAY!!!

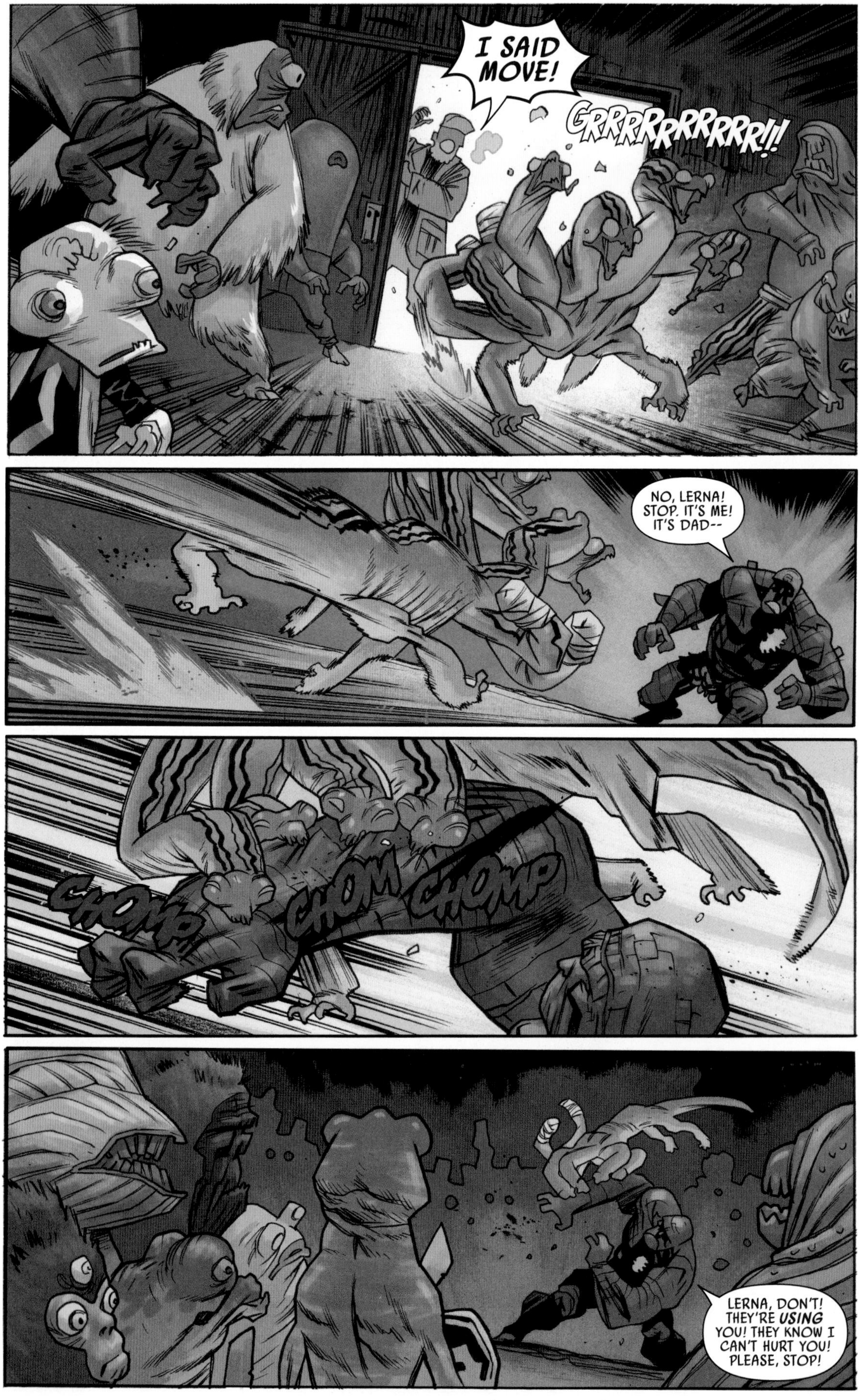
I SAID MOVE!
GRRRRRRRRRR!!!
NO, LERNA! STOP. IT'S ME! IT'S DAD--
CHOMP
CHOM
CHOMP
LERNA, DON'T! THEY'RE *USING* YOU! THEY KNOW I CAN'T HURT YOU! PLEASE, STOP!

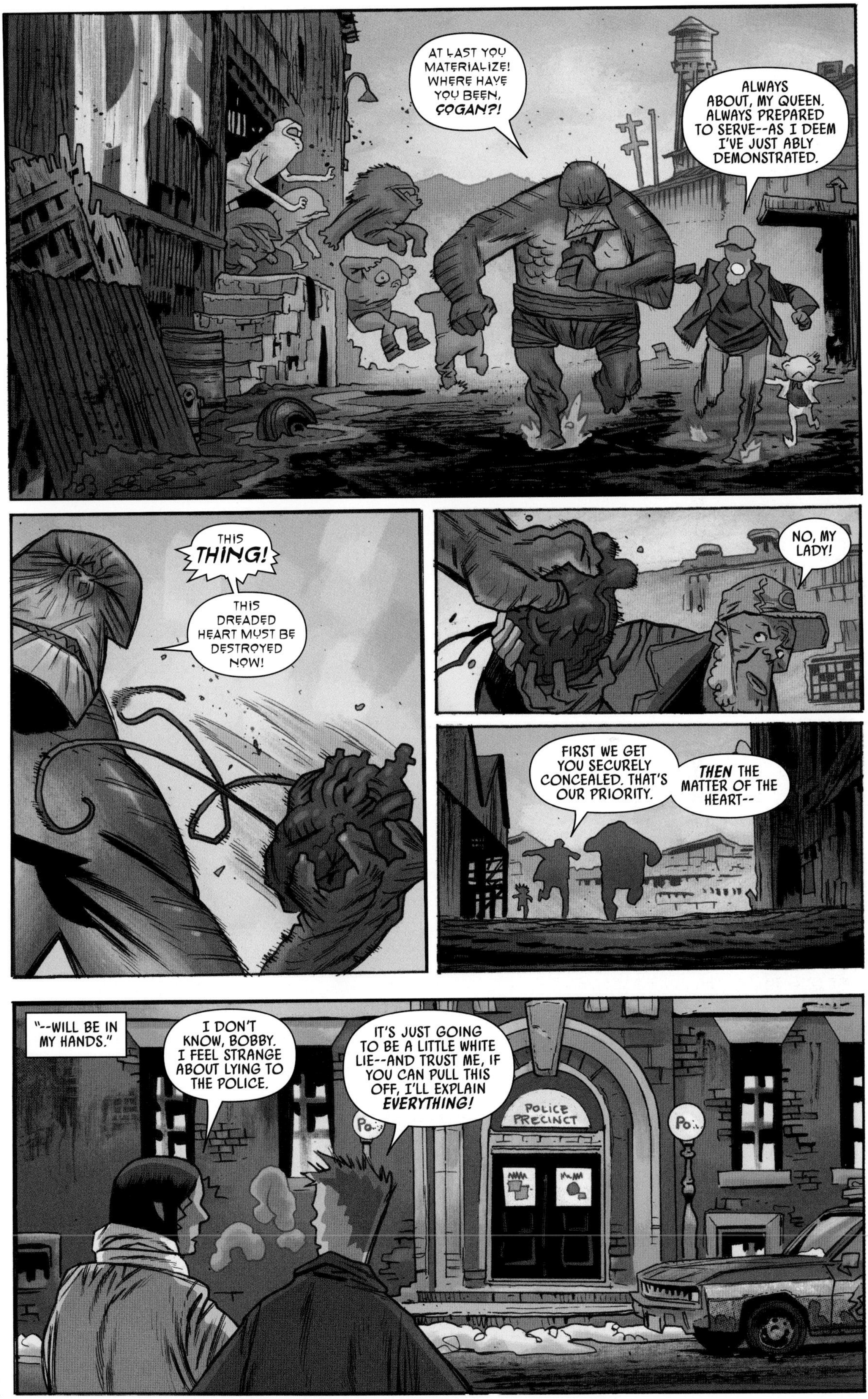
AT LAST YOU MATERIALIZE! WHERE HAVE YOU BEEN, COGAN?!
ALWAYS ABOUT, MY QUEEN. ALWAYS PREPARED TO SERVE--AS I DEEM I'VE JUST ABLY DEMONSTRATED.
THIS THING!
THIS DREADED HEART MUST BE DESTROYED NOW!
NO, MY LADY!
FIRST WE GET YOU SECURELY CONCEALED. THAT'S OUR PRIORITY.
THEN THE MATTER OF THE HEART--
"--WILL BE IN MY HANDS."
I DON'T KNOW, BOBBY. I FEEL STRANGE ABOUT LYING TO THE POLICE.
IT'S JUST GOING TO BE A LITTLE WHITE LIE--AND TRUST ME, IF YOU CAN PULL THIS OFF, I'LL EXPLAIN EVERYTHING!
POLICE PRECINCT

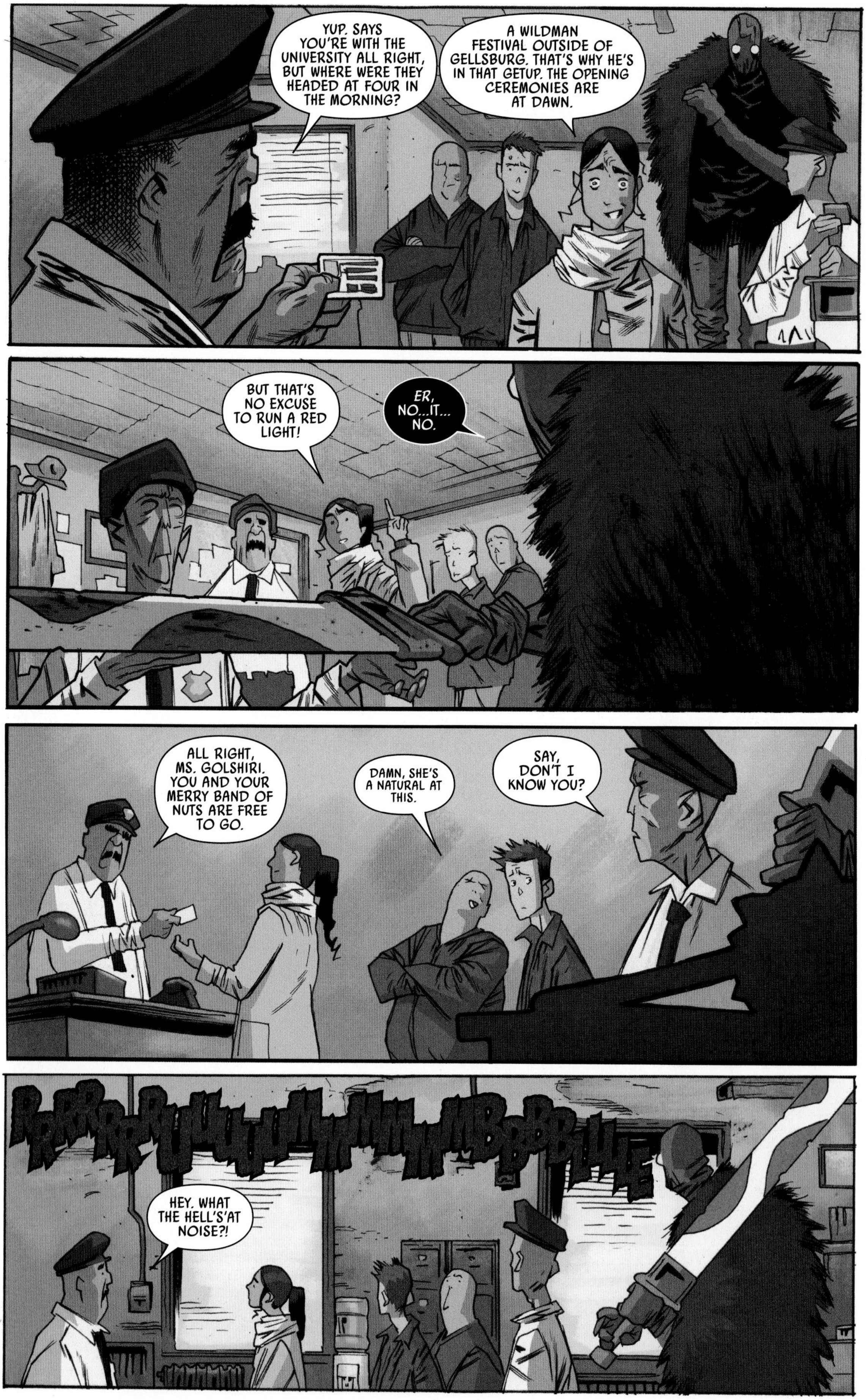
YUP. SAYS YOU'RE WITH THE UNIVERSITY ALL RIGHT, BUT WHERE WERE THEY HEADED AT FOUR IN THE MORNING?
A WILDMAN FESTIVAL OUTSIDE OF GELLSBURG. THAT'S WHY HE'S IN THAT GETUP. THE OPENING CEREMONIES ARE AT DAWN.
BUT THAT'S NO EXCUSE TO RUN A RED LIGHT!
ER, NO...IT... NO.
ALL RIGHT, MS. GOLSHIRI. YOU AND YOUR MERRY BAND OF NUTS ARE FREE TO GO.
DAMN, SHE'S A NATURAL AT THIS.
SAY, DON'T I KNOW YOU?
RRRRRRRUUUUUUMMMMMMBBBBBLLLE
HEY. WHAT THE HELL'S'AT NOISE?!

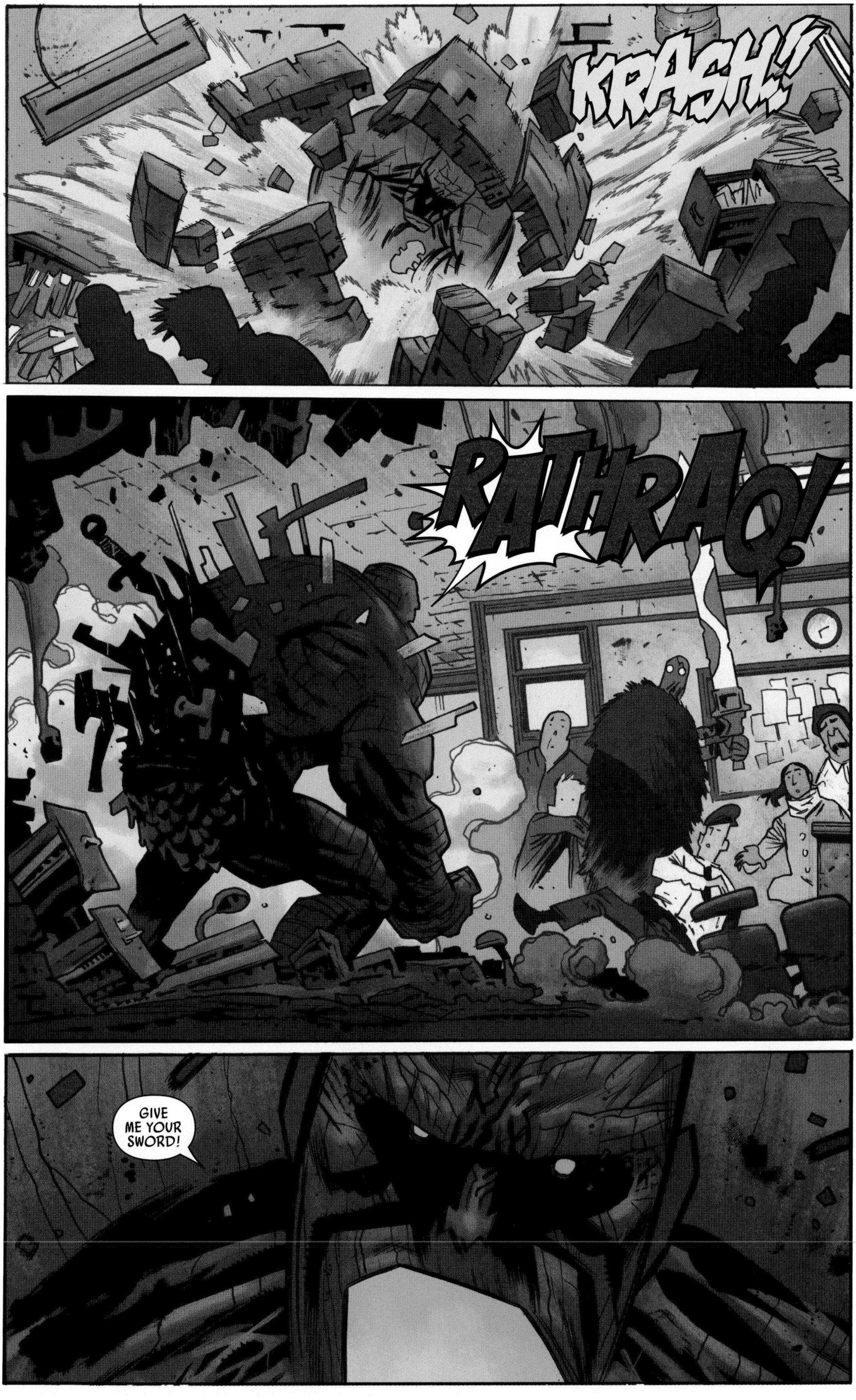
KRASH!!
RATHRAQ!
GIVE ME YOUR SWORD!

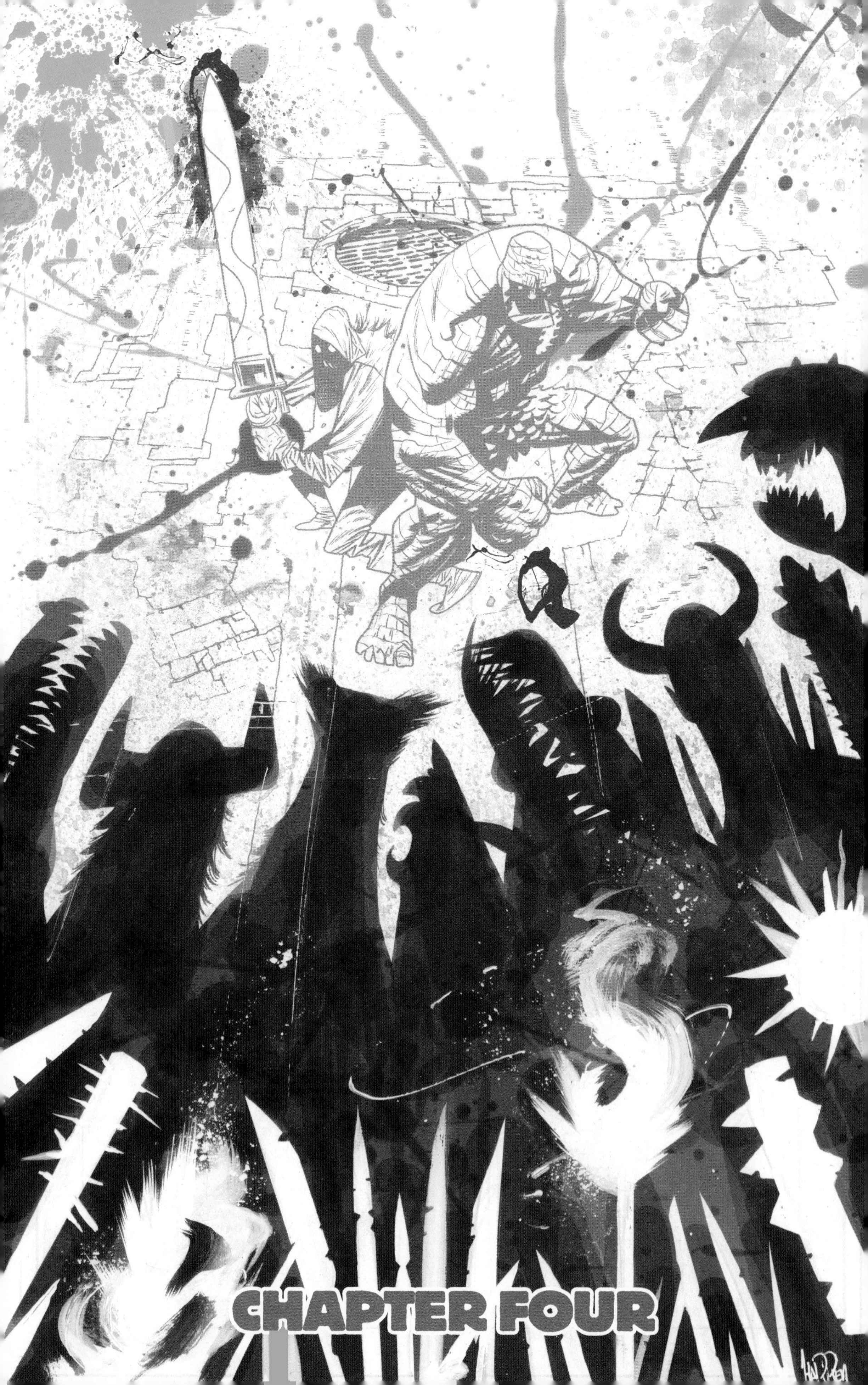
CHAPTER FOUR

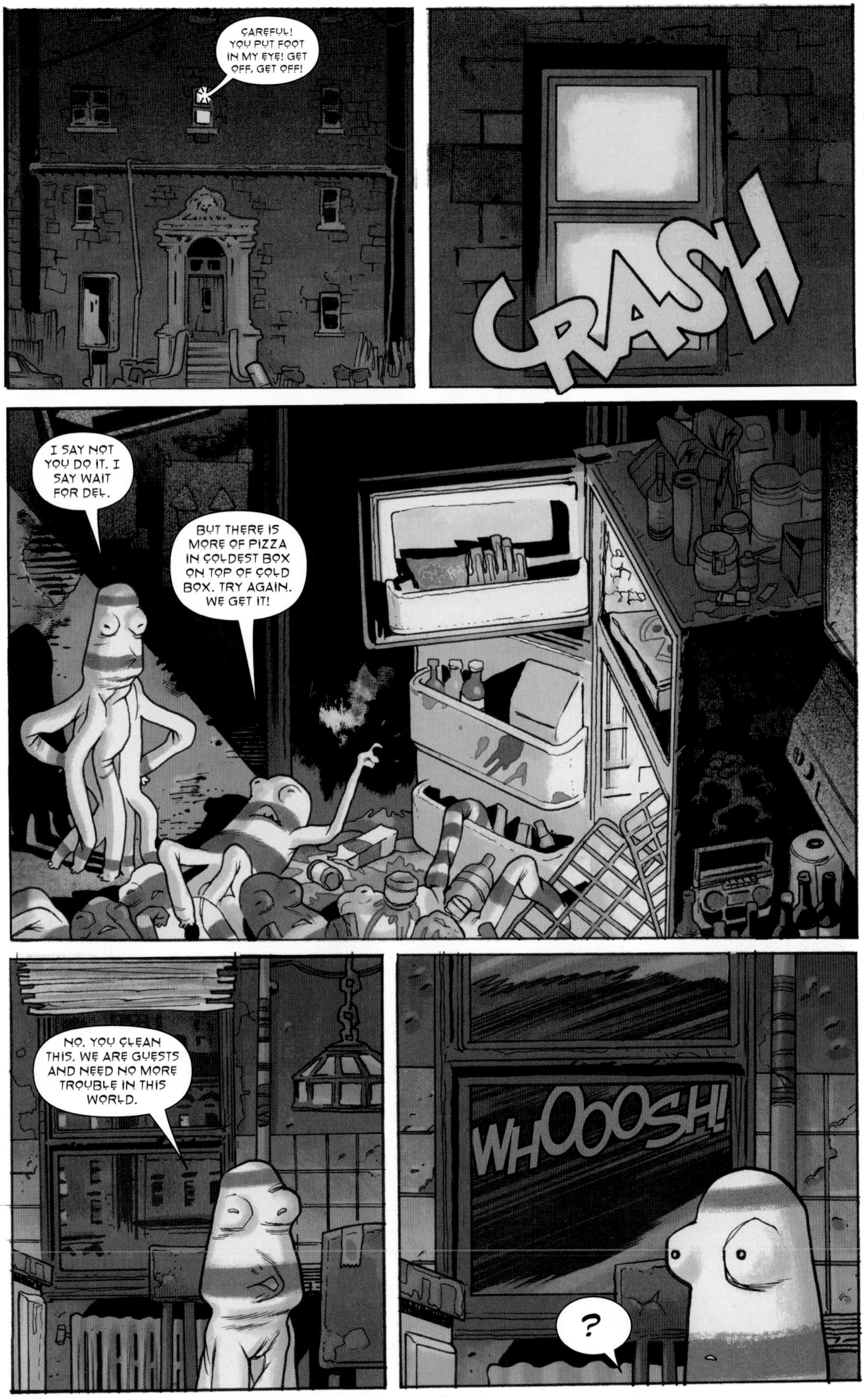
CAREFUL! YOU PUT FOOT IN MY EYE! GET OFF, GET OFF!
CRASH
I SAY NOT YOU DO IT. I SAY WAIT FOR DEL.
BUT THERE IS MORE OF PIZZA IN COLDEST BOX ON TOP OF COLD BOX. TRY AGAIN. WE GET IT!
NO. YOU CLEAN THIS. WE ARE GUESTS AND NEED NO MORE TROUBLE IN THIS WORLD.
WHOOOSH!
?

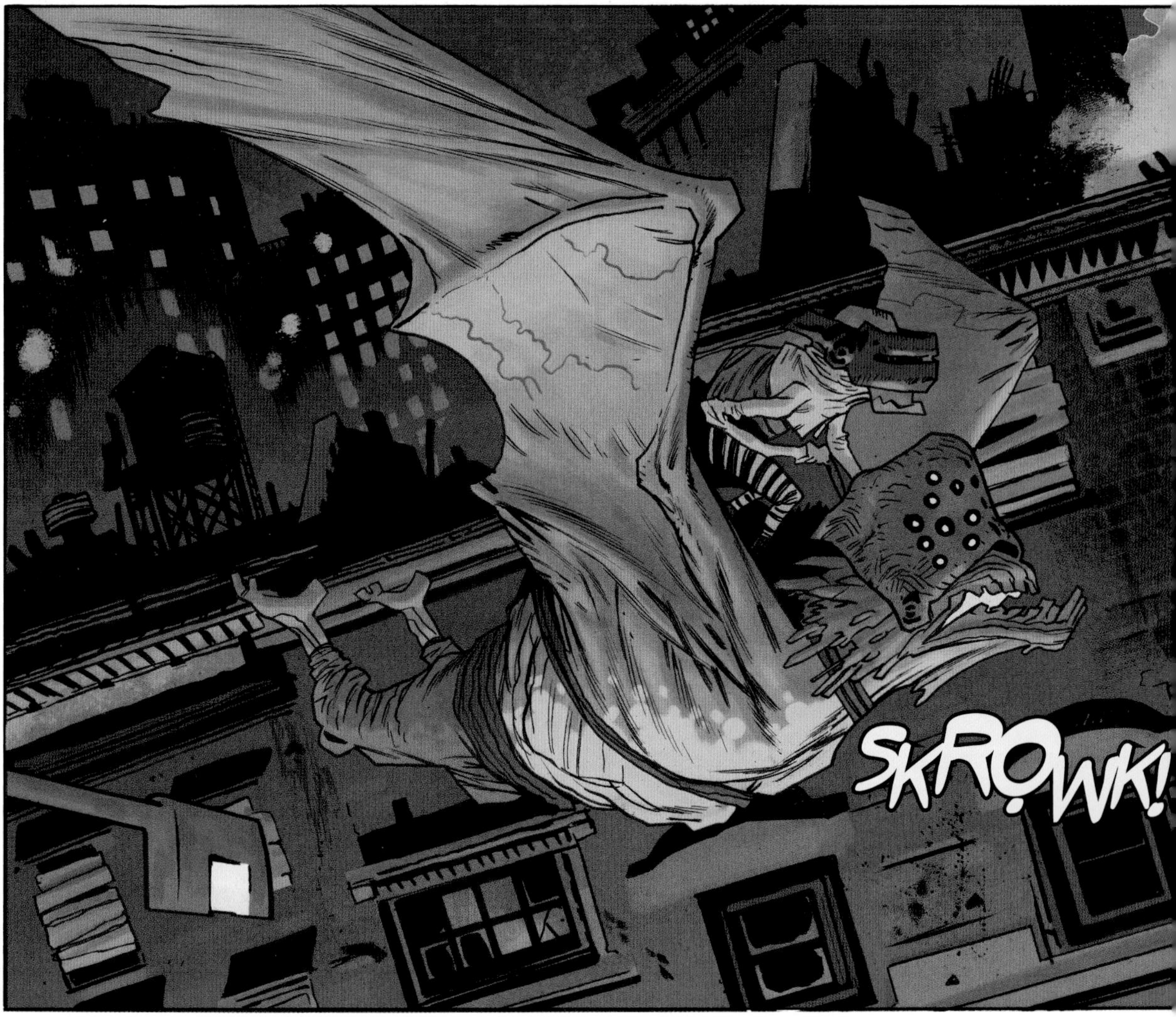
SKROWK!

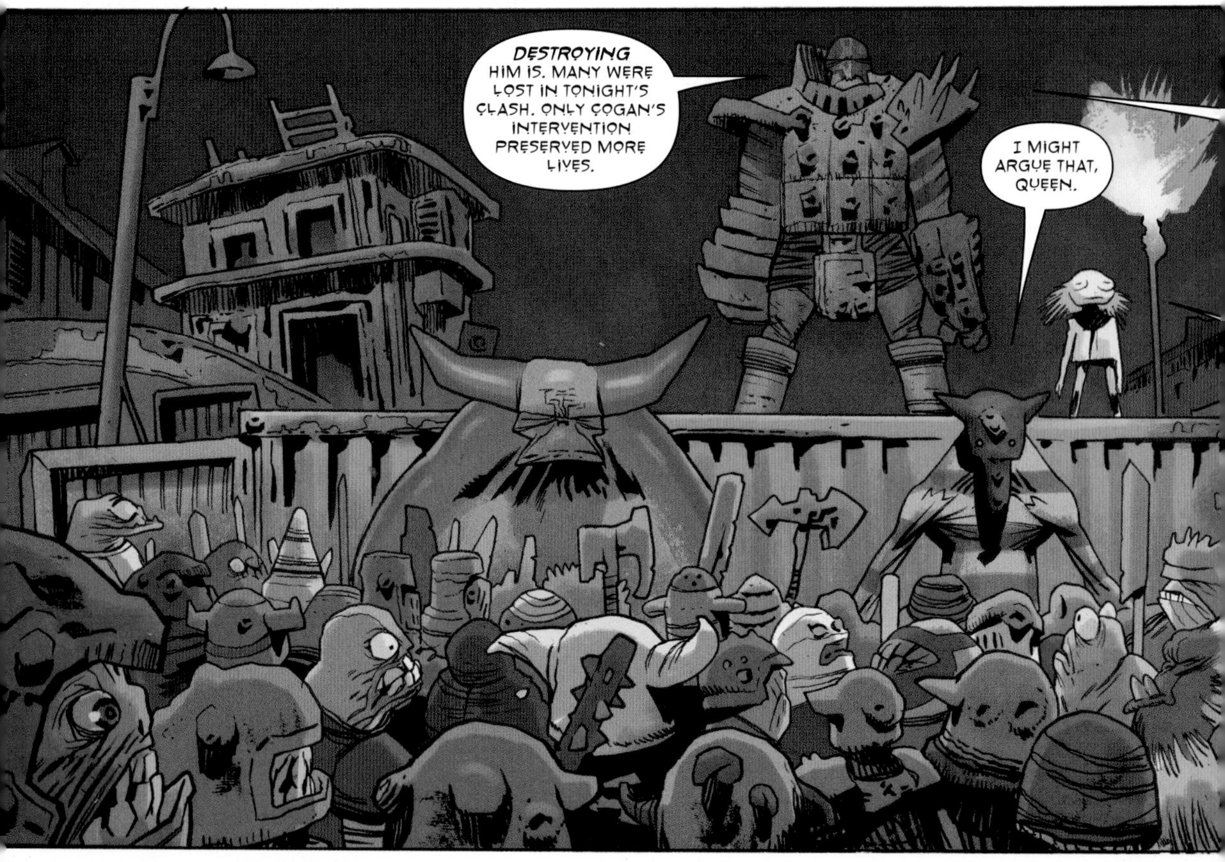
DESTROYING HIM IS. MANY WERE LOST IN TONIGHT'S CLASH. ONLY COGAN'S INTERVENTION PRESERVED MORE LIVES.
I MIGHT ARGUE THAT, QUEEN.

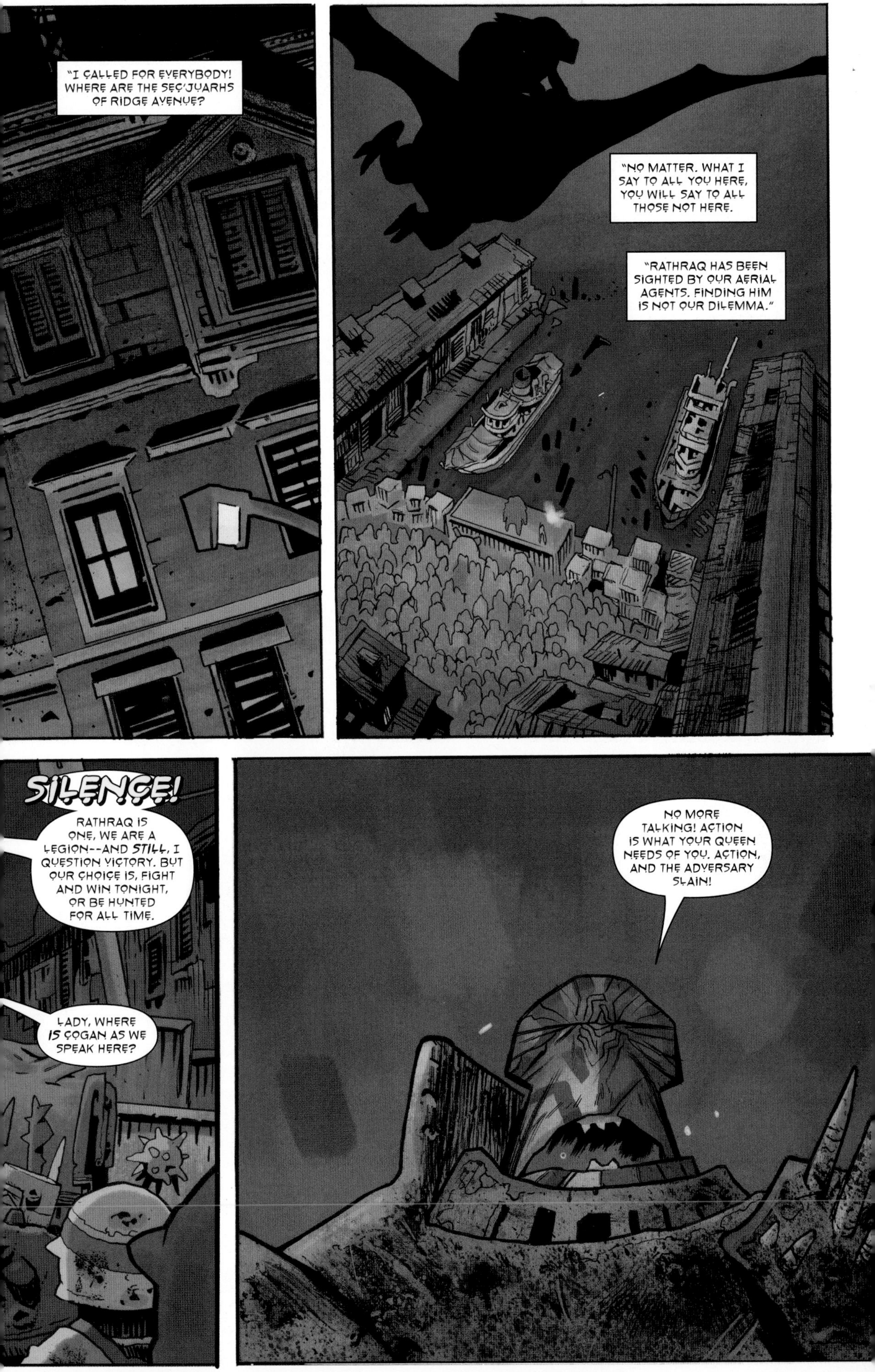
"I CALLED FOR EVERYBODY! WHERE ARE THE SEC'JUARHS OF RIDGE AVENUE?
"NO MATTER. WHAT I SAY TO ALL YOU HERE, YOU WILL SAY TO ALL THOSE NOT HERE.
"RATHRAQ HAS BEEN SIGHTED BY OUR AERIAL AGENTS. FINDING HIM IS NOT OUR DILEMMA."
SILENCE!
RATHRAQ IS ONE, WE ARE A LEGION--AND *STILL*, I QUESTION VICTORY. BUT OUR CHOICE IS, FIGHT AND WIN TONIGHT, OR BE HUNTED FOR ALL TIME.
LADY, WHERE *IS* COGAN AS WE SPEAK HERE?
NO MORE TALKING! ACTION IS WHAT YOUR QUEEN NEEDS OF YOU. ACTION, AND THE ADVERSARY SLAIN!

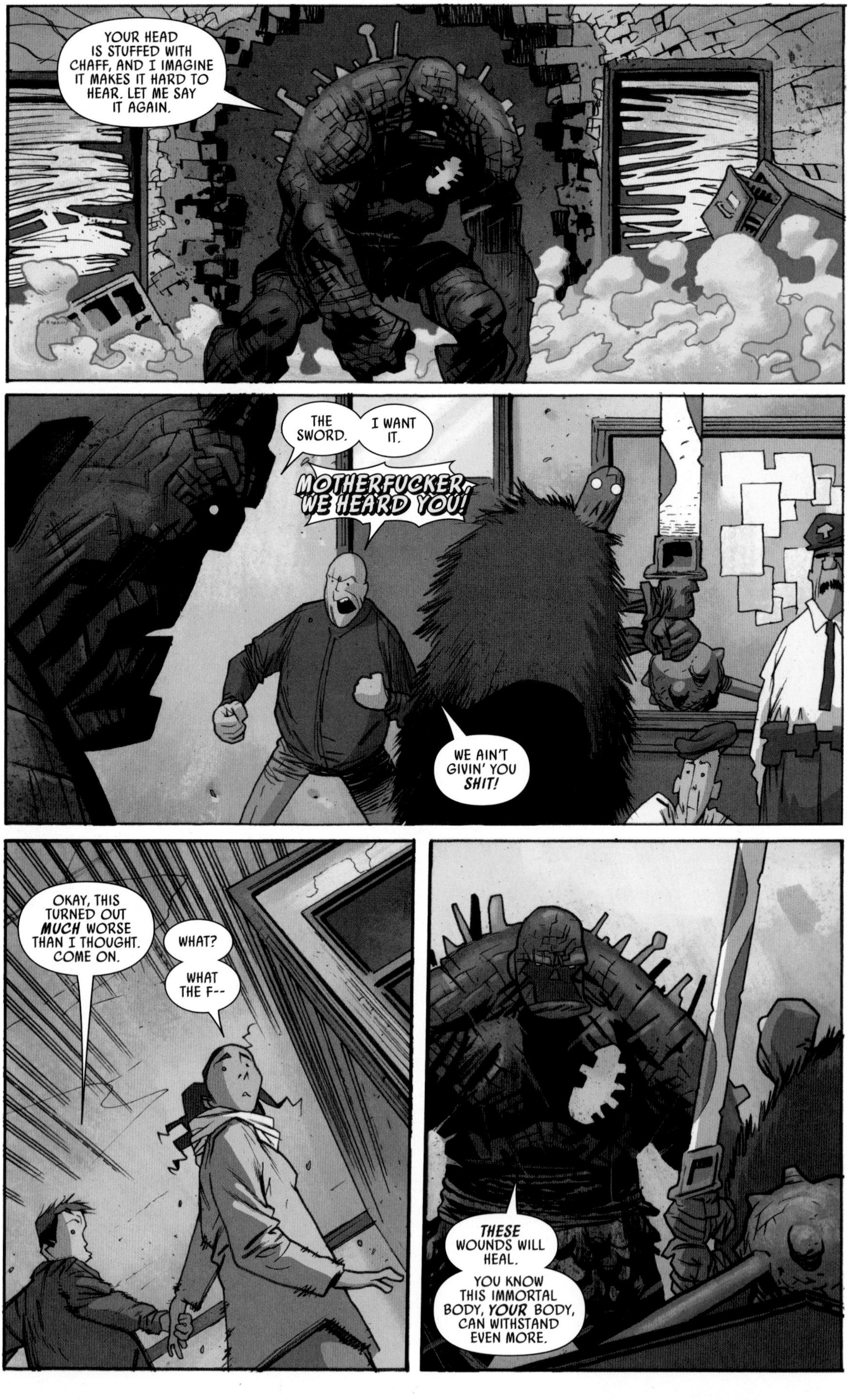
YOUR HEAD IS STUFFED WITH CHAFF, AND I IMAGINE IT MAKES IT HARD TO HEAR. LET ME SAY IT AGAIN.
THE SWORD.
I WANT IT.
MOTHERFUCKER, WE HEARD YOU!
WE AIN'T GIVIN' YOU SHIT!
OKAY, THIS TURNED OUT MUCH WORSE THAN I THOUGHT. COME ON.
WHAT?
WHAT THE F--
THESE WOUNDS WILL HEAL.
YOU KNOW THIS IMMORTAL BODY, YOUR BODY, CAN WITHSTAND EVEN MORE.

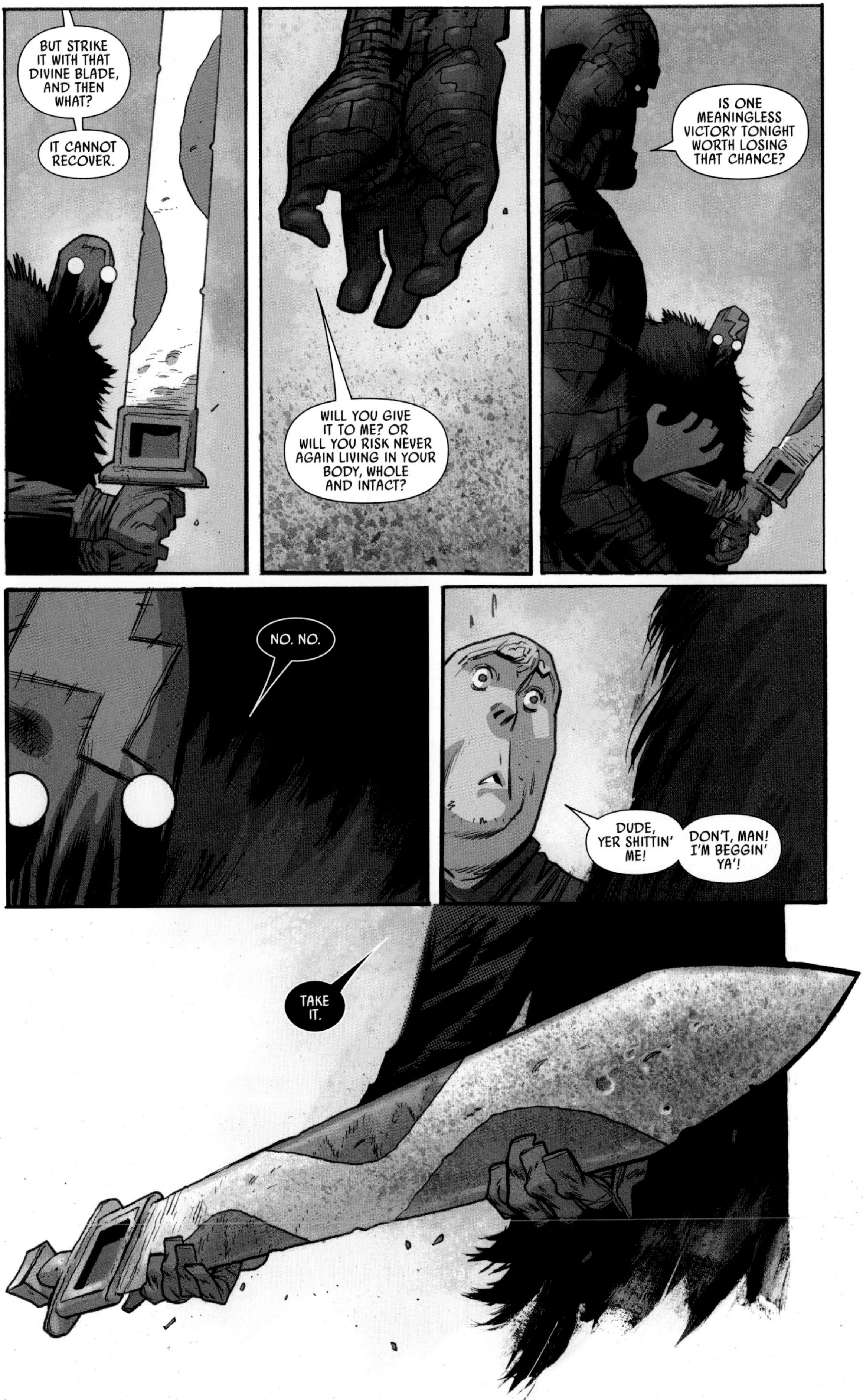
BUT STRIKE IT WITH THAT DIVINE BLADE, AND THEN WHAT?
IT CANNOT RECOVER.
WILL YOU GIVE IT TO ME? OR WILL YOU RISK NEVER AGAIN LIVING IN YOUR BODY, WHOLE AND INTACT?
IS ONE MEANINGLESS VICTORY TONIGHT WORTH LOSING THAT CHANCE?
NO. NO.
DUDE, YER SHITTIN' ME!
DON'T, MAN! I'M BEGGIN' YA'!
TAKE IT.

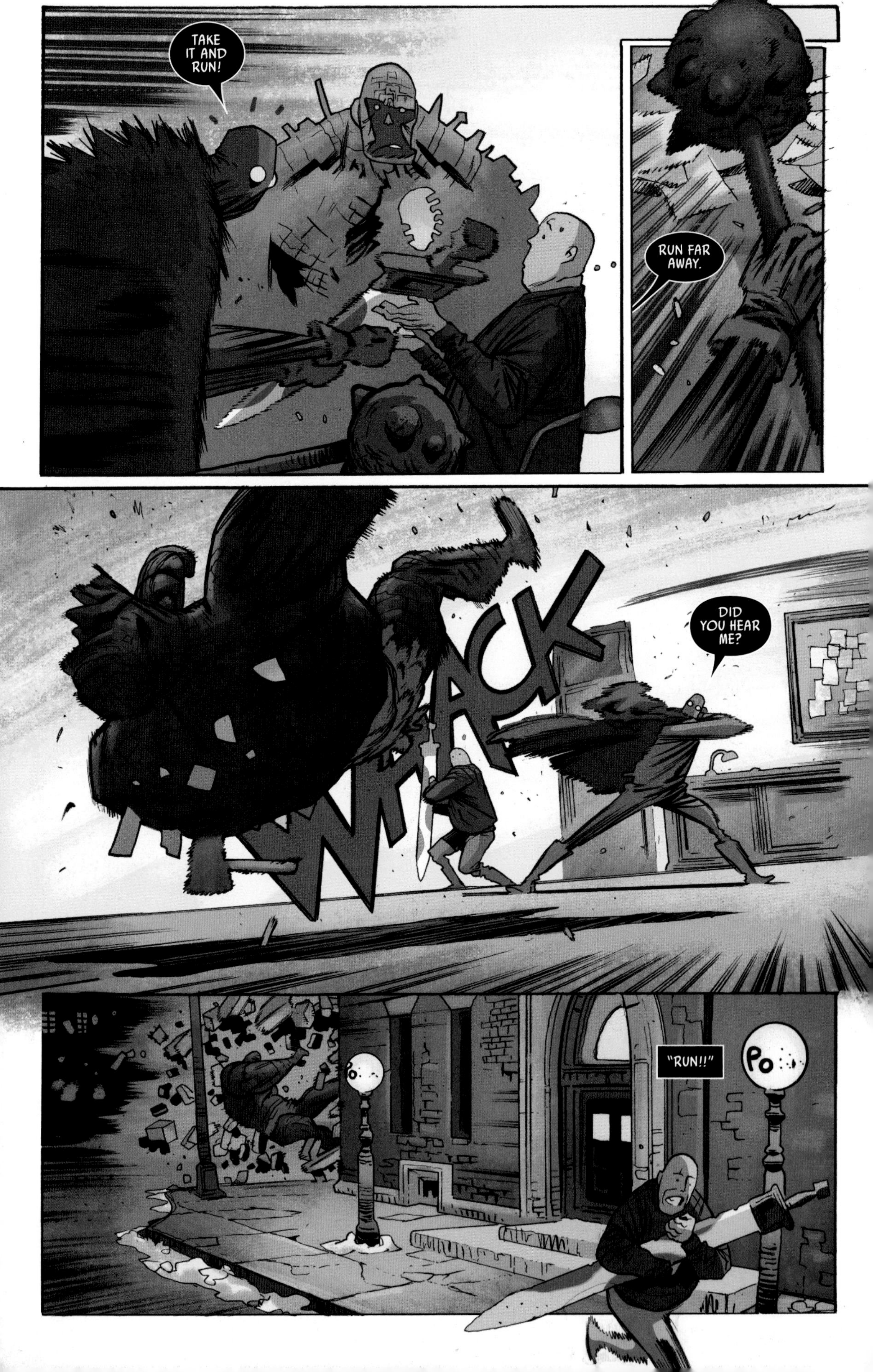
TAKE IT AND RUN!
RUN FAR AWAY.
WHACK
DID YOU HEAR ME?
PO
"RUN!!"
PO

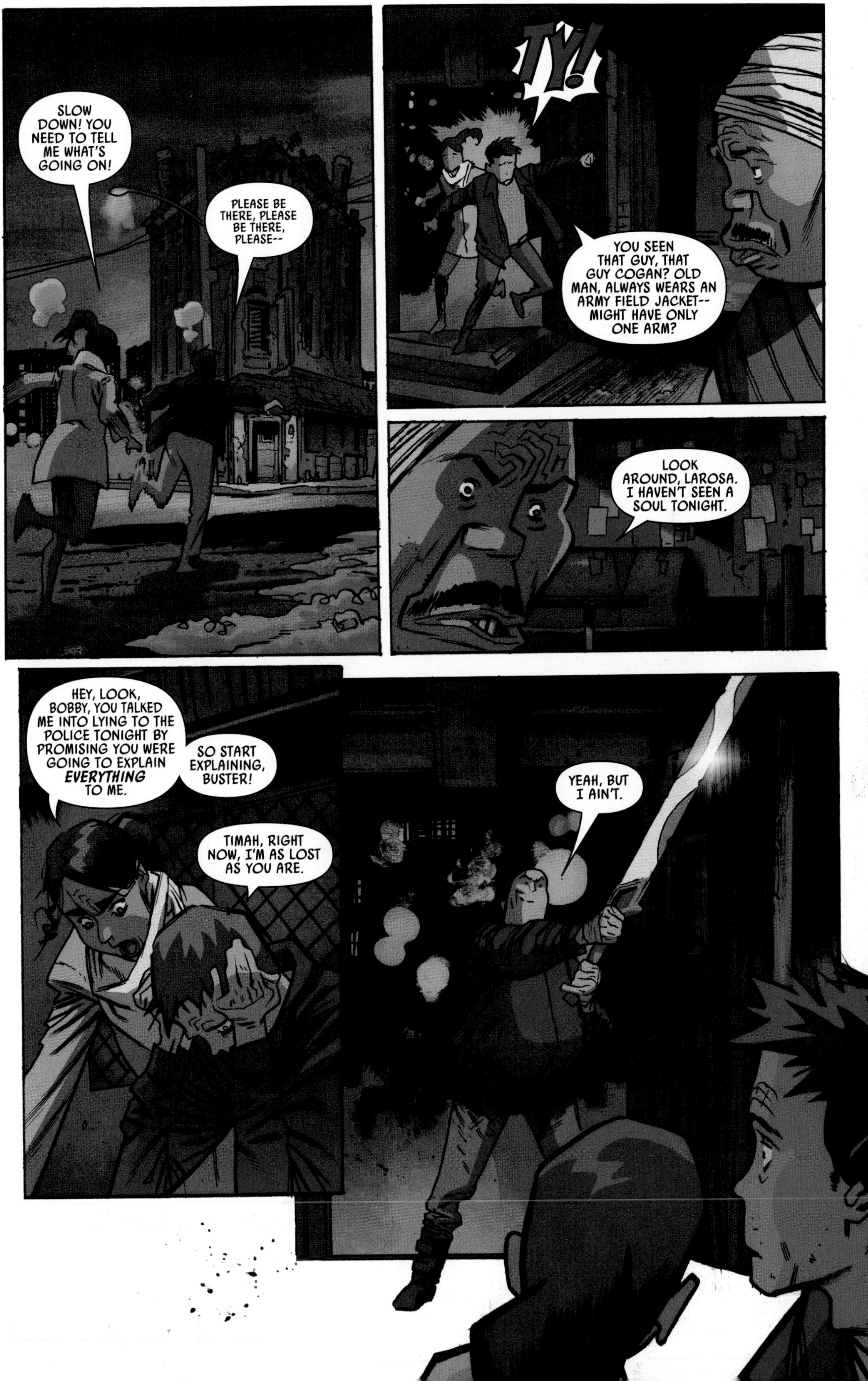
SLOW DOWN! YOU NEED TO TELL ME WHAT'S GOING ON!
PLEASE BE THERE, PLEASE BE THERE, PLEASE--
TY!
YOU SEEN THAT GUY, THAT GUY COGAN? OLD MAN, ALWAYS WEARS AN ARMY FIELD JACKET-- MIGHT HAVE ONLY ONE ARM?
LOOK AROUND, LAROSA. I HAVEN'T SEEN A SOUL TONIGHT.
HEY, LOOK, BOBBY, YOU TALKED ME INTO LYING TO THE POLICE TONIGHT BY PROMISING YOU WERE GOING TO EXPLAIN *EVERYTHING* TO ME.
SO START EXPLAINING, BUSTER!
TIMAH, RIGHT NOW, I'M AS LOST AS YOU ARE.
YEAH, BUT I AIN'T.

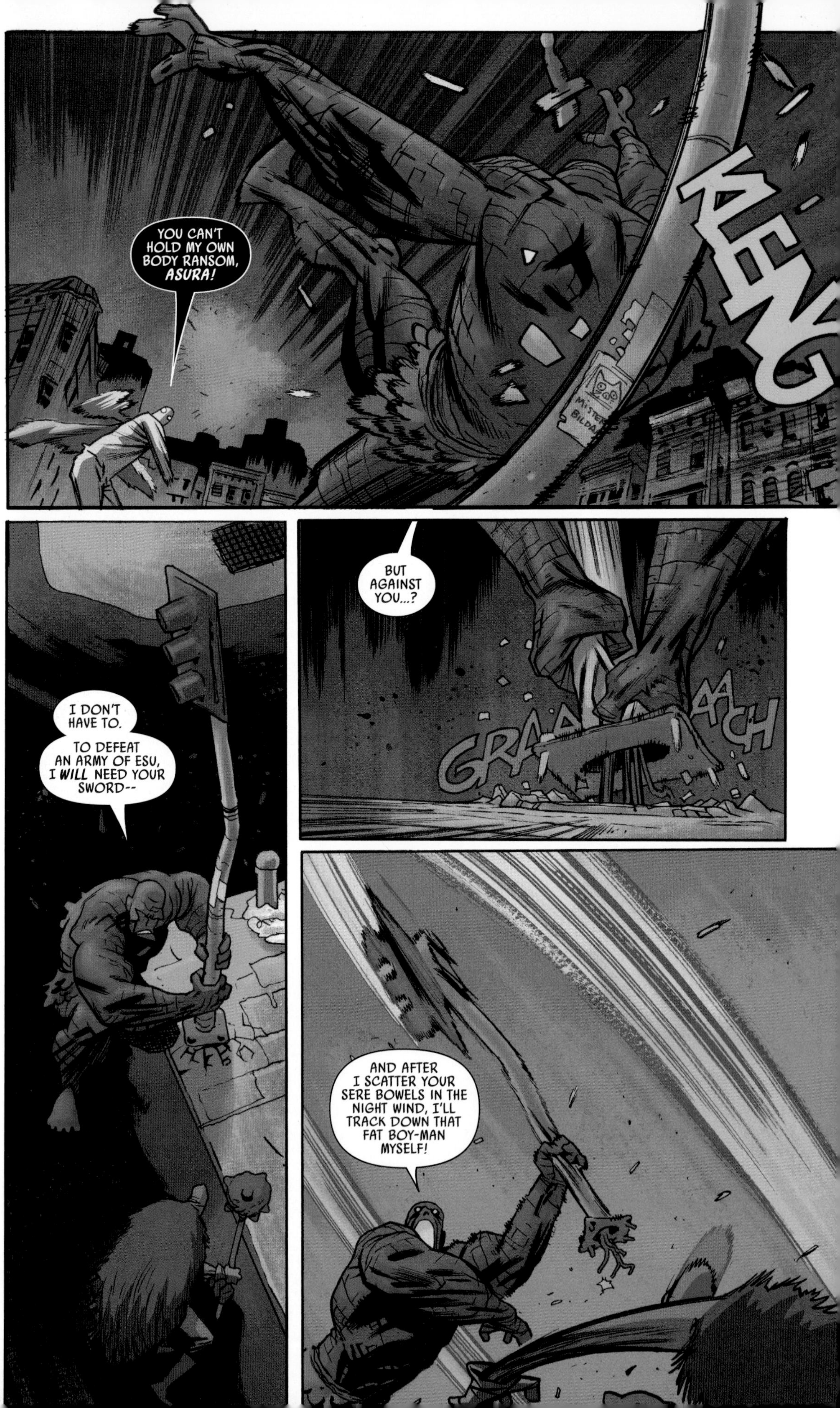
YOU CAN'T HOLD MY OWN BODY RANSOM, *ASURA!*
KLENG
MISTER BILDA
I DON'T HAVE TO.
TO DEFEAT AN ARMY OF ESU, I *WILL* NEED YOUR SWORD--
BUT AGAINST YOU...?
GRAAAACH
AND AFTER I SCATTER YOUR SERE BOWELS IN THE NIGHT WIND, I'LL TRACK DOWN THAT FAT BOY-MAN MYSELF!

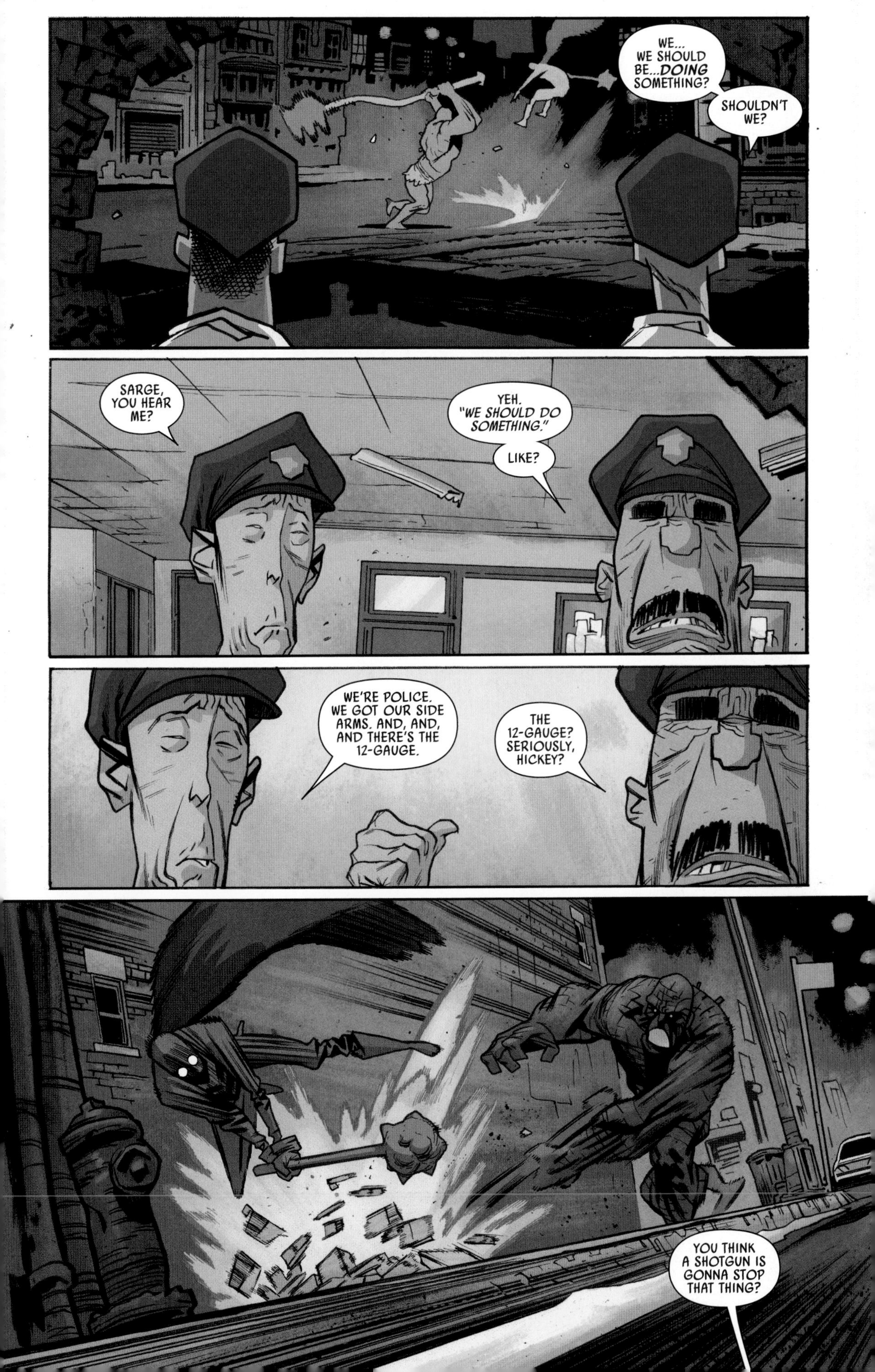
WE... WE SHOULD BE...DOING SOMETHING?
SHOULDN'T WE?
SARGE, YOU HEAR ME?
YEH. "WE SHOULD DO SOMETHING."
LIKE?
WE'RE POLICE. WE GOT OUR SIDE ARMS. AND, AND, AND THERE'S THE 12-GAUGE.
THE 12-GAUGE? SERIOUSLY, HICKEY?
YOU THINK A SHOTGUN IS GONNA STOP THAT THING?

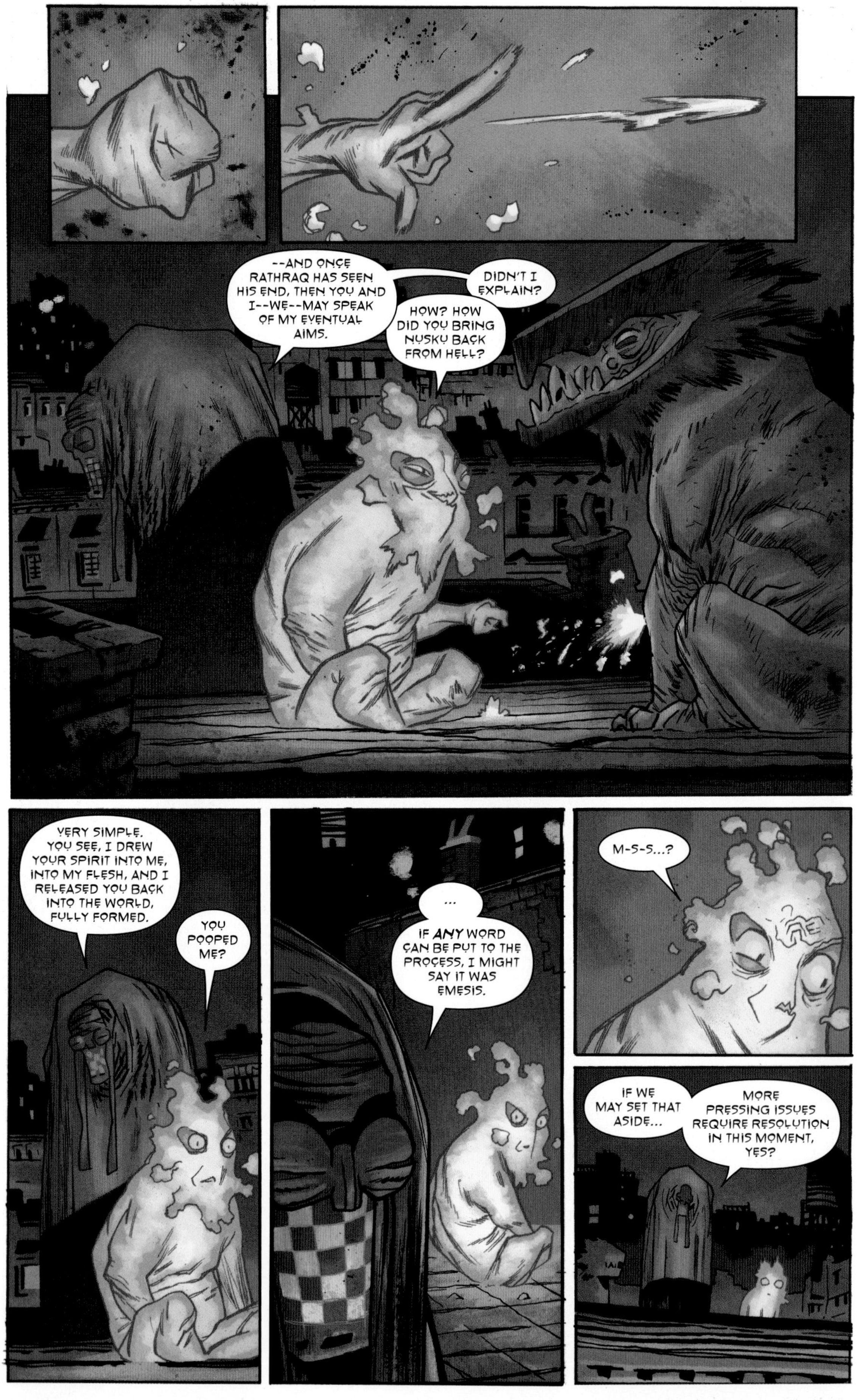
--AND ONCE RATHRAQ HAS SEEN HIS END, THEN YOU AND I--WE--MAY SPEAK OF MY EVENTUAL AIMS.
DIDN'T I EXPLAIN?
HOW? HOW DID YOU BRING NUSKU BACK FROM HELL?
VERY SIMPLE. YOU SEE, I DREW YOUR SPIRIT INTO ME, INTO MY FLESH, AND I RELEASED YOU BACK INTO THE WORLD, FULLY FORMED.
YOU POOPED ME?
...
IF ANY WORD CAN BE PUT TO THE PROCESS, I MIGHT SAY IT WAS EMESIS.
M-S-S...?
IF WE MAY SET THAT ASIDE...
MORE PRESSING ISSUES REQUIRE RESOLUTION IN THIS MOMENT, YES?

OKAY, LET ME SEE IF I GOT IT NOW. THE SOUL OF AN ANCIENT WARRIOR GOD IS STUCK IN THAT SCARECROW I SAW?

UH HUH.

AND HIS *ORIGINAL* BODY-- THE BIG MUMMY-THING I SAW--IT DOESN'T HAVE A HEART, WHICH IS WHY IT ISN'T AS POWERFUL AS IT WAS A MILLION YEARS AGO?

MILLION, GIVE OR TAKE.

BUT NOW *ANOTHER* SOUL IS INSIDE *THAT* BODY, THREATENING TO DESTROY IT.

ALL 'CAUSE OF HIS PET HYDRANT.

BUT WHY DID THE WARRIOR STAY IN THE SCARECROW? HOW IS *THAT* BETTER THAN LIVING IN THAT HUGE HULK I SAW?

WAIT... HOLD ON.

AIN'T, REALLY. JUST DIDN'T WANNA RISK DAMAGIN' HIS IMMORTAL CORPSE... IF *THAT* MAKES SENSE.

YOU SAID THIS...THIS *ASURA* GUY--THE SOUL THAT IS IN THE MUMMY--HE'S ONLY *RECENTLY* DEAD?

S'WHAT RATTRAP SAID. SEEN HIM ONLY A MINUTE AGO, RIGHT HERE IN TOWN. HE SAID.

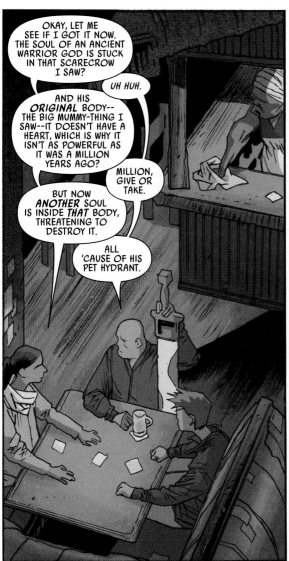

WHY ARE YOU LOOKING AT ME LIKE THAT?

BECAUSE I DON'T THINK WE HAVE TO WAIT HERE ANY LONGER! I'VE BEEN THINKING ONLY COGAN CAN HELP US, BUT I'M PROBABLY WRONG.

YOU! *YOU* CAN DO IT... I THINK. MAYBE EVEN BETTER THAN COGAN.

DECIPHER ALL THAT FOR ME IN A SECOND, BUT *FIRST*--

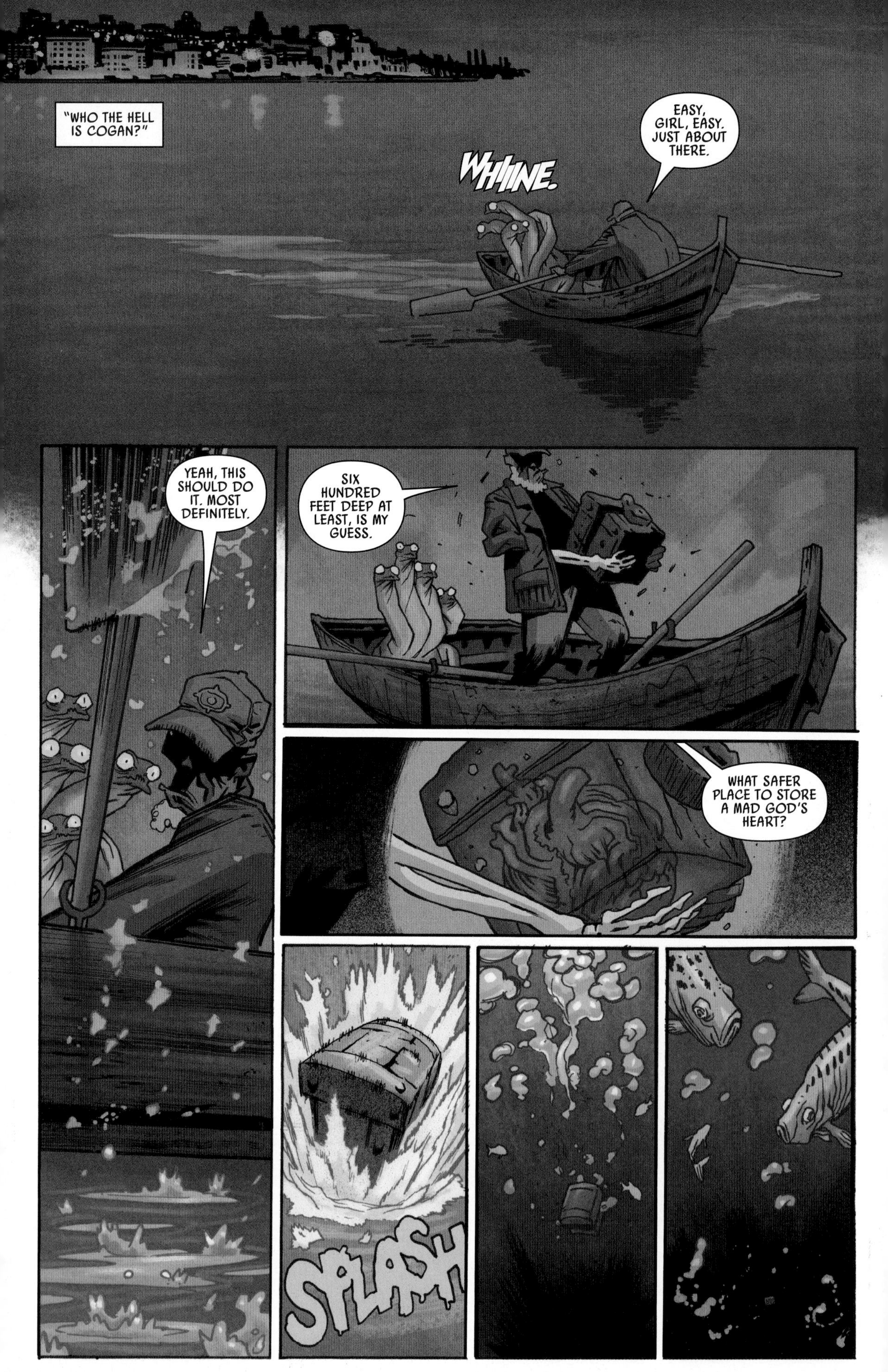
"WHO THE HELL IS COGAN?"
WHIINE.
EASY, GIRL, EASY. JUST ABOUT THERE.
YEAH, THIS SHOULD DO IT. MOST DEFINITELY.
SIX HUNDRED FEET DEEP AT LEAST, IS MY GUESS.
WHAT SAFER PLACE TO STORE A MAD GOD'S HEART?
SPLASH

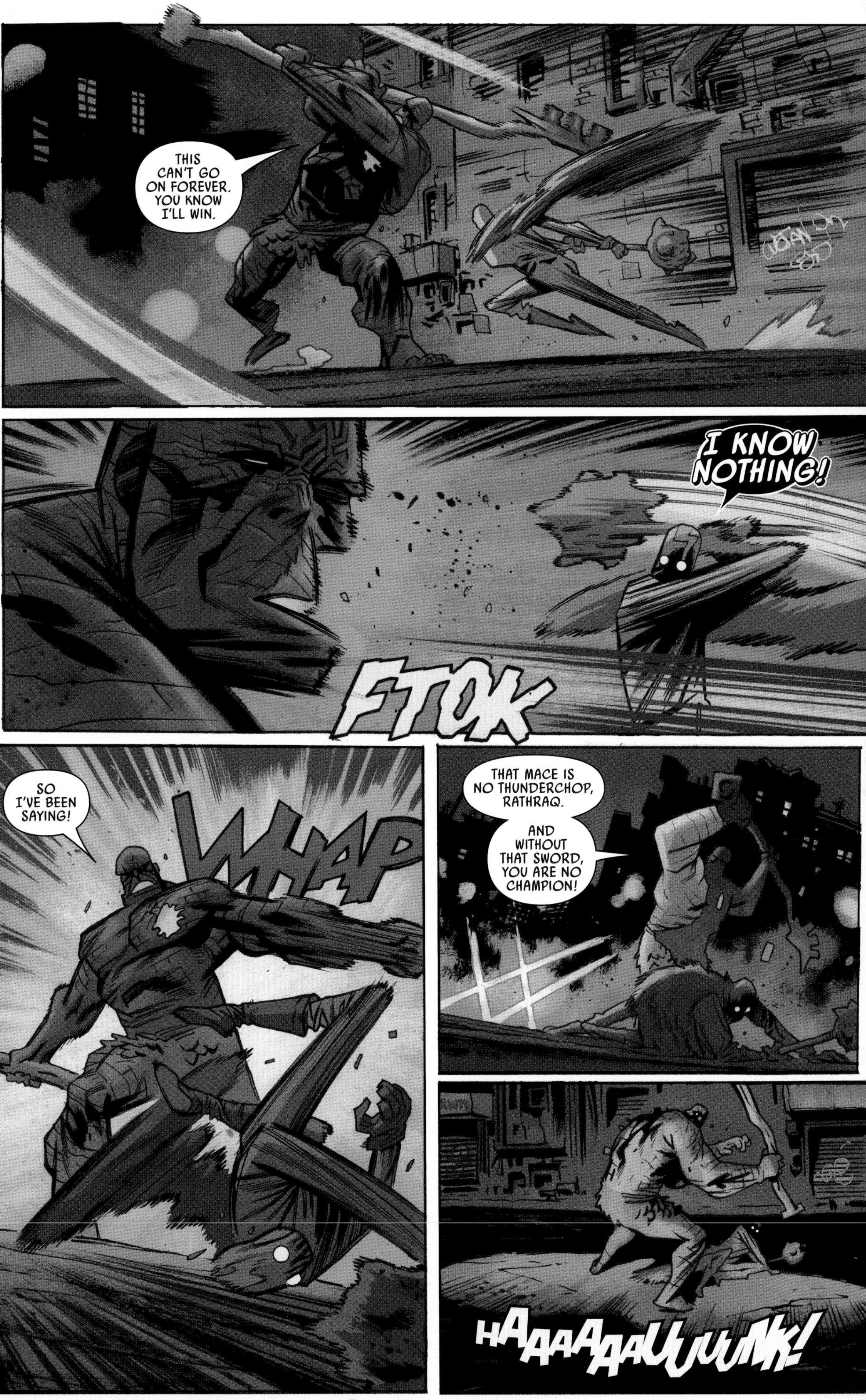
THIS CAN'T GO ON FOREVER. YOU KNOW I'LL WIN.
I KNOW NOTHING!
FTOK
SO I'VE BEEN SAYING!
WHAP
THAT MACE IS NO THUNDERCHOP, RATHRAQ.
AND WITHOUT THAT SWORD, YOU ARE NO CHAMPION!
HAAAAAAUUUUNK!

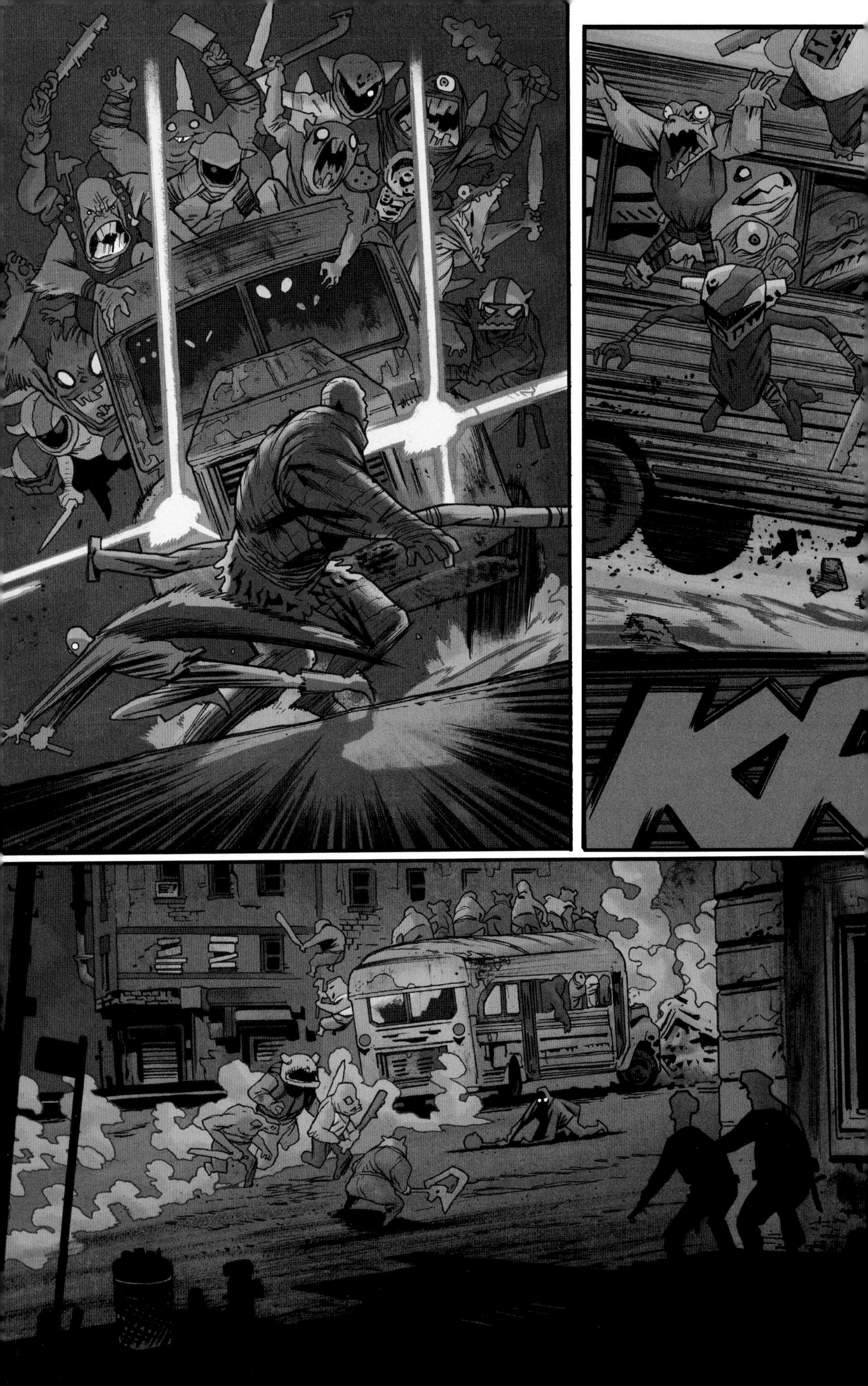

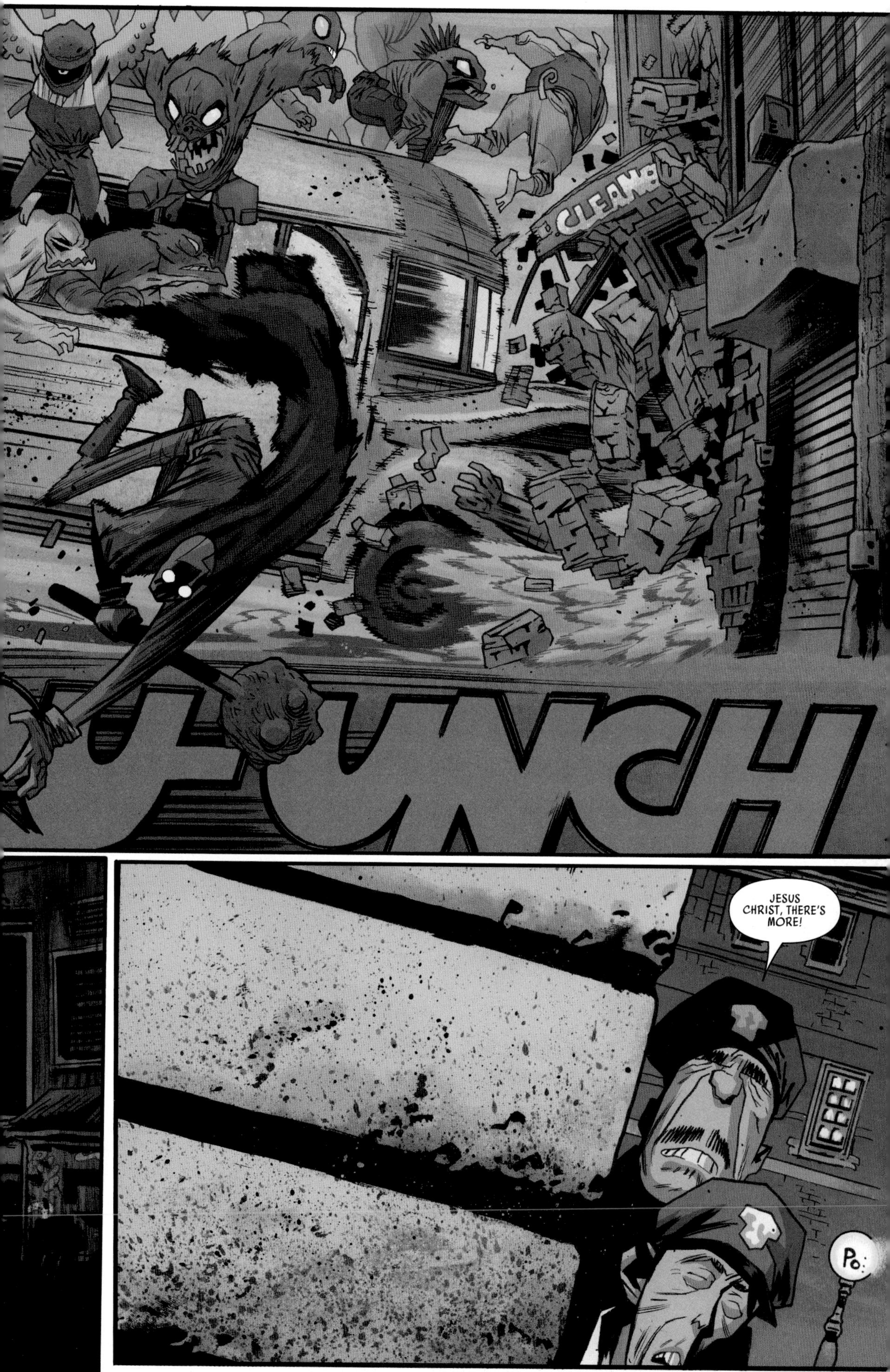
CLEAN
JESUS CHRIST, THERE'S MORE!
Po:

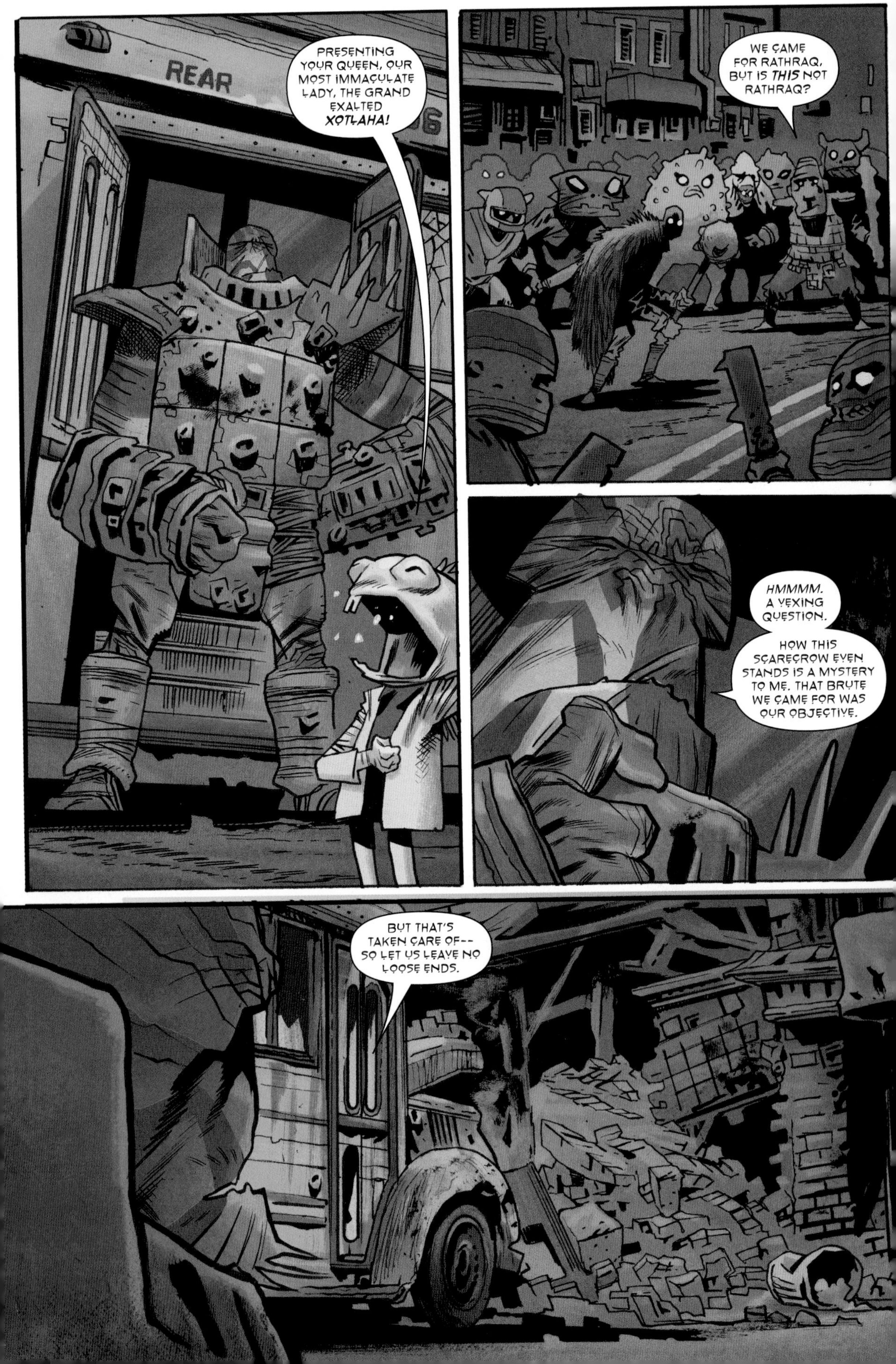
REAR
PRESENTING YOUR QUEEN, OUR MOST IMMACULATE LADY, THE GRAND EXALTED XOTLAHA!
WE CAME FOR RATHRAQ, BUT IS THIS NOT RATHRAQ?
HMMMM. A VEXING QUESTION.
HOW THIS SCARECROW EVEN STANDS IS A MYSTERY TO ME. THAT BRUTE WE CAME FOR WAS OUR OBJECTIVE.
BUT THAT'S TAKEN CARE OF-- SO LET US LEAVE NO LOOSE ENDS.

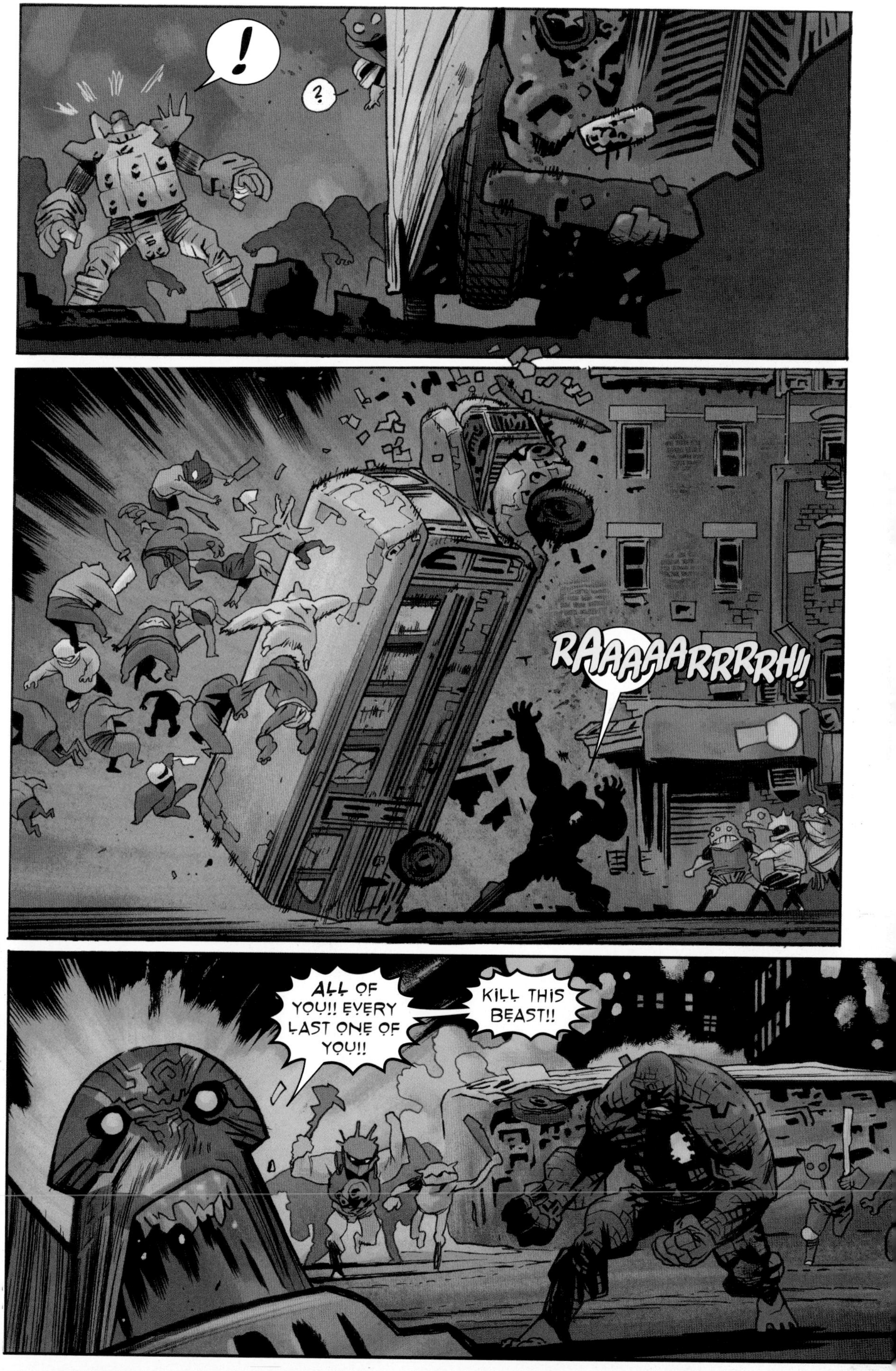
!
?
RAAAAARRRRH!!
ALL OF YOU!! EVERY LAST ONE OF YOU!!
KILL THIS BEAST!!

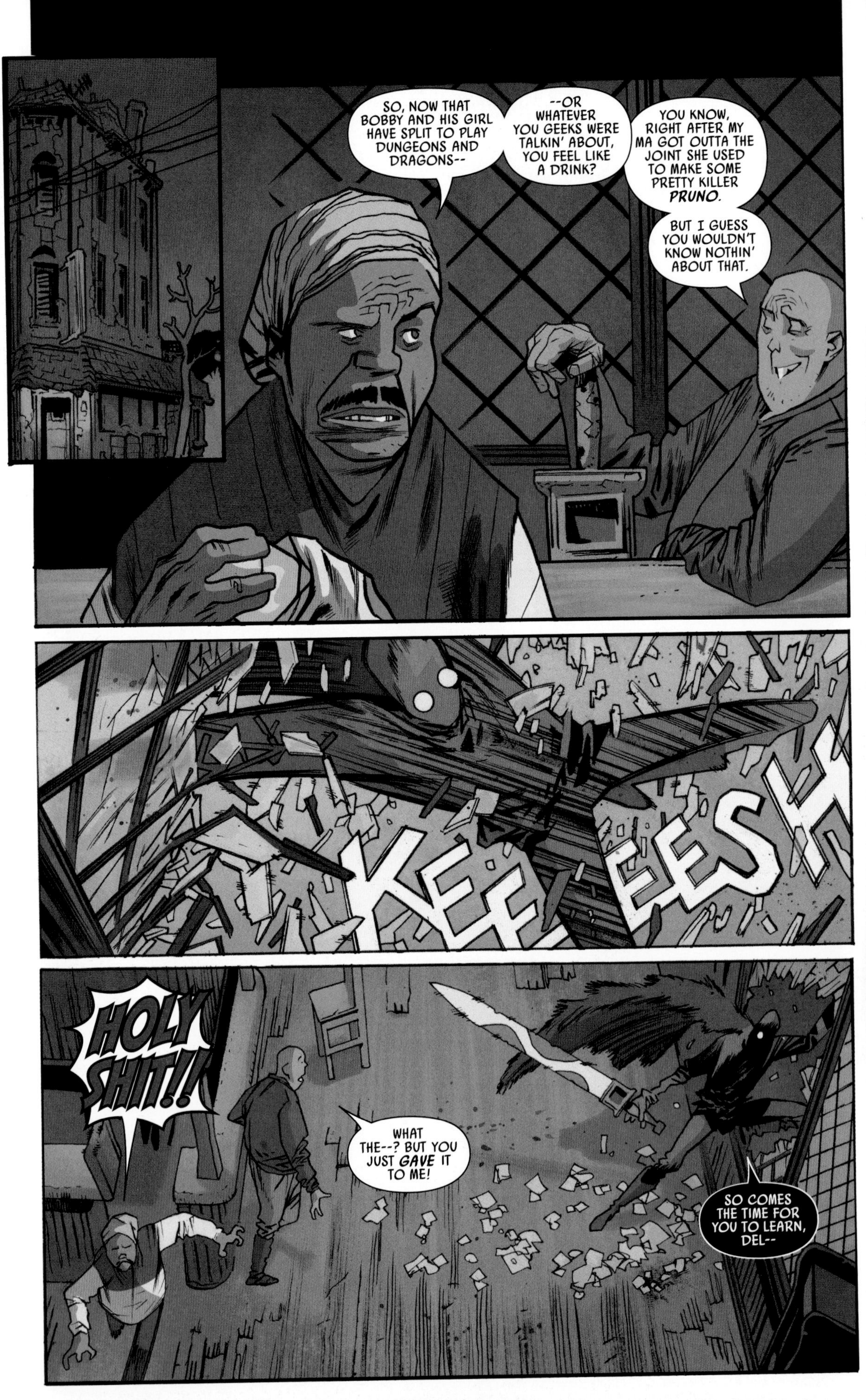
SO, NOW THAT BOBBY AND HIS GIRL HAVE SPLIT TO PLAY DUNGEONS AND DRAGONS--
--OR WHATEVER YOU GEEKS WERE TALKIN' ABOUT, YOU FEEL LIKE A DRINK?
YOU KNOW, RIGHT AFTER MY MA GOT OUTTA THE JOINT SHE USED TO MAKE SOME PRETTY KILLER PRUNO.
BUT I GUESS YOU WOULDN'T KNOW NOTHIN' ABOUT THAT.
KEE-EESH
HOLY SHIT!!
WHAT THE--? BUT YOU JUST GAVE IT TO ME!
SO COMES THE TIME FOR YOU TO LEARN, DEL--

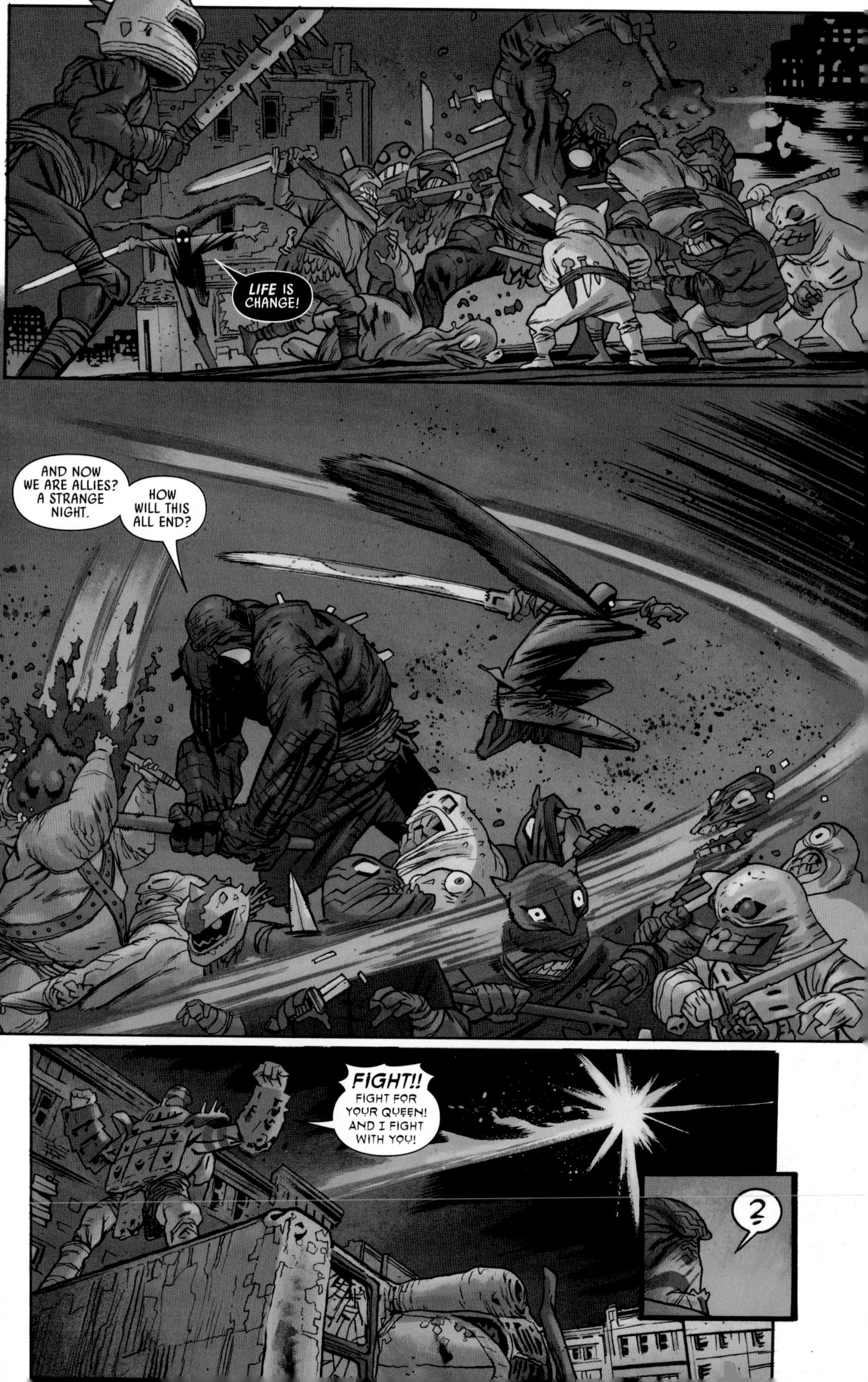
LIFE IS CHANGE!
AND NOW WE ARE ALLIES? A STRANGE NIGHT.
HOW WILL THIS ALL END?
FIGHT!! FIGHT FOR YOUR QUEEN! AND I FIGHT WITH YOU!
?

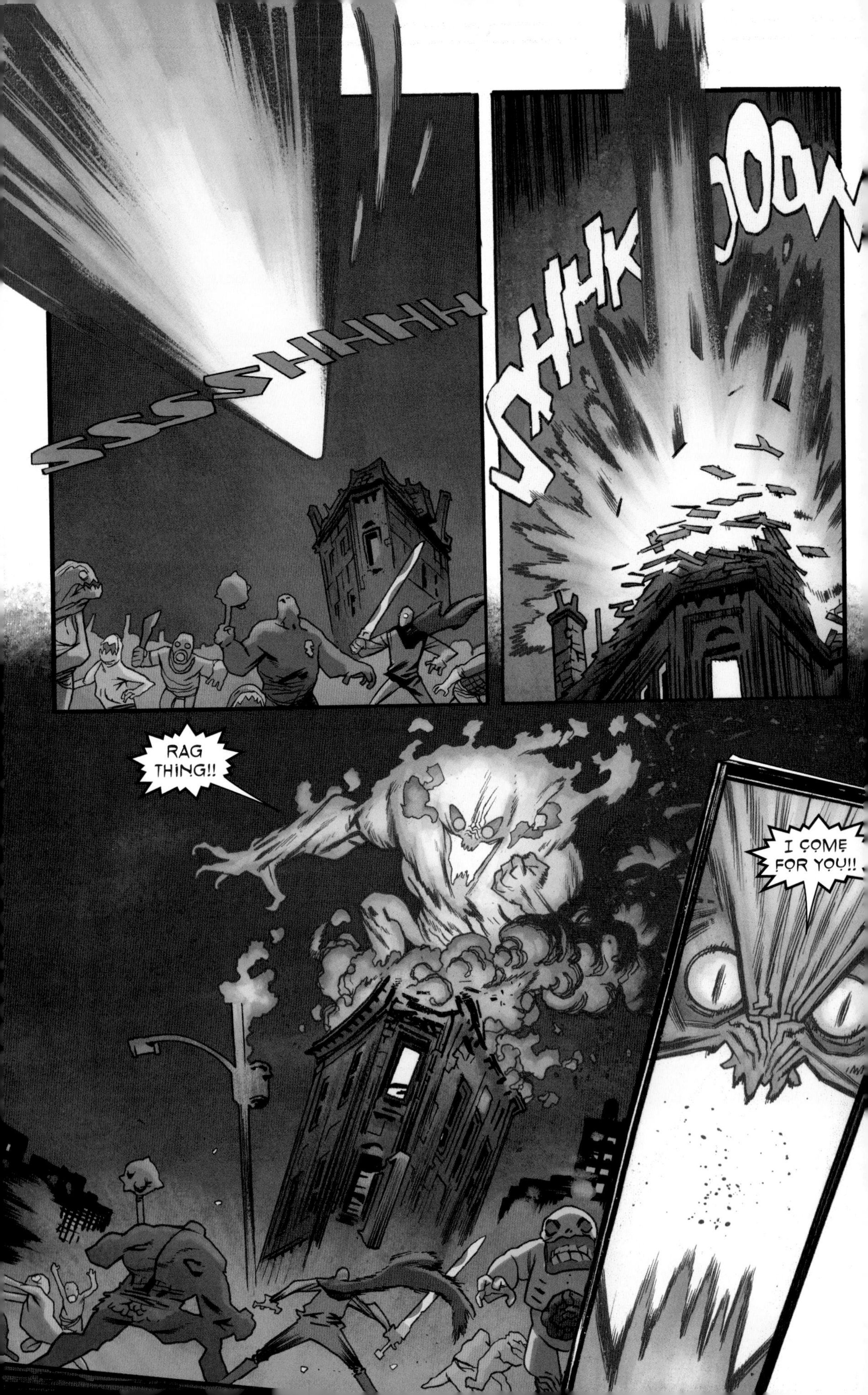
SSSSHHHHH
SHHKOOOW
RAG THING!!
I COME FOR YOU!!

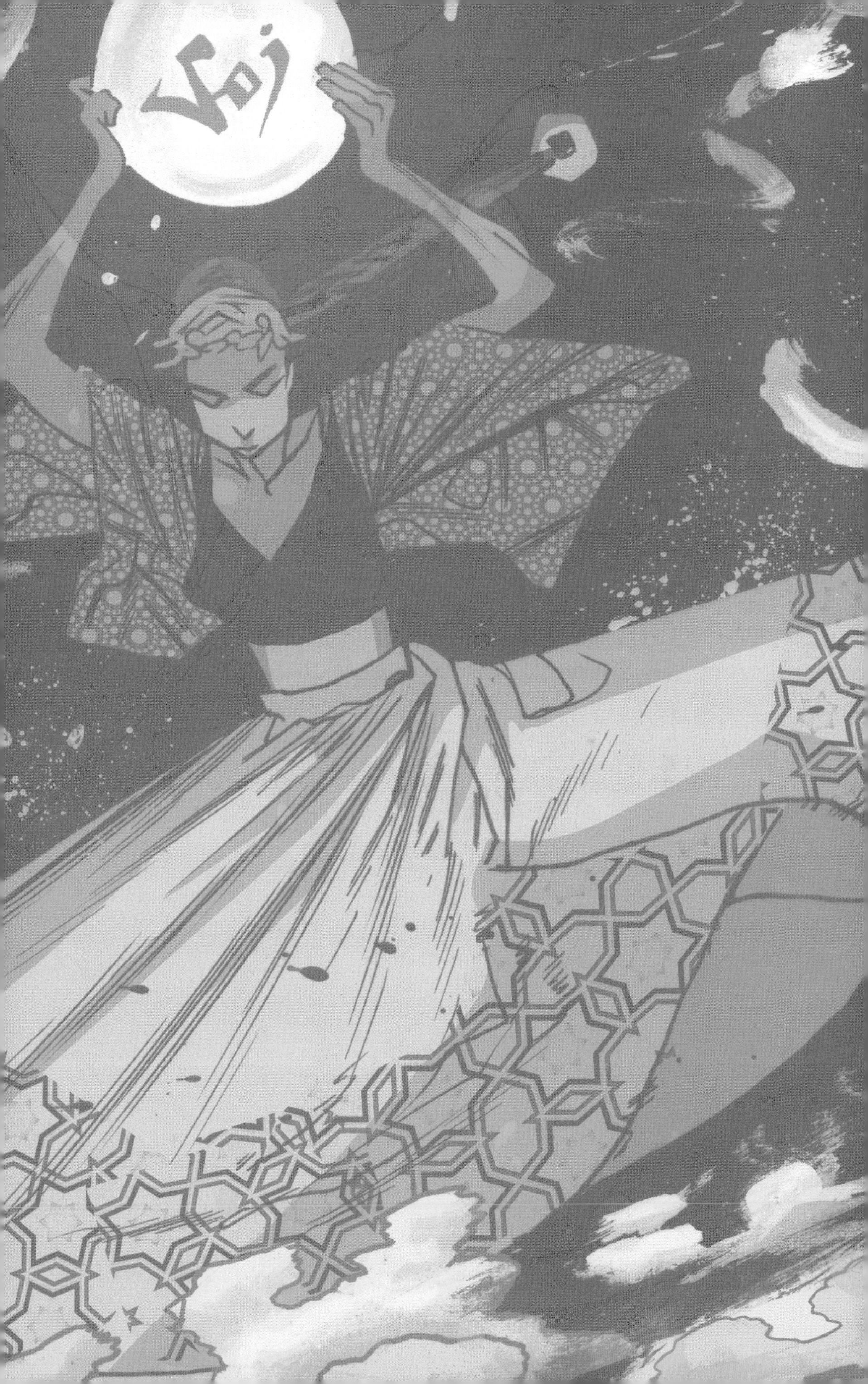

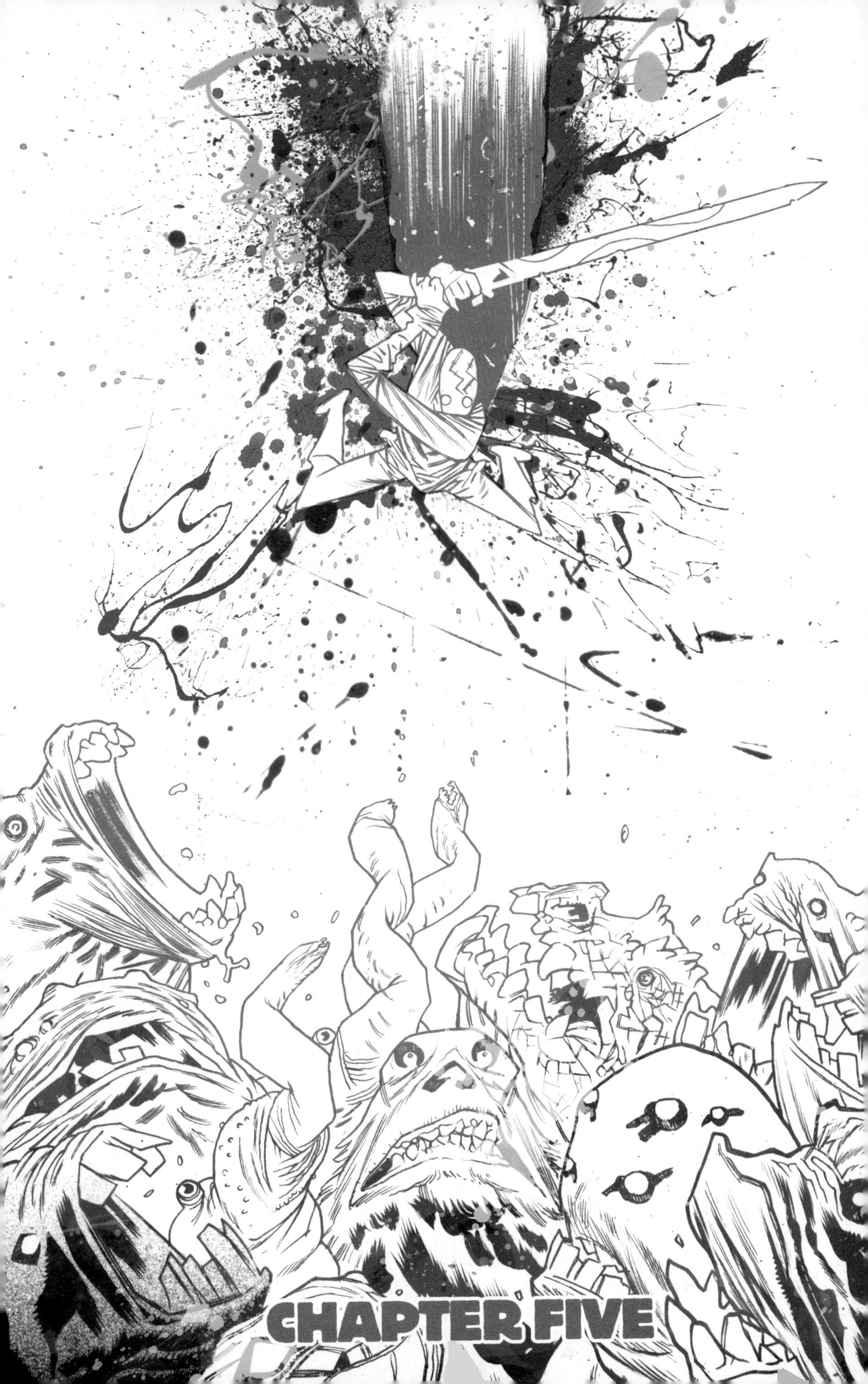
CHAPTER FIVE

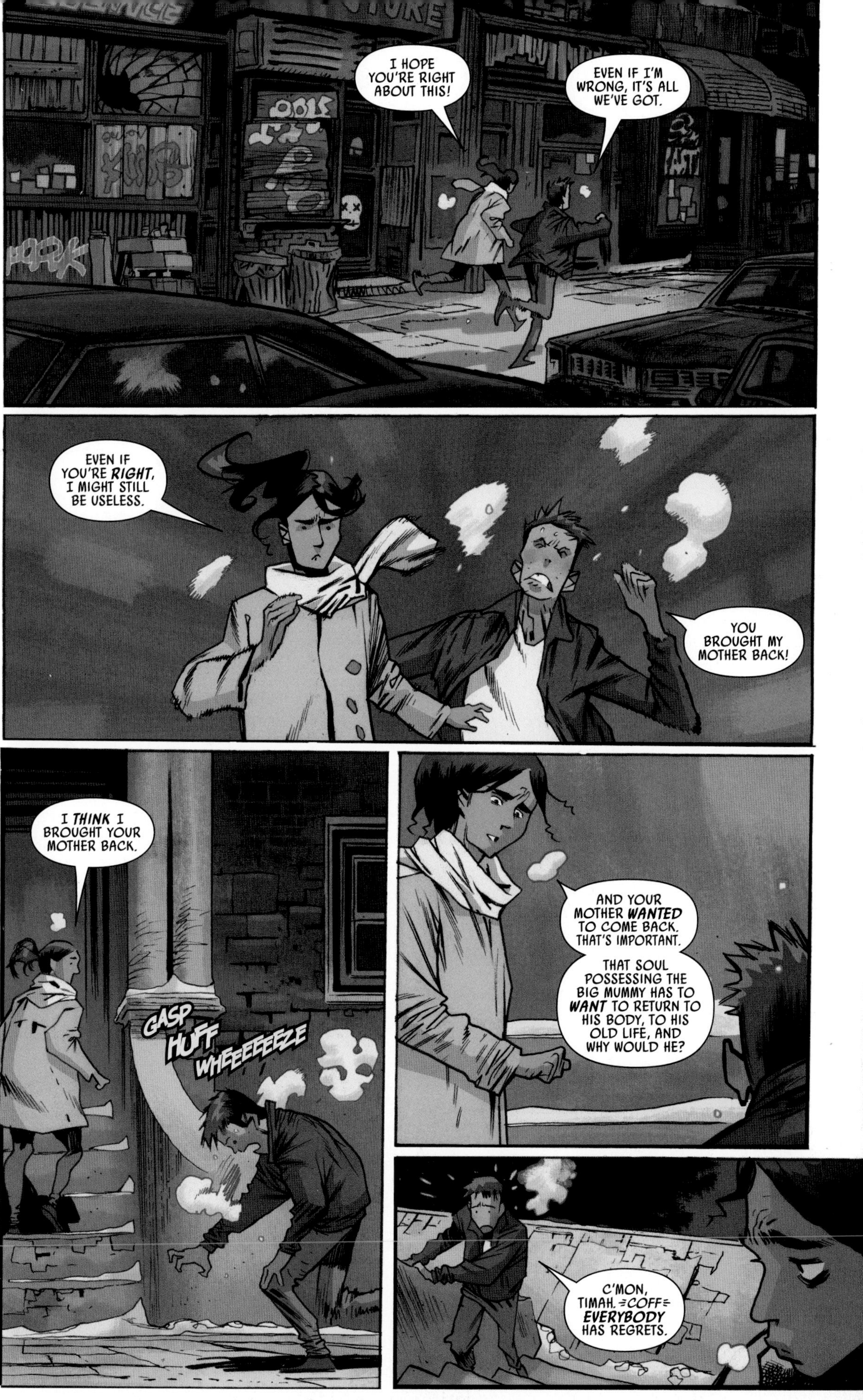
I HOPE YOU'RE RIGHT ABOUT THIS!
EVEN IF I'M WRONG, IT'S ALL WE'VE GOT.
EVEN IF YOU'RE RIGHT, I MIGHT STILL BE USELESS.
YOU BROUGHT MY MOTHER BACK!
I THINK I BROUGHT YOUR MOTHER BACK.
GASP
HUFF
WHEEEEEEZE
AND YOUR MOTHER WANTED TO COME BACK. THAT'S IMPORTANT.
THAT SOUL POSSESSING THE BIG MUMMY HAS TO WANT TO RETURN TO HIS BODY, TO HIS OLD LIFE, AND WHY WOULD HE?
C'MON, TIMAH. =COFF= EVERYBODY HAS REGRETS.

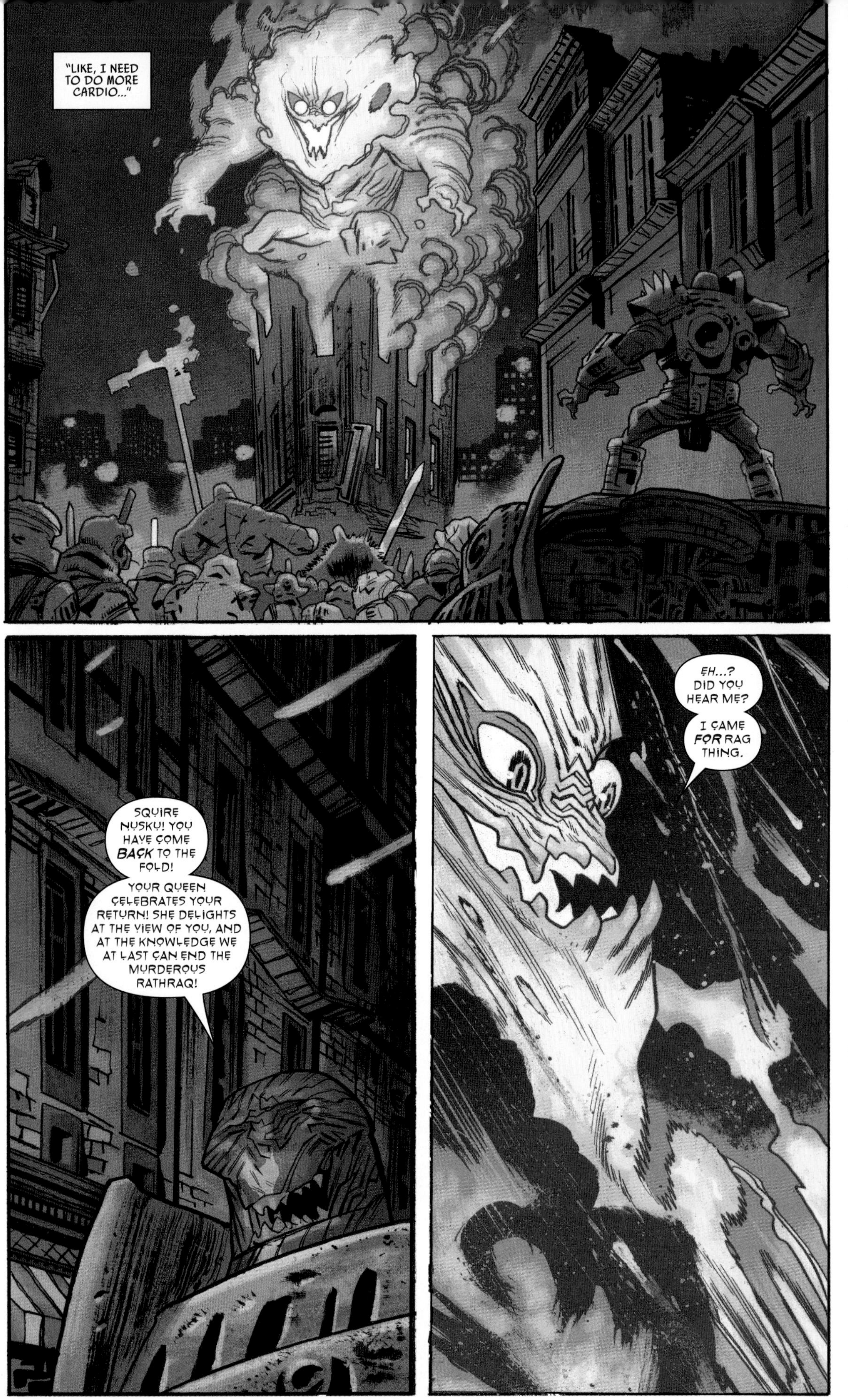
"LIKE, I NEED TO DO MORE CARDIO..."
SQUIRE NUSKU! YOU HAVE COME BACK TO THE FOLD!
YOUR QUEEN CELEBRATES YOUR RETURN! SHE DELIGHTS AT THE VIEW OF YOU, AND AT THE KNOWLEDGE WE AT LAST CAN END THE MURDEROUS RATHRAQ!
EH...? DID YOU HEAR ME?
I CAME FOR RAG THING.

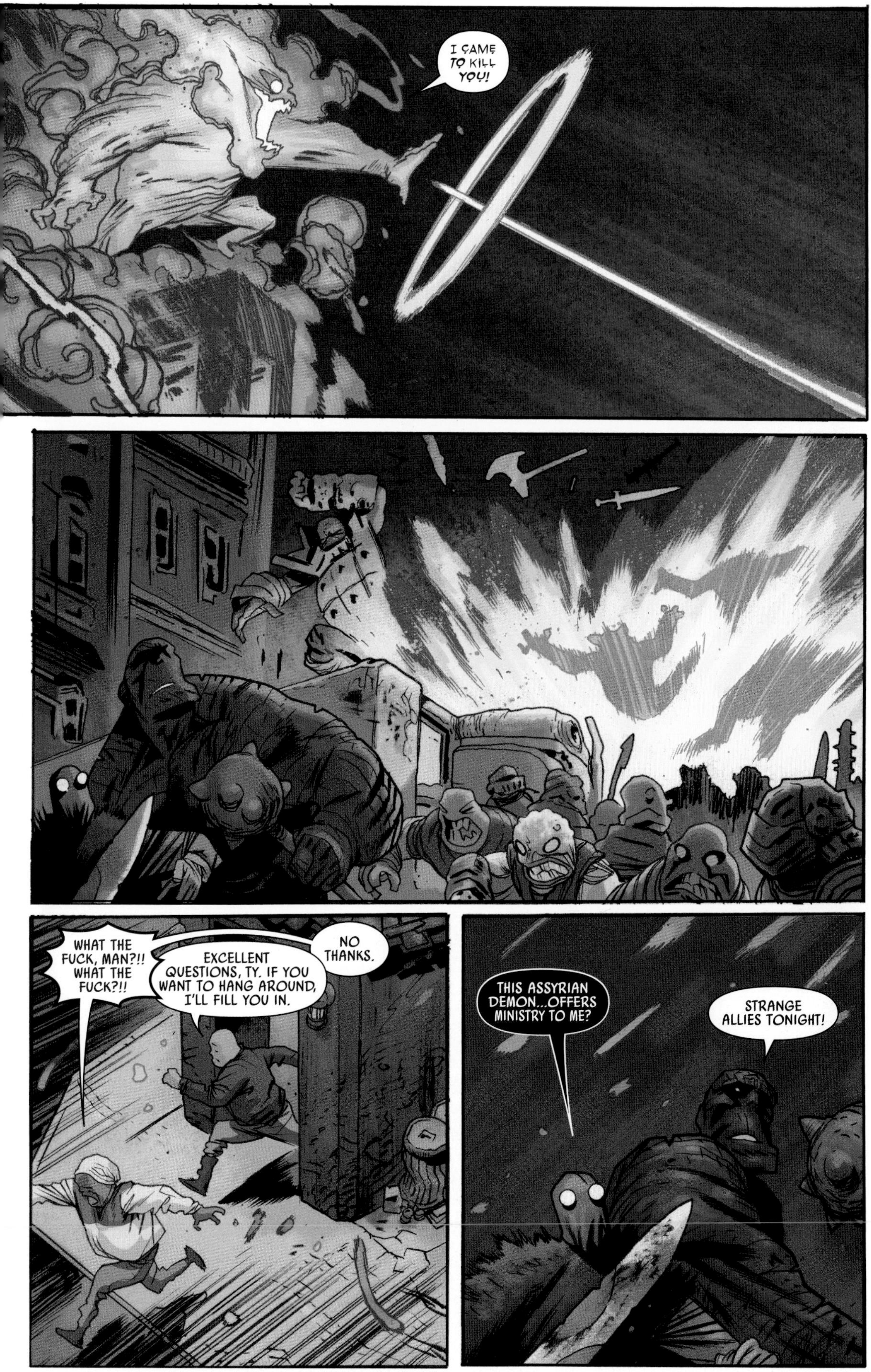
I CAME TO KILL YOU!
WHAT THE FUCK, MAN?!! WHAT THE FUCK?!!
EXCELLENT QUESTIONS, TY. IF YOU WANT TO HANG AROUND, I'LL FILL YOU IN.
NO THANKS.
THIS ASSYRIAN DEMON...OFFERS MINISTRY TO ME?
STRANGE ALLIES TONIGHT!

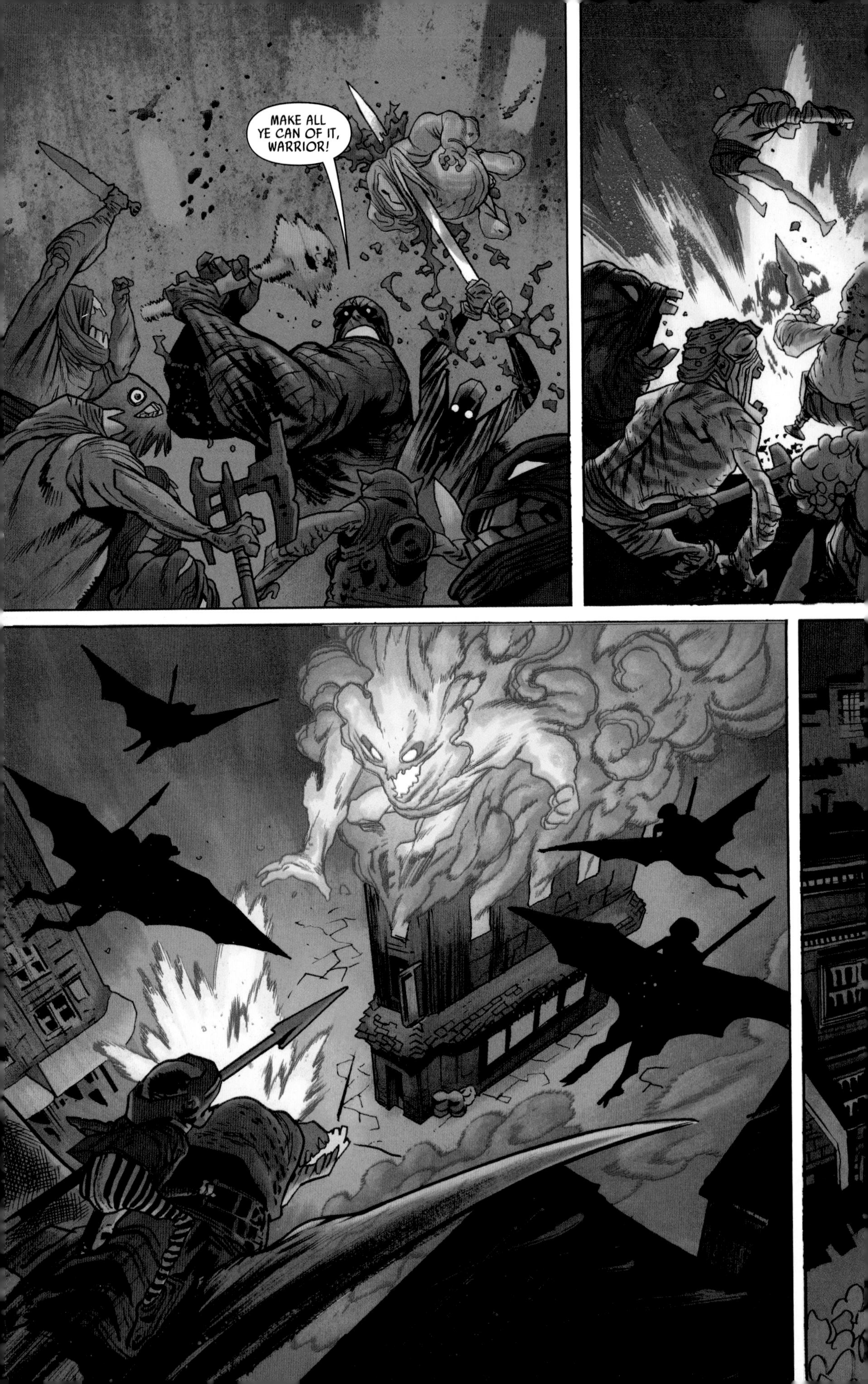
MAKE ALL YE CAN OF IT, WARRIOR!

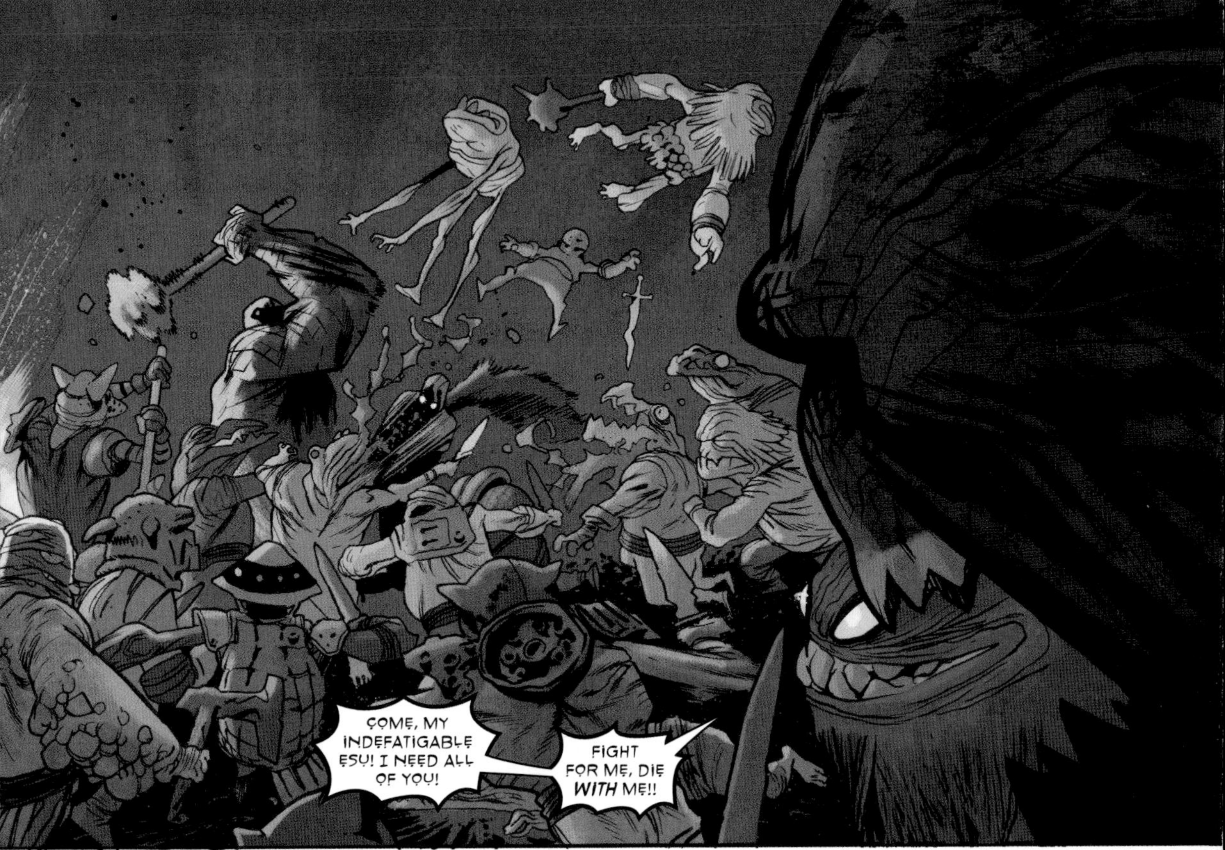
COME, MY INDEFATIGABLE ESU! I NEED ALL OF YOU!
FIGHT FOR ME, DIE WITH ME!!

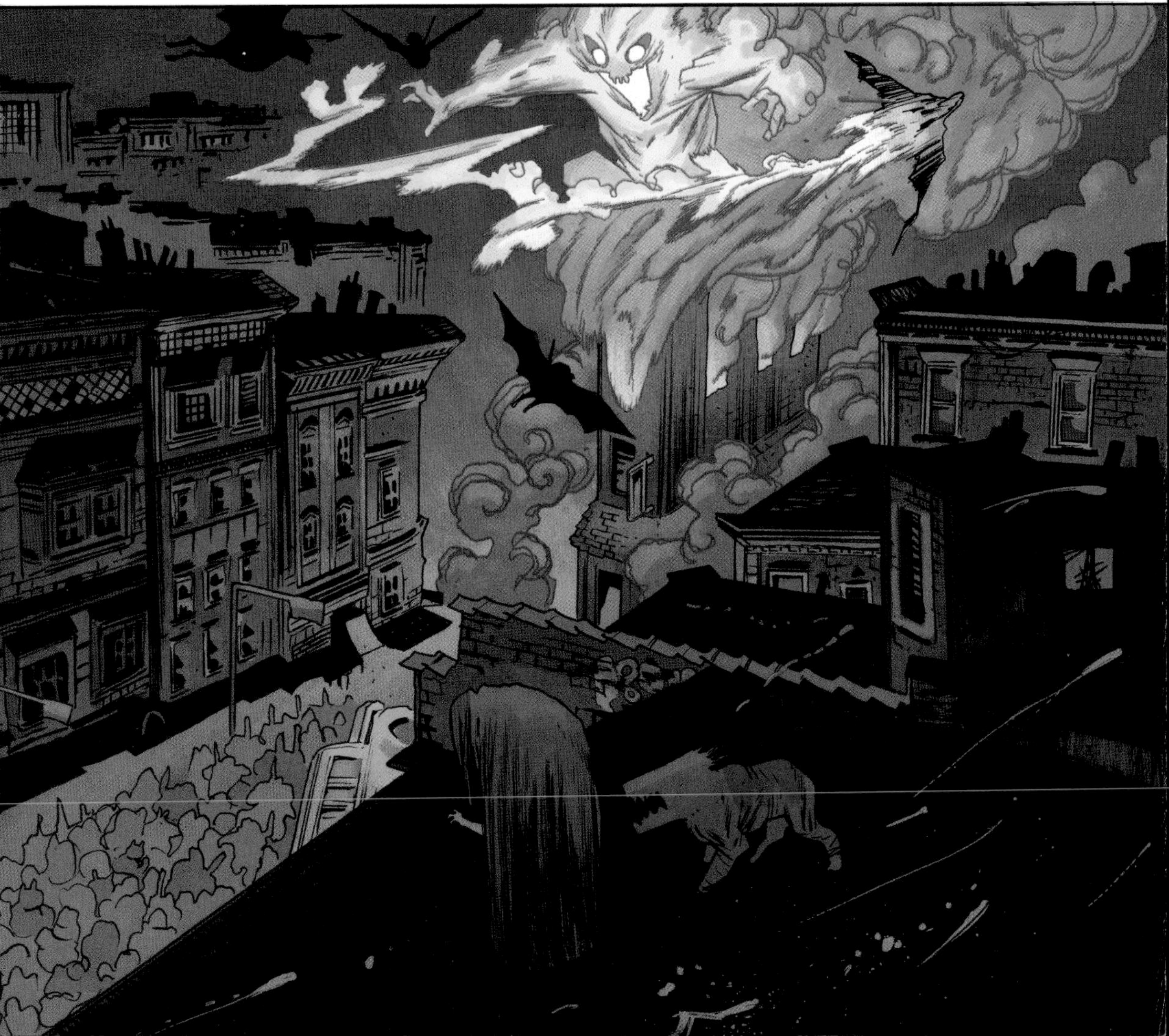

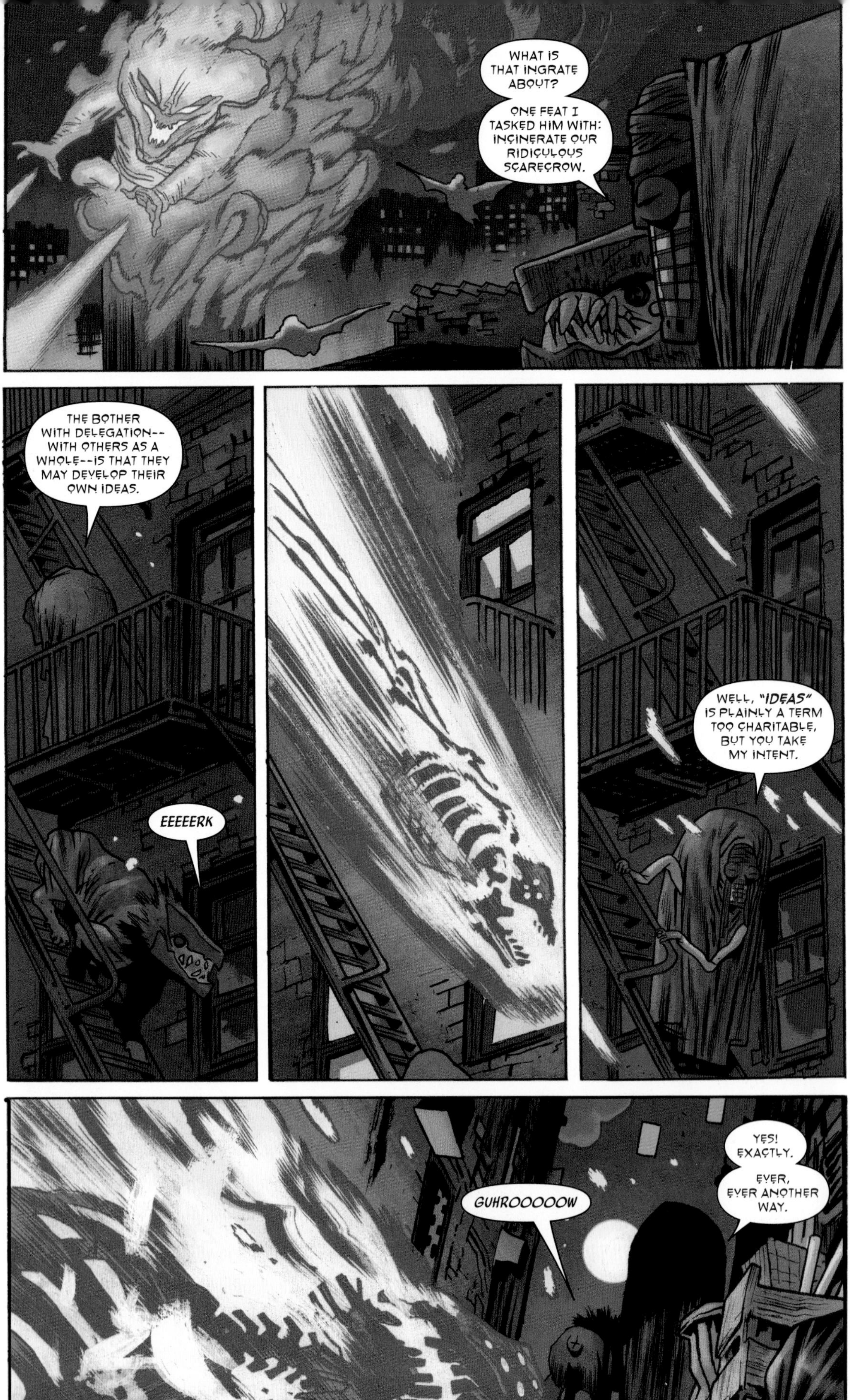
WHAT IS THAT INGRATE ABOUT?
ONE FEAT I TASKED HIM WITH: INCINERATE OUR RIDICULOUS SCARECROW.
THE BOTHER WITH DELEGATION--WITH OTHERS AS A WHOLE--IS THAT THEY MAY DEVELOP THEIR OWN IDEAS.
EEEEERK
WELL, "IDEAS" IS PLAINLY A TERM TOO CHARITABLE, BUT YOU TAKE MY INTENT.
GUHROOOOOW
YES! EXACTLY.
EVER, EVER ANOTHER WAY.

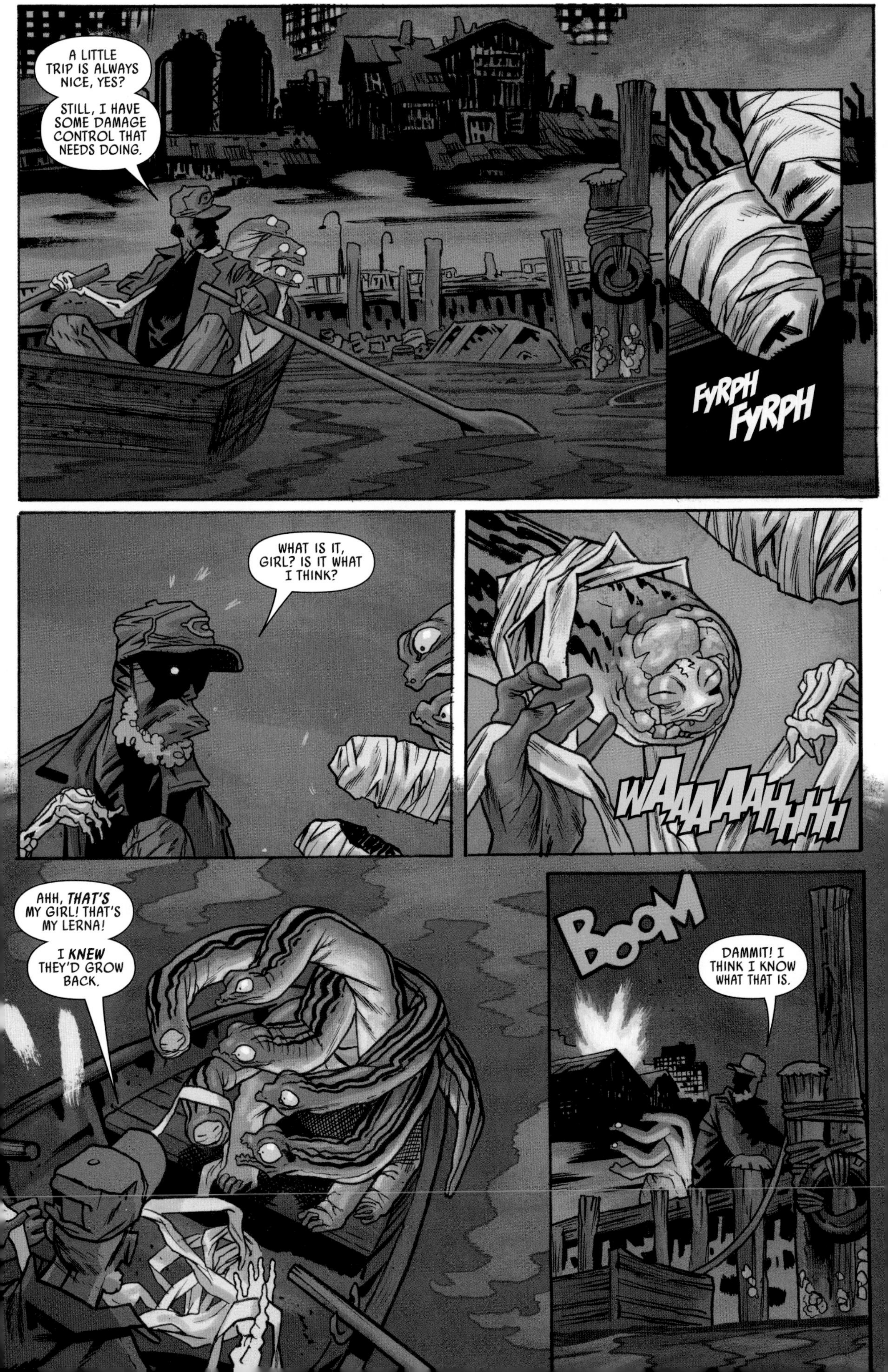
A LITTLE TRIP IS ALWAYS NICE, YES?
STILL, I HAVE SOME DAMAGE CONTROL THAT NEEDS DOING.
FYRPH FYRPH
WHAT IS IT, GIRL? IS IT WHAT I THINK?
WAAAAAHHHH
AHH, THAT'S MY GIRL! THAT'S MY LERNA!
I KNEW THEY'D GROW BACK.
BOOM
DAMMIT! I THINK I KNOW WHAT THAT IS.

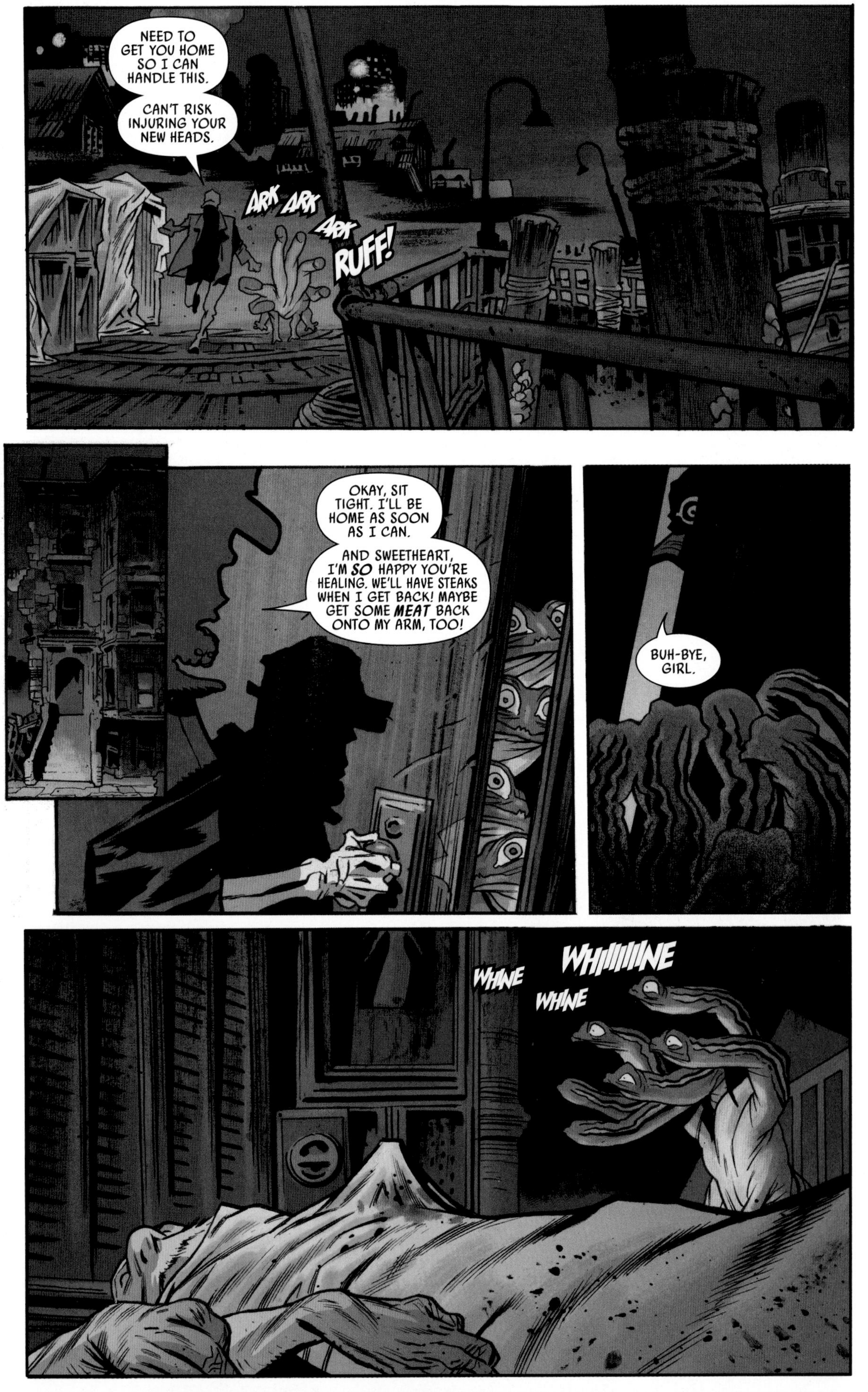
NEED TO GET YOU HOME SO I CAN HANDLE THIS.
CAN'T RISK INJURING YOUR NEW HEADS.
ARK
ARK
ARK
RUFF!
OKAY, SIT TIGHT. I'LL BE HOME AS SOON AS I CAN.
AND SWEETHEART, I'M SO HAPPY YOU'RE HEALING. WE'LL HAVE STEAKS WHEN I GET BACK! MAYBE GET SOME MEAT BACK ONTO MY ARM, TOO!
BUH-BYE, GIRL.
WHINE
WHIIIIIINE
WHINE

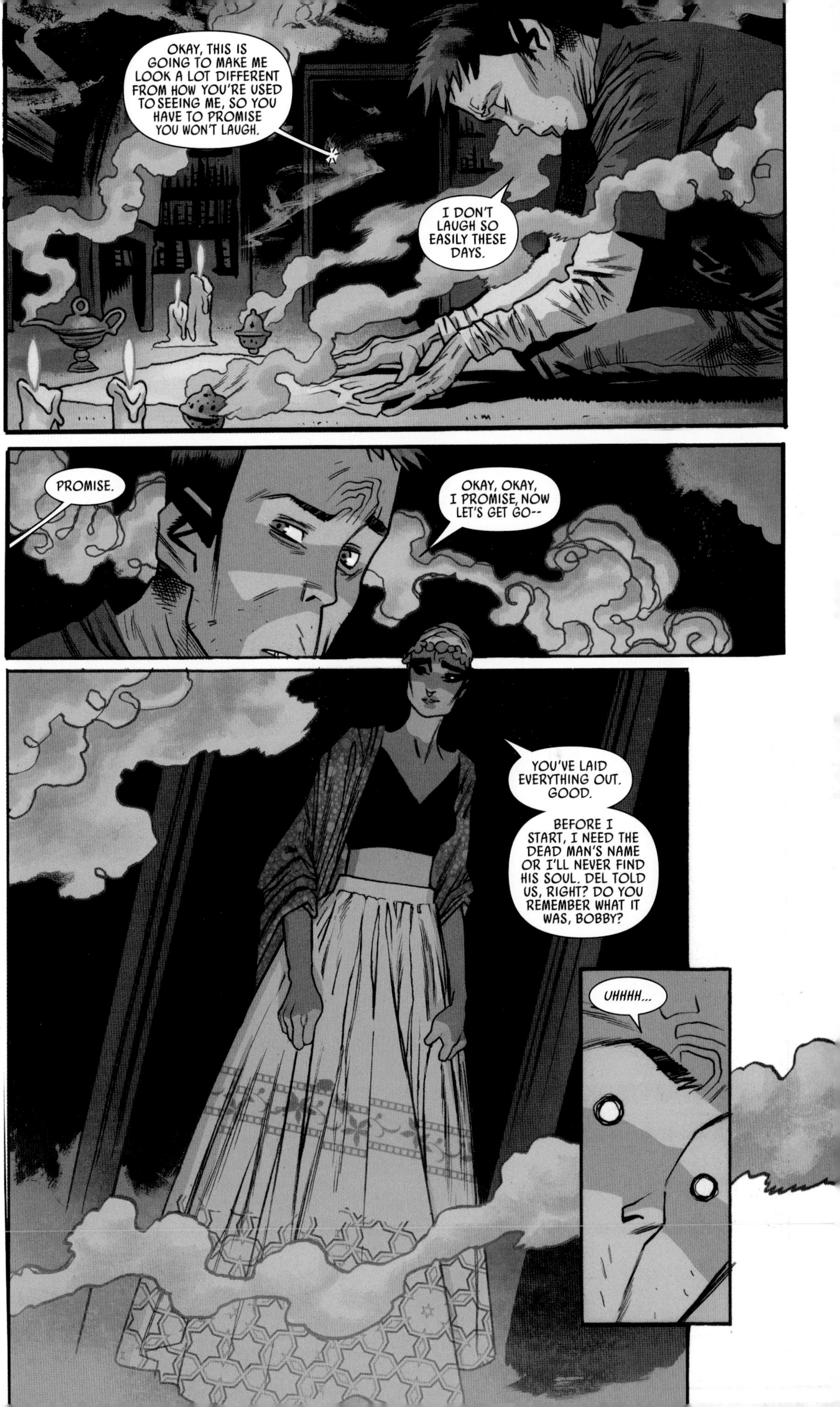
OKAY, THIS IS GOING TO MAKE ME LOOK A LOT DIFFERENT FROM HOW YOU'RE USED TO SEEING ME, SO YOU HAVE TO PROMISE YOU WON'T LAUGH.
I DON'T LAUGH SO EASILY THESE DAYS.
PROMISE.
OKAY, OKAY, I PROMISE, NOW LET'S GET GO--
YOU'VE LAID EVERYTHING OUT. GOOD.
BEFORE I START, I NEED THE DEAD MAN'S NAME OR I'LL NEVER FIND HIS SOUL. DEL TOLD US, RIGHT? DO YOU REMEMBER WHAT IT WAS, BOBBY?
UHHHH...

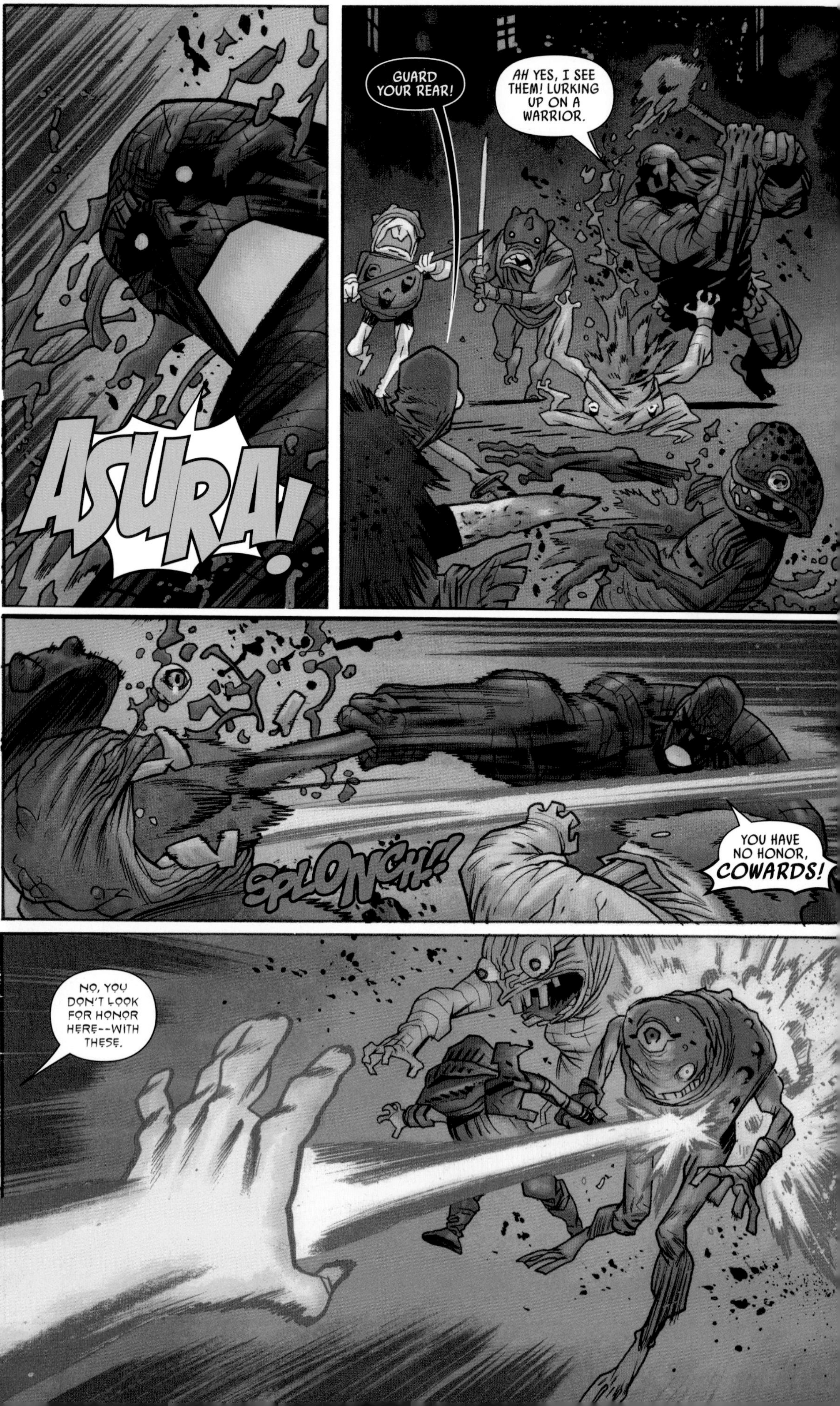
ASURA!
GUARD YOUR REAR!
AH YES, I SEE THEM! LURKING UP ON A WARRIOR.
SPLONCH!!
YOU HAVE NO HONOR, COWARDS!
NO, YOU DON'T LOOK FOR HONOR HERE--WITH THESE.

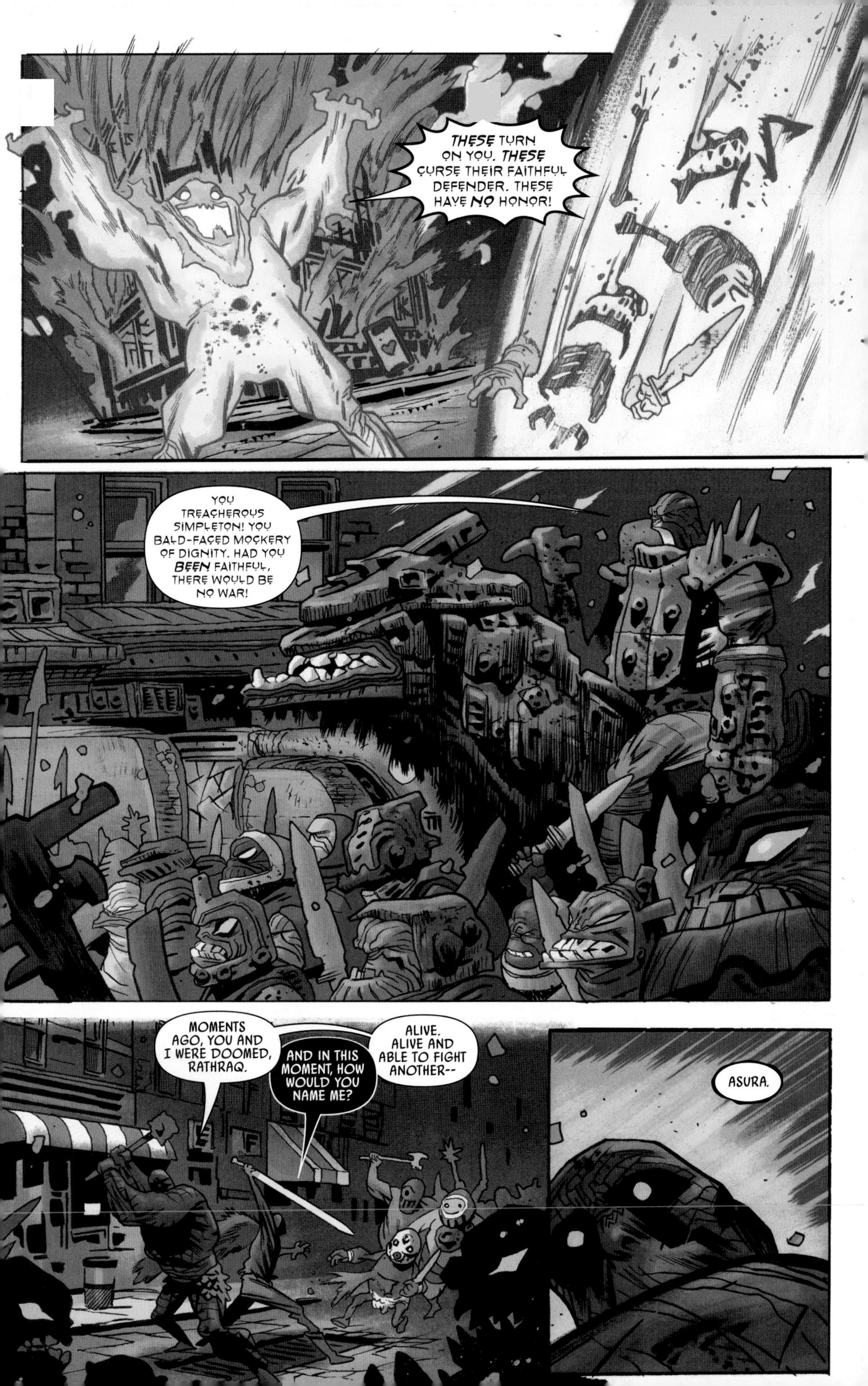
THESE TURN ON YOU. THESE CURSE THEIR FAITHFUL DEFENDER. THESE HAVE NO HONOR!
YOU TREACHEROUS SIMPLETON! YOU BALD-FACED MOCKERY OF DIGNITY. HAD YOU BEEN FAITHFUL, THERE WOULD BE NO WAR!
MOMENTS AGO, YOU AND I WERE DOOMED, RATHRAQ.
AND IN THIS MOMENT, HOW WOULD YOU NAME ME?
ALIVE. ALIVE AND ABLE TO FIGHT ANOTHER--
ASURA.

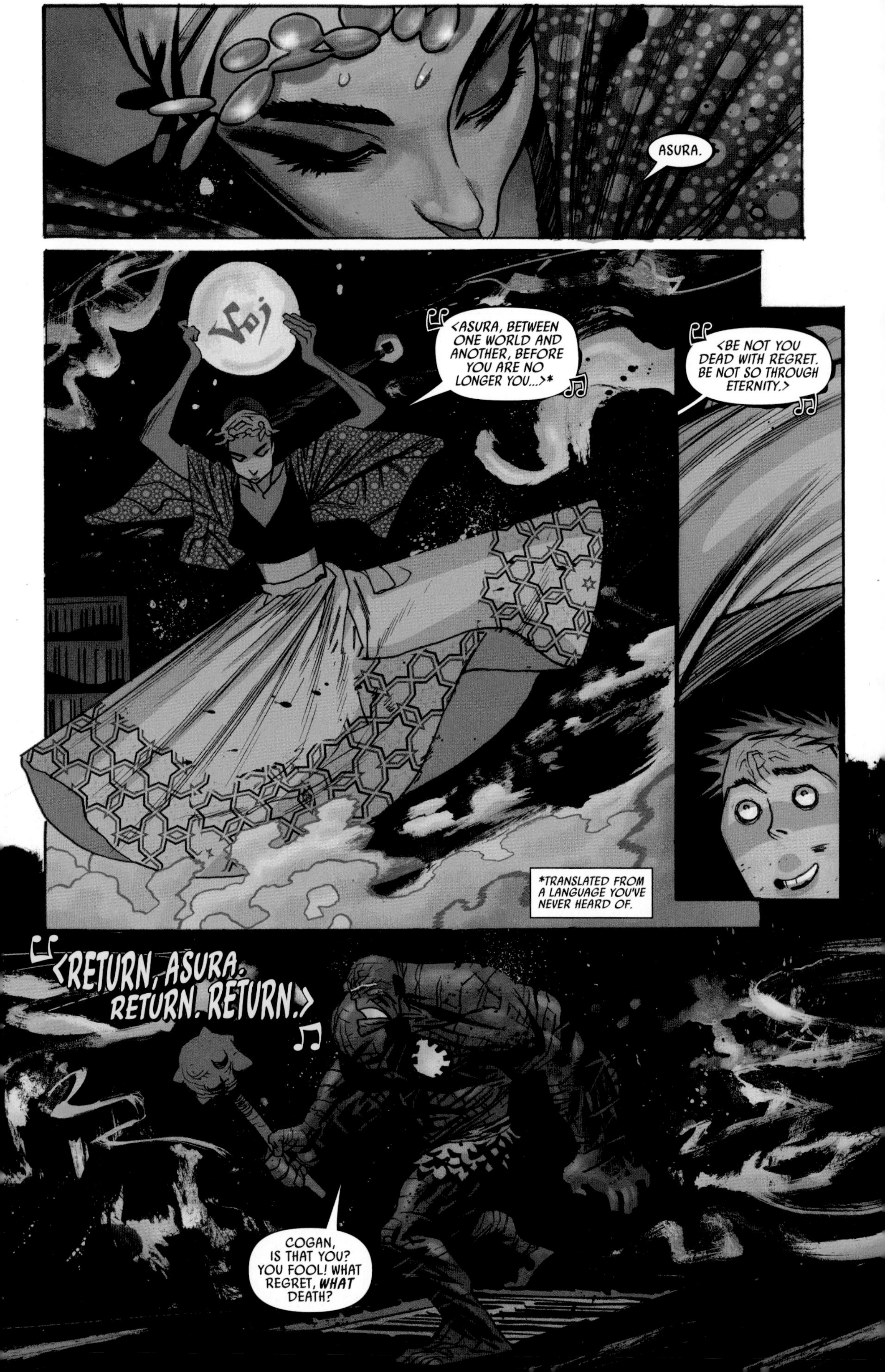
ASURA.
<ASURA, BETWEEN ONE WORLD AND ANOTHER, BEFORE YOU ARE NO LONGER YOU...>*
<BE NOT YOU DEAD WITH REGRET. BE NOT SO THROUGH ETERNITY.>
*TRANSLATED FROM A LANGUAGE YOU'VE NEVER HEARD OF.
<RETURN, ASURA. RETURN. RETURN.>
COGAN, IS THAT YOU? YOU FOOL! WHAT REGRET, *WHAT* DEATH?

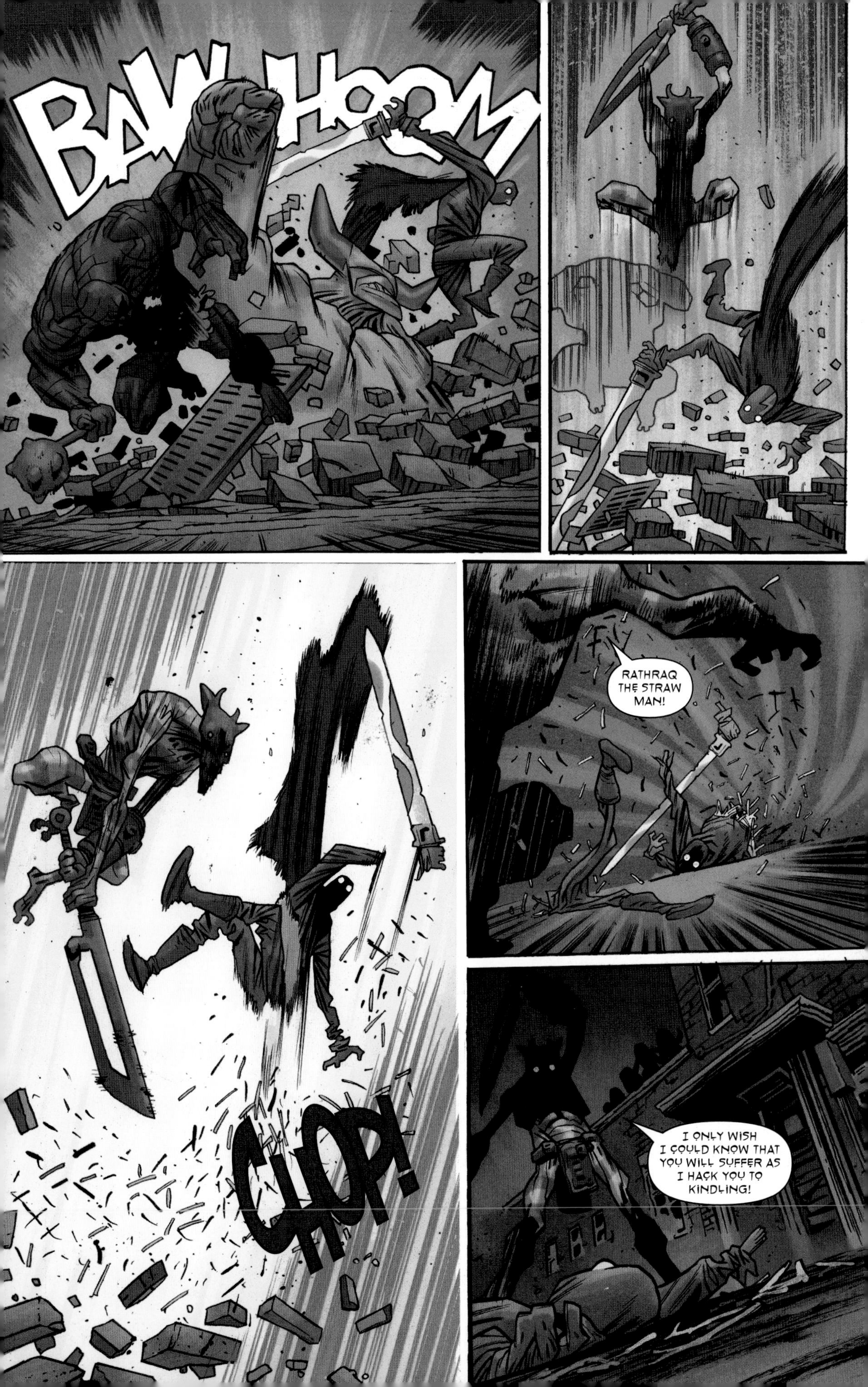
BAWHOOM
CHOP!
RATHRAQ THE STRAW MAN!
I ONLY WISH I COULD KNOW THAT YOU WILL SUFFER AS I HACK YOU TO KINDLING!

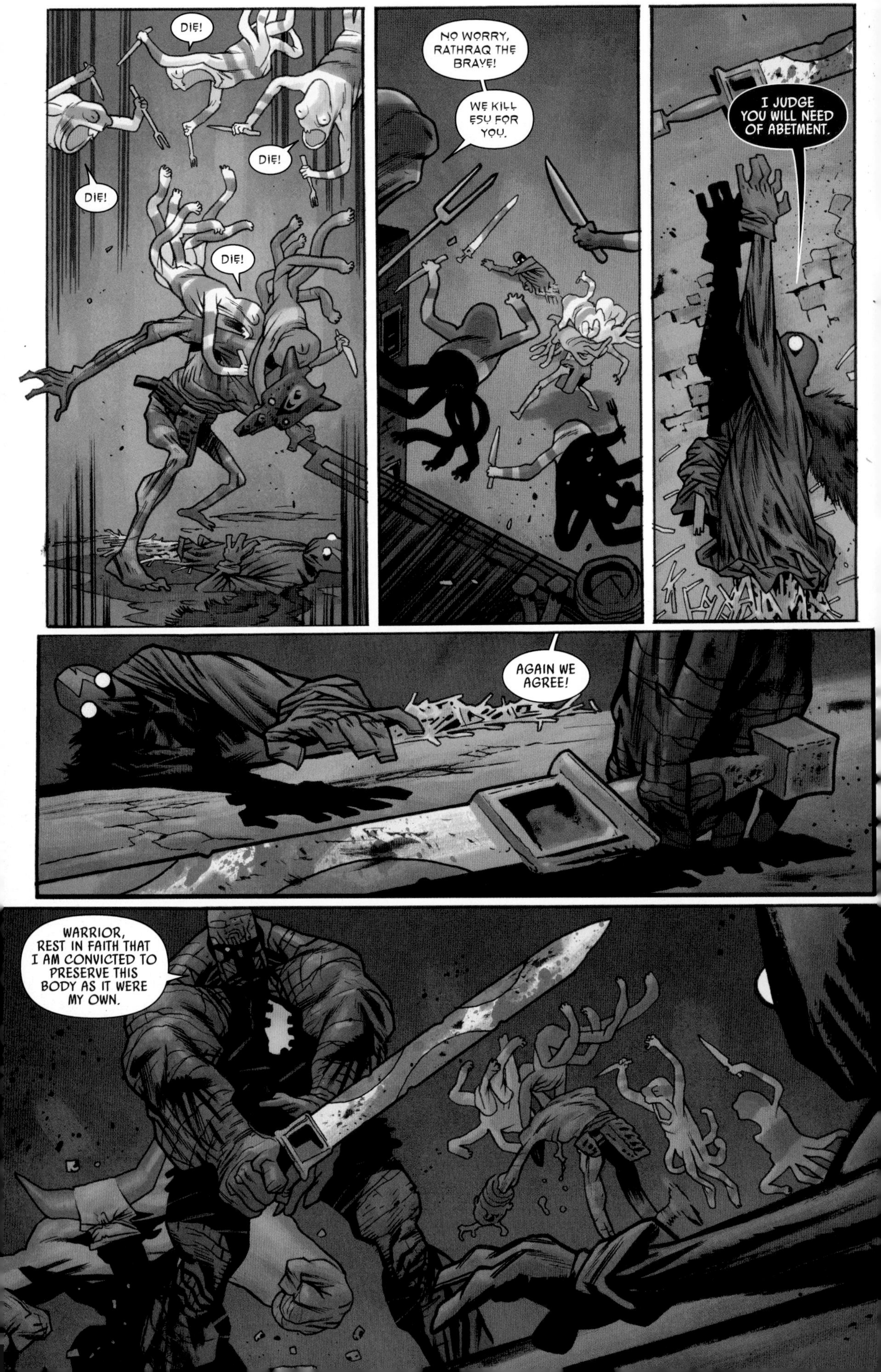
DIE!
DIE!
DIE!
DIE!
NO WORRY, RATHRAQ THE BRAVE!
WE KILL ESU FOR YOU.
I JUDGE YOU WILL NEED OF ABETMENT.
AGAIN WE AGREE!
WARRIOR, REST IN FAITH THAT I AM CONVICTED TO PRESERVE THIS BODY AS IT WERE MY OWN.

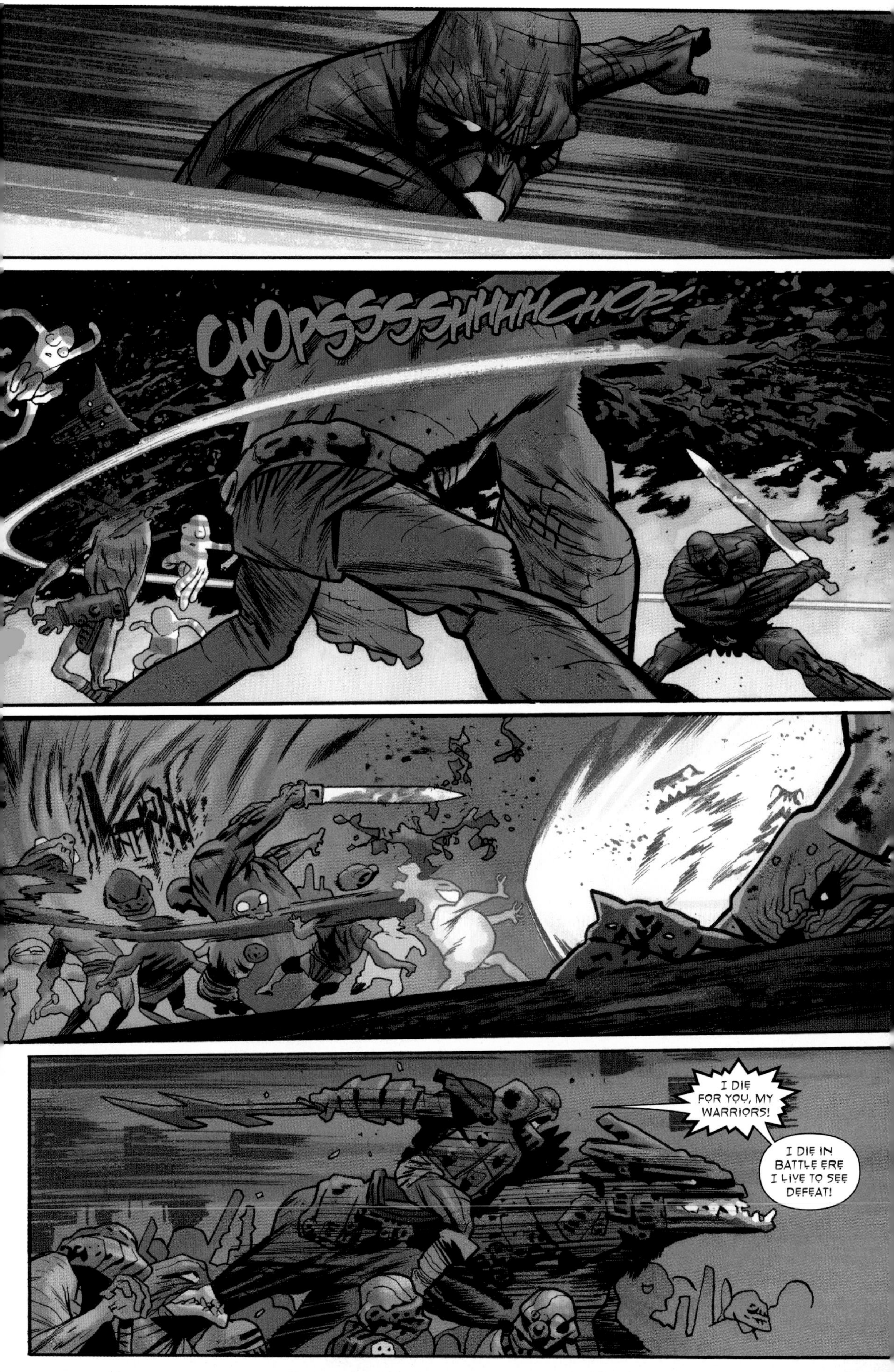
CHOPSSSSSHHHCHOP!
I DIE FOR YOU, MY WARRIORS!
I DIE IN BATTLE ERE I LIVE TO SEE DEFEAT!

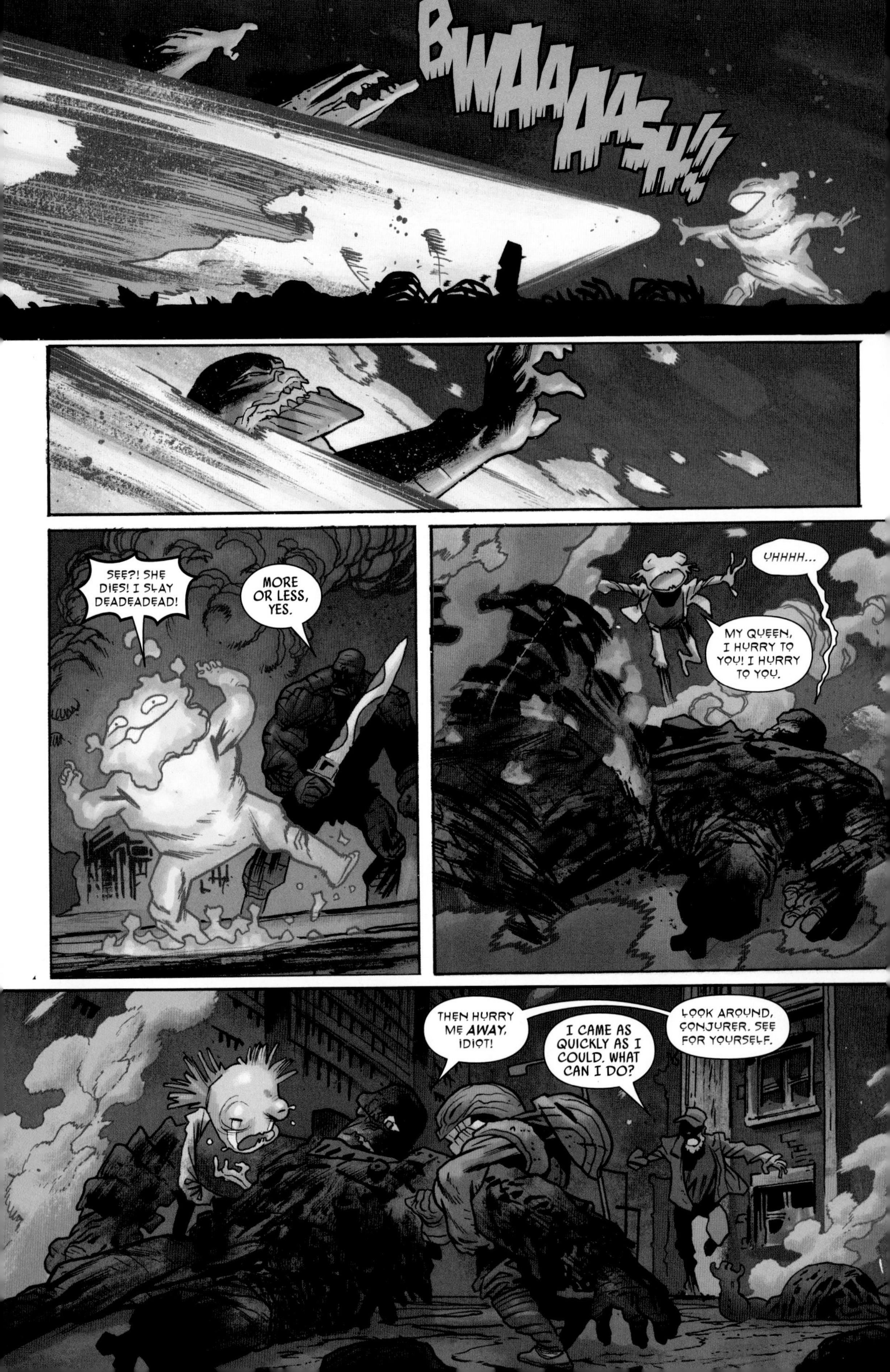
BWAAAAASH!!
SEE?! SHE DIES! I SLAY DEADEADEAD!
MORE OR LESS, YES.
UHHHH...
MY QUEEN, I HURRY TO YOU! I HURRY TO YOU.
THEN HURRY ME AWAY, IDIOT!
I CAME AS QUICKLY AS I COULD. WHAT CAN I DO?
LOOK AROUND, CONJURER. SEE FOR YOURSELF.

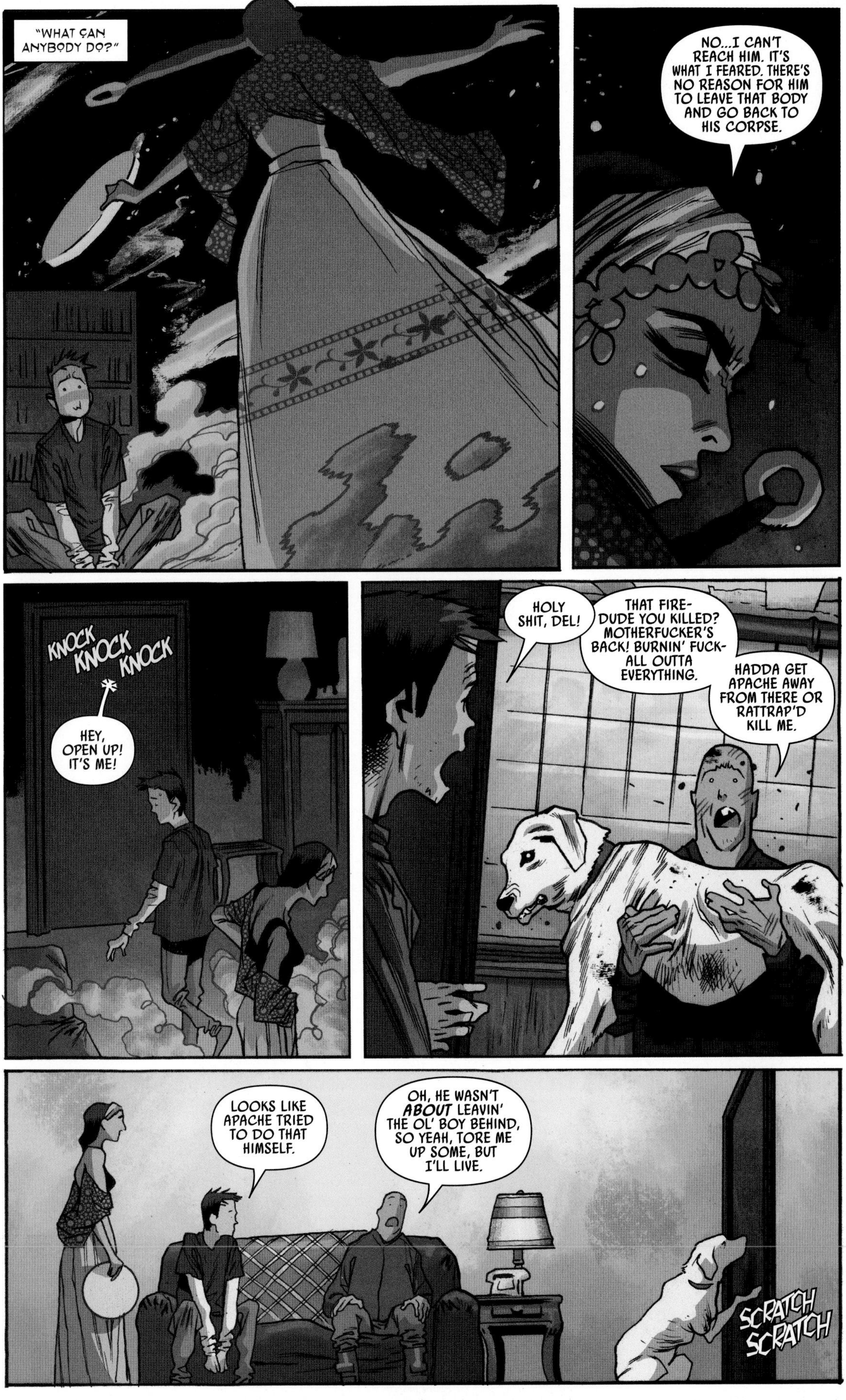
"WHAT CAN ANYBODY DO?"
NO...I CAN'T REACH HIM. IT'S WHAT I FEARED. THERE'S NO REASON FOR HIM TO LEAVE THAT BODY AND GO BACK TO HIS CORPSE.
KNOCK KNOCK KNOCK
HEY, OPEN UP! IT'S ME!
HOLY SHIT, DEL!
THAT FIRE-DUDE YOU KILLED? MOTHERFUCKER'S BACK! BURNIN' FUCK-ALL OUTTA EVERYTHING.
HADDA GET APACHE AWAY FROM THERE OR RATTRAP'D KILL ME.
LOOKS LIKE APACHE TRIED TO DO THAT HIMSELF.
OH, HE WASN'T ABOUT LEAVIN' THE OL' BOY BEHIND, SO YEAH, TORE ME UP SOME, BUT I'LL LIVE.
SCRATCH SCRATCH

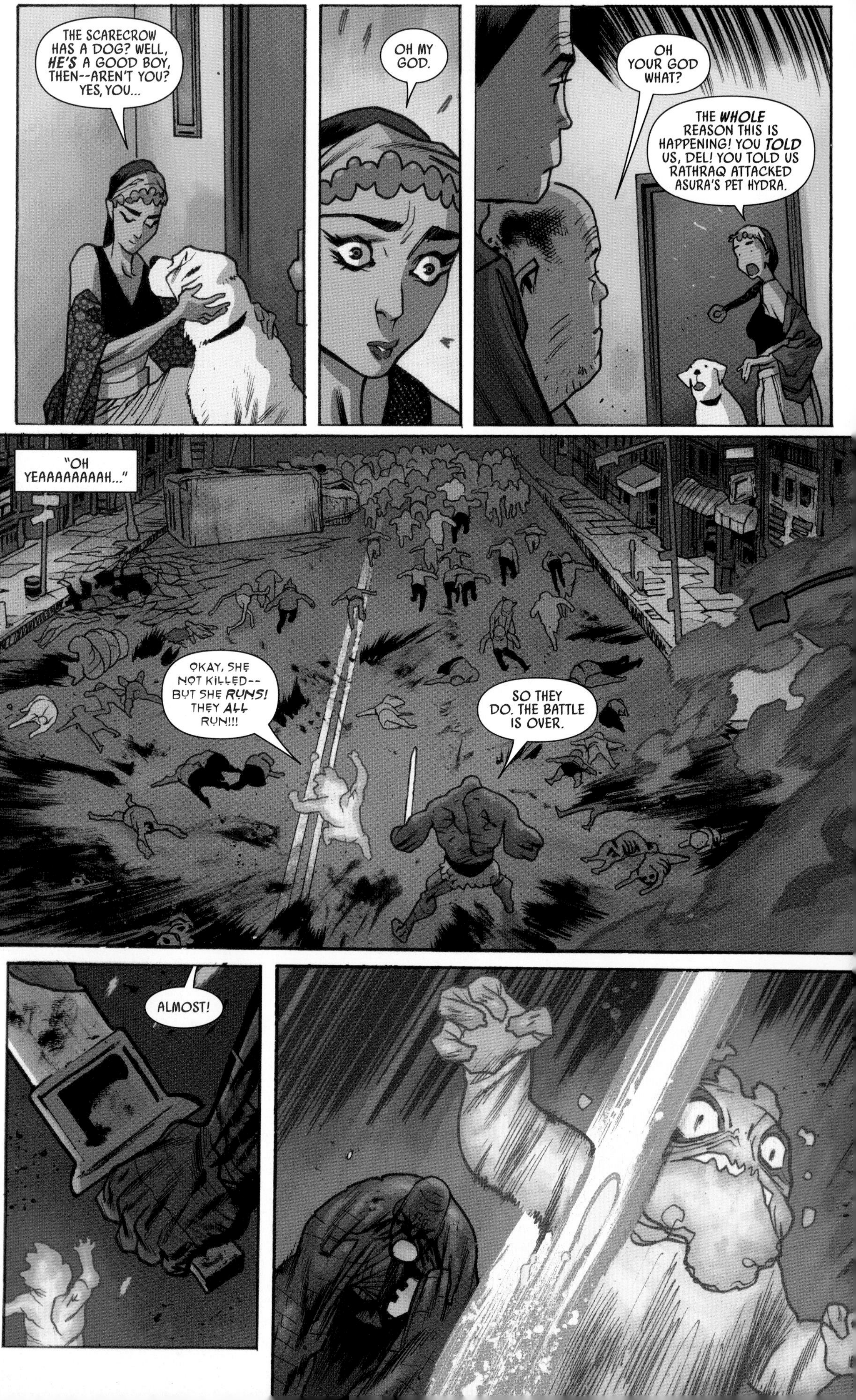
THE SCARECROW HAS A DOG? WELL, HE'S A GOOD BOY, THEN--AREN'T YOU? YES, YOU...
OH MY GOD.
OH YOUR GOD WHAT?
THE WHOLE REASON THIS IS HAPPENING! YOU TOLD US, DEL! YOU TOLD US RATHRAQ ATTACKED ASURA'S PET HYDRA.
"OH YEAAAAAAAAH..."
OKAY, SHE NOT KILLED--BUT SHE RUNS! THEY ALL RUN!!!
SO THEY DO. THE BATTLE IS OVER.
ALMOST!

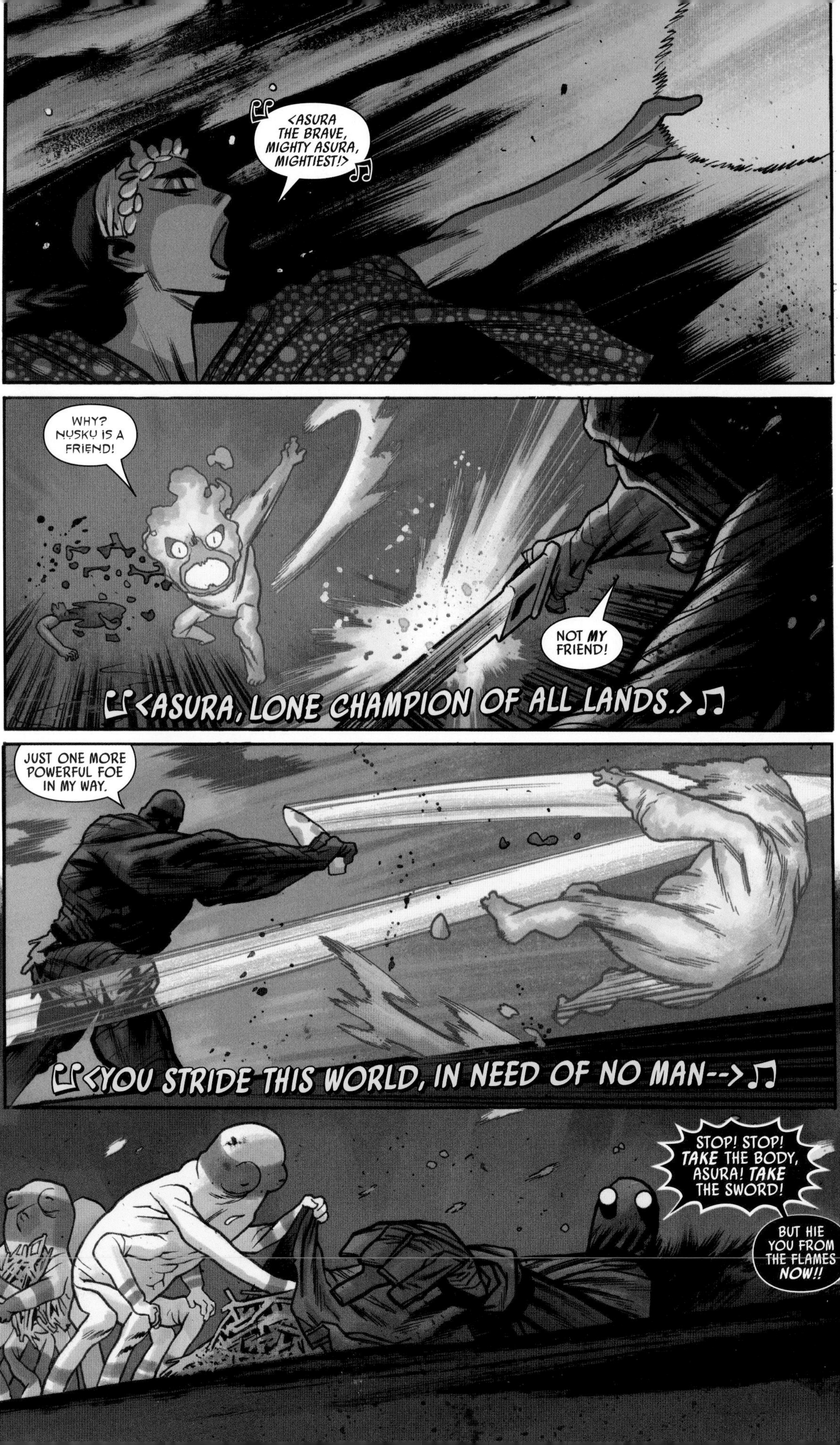

<ASURA THE BRAVE, MIGHTY ASURA, MIGHTIEST!>
WHY? NUSKU IS A FRIEND!
NOT MY FRIEND!
<ASURA, LONE CHAMPION OF ALL LANDS.>
JUST ONE MORE POWERFUL FOE IN MY WAY.
<YOU STRIDE THIS WORLD, IN NEED OF NO MAN-->
STOP! STOP! TAKE THE BODY, ASURA! TAKE THE SWORD!
BUT HIE YOU FROM THE FLAMES NOW!!

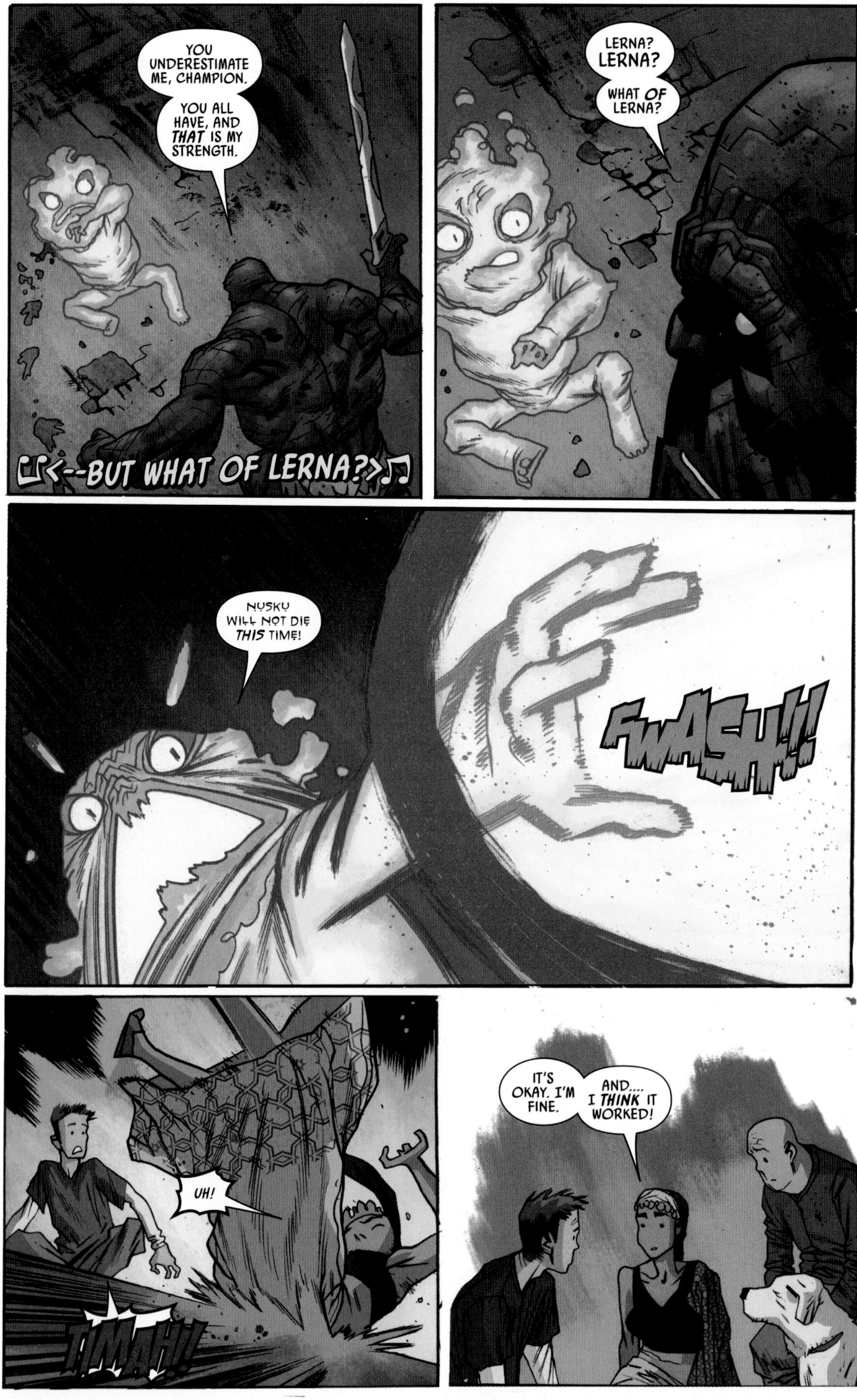
YOU UNDERESTIMATE ME, CHAMPION.
YOU ALL HAVE, AND THAT IS MY STRENGTH.
<--BUT WHAT OF LERNA?>
LERNA? LERNA?
WHAT OF LERNA?
NUSKU WILL NOT DIE THIS TIME!
FWASH!!!
UH!
TMAH!!
IT'S OKAY. I'M FINE.
AND.... I THINK IT WORKED!

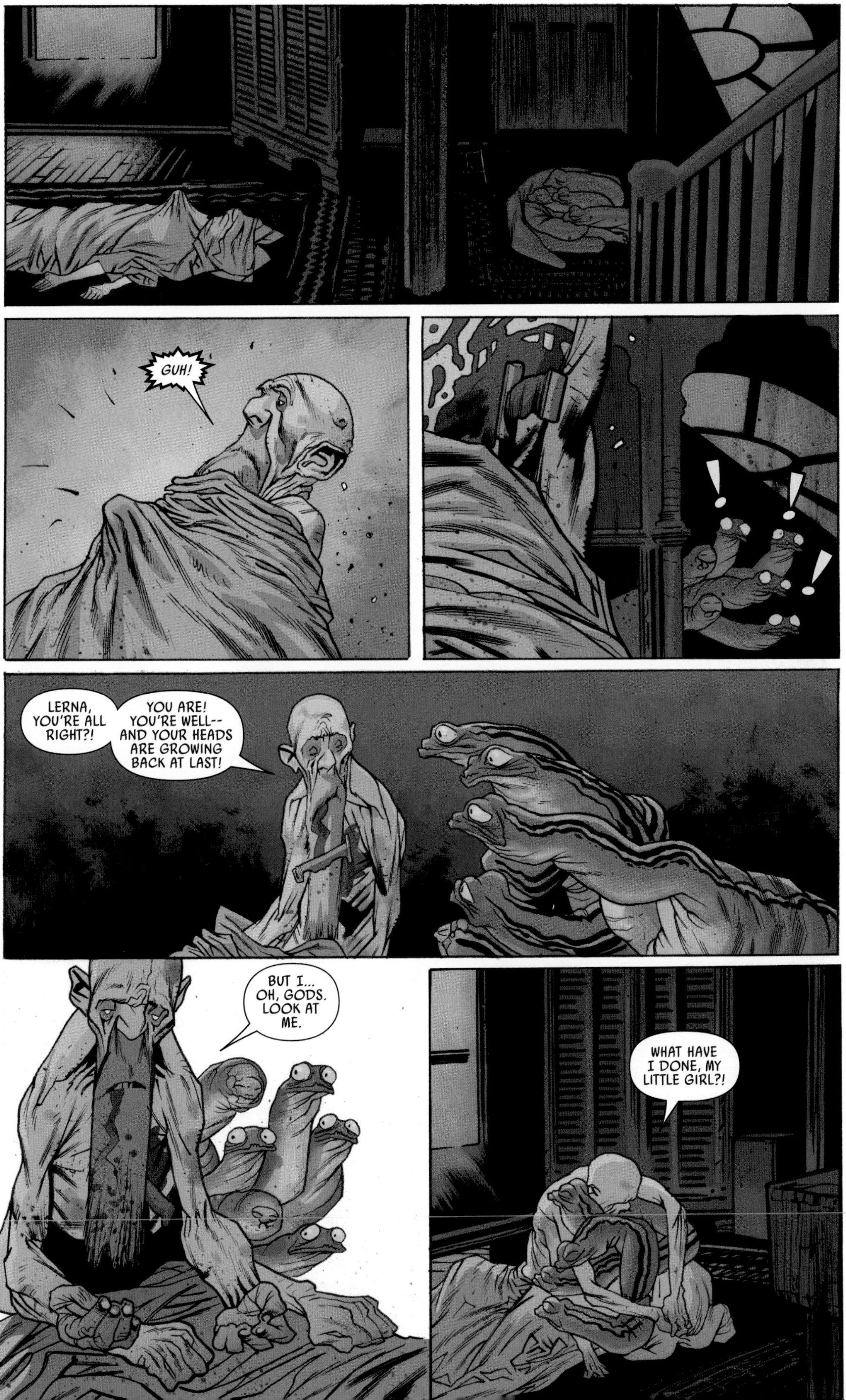
GUH!
!
!
!
LERNA, YOU'RE ALL RIGHT?!
YOU ARE! YOU'RE WELL--AND YOUR HEADS ARE GROWING BACK AT LAST!
BUT I... OH, GODS. LOOK AT ME.
WHAT HAVE I DONE, MY LITTLE GIRL?!

WHAT WILL BECOME
OF ME?

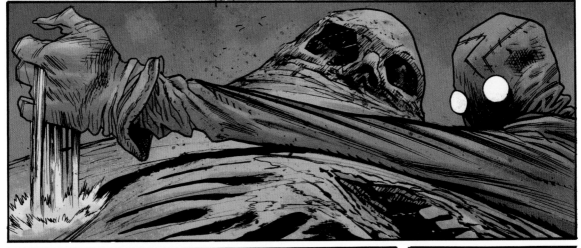

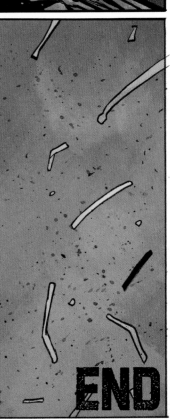

END

COVERS

ISSUES #11-15 COVER A
JAMES HARREN – art & colors

ISSUE #11 COVER B
ANDREW MACLEAN
Instagram – @andrewmaclean

ISSUE #12 COVER B
TRADD MOORE – art
DAVE STEWART – colors
Instagram – @traddmoore

ISSUE #13 COVER B
RICHARD CORBEN – art
BETH CORBEN REED – colors
www.corbencomicart.com

ISSUE #14 COVER B
SKOTTIE YOUNG
Instagram – @skottieyoung

ISSUE #15 COVER B
GEOF DARROW – art
DAVE STEWART – colors
Twitter – @geofdarrow

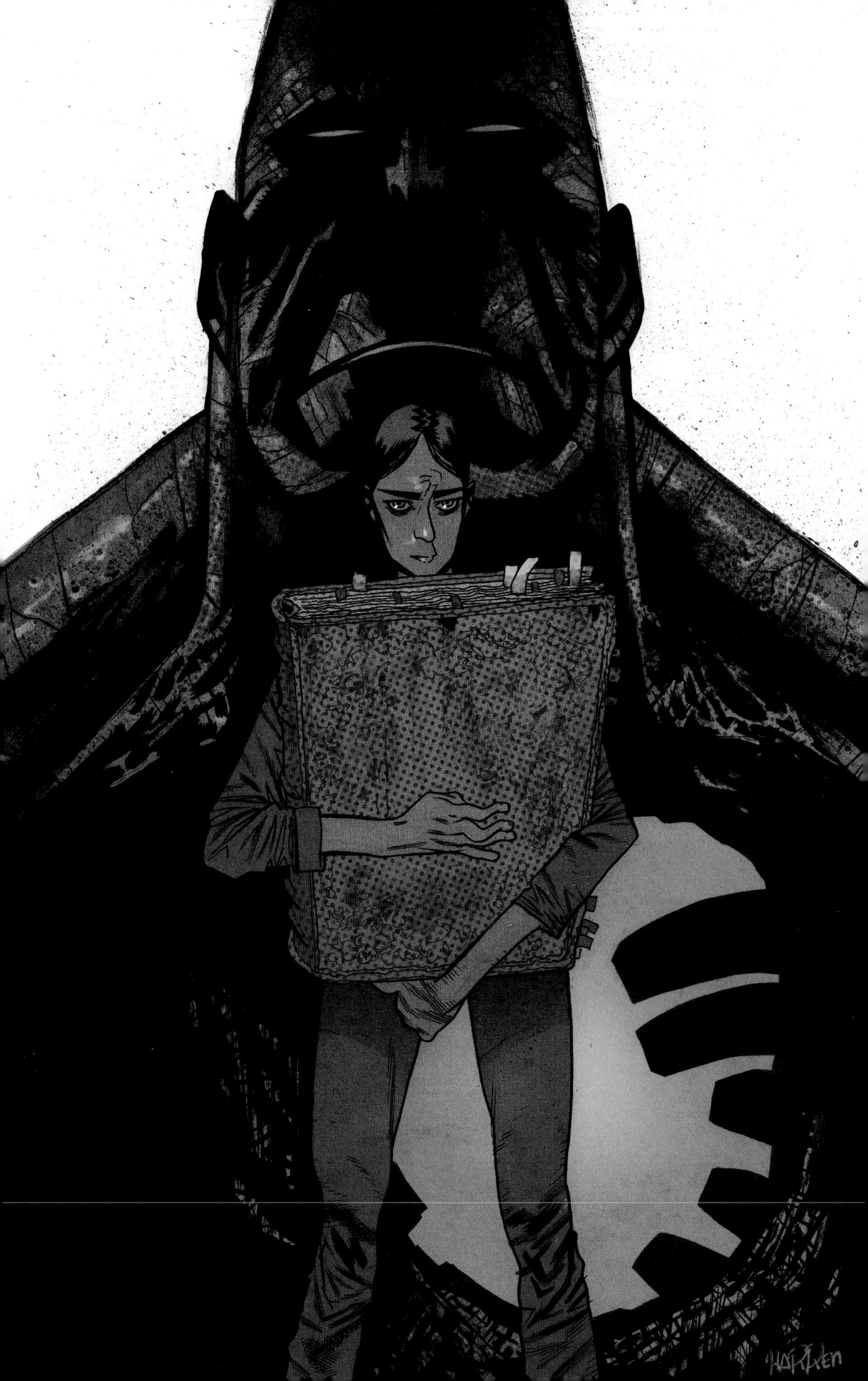

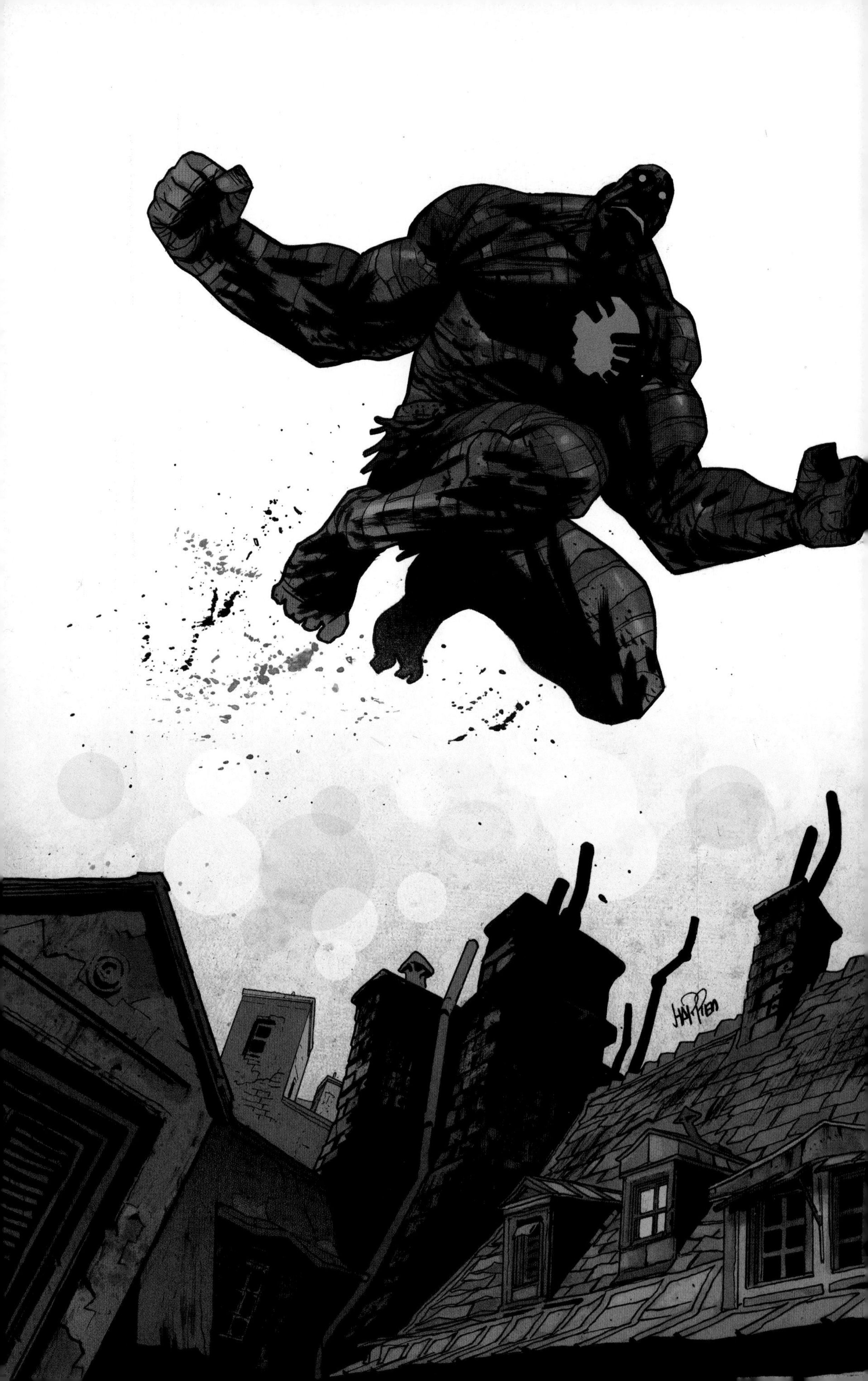

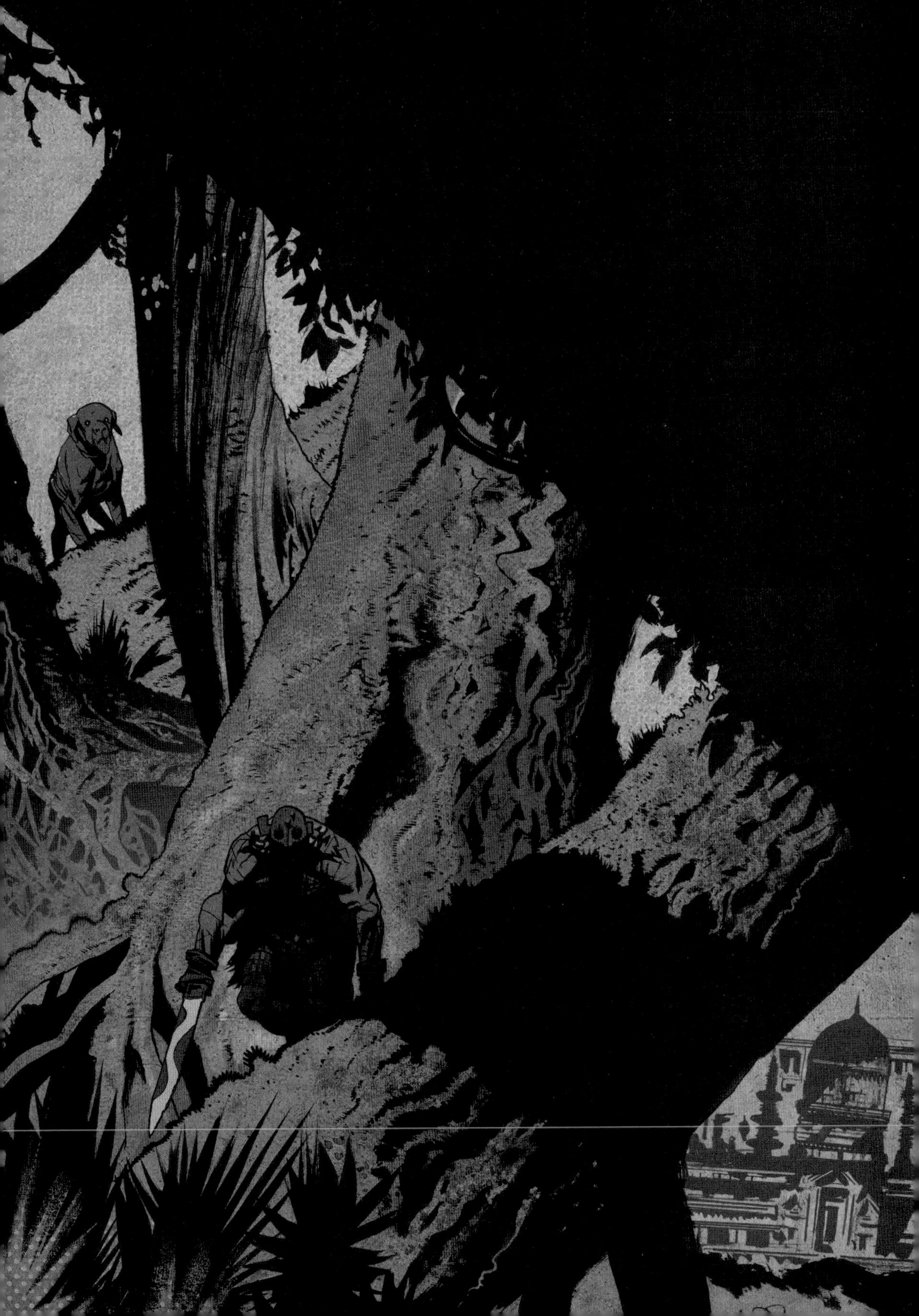

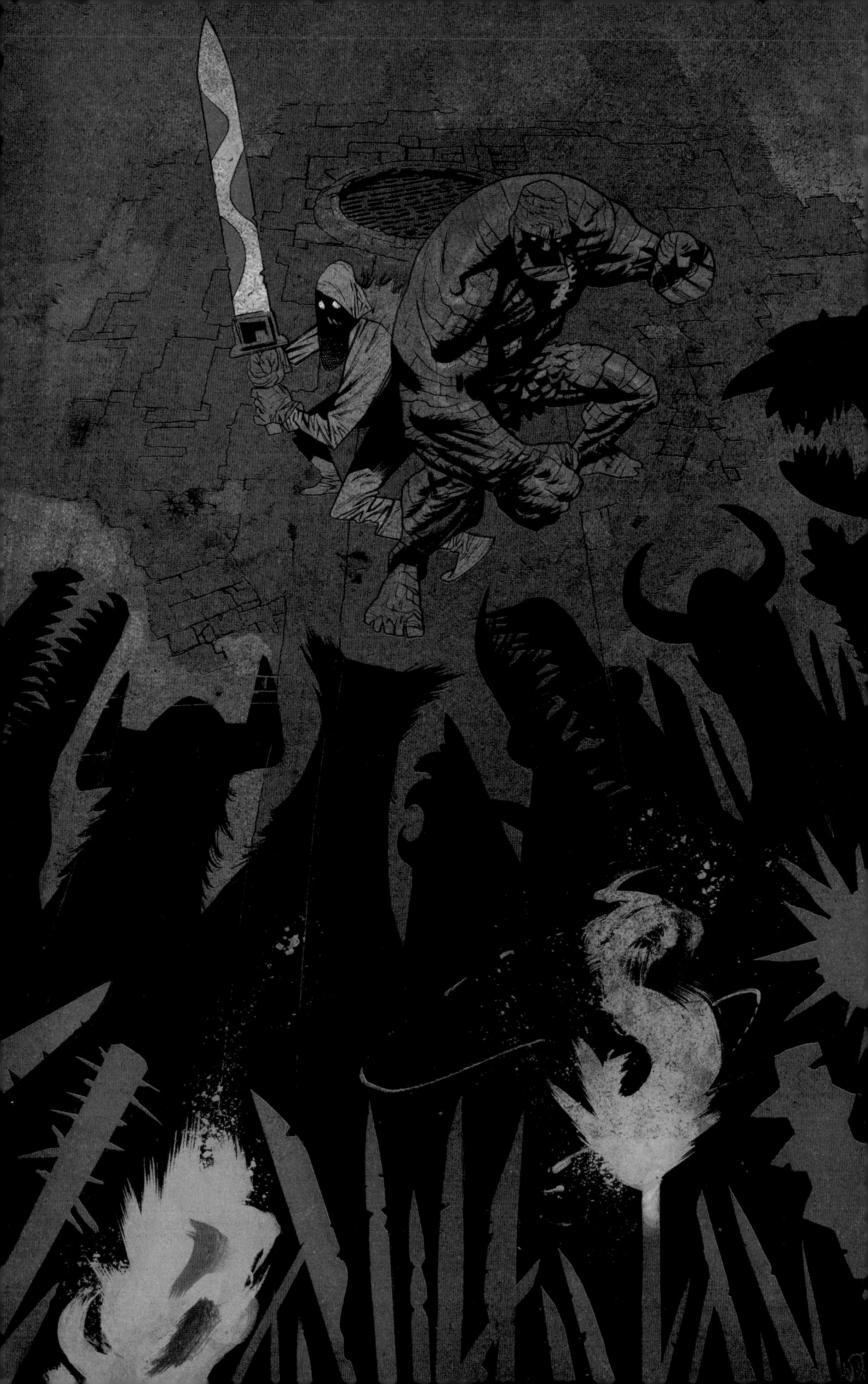

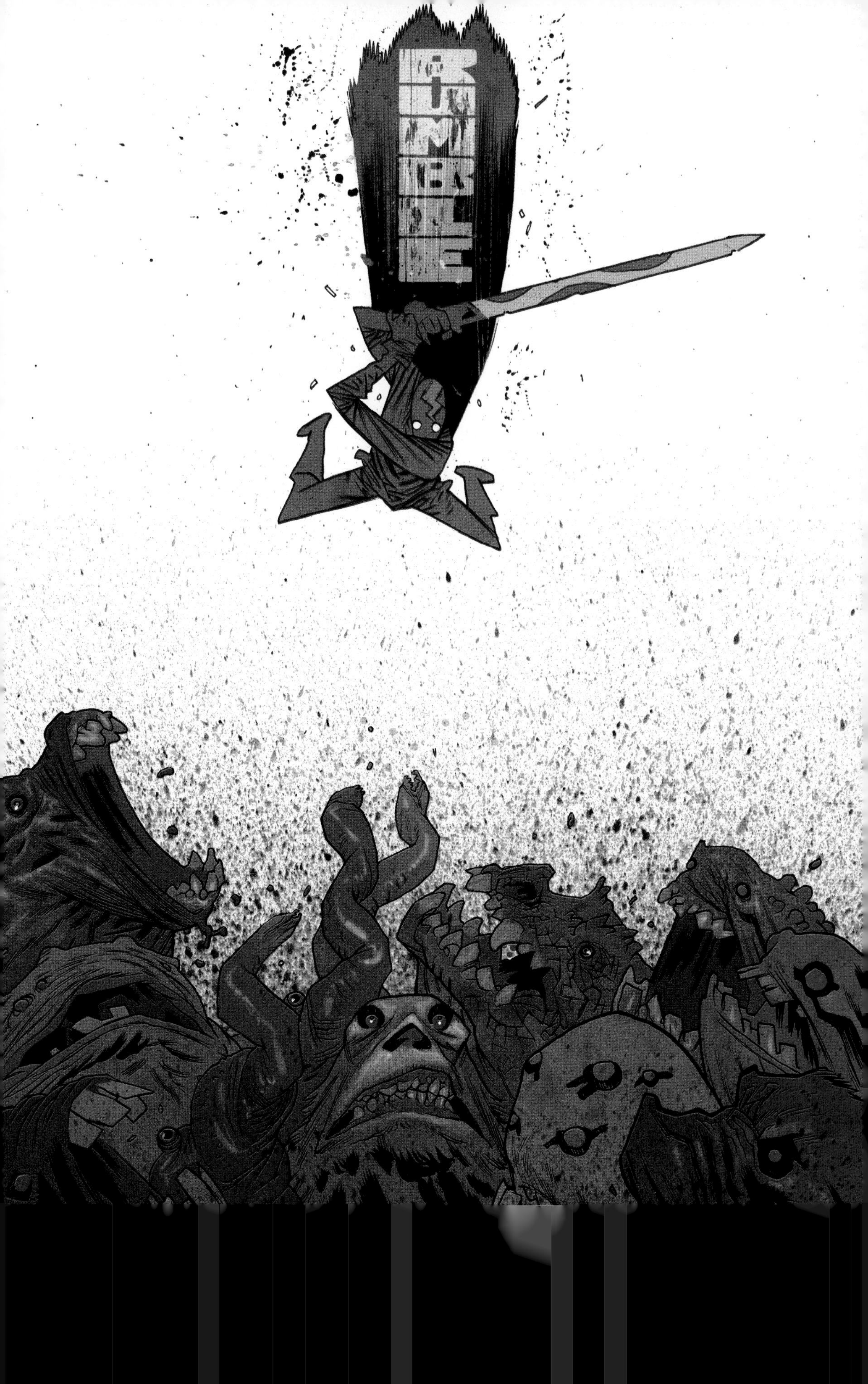
RUMBLE

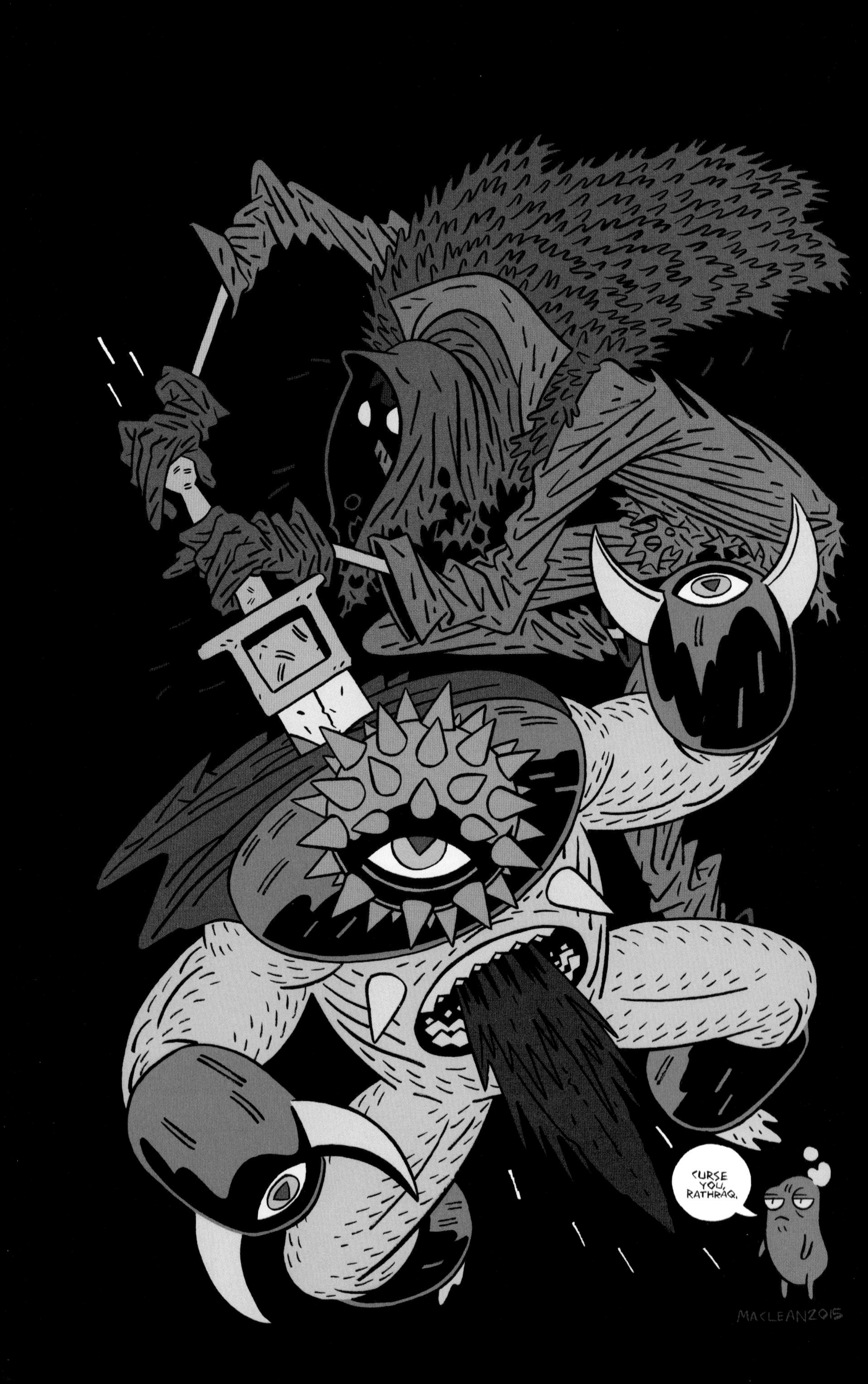
CURSE YOU, RATHRAQ.
MACLEAN2015

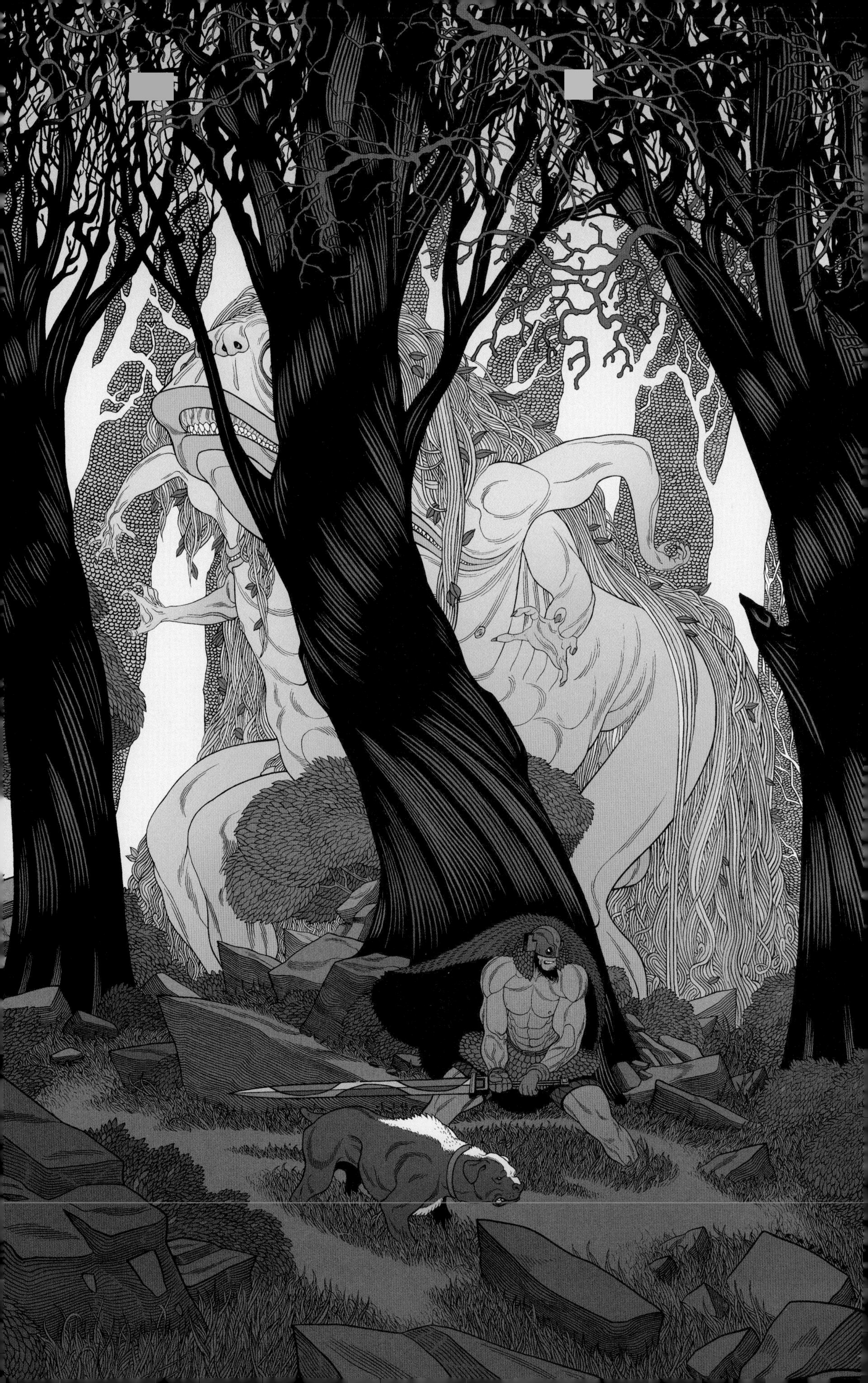

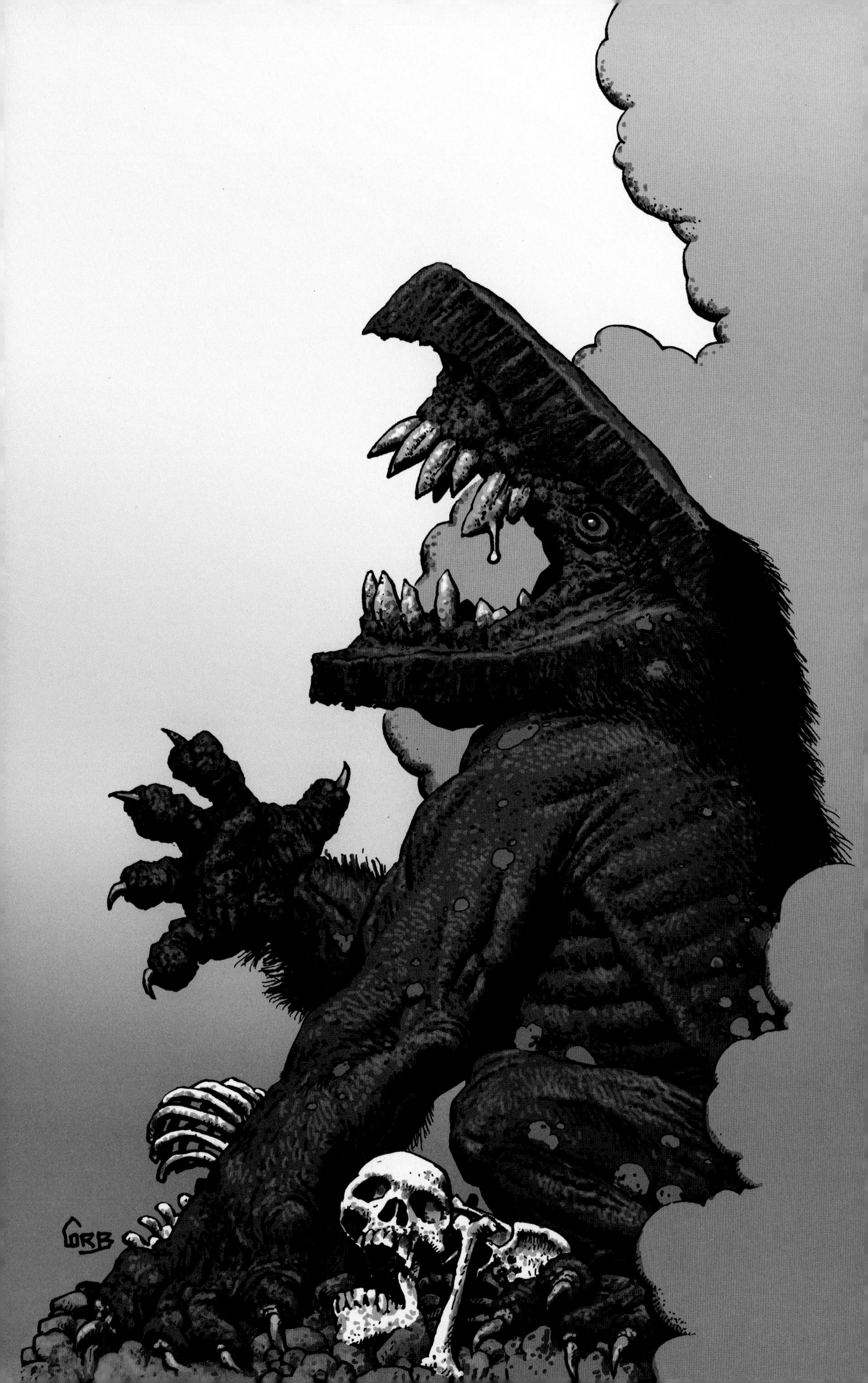
CORB

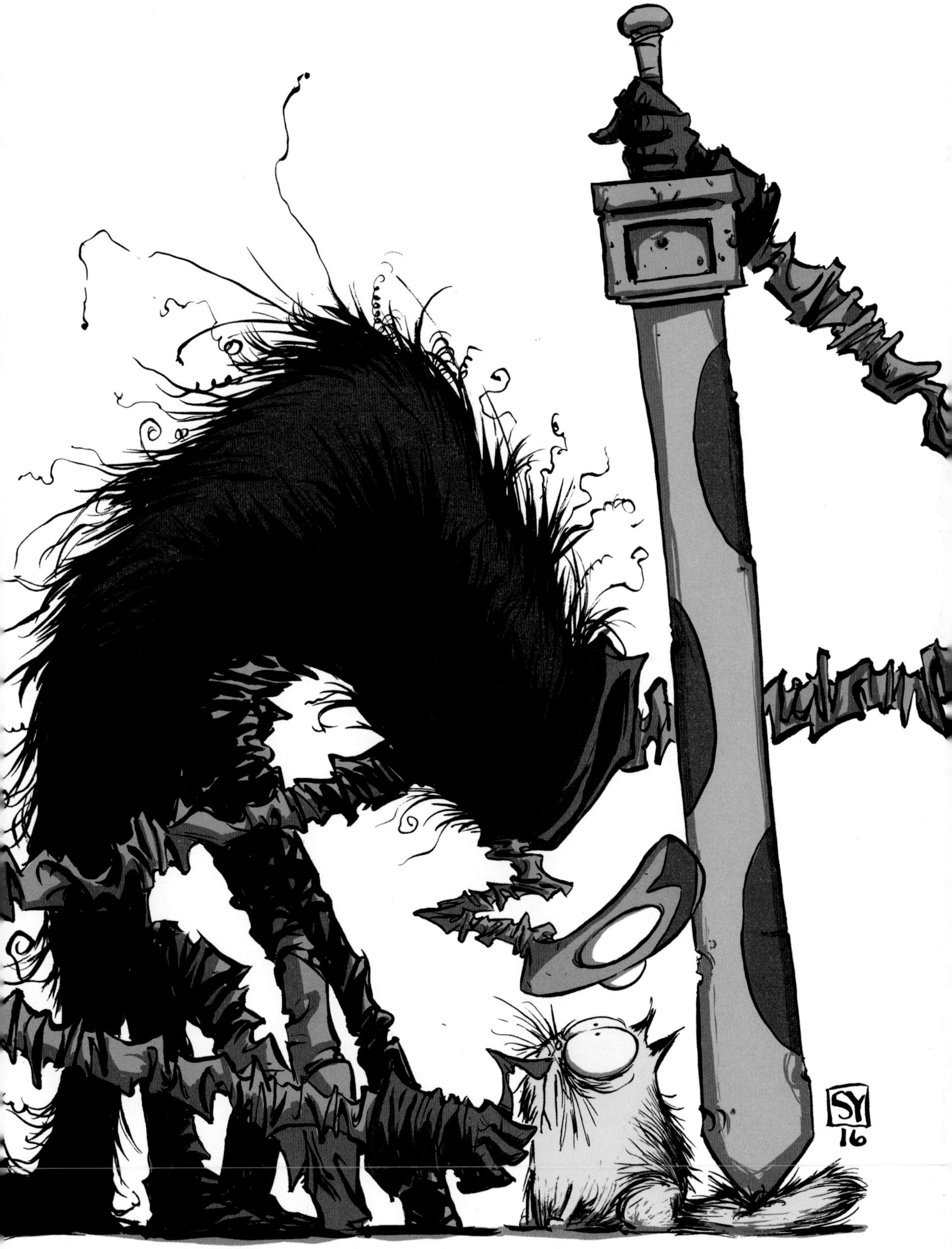
SY
16

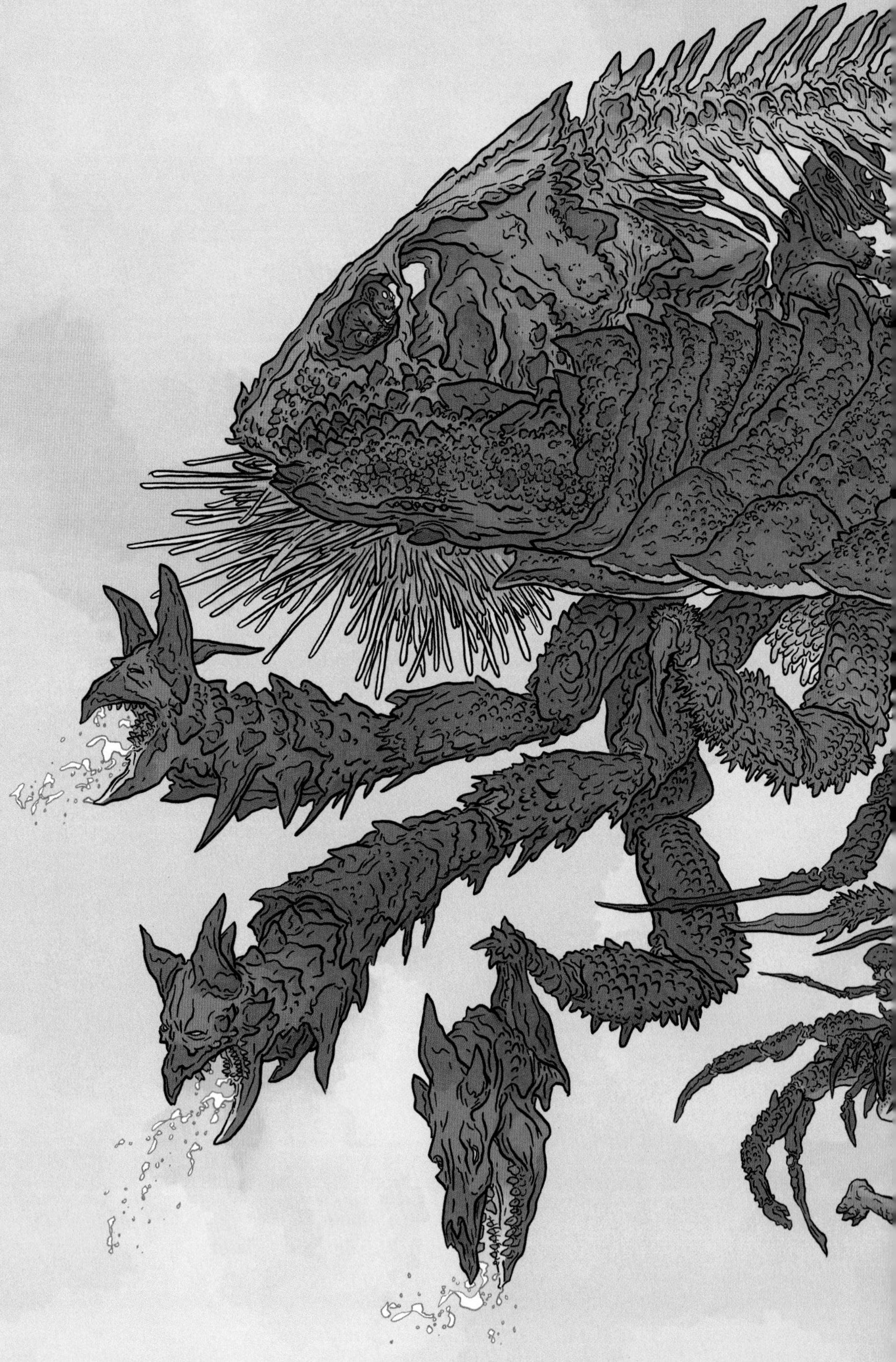

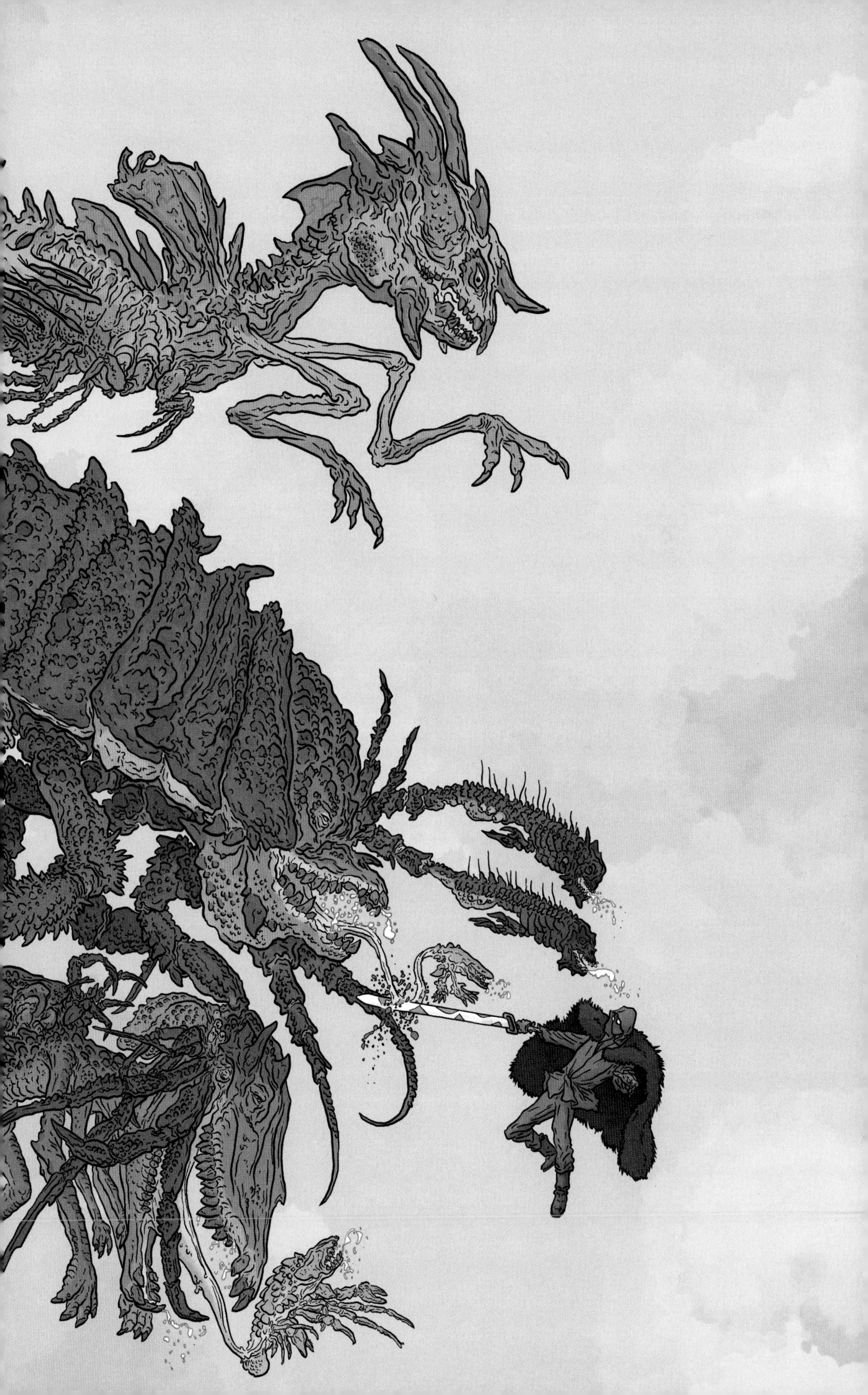

JEFFREY ALAN LOVE
Instagram – @jeffreyalanlove

CEDRIC BABOUCHE
Instagram – @cedric_babouche

CHRIS BOLTON
Instagram – @savagezombieart

PASQUAL FERRY
Instagram – @ferrypoli

TONI FEJZULA – art
ALBA CARDONA GIL – colors
Instagram – @tonifejzula & @alba.cardona3

TOM FOWLER – art
DAVE STEWART – colors
Twitter – @tomfowlerbug

LAURENCE CAMPBELL – art
DAVE STEWART – colors
Twitter – @getcampbell

PATRICK OLLIFFE
Instagram – @polliffe65

REBECCA KIRBY
Instagram – @reweki

ROBB MOMMAERTS
Instagram – @robbmommaerts

SEBASTIAN FIUMARA
Instagram – @sebafiumara

DAVID RUBIN
Twitter – @davidrubin

JOHN McCREA – art
DAVE STEWART – colors
Twitter – @mccreaman

SIMON ROY – art
DAVE STEWART – colors
Instagram – @simonamroy

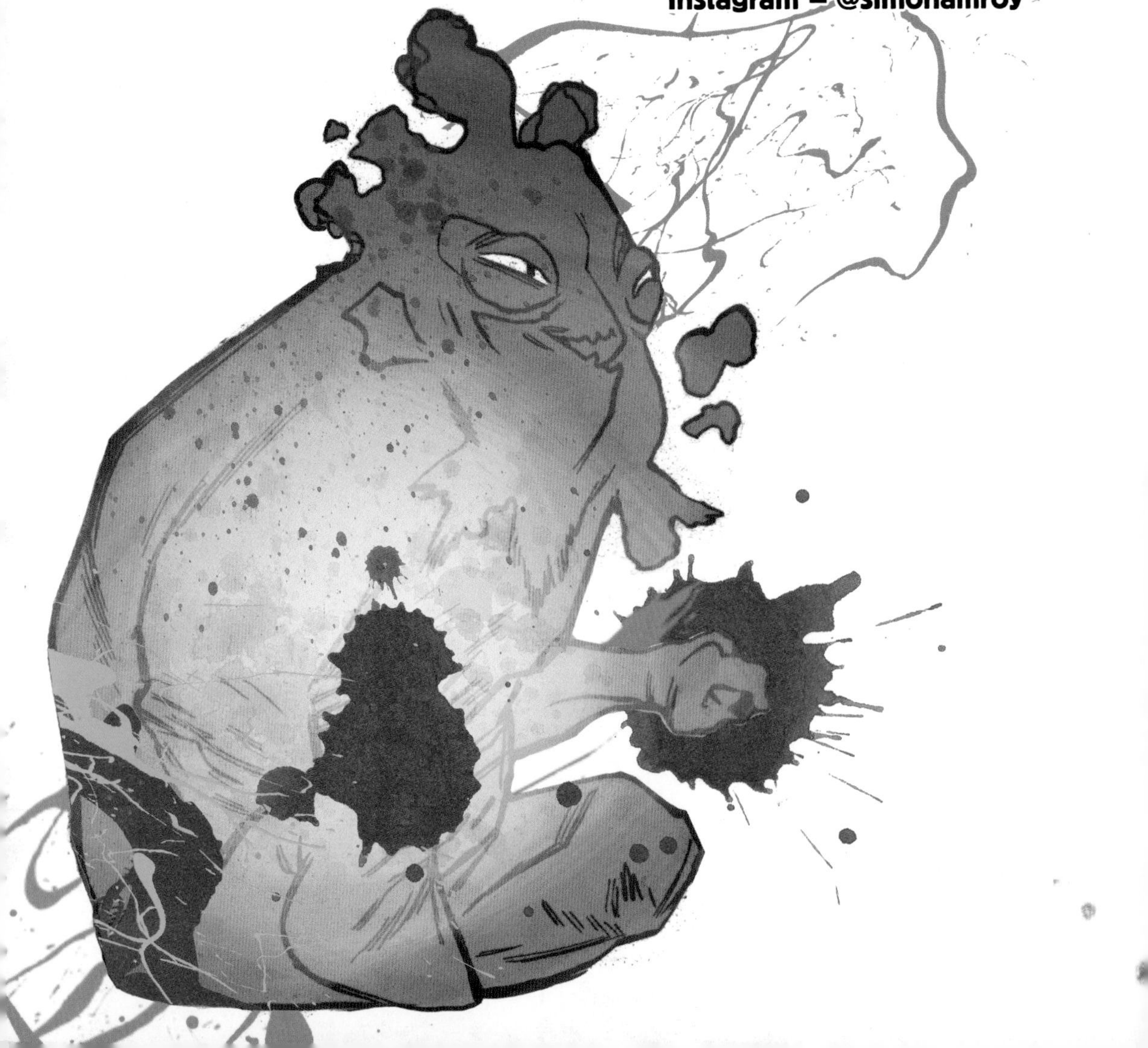

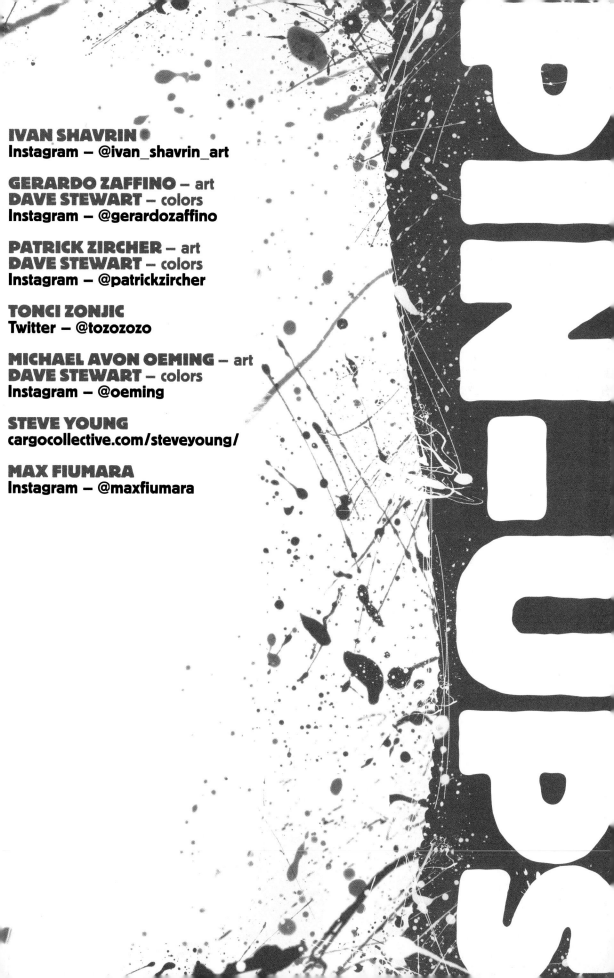

IVAN SHAVRIN
Instagram – @ivan_shavrin_art

GERARDO ZAFFINO – art
DAVE STEWART – colors
Instagram – @gerardozaffino

PATRICK ZIRCHER – art
DAVE STEWART – colors
Instagram – @patrickzircher

TONCI ZONJIC
Twitter – @tozozozo

MICHAEL AVON OEMING – art
DAVE STEWART – colors
Instagram – @oeming

STEVE YOUNG
cargocollective.com/steveyoung/

MAX FIUMARA
Instagram – @maxfiumara

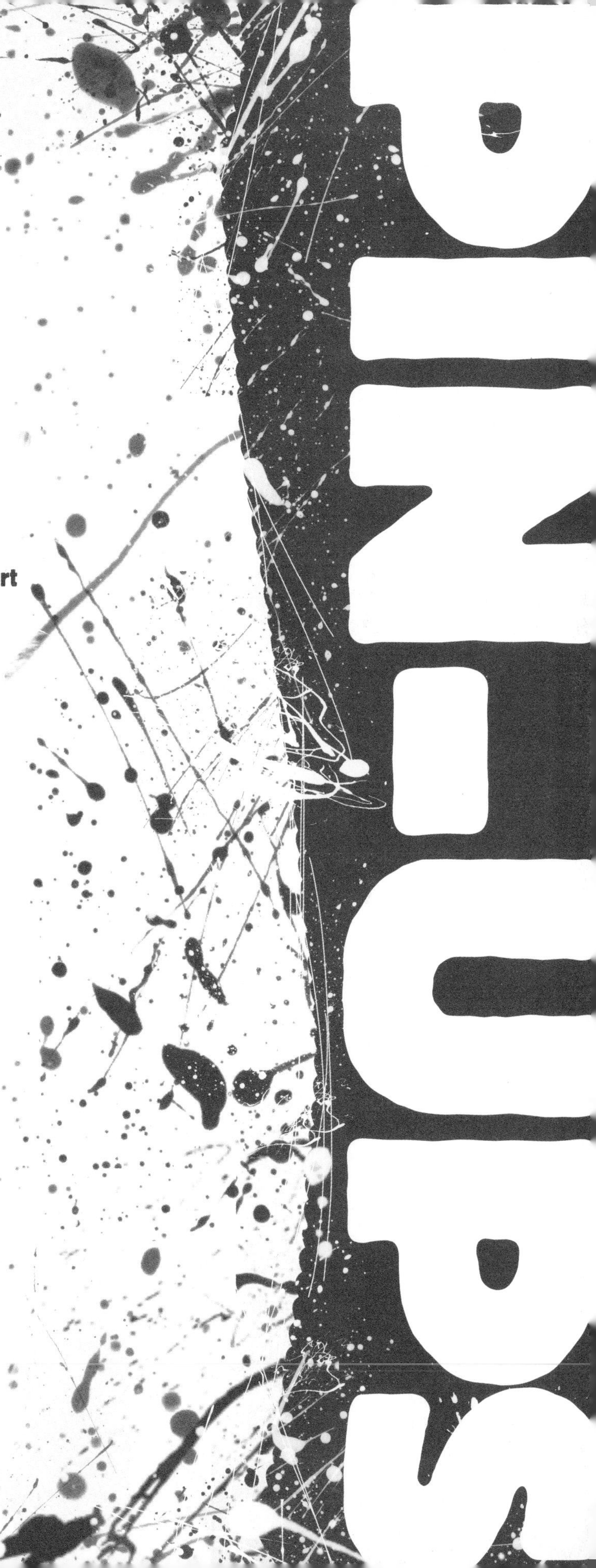

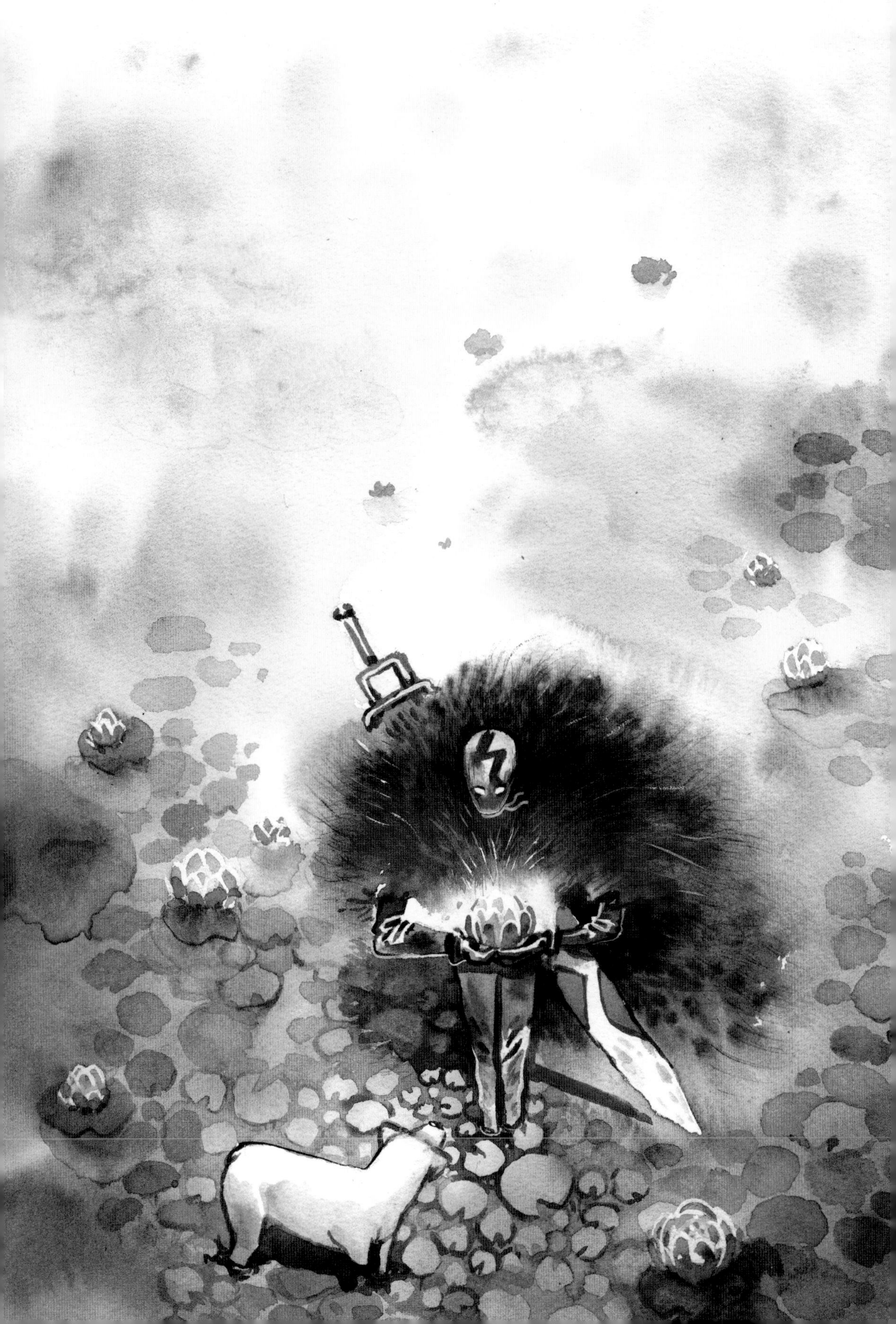

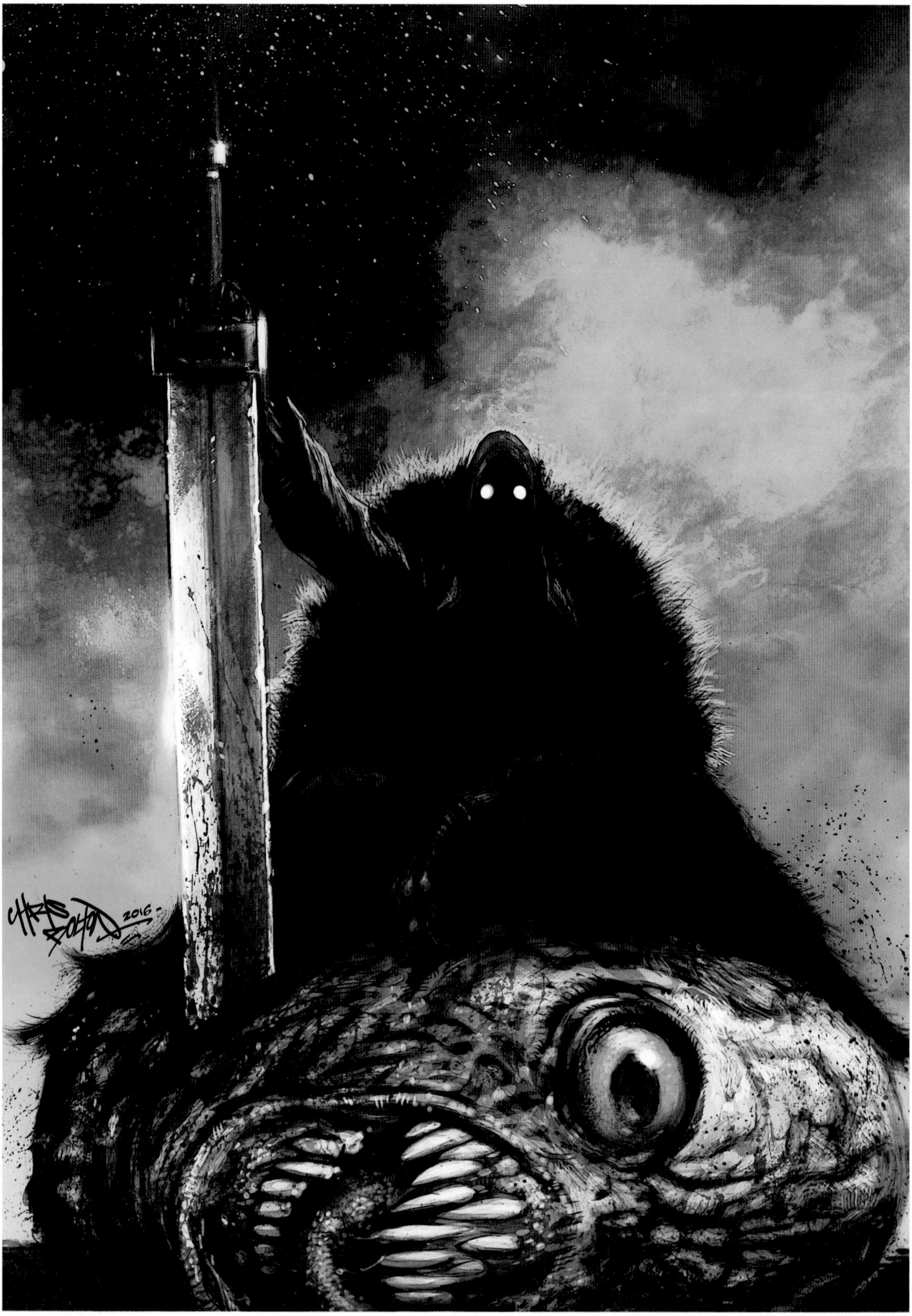
CHRIS BOLTON 2016

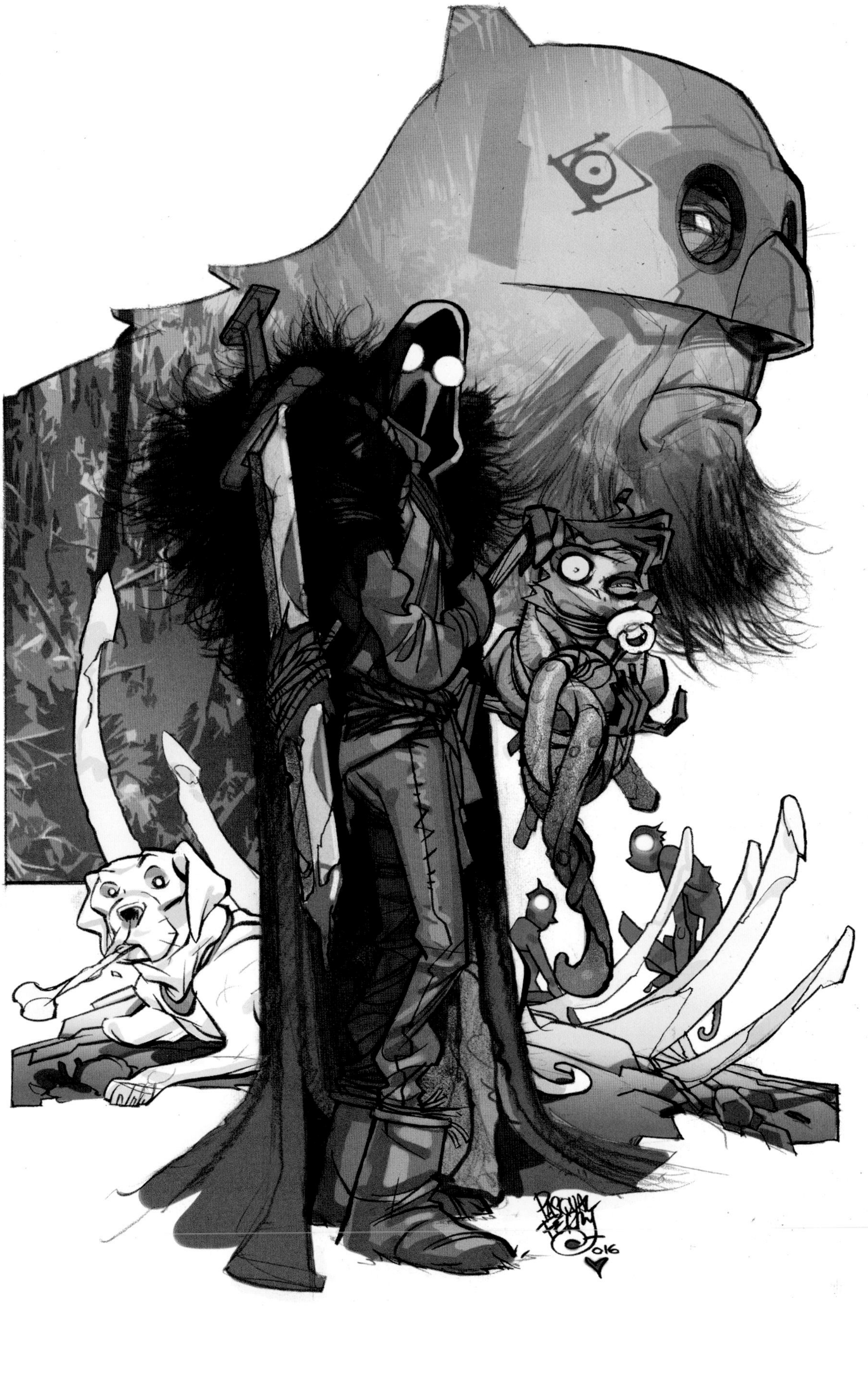

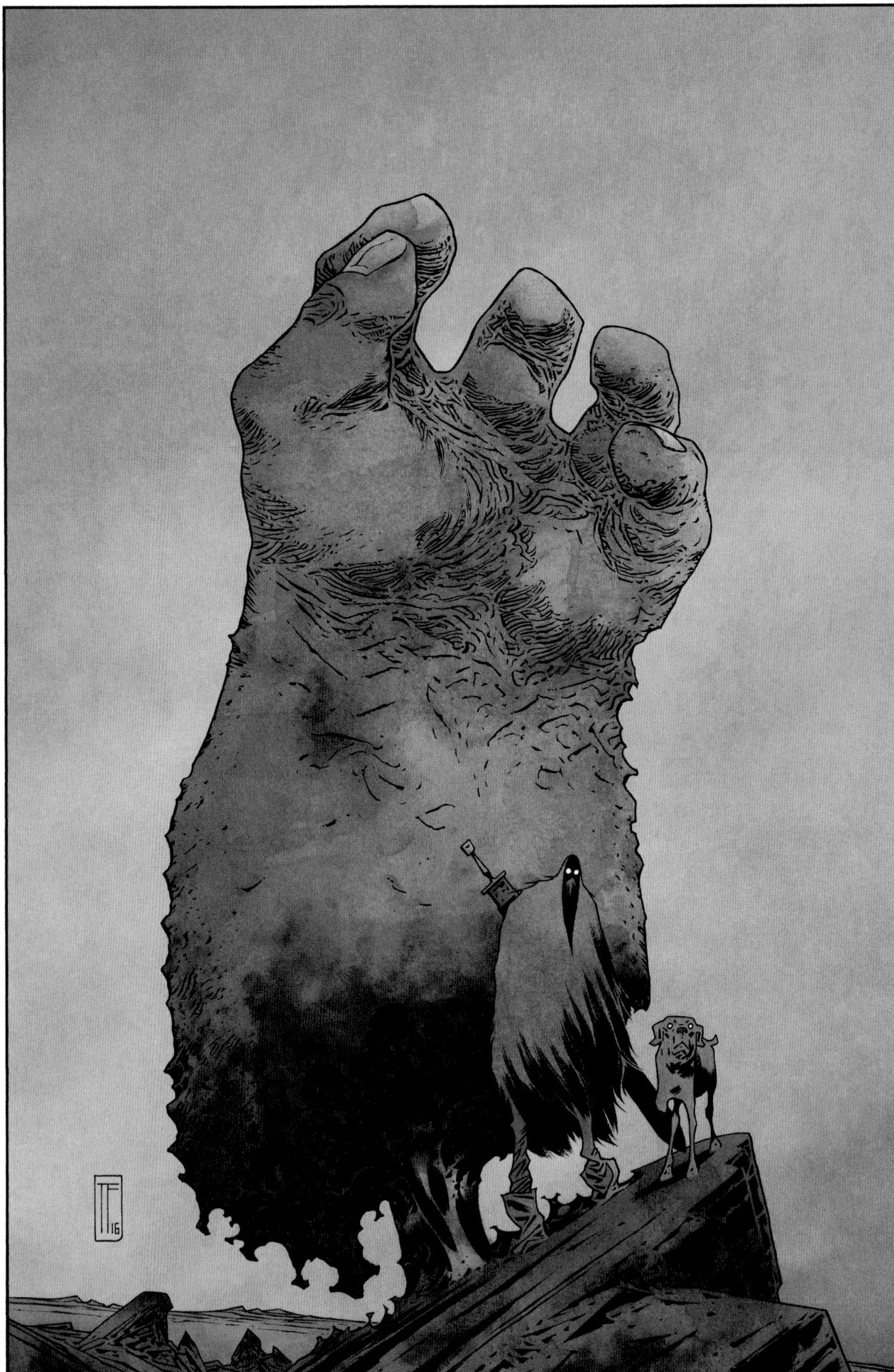

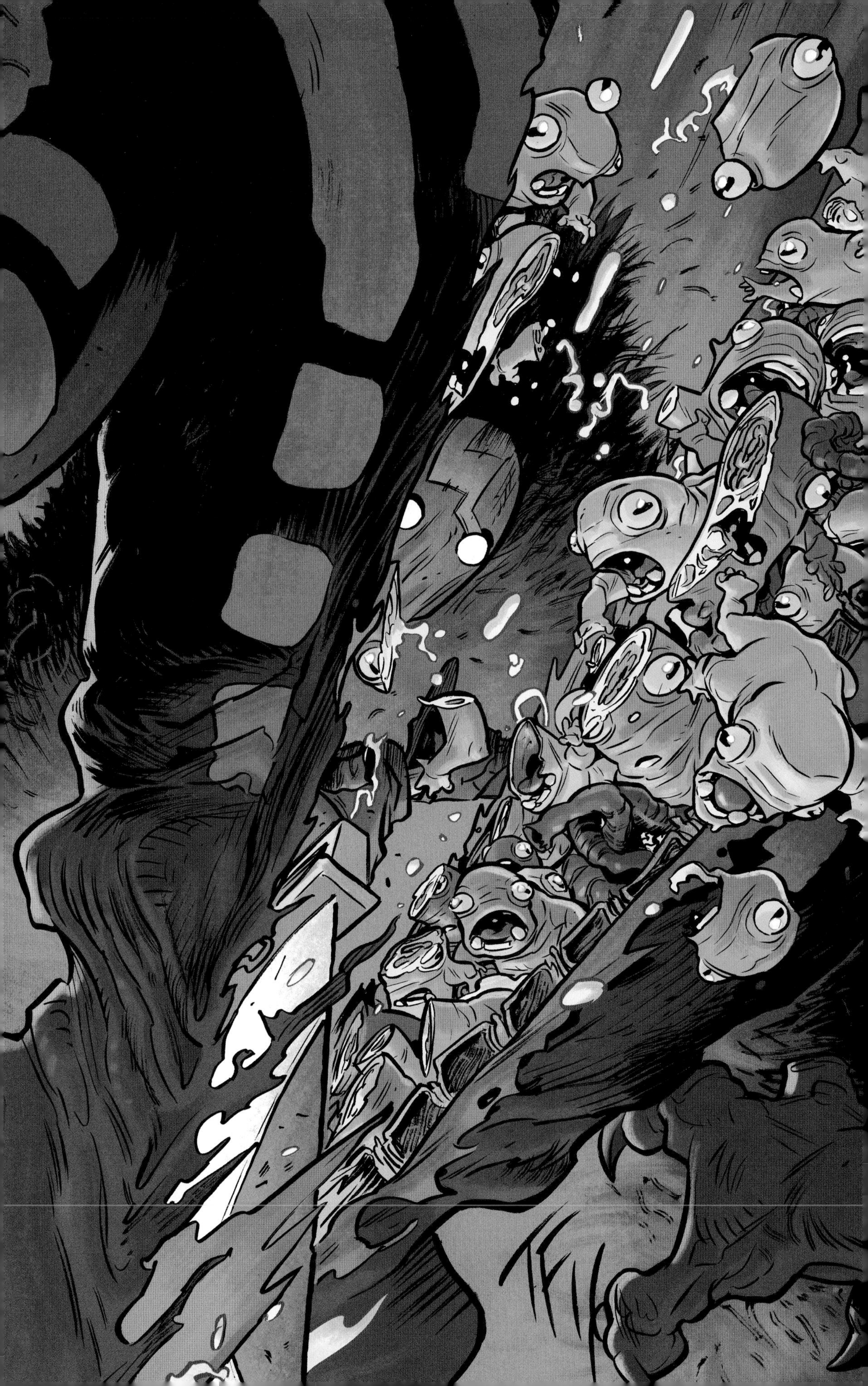

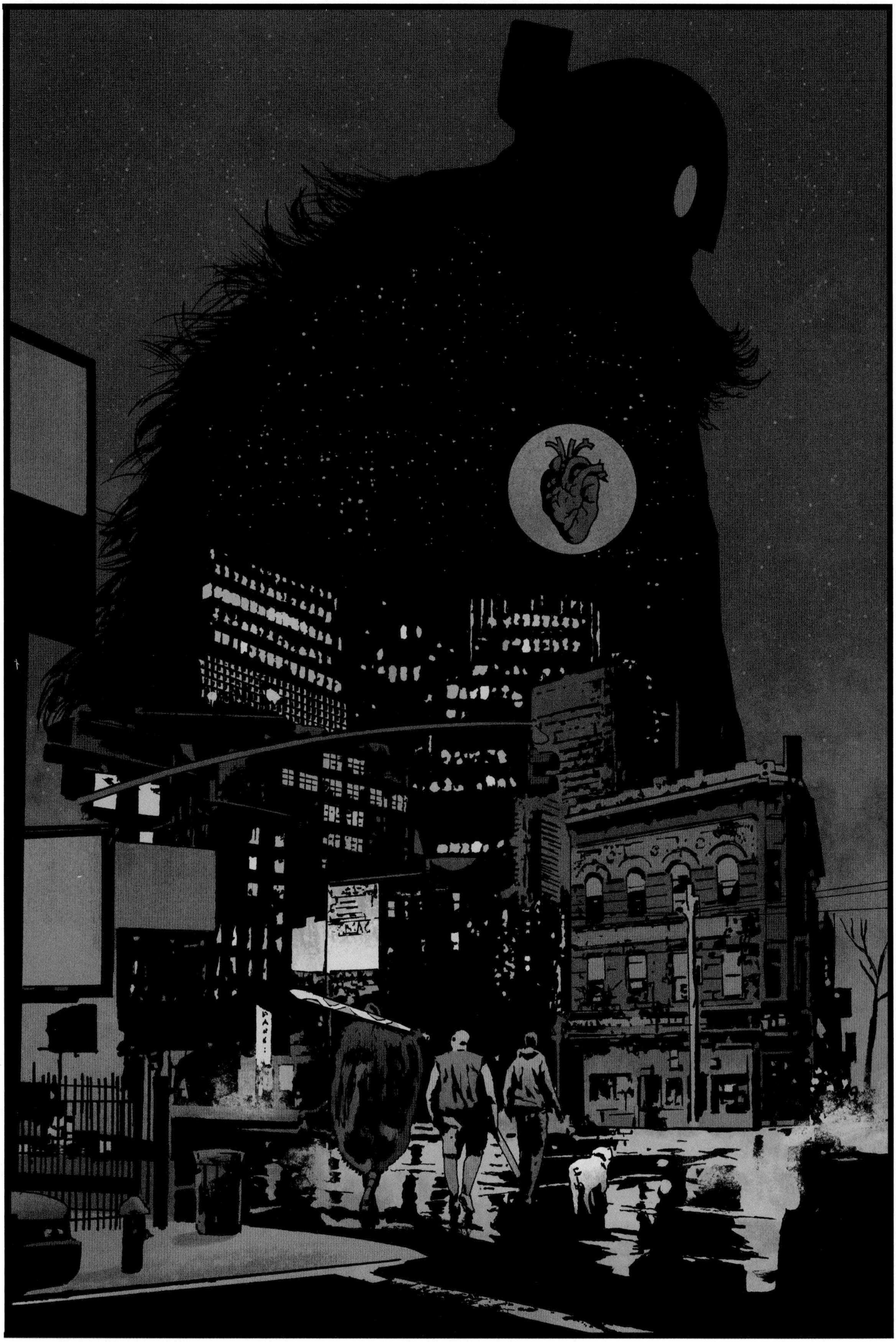

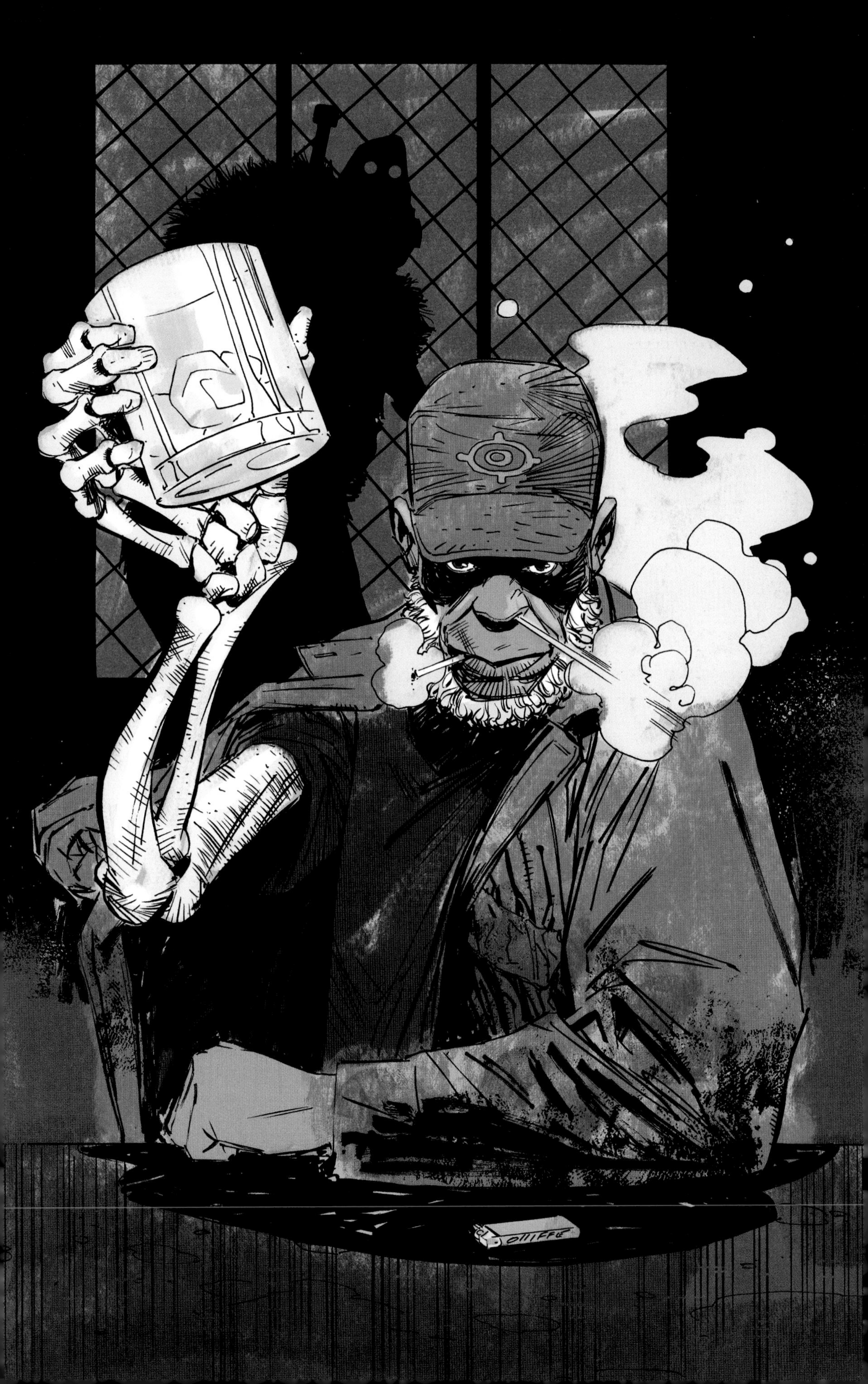
OLIFFE

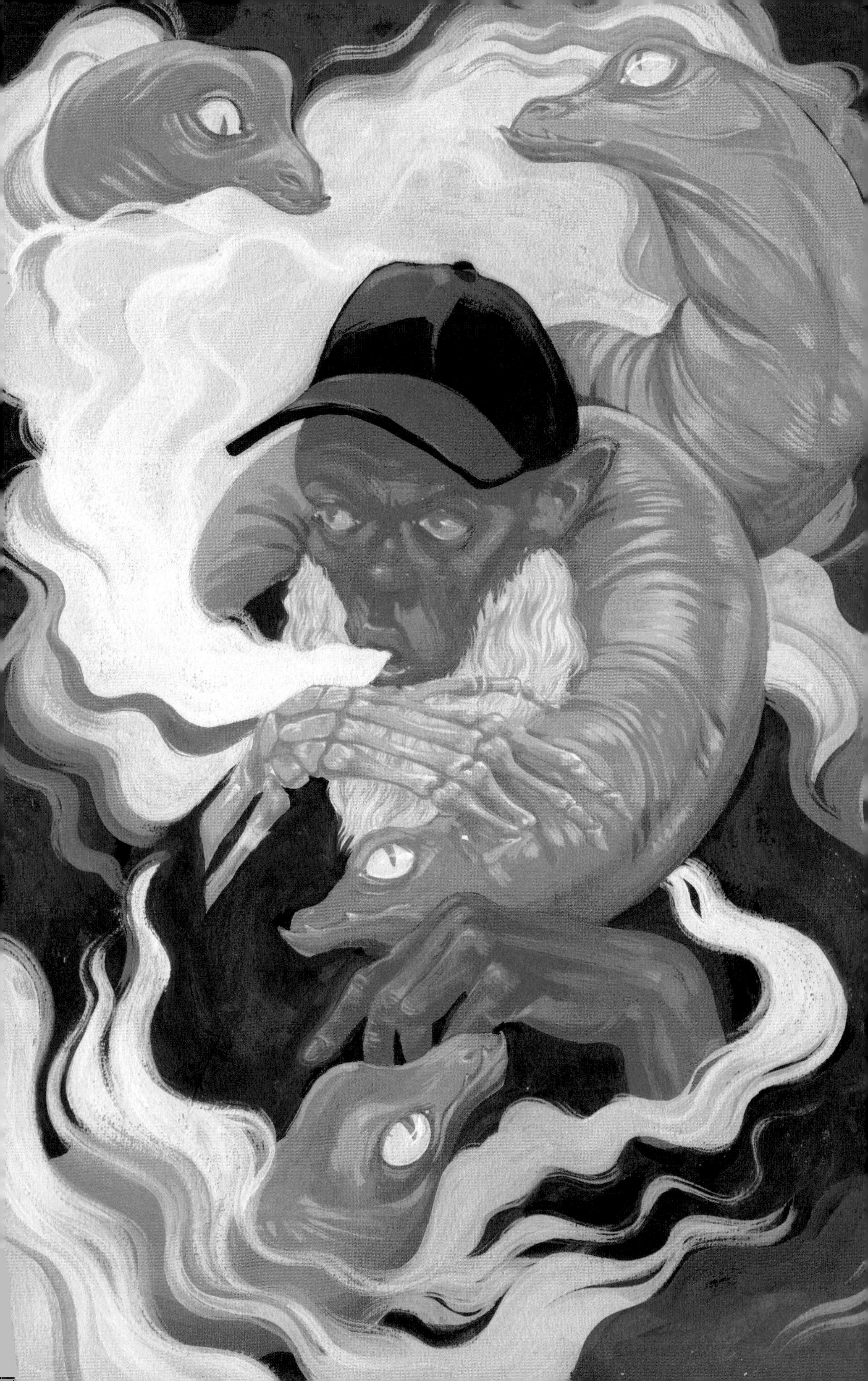

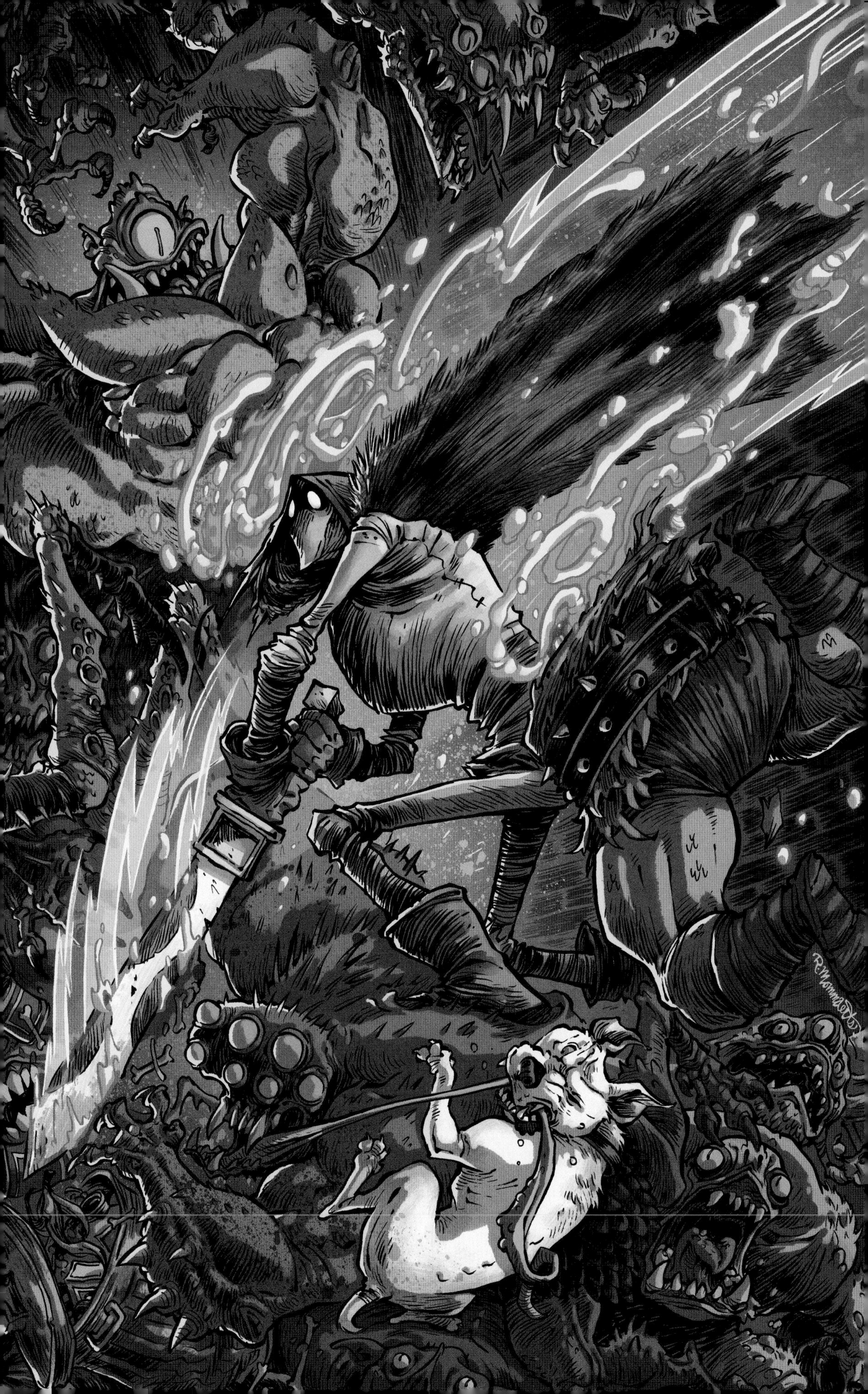

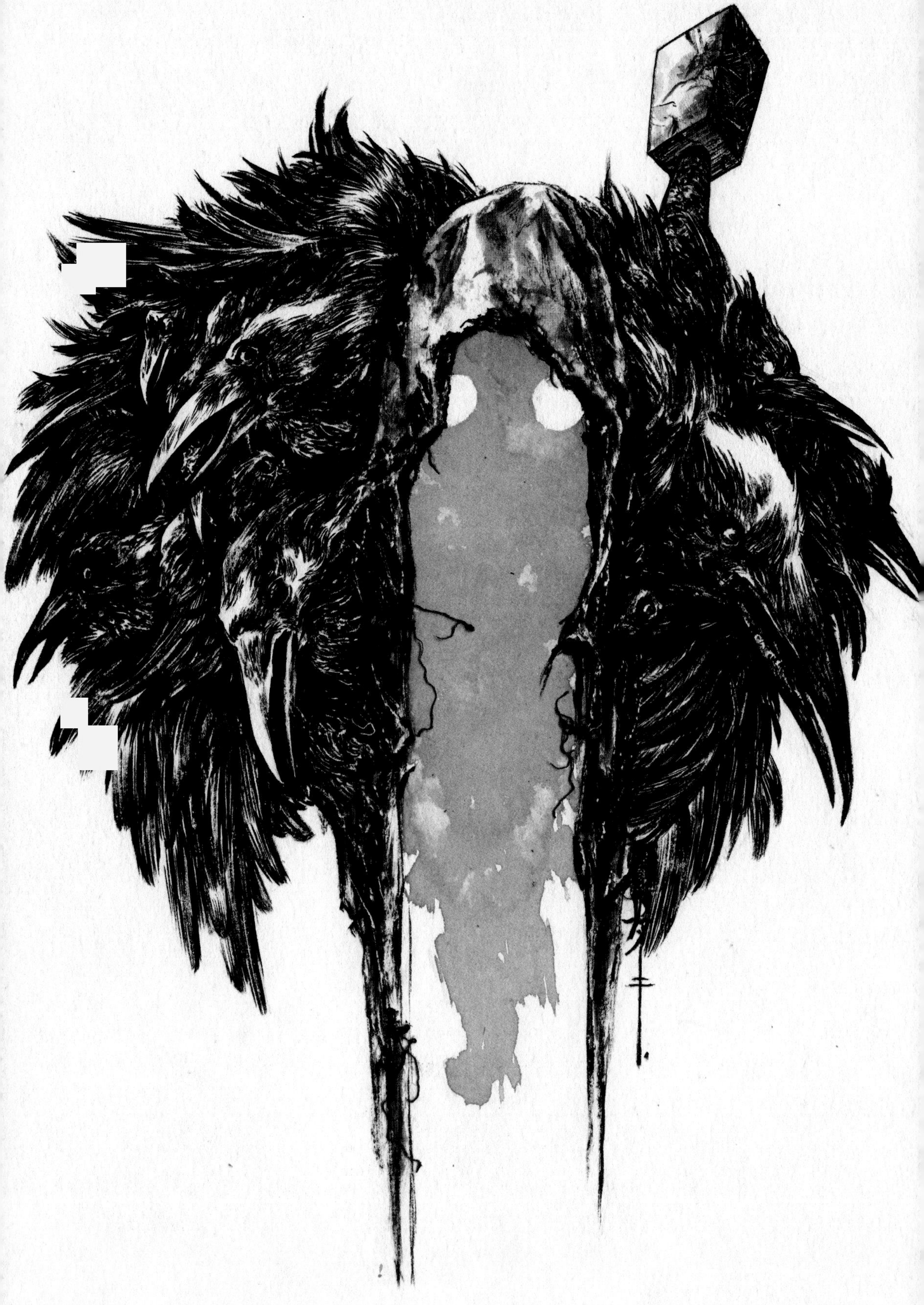

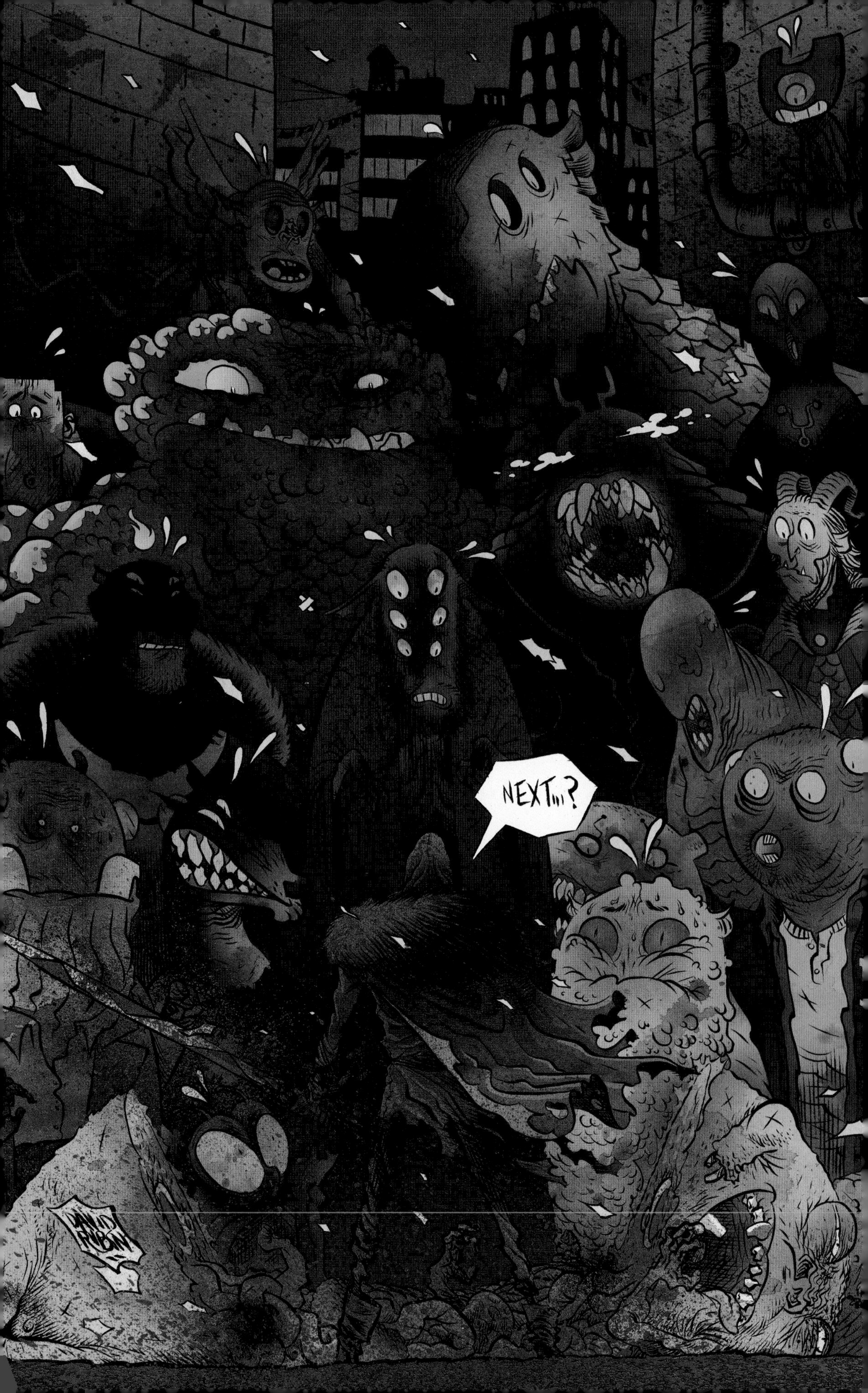
NEXT...?

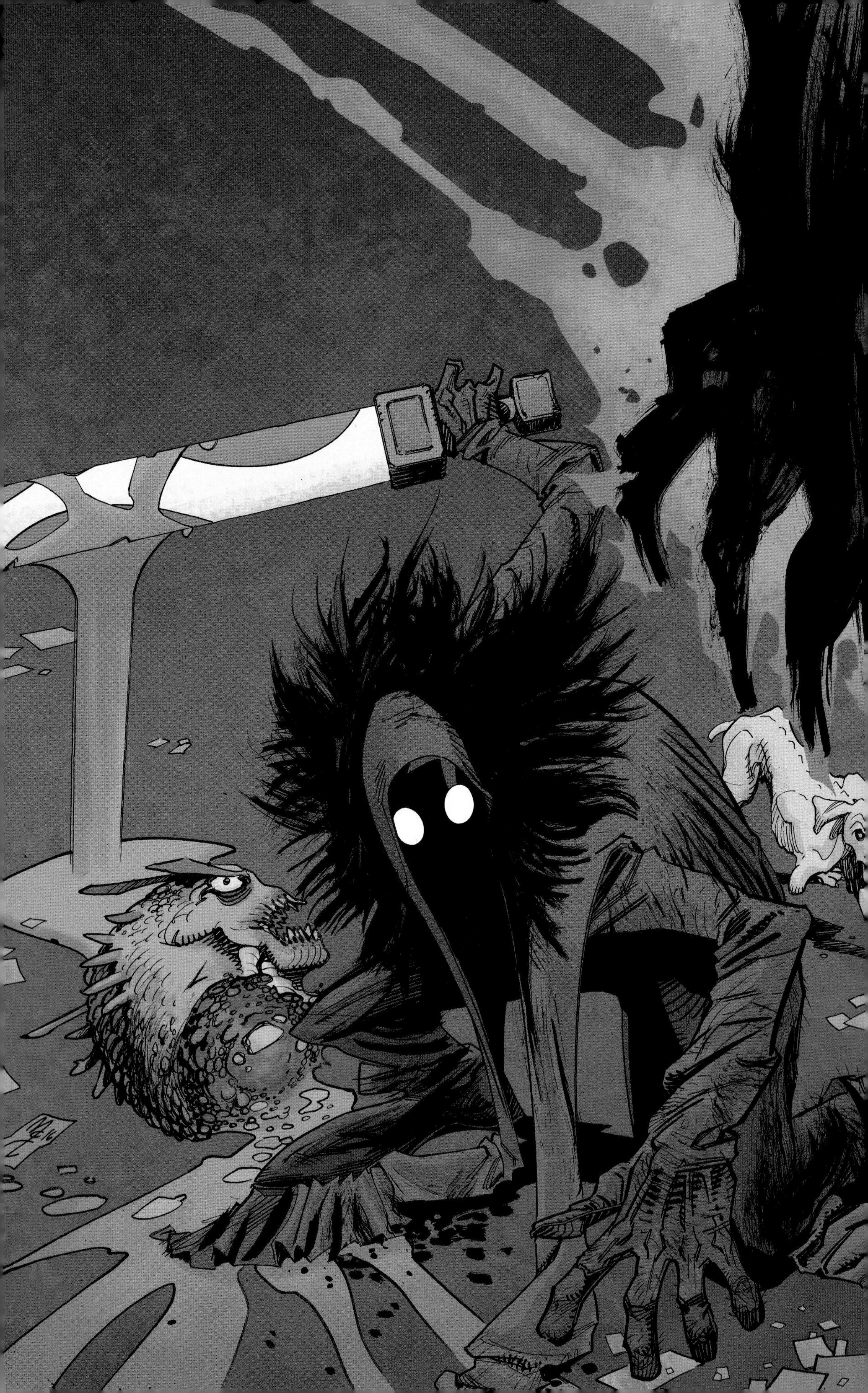

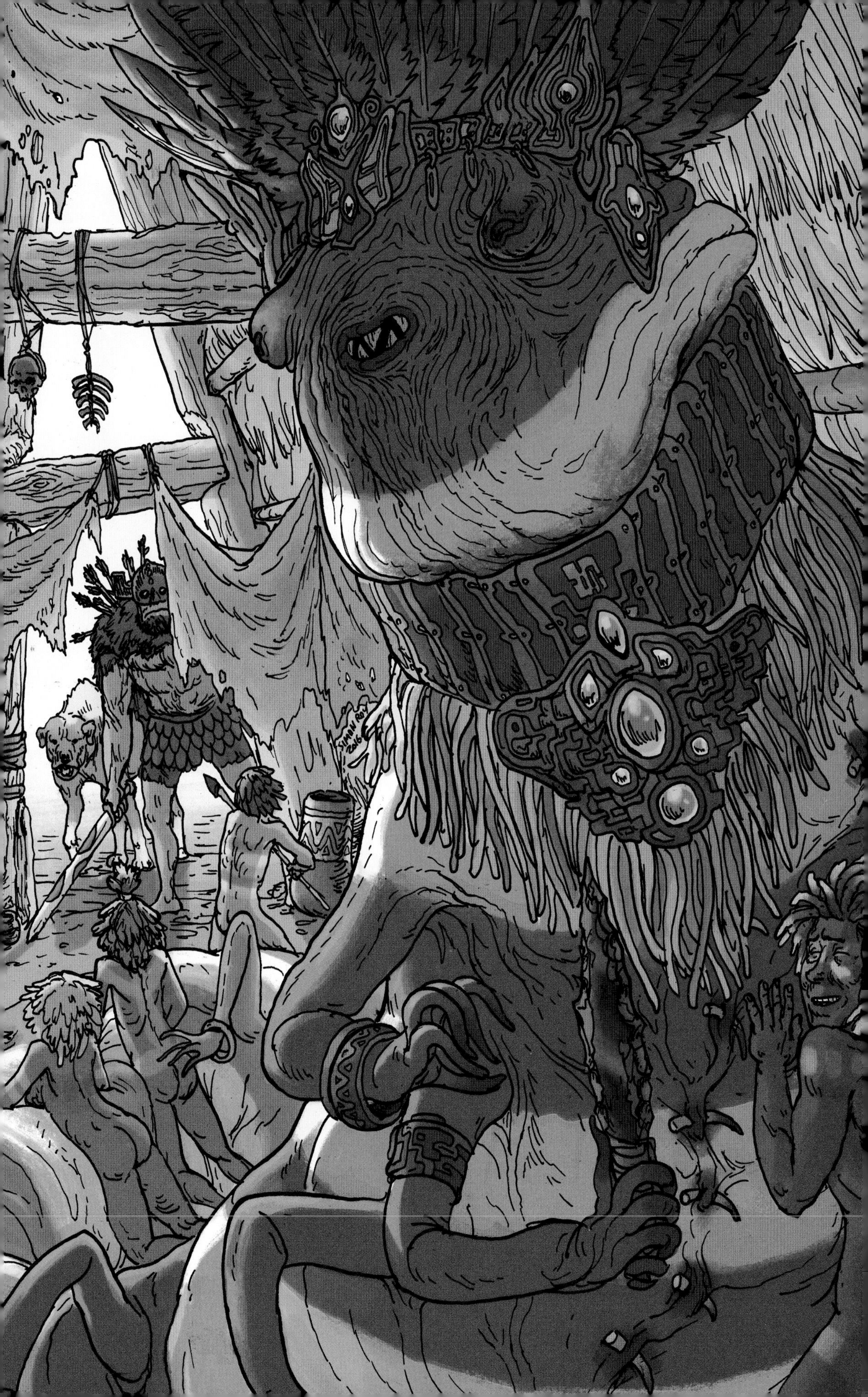
SIMON ROY 2016

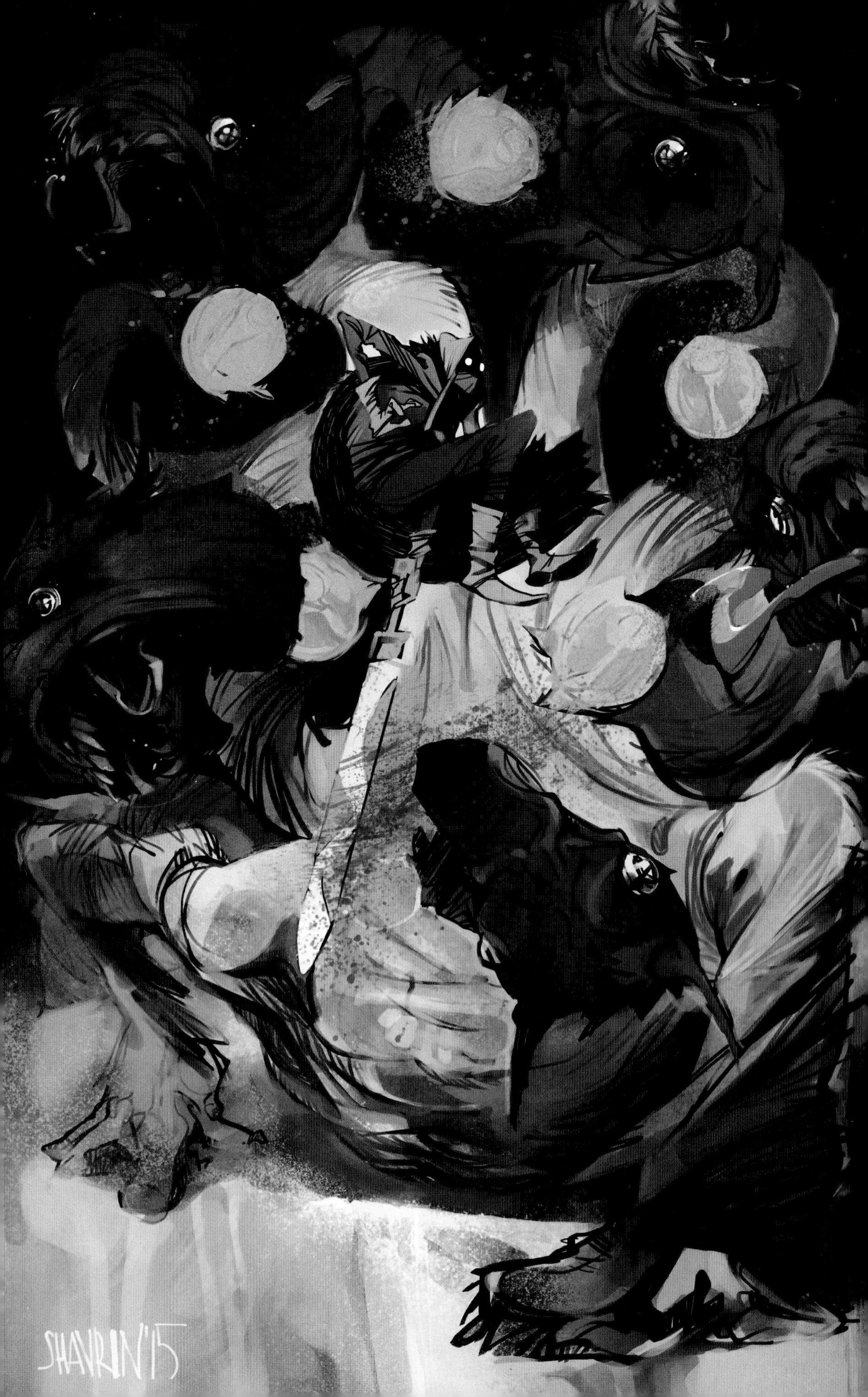
SHAVRIN'15

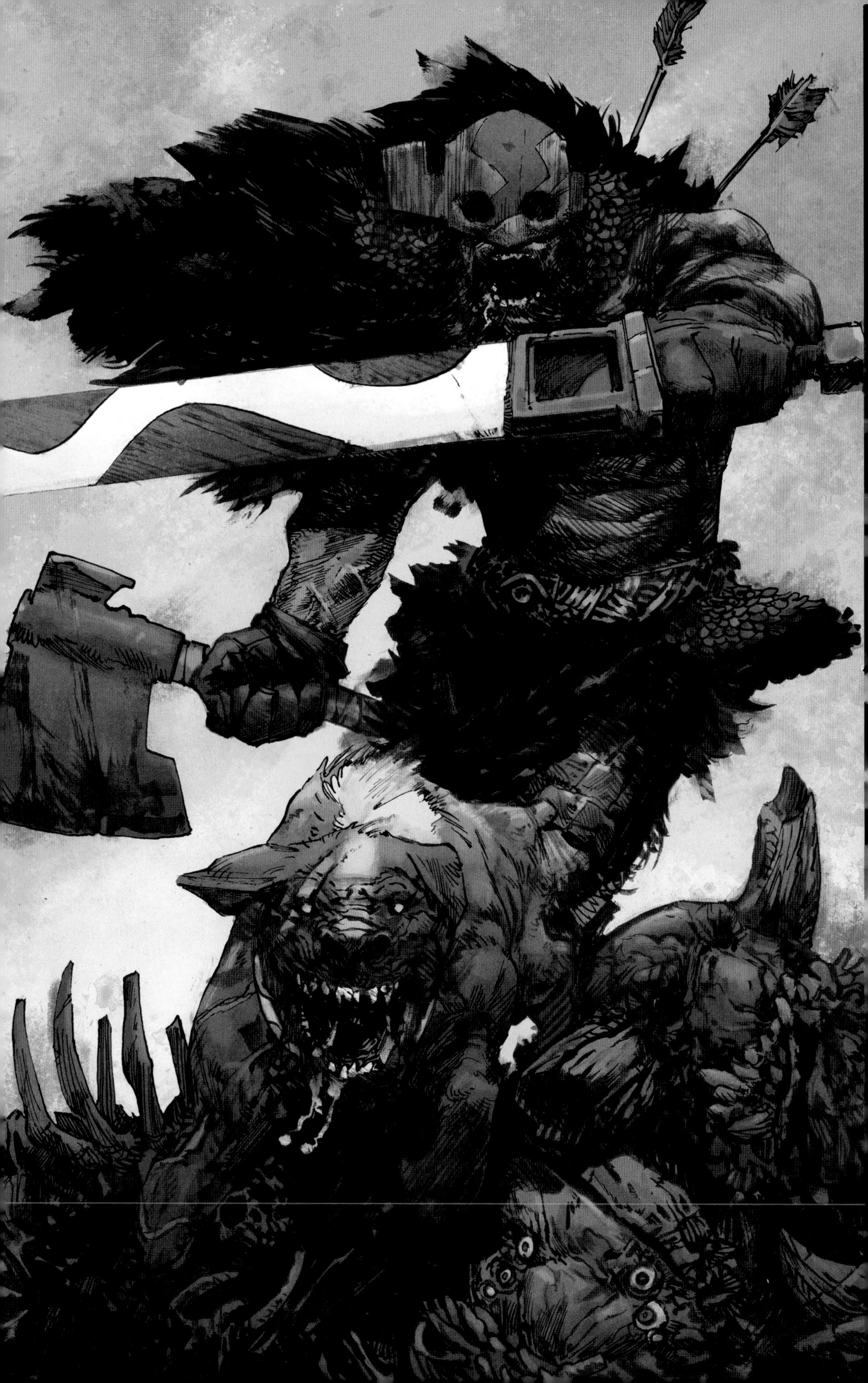

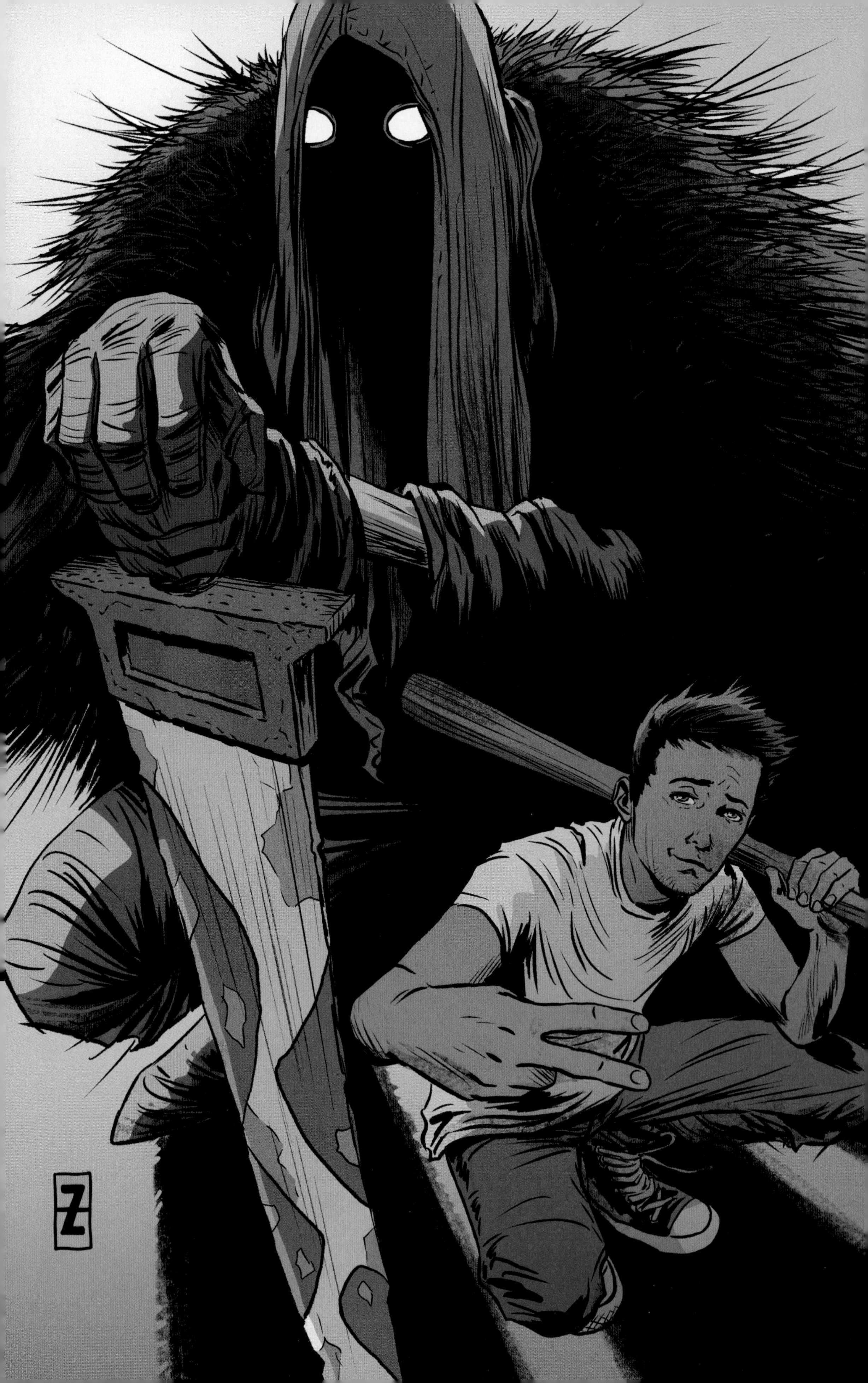

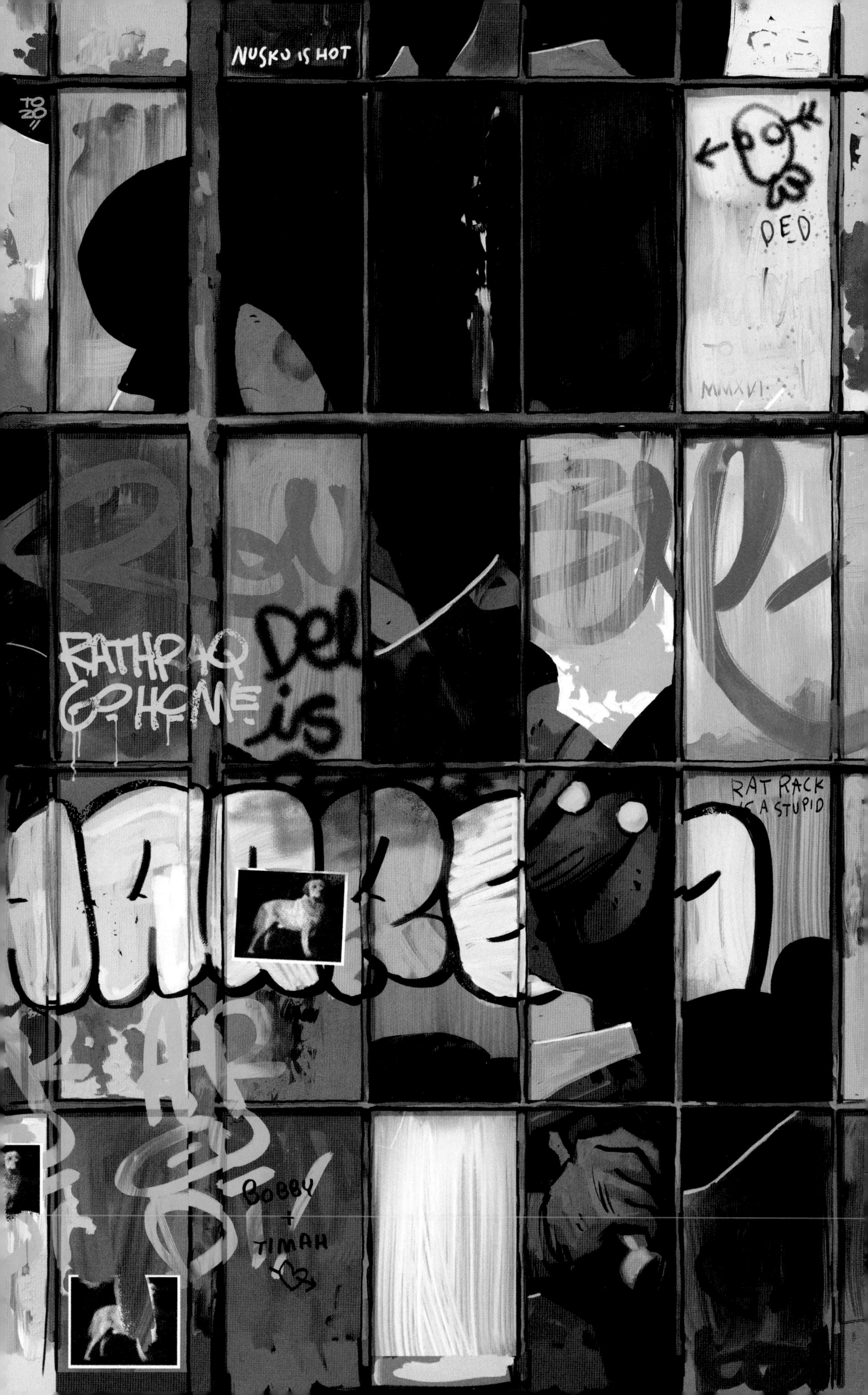
NUSKO IS HOT
DED
RAT RACK IS A STUPID
BOBBY + TIMAH

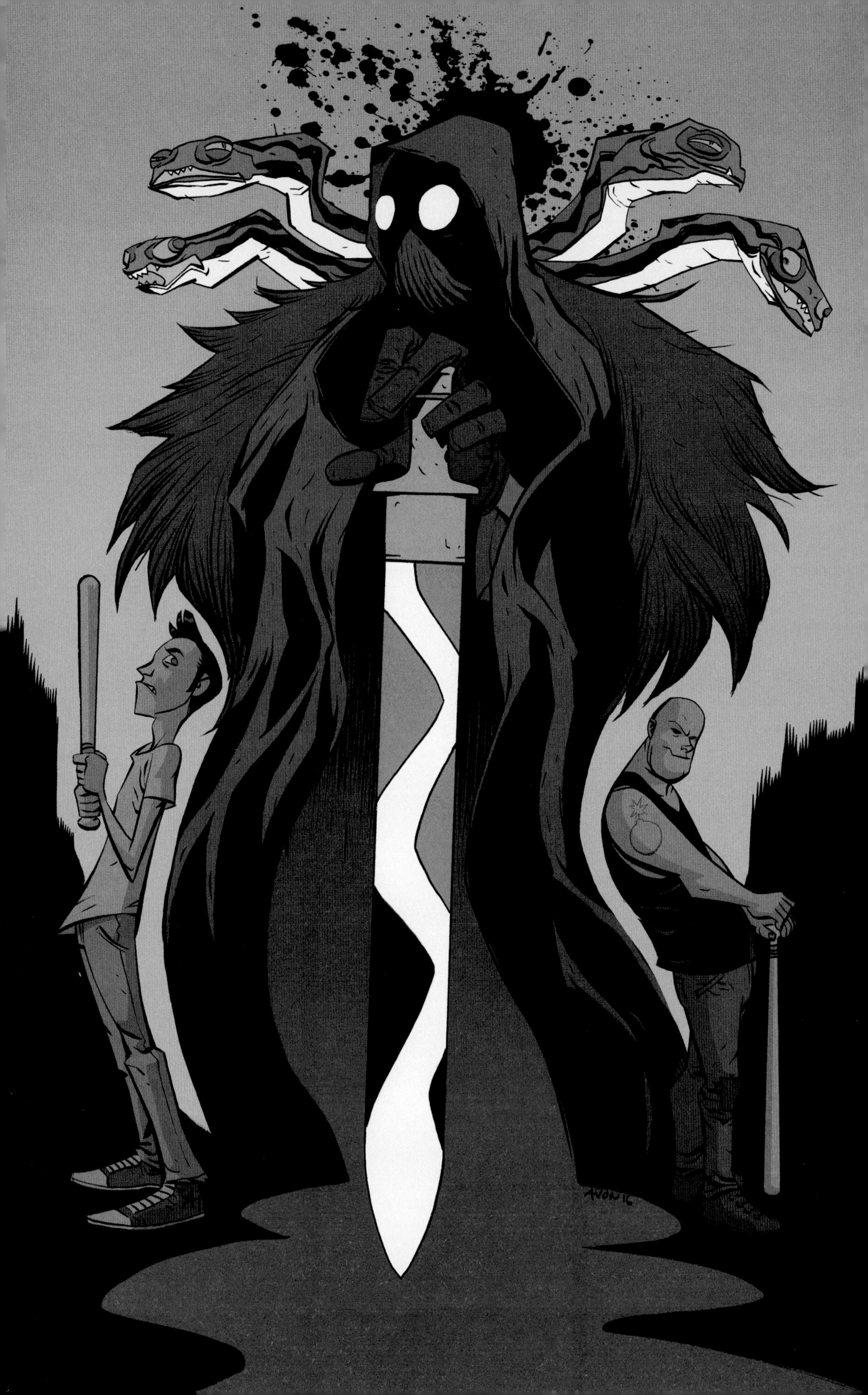

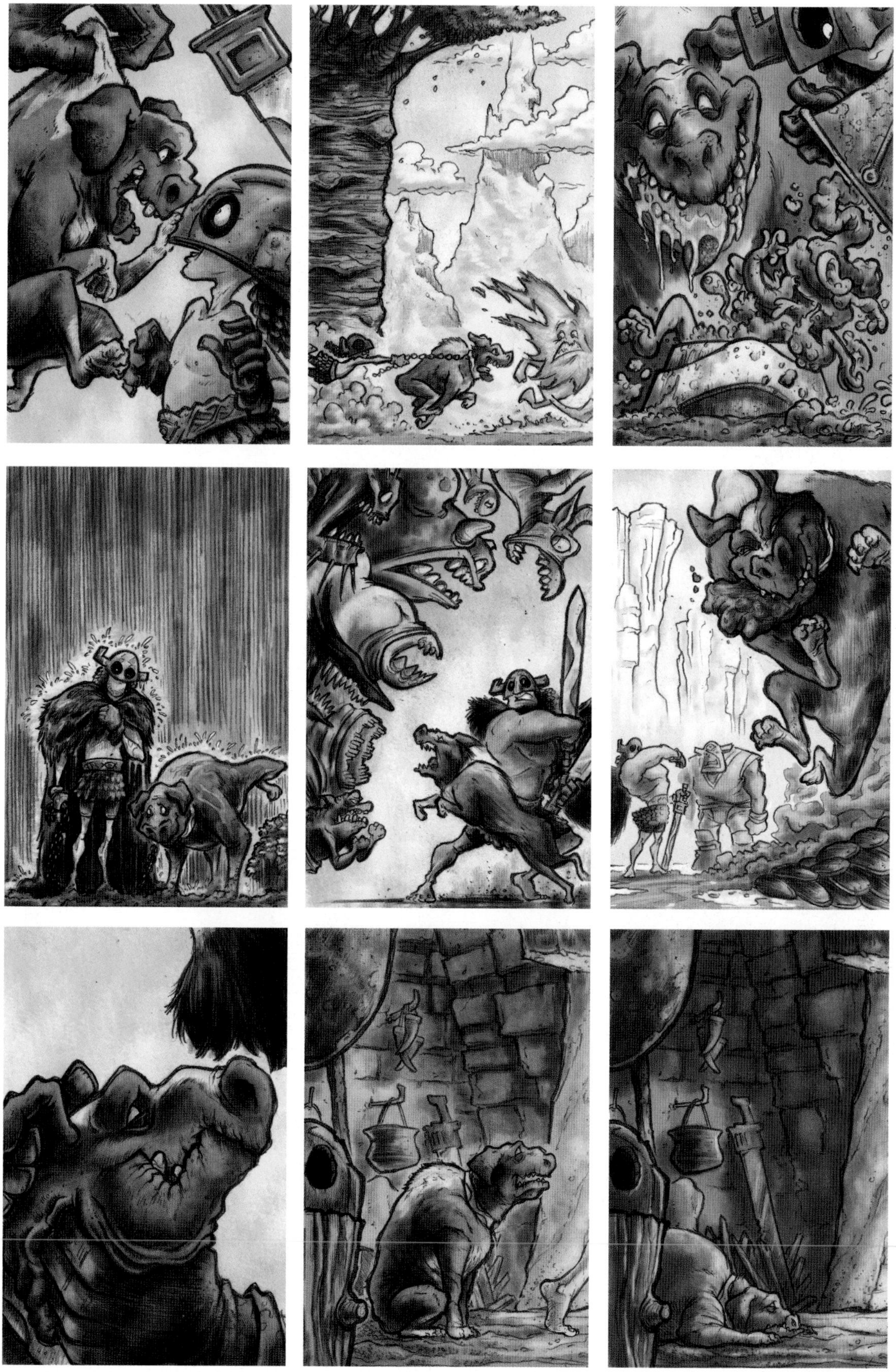

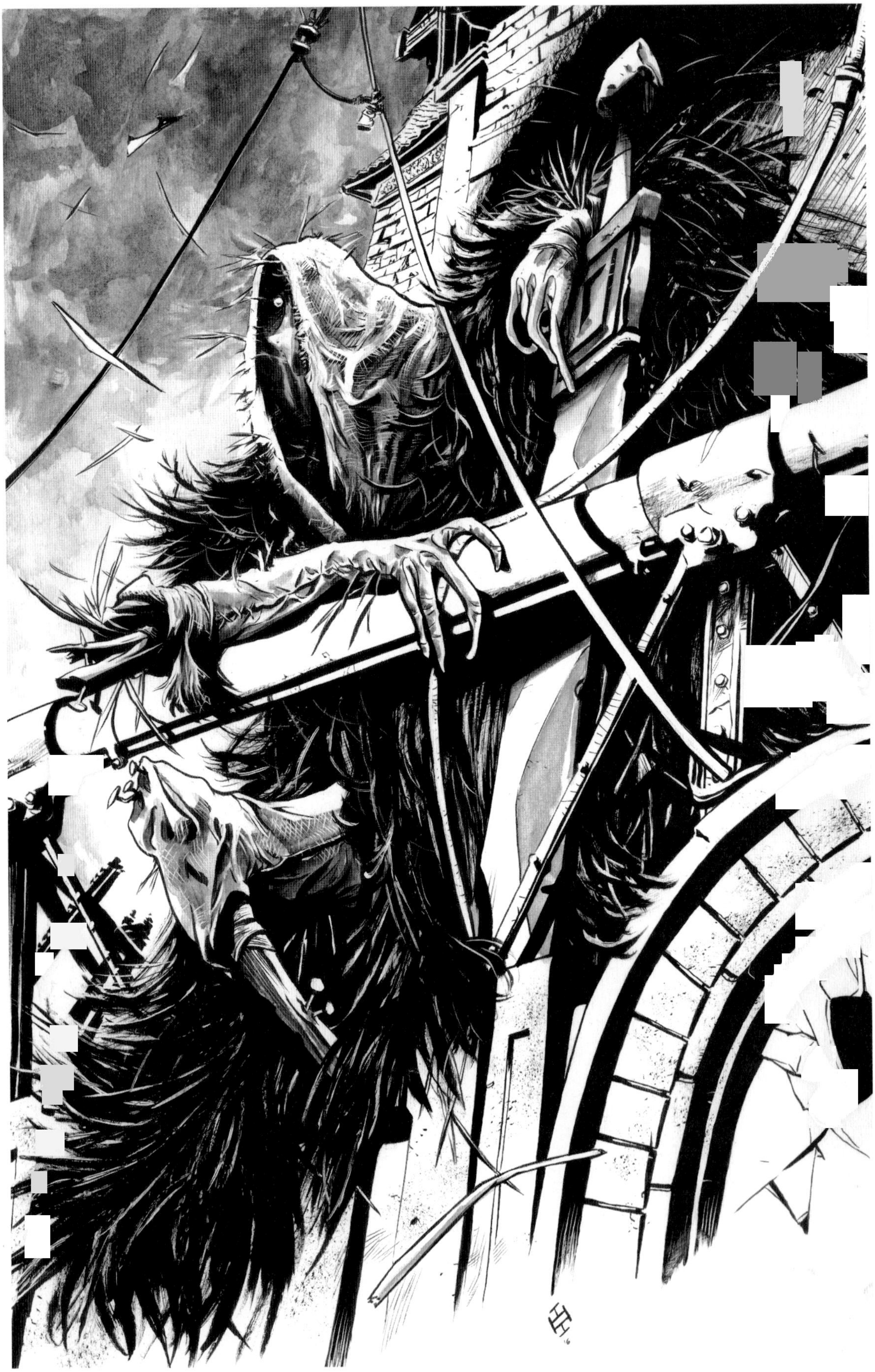

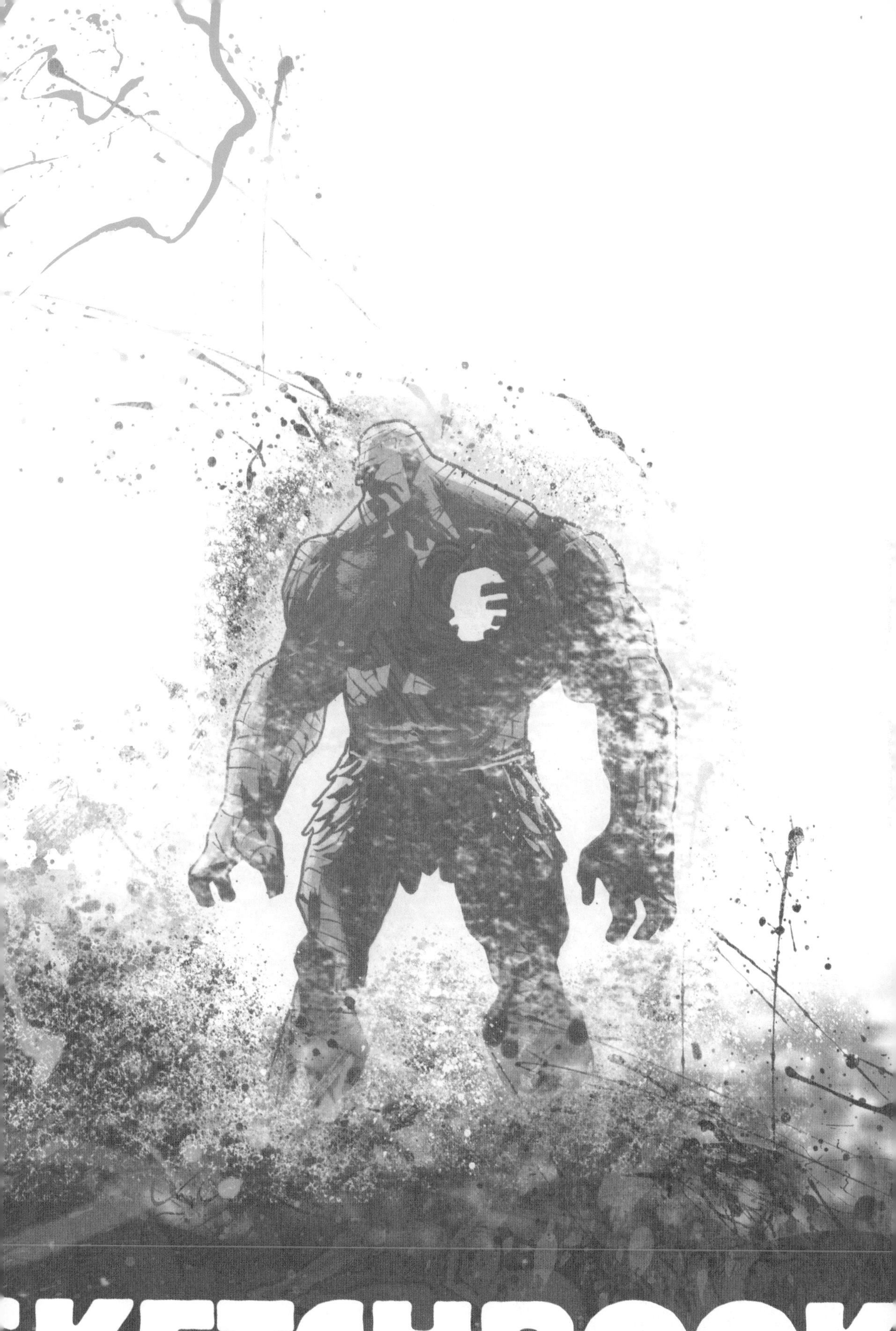

SKETCHBOOK

TOADY

Here are some passes at Toady. He was a minor character so I didn't fuss too much. I enjoy drawing his tiny suit.

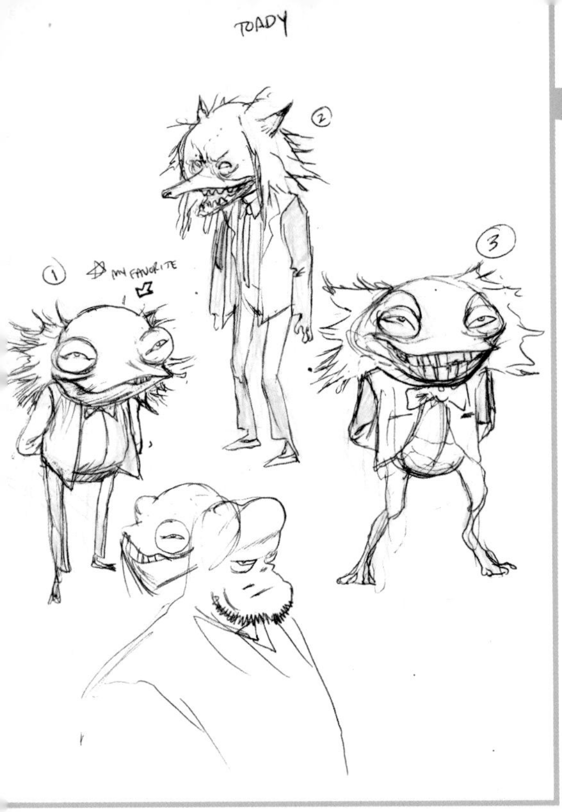
TOADY
1
MY FAVORITE
2
3

VJ

Next was the ancient King version of VJ. I went through a lot of incarnations with him. I even tried one where he's just a giant cartoon spider. Yikes!

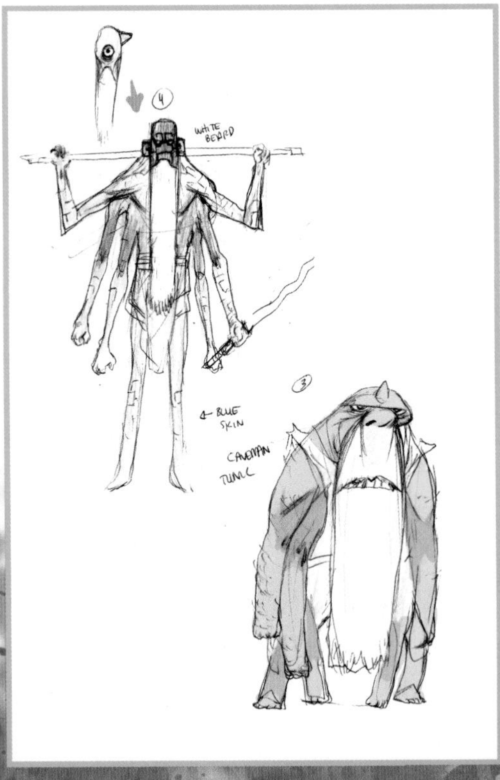
4
WHITE BEARD
3
← BLUE SKIN
CAVEMAN TUNIC

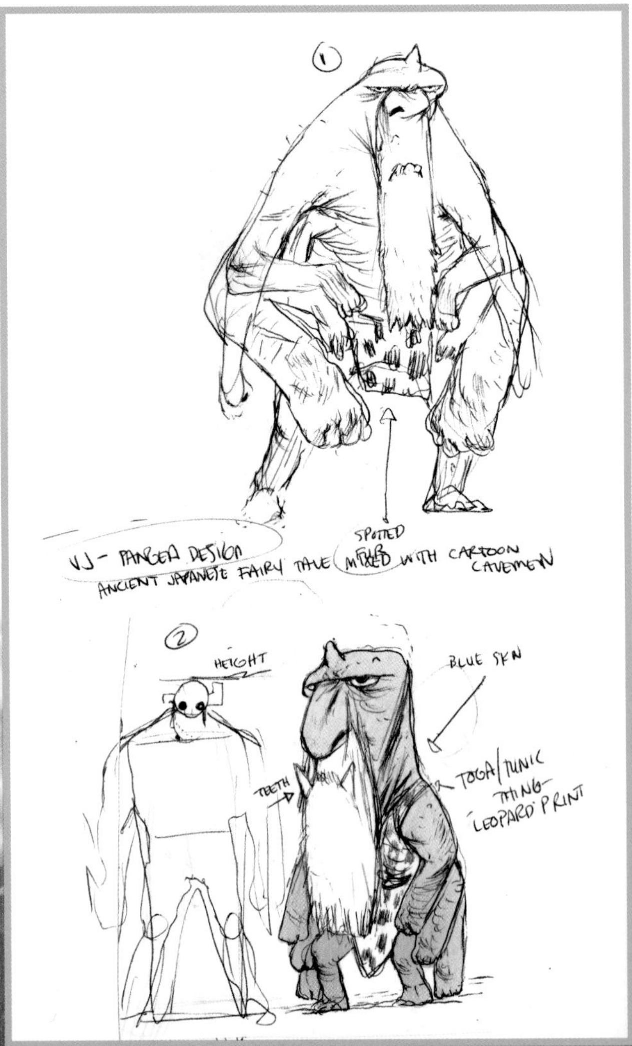
1
SPOTTED FUR
VJ - PANGEA DESIGN
ANCIENT JAPANESE FAIRY TALE MIXED WITH CARTOON CAVEMEN
2
HEIGHT
BLUE SKN
TEETH
TOGA/TUNIC THING
"LEOPARD" PRINT

My favorite version was the blue guy on the right. His proportions may have made him too "funny" and would have distracted from the emotional punch at the end of that issue, so we passed.

RATHRAQ

I think I drew these because, at this point in my journey, drawing Rath in his non-descript brown pajamas (What the hell is he wearing?! Who does the artist think he is designing the main character with a bafflingly vague wardrobe?!), was getting a bit boring. I wanted to spice things up a little.

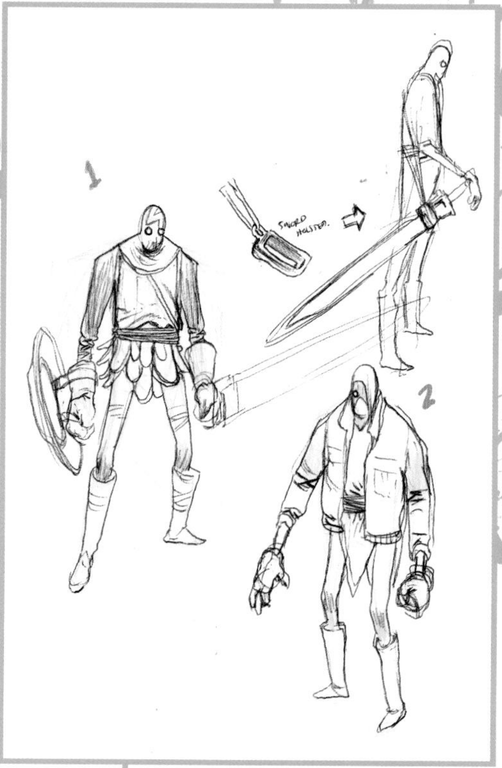
1
SWORD HOLSTER.
2

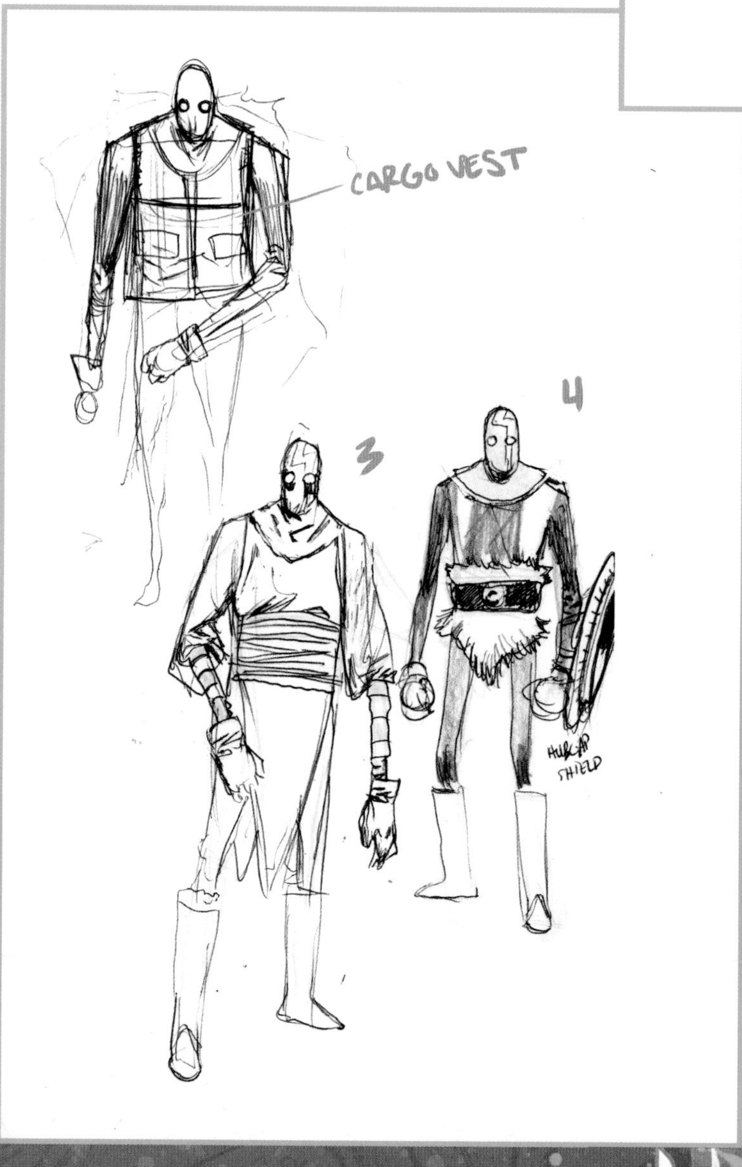
CARGO VEST
3
4
HUBCAP SHIELD

These are all me trying something different, more distinct, more specific. Maybe we'll get a chance to explore this in future issues.

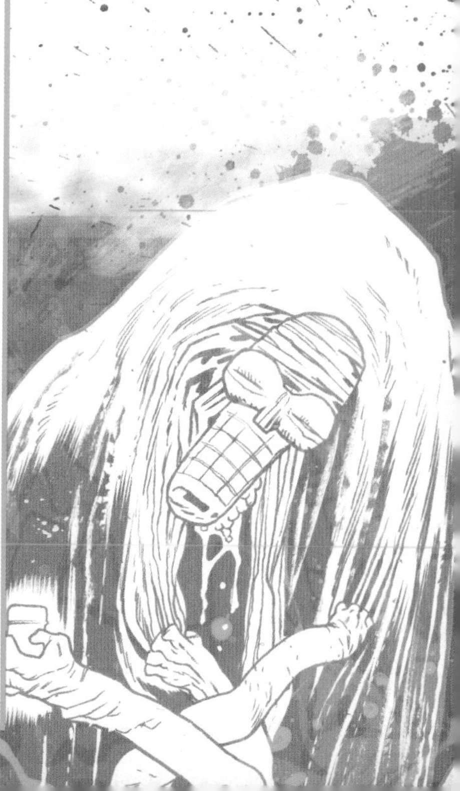

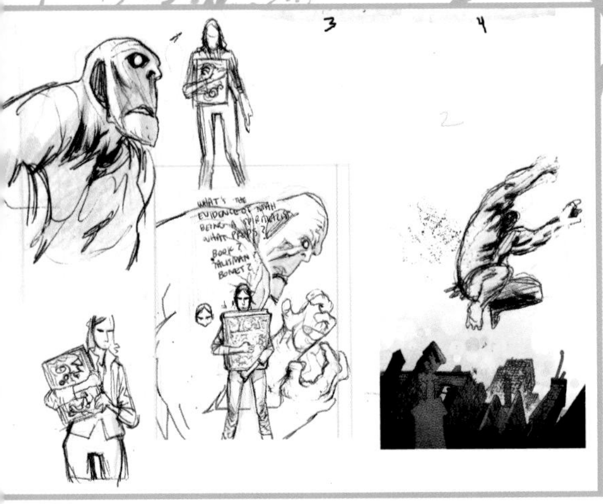
3
4

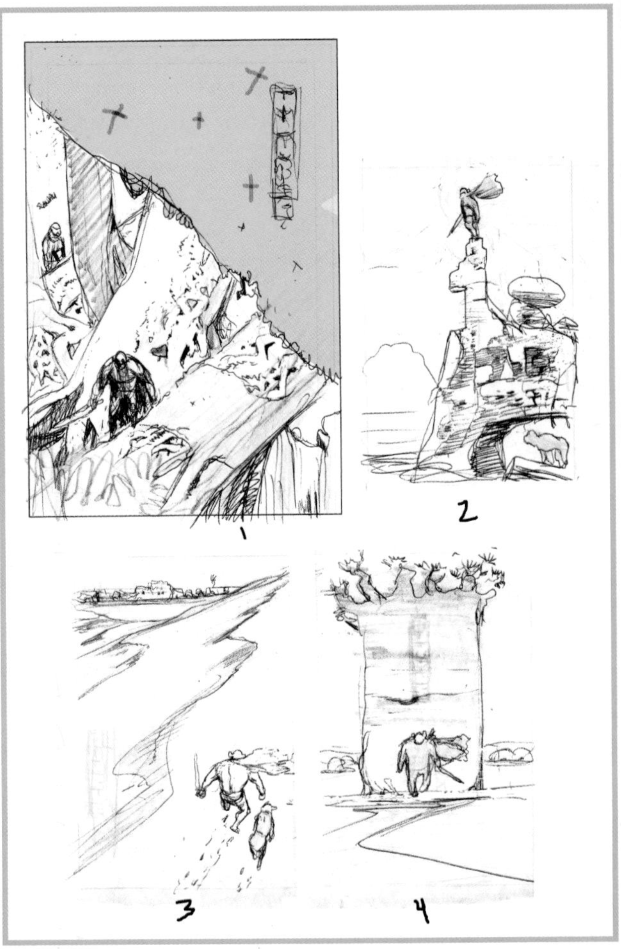
1
2
3
4

Here are some cover sketches and thumbnails. Some of those on the right might be worth returning to for a future issue.

ELEPHANT GUY

My first version was an elephant-headed giant dude with multiple arms. John said he looked too much like an action figure, so I went back to the drawing board. Had a lot of fun doing different versions of this character!

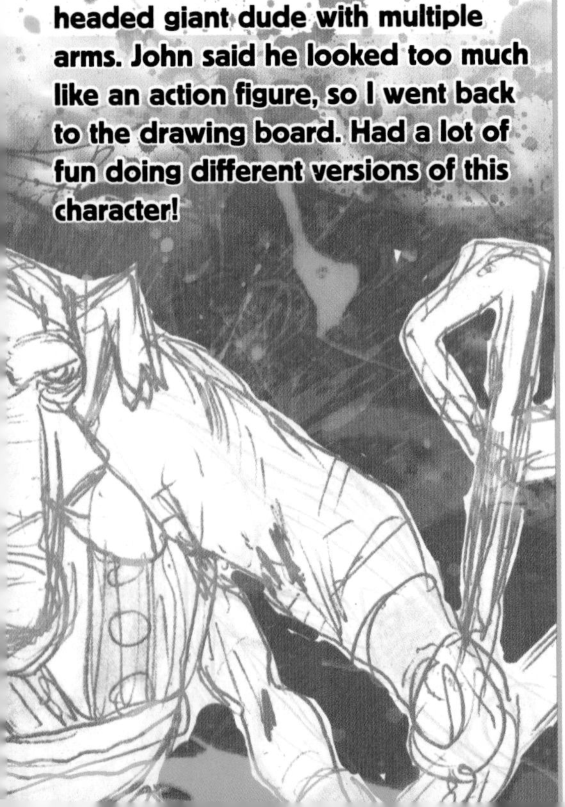

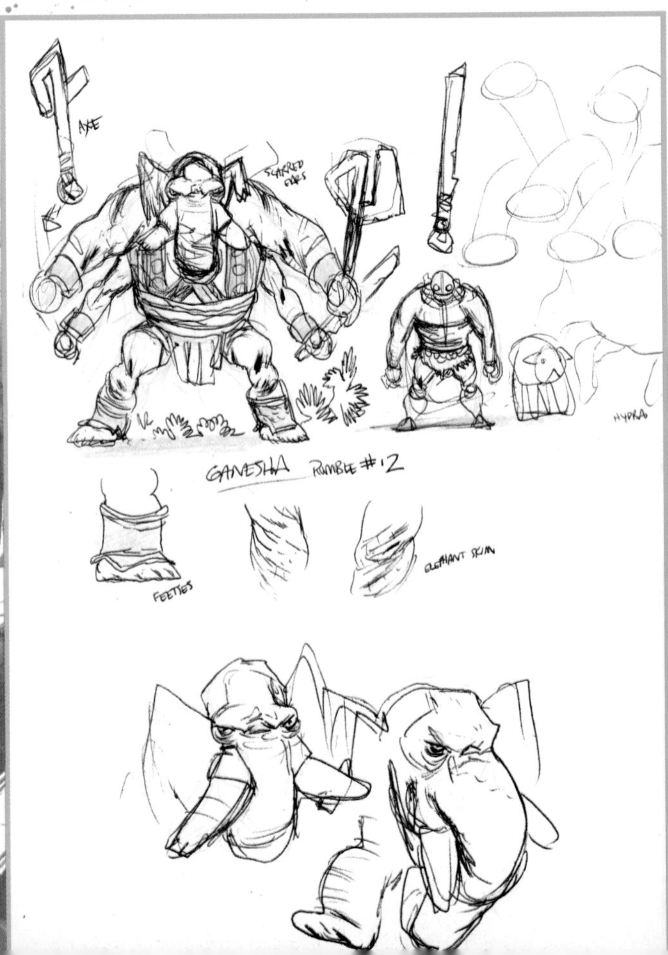
AXE
SCARRED EARS
HYDRA
GANESHA RUMBLE #12
FEETIES
ELEPHANT SKIN

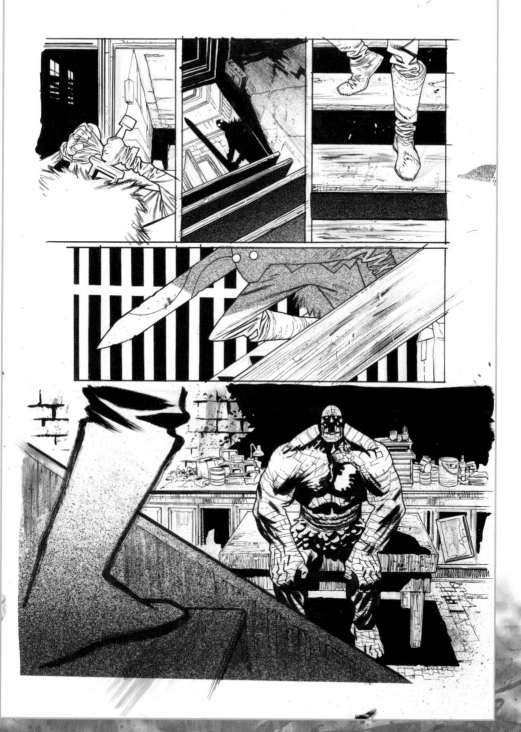

The raw inks to one of my favorite pages from issue #11.
Thought I'd give people a chance to see those traditional
screentones that you stick directly to the art. None of
that fancy digital muck-a-brack with the kids and the star
childrens and the footloosing.

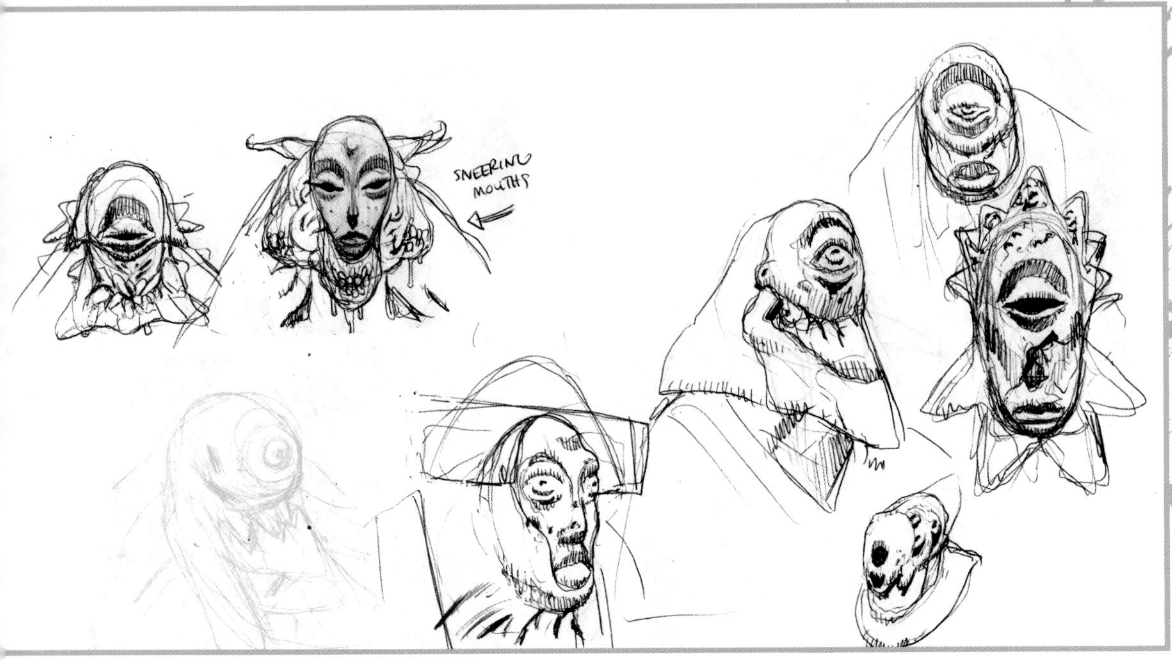
SNEERING MOUTHS

More helmets and body ideas for the ancient guard warrior guy.

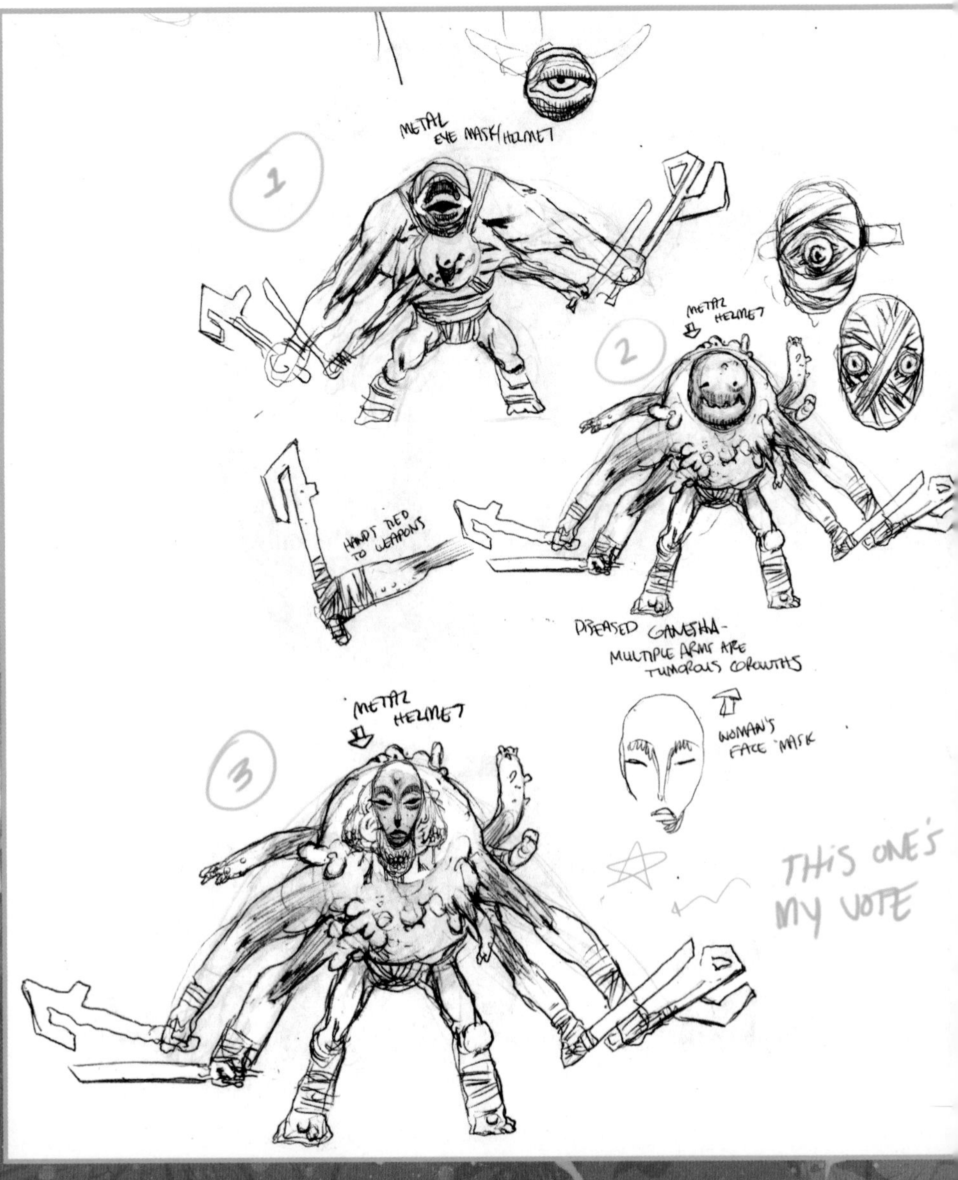
METAL EYE MASK/HELMET
1
METAL HELMET
2
HANDS TIED TO WEAPONS
DISEASED GANESHA-
MULTIPLE ARMS ARE
TUMOROUS GROWTHS
WOMAN'S FACE MASK
METAL HELMET
3
THIS ONE'S MY VOTE